Praise for Victoria Bylin

"*The Bounty Hunter's Bride* is a sweet love story, with rough edges, filled with hope, love, forgiveness and redemption. Victoria Bylin has written enough historical novels to know what readers expect, and she delivers on all levels."

—*RT Book Reviews*

"Readers will get caught up in the characters' pain, joy, sorrow and anger and believe there's hope and forgiveness for them as well as for the characters."

—*RT Book Reviews* on *The Maverick Preacher*

"*Wyoming Lawman* is a tender, charming love story filled with strong, memorable characters.... Don't miss this talented author."

—*RT Book Reviews*

Praise for Sara Mitchell

"Mitchell is an amazing, talented author who spins a tale of greed, love, family secrets and keeping the faith in oneself."

—*RT Book Reviews* on *The Widow's Secret*

"Mitchell's tale has a refreshing story line and romance, and an unexpected twist gives it new life."

—*RT Book Reviews* on *A Most Unusual Match*

"A charming love story with two characters who were made for each other."

—*RT Book Reviews* on *Legacy of Secrets*

Victoria Bylin
and
Sara Mitchell

The Bounty Hunter's Bride
&
Legacy of Secrets

HARLEQUIN® LOVE INSPIRED® CLASSICS

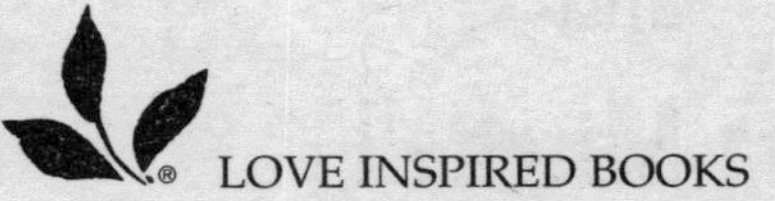

Recycling programs for this product may not exist in your area.

ISBN-13: 978-1-335-89586-8

The Bounty Hunter's Bride & Legacy of Secrets

This edition published by arrangement with Love Inspired Books.

www.Harlequin.com

Printed in U.S.A.

CONTENTS

Victoria Bylin fell in love with God and her husband at the same time. It started with a ride on a big red motorcycle and a date to see a *Star Trek* movie. A recent graduate of UC Berkeley, Victoria had been seeking that elusive "something more" when Michael rode into her life. Neither knew it, but they were both reading the Bible.

Five months later they got married and the blessings began. They have two sons and have lived in California and Virginia. Michael's career allowed Victoria to be both a stay-at-home mom and a writer. She's living a dream that started when she read her first book and thought, "I want to tell stories." For that gift, she will be forever grateful.

Feel free to drop Victoria an email at VictoriaBylin@aol.com or visit her website at victoriabylin.com.

Books by Victoria Bylin

Love Inspired Historical

The Bounty Hunter's Bride
The Maverick Preacher
Kansas Courtship
Wyoming Lawman
The Outlaw's Return
Marrying the Major
Brides of the West

Visit the Author Profile page at Harlequin.com for more titles.

THE BOUNTY HUNTER'S BRIDE

Victoria Bylin

Even the sparrow has found a home,
and the swallow a nest for herself,
where she may have her young—
a place near your altar,
O Lord Almighty, my King and my God.
—*Psalms* 84:3

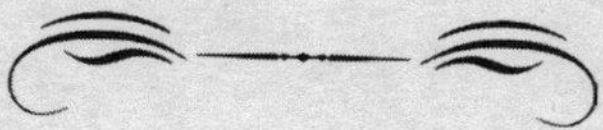

For my brother, John Bylin…
Dad would be proud of you. I know I am.

Chapter One

Castle Rock, Colorado
June 1882

"You know the story of Cain and Abel?"

"I do."

"Patrick was Abel. I'm Cain."

Daniela Baxter gaped at the man in the doorway. Unshaven and bleary eyed, he looked enough like Patrick to be his brother. Except Patrick would never have answered the door in dirty trousers and a wrinkled shirt.

Patrick and she were engaged to be married. Tomorrow. At the church she'd spotted outside of town. When he'd failed to meet her at the train depot, Dani had hired a buggy and driven the five miles to his dairy farm. She'd expected her fiancé to greet her with a smile and an apology for missing her train. Instead, a stranger had answered the door. She'd asked for Patrick by name and been assaulted by his sneering question about Cain and Abel.

Her insides knotted. "I don't understand."

"Patrick's dead."

Dani blinked. "I must be at the wrong house."

The road had forked a mile west of town. She'd guessed and taken the straighter of the two trails.

The man with Patrick's eyes studied her more closely. "Who are you?"

"Daniela Baxter. I'm his fiancée."

She and Patrick had been introduced through letters by Kirstin Janss, his cousin and Dani's best friend. They had corresponded for six months. He'd written often about the town of Castle Rock, his growing dairy business and his three young daughters.

The man's gaze stayed hard, but his voice softened like hot caramel, sweet but still sticky. "I'm sorry, miss. Patrick died five days ago."

Gasping, Dani clutched her reticule. It held her only picture of the man she loved, the one he'd taken just for her. He'd combed his thick hair with pomade and dressed in his Sunday best, a black suit with a crisp shirt. She knew his dreams. He knew hers. She loved him. She loved his daughters and yearned to be a mother, both to his girls and the babies to come.

The porch started to spin. Dani grabbed the rocking chair for support, but it tipped, throwing her to her knees. As she hit the threshold, pain shot through the marrow of her bones.

A strong hand gripped her elbow and hauled her to her feet. "Don't faint on me, lady."

"I won't."

As tears filled her eyes, he dragged her to a chair in the front room where she collapsed on the cushioned seat, taking in the horsehair divan and a scattering of flower petals. She smelled lilies and realized a coffin had sat in this room. Patrick…her love. An anguished cry exploded in her throat.

The man shouted into the kitchen. "Emma! Get some water."

Dani pushed to her feet. She'd come to be a mother to the girls, not a burden. "I'll be fine."

The man glared at her. "You don't look fine."

"Who are you?" she demanded.

Before he could answer, Patrick's oldest daughter came into the room with the glass of water. Judging by the tight pull of Emma's brows, she disliked this man. "Here," she said, shoving the glass in his direction.

He put his hands on his hips. "It's not for me." He indicated Dani with his chin.

The instant the child turned, her oval face brightened with hope. "Dani?"

"Yes, sweetie. It's me." Dani crossed the gap between herself and the child and offered a hug.

Emma clung to her like moss on a tree. Long letters had made them friends over a span of months. Grief made them family in an instant. Water from the tipped glass sloshed down the back of Dani's dress, but she didn't care. Holding Emma brought Patrick to life. He'd written proudly of his girls. Emma, Ellie and little Esther, who'd been born on Easter Sunday. *We'll have more, Dani. I want a son.* She'd written back about Edward, Ethan and Elijah. He'd countered with Earl and Ebenezer. Laughing to herself, she'd cried uncle in the next letter.

Dani released her grip on Emma, took the glass and set it on the table. "Where are your sisters?"

"Upstairs," Emma said. "Esther's taking a nap."

Emma, barely ten years old, had the tired eyes of a young mother. Who would take care of the girls now?

Not this man with tattered clothes and bristled cheeks. As Dani turned in his direction, he paced to the front window. Standing with his feet apart, he peered through the glass, studying the sky like a man expecting a storm. Dani tried to imagine Patrick striking such a belligerent pose but couldn't.

The picture in her reticule showed a man with gentle eyes. He had described himself as wiry and slight, a man with the rounded shoulders of a dairy farmer. The stranger at the window stood six feet tall and ramrod straight. Judging by his stance, he bent his knee to no one.

Dani knew better than to judge by appearances, but the stranger had declared himself to be Cain, the brother who'd surrendered to sin rather than fight for his righteousness. Cain had murdered Abel and been doomed to restless wandering. Even so, God hadn't left Cain. Cain had abandoned God.

Dani put her arm around Emma's shoulders, then spoke to the man's back. "Perhaps the three of us could sit down."

He faced her but stayed at the window. "I'll stand."

In that case, so would Dani. "We haven't been introduced."

"I'm Beau Morgan. Patrick's brother."

Emma clutched a fistful of Dani's dress. Dani took the reaction as a confirmation of a warning in Patrick's letters. He'd mentioned his brother just once. *He's not someone you should know, Dani. Not a man I'd trust with my girls.* Patrick had been vague about his brother's shortcomings but clear about his intent. *I made a will years ago, before Beau went crazy. As soon as we're married, I'll change it. I want you to adopt the girls.*

Dani's throat tightened. Why had God taken Patrick

now? Why not a year from now, after they were married and settled? Why not fifty years when they were old and gray? The questions rose like a vapor but vanished as quickly as morning mist on a hot day. God's ways were higher than hers; His knowledge greater. At her mother's funeral, Pastor Schmidt had preached from Isaiah, paraphrasing the ancient prophet. "Who among you walks in darkness and has no light? Let him trust in the name of the Lord…" Dani had leaned on those words every day since her mother's death. Isaiah had seen the future and persevered. Dani didn't have his foresight, only her faith that God was good, but she knew how to persevere.

She touched Emma's cheek. "Your pa's listening in Heaven, so I'm talking to him as well as you. No matter what happens, I won't leave you and your sisters."

Did you hear that, Patrick? Rest easy, my love.

Emma nodded in short bursts that made her eyes flicker with desperation. Dani lifted her gaze to the man at the window. What had he said to these children? Had he offered the slightest bit of reassurance? More than ever, they needed the comfort of familiar things, the promise they'd be together and that God Himself shared their grief.

Staring back at Dani, Beau Morgan sealed his lips in a hard line, then turned back to the window. Framed by lace curtains and panes of glass, he stood with his arms crossed and his feet spread wide. If he'd been wearing boots, Dani might have been intimidated. Instead she saw a hole in the heel of his sock. A tug on the yarn would unravel the entire garment. She suspected the man's life was in the same sorry shape and prayed he'd be eager to leave Patrick's daughters in her care.

Thoughts of the girls mixed with the scent of the lilies.

Looking down, she squeezed Emma's shoulders. "Can you tell me what happened?"

Emma opened her mouth but sealed it without making a sound.

Dani looked to the man by the window. Hate glinted in his eyes. "It was ugly. Emma doesn't need to relive it."

The child shook her head. "I *want* to remember. He said he loved us. He said—"

"Emma, don't." Beau Morgan glared at Dani. "Patrick was struck by lightning. Emma found him."

Dani gasped, then closed her eyes. "Dear Lord in Heaven, be with Patrick. Be with all of us."

The man snorted. "I wouldn't call the Almighty 'dear.'"

Dani stiffened at the lack of respect. "Patrick had faith. He believed—"

"That's fine for him," the man replied. "But the Almighty and I don't see eye to eye, not anymore."

Emma choked on a sob. "It was my fault. I knew a storm was coming, but I didn't tell him."

The man scowled. "It's not your fault, kid. You didn't make it rain."

"But I knew!" Her voice rose to a wail. "He went to see Pastor Josh about the wedding. I asked him to buy some ribbon for Esther's dress. If he hadn't gone to the store, he'd have been home before the storm."

Dani trembled with regrets of her own. Patrick had wanted a September wedding. She'd pushed for June. If she'd shown more patience, he'd be alive. She knew her thoughts were crazy. She didn't control the weather. A lightning strike... What were the odds? She thought of Patrick's last letter. *Storms are common, Dani. Life here is hard. Are you sure you want to marry me?*

She'd written back. *I love storms!*

Noah had built an ark. Christ had calmed a stormy sea. She'd seen blizzards in January, tasted the cold and watched tornadoes drop from summer clouds. She'd felt the fear and clung to her faith. Not once had God let her down. She refused to doubt Him now, yet how could she not wonder, just a little, if God had blinked and left Patrick to die?

Weak in the knees, she led Emma to the divan. "When did it happen?"

Mr. Morgan shot her a look of warning, then spoke to Emma. "Go upstairs. I'll tell her."

"No!" the child cried.

Did this man really think silence would spare Emma the memories? Dani had been the same age when her mother died. She'd brought home a cold from school. Leda Baxter had nursed her daughter and died of pneumonia. Silence had turned Dani's childhood home into an open grave, leaving her alone with the same twisted guilt plaguing Emma. No way would she leave the child to suffer as she had.

Dani took Emma's hand. "What happened, sweetie?"

"The storm turned the sky black." Her voice dropped to a murmur. "I sent Ellie and Esther to the cellar, then I came up here to watch for Pa. I stood right there."

She pointed to a spot in front of the side-by-side windows looking into the yard. Beau Morgan's back blocked the view, so Emma leaned to the side to see around him. Dani craned her neck, as well, but he put his hands on his hips, blocking the view with his bent elbows. When Emma walked to the edge of the window so she could see the yard, Dani joined her. Standing behind the child, she placed her hands on Emma's thin shoulders and followed her gaze down the road to a distant pine.

"Do you see that tree?" Emma asked.

"I do." Dani looked at the charred branches and blackened trunk of a ponderosa. She'd passed it on the way to the farm.

"I saw the lightning strike. The air buzzed, then everything went white and thunder shook the house. A minute later, Pa's horse galloped into the yard."

Riderless.

Against her will, Dani saw the pelting rain, the mud, the empty saddle.

Emma's voice cracked. "Lightning hit again. Everything turned as bright as day. That's when I saw that Buck had no tail. His rump had a burn on it. I could smell the hair."

Beau Morgan reached across the span of the window and touched the child's back. His sleeve rode up his forearm, revealing tense muscles and a jagged scar above his wrist. "Don't do this to yourself."

As the child stared into the yard, Dani stroked her arms. The images in Emma's mind were sacred, hers to share or bury as her heart demanded. The clock ticked. Chickens pecked the dirt by the barn as Dani stared at the gouges left in the mud by Patrick's horse. Next time it rained, she'd stomp them flat.

Emma saw the marks, too. "I knew Pa was hurt, so I ran outside. Buck died right in front of me."

Dani held in a groan that would do no good. As a child she'd embroidered samplers with her favorite Bible verses. *For God so loved the world... Peace I give to you...* Staring into the empty yard, she felt the thinness of the thread shaping those words. She'd snapped it with her teeth or snipped it with scissors. Listening to Emma, Dani felt a new tension stretching her faith.

Emma's shoulders sagged. "I found Pa by that pine tree. His clothes were burned and he was lying in the mud, but he was still alive."

Why, Lord?

It wasn't like Dani to doubt God's ways, but she couldn't stop the anger welling in her middle. These children had already lost their mother. Why had God taken Patrick, too? She stared at the window where a pale reflection of Emma's face stared back. Tears trickled down the girl's cheeks, glistening like silver ribbons.

Emma squared her shoulders. "He looked me right in the eye, then he touched my nose like he did when I was little. He said he loved us, then he saw Mama. I know, because he called her name."

Dani refused to be jealous. Patrick had loved his first wife with a dedication she admired and wanted for herself. He'd called her Beth, short for Elizabeth. They'd been childhood friends. Two years ago, Beth had died of a ruptured appendix.

Dani gripped Emma's shoulders. "He's with your ma now. I know for a fact he's looking out for you right this minute."

"He loved you, too." Emma wiped her eyes, then faced Dani. "You said in your letters that you'd be our new mother. Pa's gone, but—"

"I'm keeping that promise."

Dani hugged the girl hard. They sobbed together until the river of tears turned to a trickle. Grief would rain on them again, filling the wells, but for now they were spent.

Beau Morgan cleared his throat. "You may not be aware, Miss Baxter. I'm the girls' legal guardian."

Dani straightened, then met his gaze. "I'm very aware, Mr. Morgan. Patrick named you as executor several years ago." Her next words would settle the issue for good or start a battle she couldn't lose. "I have a letter in my trunk. It clearly states his more recent intentions."

"And what were those?"

"He asked me to adopt the girls."

"Contingent on marriage?"

"Of course."

Mr. Morgan raised one thick brow. "And the farm? Would he want you to have that, too?"

Dani hadn't thought that far. "I suppose." She needed a way to support the children.

Beau Morgan rocked back on his heels. "Miss Baxter, you're either naive or a con artist."

Dani's mouth gaped. "How dare you!"

"No, how dare *you*." His voice stayed as flat as a coin. "I'm a blood relative with legal authority. You waltz in here and announce you want my nieces and a farm that's worth a good amount of money."

"I don't care about the money!"

"Of course, you don't." His lips curled with contempt. "Frankly, it doesn't matter what you want. I have an obligation to see to my nieces and I intend to meet it."

Staring into the man's eyes, a green that reminded her of dying grass, Dani saw good reason to trust Patrick's assessment of him as crazy. She judged him to be in his midthirties, a few years older than his brother, but far less settled. Judging by the ragged ends of his hair, he'd cut it himself with a knife. The dark blond strands brushed his collarless shirt like a worn-out broom. Dani's eyes skimmed across the denim that had once been green or blue. She couldn't tell which. The sun had bleached it to turquoise, a soft color that blended with the dust on his brown trousers and the unraveling yarn of his gray sock.

If he couldn't take care of himself, how could he manage three young girls? Maybe he didn't want to… Perhaps he was eager to turn over guardianship and needed assurance of her honorable intentions. A woman could beat a mule with a stick or coax it with a carrot. Dani opted for the carrot. "I appreciate your concern, Mr. Morgan. In fact, I admire it."

"Good."

"Once you see Patrick's letter, I'm sure you'll agree with me."

"Don't count on it, Miss Baxter. The world's full of liars. How do I know you're not one of them?"

Emma thrust herself between them. "Pa loved Dani!"

The man looked Dani up and down, assessing her appearance without really seeing her. Before leaving the train, she'd put on her prettiest outfit, a pink taffeta suit with a snug jacket and ruffled skirt, and a sweeping straw hat that dipped across her brow. The outfit made her feel pretty. She'd dressed for Patrick, not this rude man with holes in his socks.

His eyes darted back to her face. "Men are fools, Miss Baxter. Especially lonely ones. Patrick fit that mold."

Dani had never felt so insulted in her life, or so alone. Back home, her reputation had shone like gold. No one would have questioned her motives for taking in three orphaned girls. Then again, no one in Walker County, Wisconsin, had Beau Morgan's suspicious nature. Dani couldn't help but wonder who'd kicked him in the shins.

His eyes focused on hers. "A train leaves for Denver in the morning. I want you on it."

"Absolutely not."

"I'll pay your fare home."

Dani had fifteen dollars in her reticule, enough for a week in a hotel but not much else. Her brother would send money if she asked, but she refused to consider it. She'd made a promise to Patrick and intended to keep it, but she'd also left Wisconsin for a reason. When their father died, her brother had inherited the family dairy. A year ago, he'd married. Ever since, he'd been pushing Dani to leave. *This isn't your house, Dani. It's mine and Marta is my wife. You need a home of your own.*

Dani thought so, too. Some time ago, she'd been engaged to a young man named Tommy Page. They'd been childhood friends, but Dani hadn't felt any of the excitement she'd expected. Tommy had wanted to kiss and hug, but she'd said no. He was a brother to her, nothing more, so she'd ended the engagement. Dani wanted the right husband, the man God had made just for her. She'd been willing to wait, but her brother had lost patience with her. Against her will, he'd encouraged Archie Weldon to court her. A widower with a bad back, Archie had wanted a housekeeper, not a wife. Lars Jenson, a man who spoke in grunts, had been next on her brother's list. And so on… until Dani had met every bachelor in Walker County.

Eventually she'd given in and agreed to marry Virgil Griggs. She'd liked Virgil, but she hadn't loved him. A week before the wedding, she'd broken their engagement, embarrassing Virgil and shaming herself. *That Dani Baxter is fickle...* She'd heard the talk and been embarrassed and angry. She didn't have a fickle bone in her body. She simply couldn't lie to herself or to Virgil, who deserved better than a wife who couldn't bear the thought of kissing him. Dani had been near despair when Kirstin had mentioned her cousin in Colorado, a widower who needed a wife and mother for his three daughters. Dani had given Patrick permission to write. After three letters, she'd fallen in love with him.

Now he was gone and his wayward brother had the girls and wanted Dani to leave. She simply couldn't do it, not with Patrick's letter in her trunk. But neither could she stay at the farm with this man. Her best hope lay in convincing him to leave. Dani wasn't wise in the ways of the world, but she knew a little about men and carrots.

"I have a suggestion, Mr. Morgan."

"What's that?"

"There's a nice hotel by the railroad station. I'm sure you'd enjoy a good night's sleep."

His eyes flickered. Either he enjoyed a fight or he was tempted by the comforts of a hotel room. Judging by the dark crescents under his eyes, he hadn't slept in days.

Dani sweetened the deal. "The hotel has a restaurant. I saw it when I rented the buggy. Today's special is roast beef with raspberry pie for dessert."

His mouth hardened. "No, thanks, Miss Baxter. Emma's a good cook."

Dani doubted it. The child had written about her kitchen foibles. *Will you teach me to make biscuits? Mine are rock hard, but Pa eats them and smiles.*

A lump pressed into Dani's throat. She'd trusted Patrick with her life, her reputation. She had no such faith in the man standing in his place. She also had nowhere else to go. She didn't like what she was about to say, but she had to get Beau Morgan to leave. "There's a saloon, too."

His eyes twinkled with mischief. "You want a drink?"

"No!"

"Me, neither." The corners of his mouth tipped up. "I'm not a drinking man, Miss Baxter. Never have been."

Was that good news? Dani didn't know. She wanted this man to be so low that any judge in Douglas County would deny him custody. Instead he sounded like her Aunt Minnie.

He leaned against the wall, crossing his sock-covered feet. "I'm also good at hearing what isn't said. I'm guessing you have about ten dollars in your bag and don't know a soul."

She blushed.

"That's what I thought." He eyed her thoughtfully. "I'd be glad to pay your room and board in town, but I suspect you're too stubborn to accept."

"It's not a matter of stubbornness." She reached for Emma. "I promised Patrick—"

"I know what you promised." His voice turned gentle. "I also know what it's like to be grief-stricken. It leaves you numb, but only for a while. Once the shock passes, you wake up screaming. It'll eat you alive if you let it."

Peering into his eyes, she saw a kinship born of suffering. Dani had grieved her mother and still cried for the woman who'd given her blue eyes and wheat-blond hair. Who had Beau Morgan mourned? The connection, as brief as lightning and as bright, frightened her.

If he felt the spark, he didn't let it show. Standing straighter, he looked ready for business. "If you're willing to bend a bit, I'm prepared to offer a compromise."

"What do you have in mind?"

"I'll move to the barn while we sort things out. You get room and board in exchange for keeping house."

Emma looked up at Dani. "It's time to start the garden. We could do it together."

For a thousand miles, she'd dreamed of planting tomatoes in Patrick's side yard. She loved the feeling of loamy earth and the scent of herbs growing in a window box. She'd imagined flowers, too. Tulips in the spring, roses in June. She had learned from her mother that touches of beauty nourished a family as much as good food.

Her gaze drifted to the hole in Beau Morgan's sock. His big toe curled as if to hide, then stretched in defiance. "As you can see, my clothes could use some mending."

"And a good scrubbing," she added.

"That's a fact."

His voice held a yearning that put Dani on alert. Which was more dangerous? The snake that rattled as it slithered or the one sleeping in the sun?

Emma squeezed her hand. "Stay, Dani. Please."

She wanted to say yes, but she had to protect her reputation as well as the children. "I'd prefer the hotel," she said. "But only if the girls can stay with me."

"I can't allow it."

"Why not?" She tried to sound confident. "It would be a change for them."

"You're naive, Miss Baxter."

Dani bristled. "I've just traveled a thousand miles—"

"And I've traveled ten thousand." He raised his chin. "Have you ever seen a pack of wolves?"

She'd heard howling in the forest near her father's farm, but the wolves had stayed out of sight. "No, I haven't."

"I have," he said. "The kind with two legs."

"Castle Rock seems safe to me."

His eyes glittered like broken glass. "It was—before I got here."

Chapter Two

Looking at Daniela Baxter, Beau felt the cut of sudden change. The last time he'd seen Patrick had been five years ago. His brother had come to the funeral for Beau's wife, traveling alone because his own wife, Beth, had been close to delivering their third child. Beau and his brother hadn't been close, but he'd appreciated the kindness. Patrick had made him promise to write now and then. He'd even offered him a place to stay.

Beau had said he'd keep in touch, but he'd broken the promise so badly he hadn't known about Beth's passing. He hadn't known a lot of things when he'd arrived in Castle Rock two days ago. Hot on the trail of an outlaw named Clay Johnson, Beau had found himself within a few miles of his brother's farm. He'd decided to pay a visit and had arrived to find a fresh grave and an old man in the barn. The fellow and his wife were neighbors who'd come to care for the cows and the girls until other arrangements could be made.

The girls could have been farmed out to friends, but the cows needed their routine. A lightning strike…of all the foolish things. Even more surprising was the news from Patrick's attorney. Seven years ago, Patrick had written a will. It named Beau as guardian of his children—a fact Beau vaguely remembered. He'd have made a good guardian in the past, but not anymore. An ex-lawman, he sold his gun to the highest bidder. Like most shootists, he lived in the canyons between good and evil. He enjoyed the freedom and the money, but mostly he burned with the need to bring Clay Johnson to justice.

Whether God or the devil had given him a thirst for Johnson's blood, Beau didn't know. He only knew that Clay Johnson had killed the most precious person in his life. Lucy, his young wife, had put on her prettiest dress, a pink thing with puffy sleeves, and brought him supper at the sheriff's office. What happened next was an abomination. Beau no longer dreamed about that day, but he remembered every detail. Looking at Miss Baxter in her pink dress, he swallowed a mouthful of bile. He hated that color and the memories it brought. He always would.

Sending her to the hotel tempted him as much as that roast beef dinner. He'd lied about Emma's cooking. The girl made a mean pancake, but a man needed more than starch in his belly to do a day's work. He also needed to sleep at night, something Beau hadn't done since he'd arrived. He couldn't. Since Lucy's murder, he and Johnson had been playing a game of cat and mouse. Sometimes the outlaw vanished for months, leaving Beau to search aimlessly for his prey. Other times Johnson went on the prowl, leaving threats for Beau at local saloons. Sometimes he wrote notes. Sometimes he left tokens that chilled Beau's blood.

Daniela Baxter's eyes drilled into his. "Who are you, Mr. Morgan?"

"I told you. I'm Patrick's brother."

"That's not what I meant."

Beau held back a smart remark about jabbering females. If Miss Baxter ended up at the hotel, she might blather to every busybody in town. She looked like the kind of woman who'd want to go to church on Sundays. Beau knew all about gossip cloaked in prayer. He'd been the focus of his share after Lucy's death. Wishing he'd been less of a blowhard, he tried to smile. "Forget the bluster. I'm no one."

"Somehow, I doubt that."

Beau said nothing. In truth, his reputation stretched from Bozeman to El Paso, across the plains and over mountains that dwarfed a man's pride but not his pain. If word spread he was in Castle Rock, anyone he touched would be a target for Johnson. That included Miss Baxter. He didn't need another female in his care, but honor required him to see to her safety. Like it or not, he'd have to keep an eye on her.

No hardship there… Daniela Baxter was just plain pretty. Slender but womanly, she filled out the dress in all the right places. Not that Beau cared. Being a man, he couldn't help but notice her looks, but he knew the rules. When he'd married Lucy, he'd promised to love, honor and cherish his wife until they were parted by death. Lucy was gone, but Beau took comfort in keeping his vows. His eyes locked on Miss Baxter, saying things with a look that acknowledged the deepest of truths. He was male. She wasn't. He had the power to harm her. She needed to know he never would. He made his voice solemn. "I'm an honorable man, Miss Baxter."

"You're the one who mentioned wolves," she replied. "I understand they come in sheep's clothing."

"I'm not one of them."

Before she could reply, footsteps padded on the landing at the top of the stairs. He turned and saw Ellie and Esther peeking around the corner. Esther, as always, had her thumb in her mouth. She was five and too old for the habit, but Beau hadn't tried to stop her. Human beings, no matter their age, took comfort where they could find it.

"Are you Dani?" Ellie asked.

"I am."

The girls hurried down the steps and threw themselves into her arms. More hugs, more tears. Beau was tired of the flood but knew the girls would pull on Miss Baxter's heart in a way common sense couldn't. With a throat as dry as sand, he watched the swirl of pink and ribbons and locks of golden hair. All four of them were blonde, though the girls' hair would darken with time as Patrick's had. Beau's hair had lost its shine a long time ago, though it lightened up in the summer.

He watched as the woman kissed Ellie's forehead, then lifted Esther on to her hip. In a voice choked with tears, she rambled about God and Patrick looking down from Heaven.

They loved you, brother. I wish I'd known you better.

Even as he thought the words, Beau stifled his regrets. He'd learned to live one day at a time. To take what pleasure he found and be content with it. A can of beans for supper. A lantern on a moonless night. If a man didn't have a home, he couldn't lose it. If he didn't love, he couldn't get hurt. Beau had drawn that line the day Clay Johnson shot Lucy and not once had he crossed it. He hoped Daniela Baxter would be wise and draw a similar line for herself. She had no future in Castle Rock. Even if he'd wanted to hand her custody of the girls, he couldn't do it. Running a farm required both brains and muscle.

The thought of leaving a woman and three children at the mercy of hired hands struck him as gutless.

Beau glanced at the mantel clock. In two hours, he had an appointment with Trevor Scott, the attorney handling Patrick's will. If things went as planned, the girls would leave for boarding school at the end of the month.

Ellie, a tomboy in coveralls, broke the hug and looked at Dani. "You're staying, aren't you?"

Miss Baxter tousled the child's hair, then looked at Beau. Her eyes soothed his soul and laid it bare at the same time. "Can I trust you, Mr. Morgan?"

"With your life."

"In that case, we have a deal. If you'll stay in the barn, I'll tend to the house."

When she held out her gloved hand, Beau noticed the cupped shape of her fingers. His own hand, loose and open, was just a clench away from the violence that defined his life, but he offered it in good faith. He expected to see trepidation in her eyes. Instead she squeezed back with surprising firmness. The grip, he realized, came from hard work. The grit came from her heart. Beau saw her pink dress, the shadow of roses in her cheeks, and pined a moment for Lucy. How did it feel to grow old with a woman? To see your daughters marry and your sons grow strong? To live without the thirst for Clay Johnson's blood? Beau would never know. Most of the time, he didn't want to know. He let go of Miss Baxter's hand. He'd had all the innocence he could stand for one day.

He'd seen a rented buggy out front. "Where's your trunk?"

"At the train station."

Beau thought of his appointment with Patrick's attorney. "I have to go to town this afternoon. I'll take you and the girls and we'll pick it up."

"Thank you," she said.

Beau looked down at his nieces. "Get going. We leave in ten minutes."

They scurried up the stairs like frightened mice, leaving Beau to wonder what he'd done to scare them. He wished he could be less stern, but he had a melancholy nature. Miss Baxter had turned her head to watch the girls. Even with tears on her cheeks, she seemed like the cheerful sort. Beau hoped so. The girls needed a woman's tenderness.

Leaving Miss Baxter at the stairs, he strode into Patrick's bedroom, where he changed into a clean shirt, then balled up his laundry and slung his saddlebag over his shoulder. As he came out of the dark room, he saw Miss Baxter sitting on the bottom step with her head bowed.

Beau feared God but didn't much like Him. Taking Patrick's life struck him as wrong. Leaving this young woman to cope alone counted as cruel. He stopped a few feet away. "Miss Baxter?"

She looked up with damp eyes. "Yes?"

"I'm truly sorry for your loss."

"Thank you."

Beau shifted his weight. Handing her his dirty clothes didn't seem right, so he headed for the door.

When she called his name, he turned but said nothing.

"Is that your laundry?" she asked.

"Yes, it is."

"I expect to keep my end of the bargain. Leave your clothes and I'll wash them tomorrow."

Beau stepped back to the staircase where she'd pushed to her feet. Judging by the twitch of her nostrils, the smell of the barn reached her before he did. He had three horses in his care, his roan and Patrick's two workhorses.

"You've been mucking out stalls," she said.

"Someone had to do it."

"And the milking?"

"Of course."

What did she think? That he dozed in a hammock all day? Patrick had ten Jersey cows. They might have been "ladies" for Patrick, lining up at the gate at milking time, but they hadn't taken to Beau. Each one had bawled and squalled while he looped a rope around her neck and led her to the barn for milking. He'd felt ridiculous on a little three-legged stool, and his clumsy hands annoyed the cows until Emma had given him pointers. She'd also informed him the cows had names and liked it when her pa sang hymns. Beau had grunted, then listened to the child crooning words to a song he'd made a point of forgetting.

Blessed assurance, Jesus divine!

Oh what a foretaste of glory is mine...

Beau hadn't set foot in a church in five years and he didn't intend to start now. He handed his clothes to Miss Baxter. They needed a good scrubbing. So did he, but a visit to the bathhouse was out of the question with four females in his care and Clay Johnson nearby. With the saddlebag dragging on his shoulder, Beau headed for the barn. Maybe Trevor Scott had found a school. Beau hoped so. He didn't know how much purity and light he could tolerate.

Dani carried Beau Morgan's laundry through the kitchen and out to the back porch. Where did Patrick

"Not exactly," the girl explained. "The gun's empty but I can hear it click. He does it over and over, like he's aiming at someone he can't see."

That settled it. The man was crazy. He was either wanted by the law or protecting them from a danger he'd brought to Castle Rock himself.

The front door swung open. Heavy boots thudded on the wooden floor. "Ladies?"

Dani whispered into Emma's ear. "We'll talk later."

As she stood straight, Beau Morgan stepped into the kitchen and crossed his arms as though he meant business. A tan duster hung from his shoulders but gaped at the waist, revealing a wide leather belt and the front edge of a cross-draw holster. He pulled his mouth into a smile that bordered on a sneer. "Pray tell, ladies. My ears are burning. I don't suppose you were talking about me?"

"No, sir."

Emma had lied, but Dani didn't correct her. She wanted to hide the girls under her skirts. No way could they share their home with a man who armed himself for a trip to town. She'd spotted the church from the window of the train. She'd never met Pastor Blue and his wife, but Patrick had said they were kind. Surely the couple would take them in until Dani could find safer accommodations.

"Let's go," she said with false cheer.

Mr. Morgan led the way out the door, grabbing the hat he'd left on a peg in the entry hall. As he pulled it low, the girls followed him down the steps with Dani bringing up the rear. In the front yard she saw the livery buggy and the family wagon. He was standing by the buggy, watching them like a coyote spying a flock of chickens.

He pointed his chin at the wagon. "The girls can ride in the back."

Dani steered them to the buggy. "I think we can fit. Don't you, girls?" The rig had a single seat. It would be a squeeze.

Mr. Morgan shrugged. "Suit yourselves."

When she bent to lift Esther, he reached for the child at the same time. Their hands overlapped on the girl's waist with Dani losing the race.

His eyes narrowed. "Let me. She's heavy."

"I can manage."

Esther grabbed for Dani, but Mr. Morgan scooped her up and plopped her on the seat before she knew enough to cry. Scowling, he offered his gloved hand to Ellie, then Emma, and finally to her. Looking at the leather, Dani wondered what it hid. Some people thought a man's eyes revealed his soul. Dani looked at hands. Calluses testified to hard work. Soft skin hinted at laziness or vice. If Mr. Morgan removed the gloves, what would she see? The trim nails of a gambler? The knuckles of a brawler?

His eyes glinted. "I won't bite, Miss Baxter."

Satan had said the same thing to Eve. Ignoring his hand, she climbed into the buggy.

He went to the wagon. "Stay in front of me."

She took the reins and drove out of the yard with Ellie pressed against her ribs and Esther in Emma's lap. The top of the buggy shielded them from Mr. Morgan's stare, but the creak of the wagon kept him close.

Ellie squirmed closer to Dani. "He's nothing like Pa."

Emma stared straight ahead. "Pa's gone. We have to get used to it."

"I don't want to!" Ellie cried.

"There's no choice." Emma tightened her grip on Esther's waist. "I'm the oldest. That means I have to look out for you."

Dani's heart broke for the girl. She knew how it felt to grow up overnight. They rode in silence, listening to the rhythm of Esther sucking her thumb and the creak of the harness. Behind them, Beau Morgan clicked to the horses, crowding the buggy in spite of the empty road. Dani wondered if he'd watch them this closely in town. The closer he rode, the more determined she became to escape. But how? She needed a plan. "Do you know where Mr. Morgan's going?" she said to Emma.

"Probably to see Mr. Scott."

"Who's he?"

"Pa's attorney. He sent Mr. Morgan a message."

Ellie frowned. "He said to call him Uncle Beau."

"I don't care," Emma replied. "I want him to leave."

So did Dani. She considered barging into his meeting with the attorney, but getting the girls to Pastor Blue and his wife took priority. "Where's Mr. Scott's office?"

"On Fourth Street."

The church was on the west side of town. The livery was on First Street. If she could convince Mr. Morgan to allow her to watch the girls while he met with Mr. Scott, they could make a run for the church.

"What are we going to do?" Ellie asked.

The older girls would understand, but Esther wouldn't. She gave Emma and Ellie a conspiratorial glance. "When Mr. Morgan visits the attorney, we'll pay a visit to Pastor Blue and his wife."

Emma's eyes dimmed. "The church is far."

"About a half mile," Ellie added.

Dani's heart sank. Her new shoes had dainty heels. Pretty or not, they hurt her feet. Esther posed another problem. Unless Dani took the wagon, she'd have to carry the child a good part of the way. The more she thought about sneaking the wagon out from under Beau Morgan's nose, the more she liked the idea. By then, they'd have picked up her trunk and she'd have possession of Patrick's letters. Unless he changed his mind about custody, she'd need them in a court of law.

Aware of three pairs of blue eyes on her face, Dani nudged the horse into a faster walk. "We'll make it," she said to the girls.

"I don't see how." Emma sighed.

Dani put iron in her voice. "Do you know the story about Daniel in the lion's den?"

"It's scary," Esther said.

"That's true, but God kept Daniel safe." Dani let the words sink in. "If God can put lions to sleep, He can get us to the church."

"We can see Miss Adie," Ellie said.

"That's right."

Esther pulled her thumb out of her mouth. "She has kittens!"

A lump pushed into Dani's throat. Emma, sensing her sister's need, chatted about the cats. Ellie joined in, leaving Dani to ponder her plan as she navigated the stretch of road into Castle Rock. With a little luck, she and the girls would be spending the night at the parsonage and Beau Morgan would see the wisdom of leaving them alone.

With the wagon rattling in the buggy's wake, Dani took in the rippling grass and patches of pine dotting the horizon. In the distance stood the dome of granite that gave the town its name. Round and high, the fortress-like stone capped a mesa jutting up from a meadow. To the east, Dani saw rows of buildings. Most were made of wood, but a few showed off the pinkish rhyolite stone that had given the town its birth. Twenty years ago, Castle

Rock had been nothing more than a cattle stop. Now it boasted a school, two churches and dozens of businesses. Patrick had described it in his letters, filling her with excitement at the prospect of being a part of something new.

As they neared the train station, Dani saw the tracks stretching as far south as she could see. The train that brought her had left hours ago. Nothing remained. Not a trace of steam, not the six people who had disembarked with her. The only sign of humanity was her trunk sitting on the platform. It looked the way she felt…alone, abandoned and packed for a trip it would never take.

Dani reined in the livery mare. Beau Morgan halted the wagon next to her, climbed down and opened the tailgate. As he strode to the platform, she leaped down from the buggy and followed him.

"That's my trunk," she said.

"I figured."

"It's heavy. You'll need help."

Ignoring her, he hoisted it as if it held feathers instead of her life and lugged it down the three steps. Dani hurried to the back of the wagon where she saw a pile of quilts. Had Patrick kept them there for the girls? Or had Beau Morgan thought to bring them for the bumpy ride? Dani didn't know, but she doubted Patrick kept blankets in his work wagon. She knew from his letters that he owned a two-seat surrey the family took to church, yet kindness didn't fit her impression of Beau Morgan.

Now, Dani... The voice belonged to her father. Walter Baxter had been quick to love and slow to judge. She could imagine his words. *For all you know, Beau Morgan's an upstanding citizen. Judge not, daughter.*

Dani tried to keep an open mind, but she couldn't erase the picture of this man dry firing a pistol into the dark. As he latched the tailgate, she went back to the buggy. He took the reins of the wagon and led the way to the livery stable. The wagon rattled as they passed a feed store, then a mining office where men stood in a line. People on the street noticed them. Some smiled and a few waved to the girls, but Dani had no way to signal for help.

When they reached the livery, Mr. Morgan stopped the wagon. Without a word, he went into the barn and disappeared into the shadows.

"Let's go!" Dani cried.

She leaped out of the buggy and turned. Emma shoved Esther into her arms, then jumped out the other side with Ellie behind her. As the older girls piled into the wagon, Dani boosted Esther over the tailgate, then hurried to the front seat. Before she could hoist herself up, Beau Morgan strode through the doorway.

Faking a smile, Dani put a ring in her voice. "We're ready to go."

"I see." He handed her a silver dollar. "Here."

"What's this?"

"Miller's refunding the rental."

It wasn't much, but every dollar would help. As she took the money, her fingers brushed his glove. He stepped back as if she had the pox, then glanced across the street to a row of shops that included an emporium. Looking befuddled, he cleared his throat. "You've had a long trip. Is there anything you need while we're in town?"

Yesterday Dani had imagined browsing the shops with Patrick's daughters. That dream had died. "No, thank you."

"I'd pay."

"I'm fine, Mr. Morgan." She wanted to run, not shop.

"Suit yourself," he said with a grunt.

Intending to ride with the girls, she headed for the back of the wagon. As she turned, strong fingers caught the bottom of her forearm and turned her back to the seat. His touch was light, nothing more than a brush, but it felt like a shackle. His voice went low, barely a whisper. "You'll ride up front with me."

"I'd rather sit with the girls."

"I'm not asking what you want," he replied. "I'm telling you what's best."

"I don't see why—"

"That's right. You don't."

Dani pulled out of his grip but didn't move. His eyes tensed with the same worry she'd seen on her father's face just before the worst storm of her life had swept across their farm. As he'd ordered her to the cellar, a tornado had funneled down behind the barn. She'd learned that day to trust her father's instincts.

Beau Morgan's expression shifted to the mix of a smile and a scowl she'd seen in the kitchen. Her father had known best. Did Beau Morgan?

"Is there a reason?" she asked.

"None I care to give."

Dani opened her mouth to argue, then sealed her lips. It didn't matter where she sat in the wagon as long as he took them to a place where they could make a run for the church. When he offered his hand, she accepted his help onto the seat. He walked to the other side, climbed up and steered the wagon into the street. Anyone on the boardwalk would think they were a family.

And that, Dani realized, explained why he'd insisted she sit at his side. She and the girls were part of a disguise. They turned Beau Morgan into a family man. Who was after him and why? Dani's stomach clenched. With each block, they traveled farther from the church. Staring straight ahead, she risked a question. "Where are we going?"

"To see Patrick's attorney."

Dani thought of Emma's guess. The child had a good mind. "It must concern the girls."

The man glanced over his shoulder. Dani did the same and saw them huddled as far from the seat as they could get.

Looking straight ahead, he lowered his voice. "I haven't told them yet, but you might as well know. I'm selling the farm and sending them to school."

"You can't!" The whisper scraped her throat.

"It's for the best."

Dani knotted her hands in her lap. Was it wiser to make a break for the parsonage or insist on seeing Trevor Scott herself? Patrick had never mentioned Mr. Scott. On the other hand, he'd spoken well of Pastor Blue. She was weighing the choice when they stopped in front of an ice-cream parlor. Mr. Morgan hooked his thumb toward the office building across the street. "Scott's office is on the second floor. I thought you and the girls might enjoy some ice cream while I take care of business."

Dani saw the answer to her prayer. "I'm sure they would."

"Can I trust you to watch them, Miss Baxter?"

"Of course." She'd told the truth. She wouldn't let the girls out of her sight until they reached the church.

He reached into his pocket, extracted a few coins and handed them to her. With her heart pounding, she put the money in her reticule and climbed down from the wagon.

As the girls scrambled to her side, Mr. Morgan stood

in front of them with his hands on his hips. "I'll be keeping an eye on you."

If Patrick had spoken those words, they'd have promised protection. Coming from his brother, they made her skin prickle. Forcing a smile, Dani looked at the girls. "Mr. Morgan is treating us to ice cream."

Emma and Ellie murmured a polite "thank you." Esther squealed with delight and ran to the door.

"Don't leave the store," he said to Dani. "I'll meet you inside."

Feeling his eyes on her back, she led the girls into the ice creamery, then watched through the window as Mr. Morgan neared the attorney's office. He had to climb a flight of stairs, knock on a door and wait in a lobby. Dani grabbed Esther's hand. "Let's go."

Emma and Ellie headed for the door, but Esther dug in her heels. "I want ice cream!"

"Later, sweetie."

"Now!"

"Esther, we have to go."

Her bottom lip trembled. "But you said!"

The child wasn't being stubborn. She was a frightened little girl whose daddy hadn't come home for five days. Ice cream promised a bit of happiness. Dani searched her mind for something more appealing, found it and dropped to a crouch, putting herself at eye level with Esther. "Remember Miss Adie and the kittens?"

The child nodded.

"That's where we're going."

Esther tipped her head to the left, then to the right. The choices seesawed in the child's mind, then hit the ground with a thud. "I want ice cream!"

The woman behind the counter looked over the jars of

penny candy with an arched brow. Dani thought of scooping Esther into her arms and running, but she couldn't risk creating a scene. Besides, they'd lost two valuable minutes. By now, Beau Morgan would be with Trevor Scott.

Straightening, she gave the clerk a wry smile. "I guess we're having ice cream."

As the girls placed their orders, Dani turned and peered at the window marking the attorney's office. Beau Morgan loomed behind the glass with crossed arms and an expression that gave her chills.

Chapter Three

"Have a seat, Mr. Morgan."

"I'll stand, thanks."

Beau was tired enough to sleep on his feet, but he planted himself at the window and focused on the ice-cream parlor. The odds of Clay Johnson walking down the street were slim to none, but Beau refused to let down his guard.

He also had doubts about Miss Baxter. Ever since he'd walked into the kitchen, she'd been giving him the evil eye. Her judgment of his character irked him. Time had tarnished his manners, but he'd tried to be considerate. He'd tossed blankets in the wagon for the girls, and he'd bargained with the livery owner for Miss Baxter's refund. A long time ago, simple courtesy had come naturally to him. So had conversation. He'd gone to church socials and asked pretty girls to dance. That's where he'd met Lucy. Miss Baxter reminded him of that happy time… and the hard time that had followed. She'd grieve for Patrick as he'd grieved for Lucy. Staring through the glass, Beau watched as she and the girls circled a small table.

Trevor Scott cleared his throat. "I have good news, Mr. Morgan."

"You've found a school?"

"Not exactly. I've located another relative, a Miss Harriet Lange."

"Who is she?"

"A great-aunt on Elizabeth's side of the family."

Beau frowned. She sounded old. "Where does she live?"

"Minnesota."

"It's cold there."

"There's another problem," Scott said.

"What's that?"

"She'll take Emma but not the younger girls."

The offer rubbed Beau the wrong way. He could see his nieces now, licking ice cream from glass bowls. Each one had impressed him. This week had been the worst of Emma's life, but she'd stepped up like a grown woman. He'd seen Ellie carrying a bucket of water to her daddy's grave. He didn't know what kind of flowers she'd planted, but she'd come to the house with muddy knees. And Esther...she'd never stop sucking her thumb without her sisters.

"Why Emma?" he asked.

Scott leaned back in his squeaky chair. "Miss Lange is an elderly spinster. I assume she wants companionship."

Or a servant, Beau thought. It made sense, but he knew he'd become cynical. He had a talent for spotting weeds but rarely noticed flowers, even when they filled a meadow. Maybe the woman had a kind heart but couldn't feed two more children. "Does she have an income?"

"She clerks at a bank."

A job that paid little money. Beau hooked his thumbs

in his belt. He earned top dollar and saved most of it. "If money's the problem, I can solve it."

"With the sale of the farm?"

"No, that's going in the bank." He wanted the girls to have a nest egg for later in life. "I'll pay for what they need."

"It's generous of you."

Maybe, but Beau felt no pride. What the girls needed most, money couldn't buy. They needed a home, parents who'd love them and tuck them in at night. He couldn't do those things.

Scott shifted in his chair. "If you'd like, I can present an offer to Miss Lange."

"Do it," Beau said. "Tell her it's all three or nothing. If she agrees, we'll discuss a monthly allowance."

"And if she says no?"

"We'll look for a school."

"I don't envy you, Mr. Morgan. The situation calls for the wisdom of Solomon."

Beau knew the story. Two women claiming the same child went to the Biblical king to resolve their differences. When he'd threatened to cut the baby in half, the real mother had given up the fight to save her child's life. Beau felt the same pressure. He'd do anything to keep the girls together. Anything except stay in Castle Rock. Peering through the window, he saw Miss Baxter wiping Esther's face with a white hankie. Someday she'd make a good mother. He hoped Harriet Lange would be as kind.

The attorney cleared his throat. "If you'll excuse my boldness, Mr. Morgan, there's another solution."

"What's that?"

"You could raise the girls yourself."

Beau laughed out loud. "Not in a million years."

"Why not?"

The duster covered his Colt .45, but the weapon weighed heavy on his hip. Even if he'd felt inclined to settle down, he couldn't do it until Clay Johnson had taken his last breath. Beau turned from the window and glared at the attorney. The balding man had spectacles, but that didn't mean he could see. One look at Beau's worn gun belt should have answered his question.

After staring for a bit, Beau stated the obvious. "I'm not inclined to settle down, Mr. Scott."

"Why not?"

"It's none of your business."

"You can't blame me for asking," the man said. "I knew Patrick well. We served together as elders at the church. He'd want his girls to be raised in Castle Rock."

"That's not possible."

Beau thought of Daniela Baxter but dismissed the idea of allowing her to adopt his nieces. Someday she'd marry and have babies of her own. Besides, what did she know about running a dairy farm? Since he'd been doing Patrick's work, Beau had come to respect farmers in a new way. The cows had no mercy when it came to being milked on time. Exhausted or not, Beau pulled himself out of bed at dawn, headed to the meadow to fetch the first cow, then milked them one at a time until he'd finished all ten. At night, the cows came to the gate bellowing precisely at five o'clock.

The milking started the day and ended it. In between, the driver from the local cheese factory picked up the milk cans and replaced them with empty ones. Beau had buckets to scrub and horse stalls to muck out. He also had a new field of alfalfa to plant. Patrick's first field, the one he'd planted seven years ago, would die out in a few years and no longer meet the needs of his growing herd. The cows had all given birth in March. Patrick had kept four heifer calves and sold the rest. The herd needed more forage, so he'd made plans for a second alfalfa crop. Beau had seen the half-plowed field and the seed bags in the barn. After just two days of work, he'd taken his hat off to his brother's dedication.

Hardworking or not, Patrick had died, leaving the work unfinished. In a blink the Almighty had cut him down. Beau turned back to the window. Instead of four blond heads, he saw four bowls of melting ice cream.

"What the—"

He scanned the boardwalk and saw Miss Baxter shepherding the girls to the wagon. When she glanced at the window, Beau saw the fear of a fugitive and bolted for the door.

"We're not done!" Scott called.

"Write to Miss Lange," Beau shouted from the stairwell. "Do it today!"

He raced through the door to the street where the wagon sat empty. He looked to the left but saw nothing. He snapped his eyes to the right and saw a pink skirt whipping around a corner.

He broke into a run, but the females had a two-block lead. When he reached the alley where they'd turned, he saw nothing but empty stairs, trash and piles of wood. Muttering an oath, he strode between the buildings, swiveling his head to look down each street and alley for another flash of pink.

He spotted them on Cantril Street. Miss Baxter and his nieces had slowed to a fast walk, a pace that would look hurried to bystanders but not panicked. Beau didn't know what to make of their flight. He didn't know much about little girls, but he'd tried to be pleasant. He hadn't raised his voice, and he'd cussed only once when a cow had stepped on his foot.

With Miss Baxter and the girls in plain sight, he followed at a distance, staying close to the buildings and ducking into doorways whenever the woman looked over her shoulder. He had to admire her instincts. She took numerous turns, blended with strangers and kept the girls at her side. Beau had no idea where she was headed. They'd passed the Garnet Hotel, the sheriff's office and the courthouse. He figured the girls had friends, but the houses in Castle Rock lay mostly to the east. Tired of the chase, he lengthened his stride. With his coat flapping and his boots thudding, he didn't have to maneuver around folks on the boardwalk. They jumped out of his way.

At the corner of Lewis and Sixth Streets, Miss Baxter glanced over her shoulder. Instead of taking cover, Beau stayed in plain sight. "Wait up!"

Her eyes rounded with fear. Breathless, she lifted Esther and ran with Emma and Ellie flanking her sides.

Beau broke into a run but stopped. He couldn't stand the thought of Miss Baxter catching a heel in the boardwalk. If she fell, she'd twist an ankle or worse. He'd also figured out her destination. The fool woman could have saved herself a lot worry if she'd stayed and finished her ice cream. Beau, too, had business with Josh and Adelaide Blue. With his hat low, he followed the females to the parsonage.

"Keep going!" Dani said between breaths. "We're almost there."

She didn't dare look over her shoulder. She'd spotted

Beau Morgan near the bank but hoped they'd lost him by zigzagging through the grid of streets. The church rose in the distance, a wood frame building painted white with a bell and a tin steeple. The sun struck the metal, reminding her of the swords in the Bible. The Lord had told His people to turn some into ploughshares. Others were used for battle. As the steeple glinted in the sun, she thought of the sword of truth, a two-edged blade sharp enough to separate flesh from bone, truth from lies. Mr. Morgan hadn't been overtly dishonest, but neither had he been forthcoming. With three girls in her care, Dani couldn't take chances. If Pastor Blue and his wife would watch the girls, she'd go in search of the town judge. She'd show him the letters and—

"Oh, no," she mumbled.

"What is it?" Emma asked.

"Your pa's letters are in my trunk."

The girl whimpered. "That's the proof he wanted you to adopt us."

"That's right."

"Can we get them?" Emma asked.

"Not easily." Dani's plan to take the wagon had changed the instant she'd locked eyes with Beau Morgan through the window. She'd told him about Patrick's letter with good intentions, but now she wished she'd been more reserved. If he wanted to play dirty, he could destroy the letters. A custody battle would turn into a war of words.

Please, Lord. I need Your help.

With mud sticking to her shoes, Dani focused on the house across from the church. Red curtains hung in the windows and flowerpots lined the railing on the wide porch. Behind the slats, she saw a hodgepodge of chairs.

A large wooden spool, probably used for telegraph wire, served as a table, and a lantern sat on a barrel. The house called out a welcome.

Come and sit. Share your burdens.

Patrick had considered Reverend Blue a good friend and he'd spoken well of the man's wife. *They'll help you get settled, Dani. Pastor Josh tells stories that make the Bible come alive, and no one's kinder than Adie.* Looking at the chairs, Dani imagined pouring out her heart to a serene man of the cloth and his gentle wife.

"There she is!" Ellie said.

A red-haired woman in a green print dress and white apron stood in the doorway. At the sight of Dani and the girls, her eyes sparked with recognition, then clouded as she spied the man following in their steps. Leaving the door ajar, Adelaide Blue slipped out of sight. Clinging to Esther, Dani ran faster, praying she wouldn't stumble. Emma stayed at her side. Unburdened, Ellie outdistanced them. They had a hundred feet to go, then seventy, fifty… Dani could see the lilacs by the front door, the checks on the gingham curtains.

When they reached the yard, Adie waved them inside. The girls sped past her and collapsed on the floor. Dani spun around and saw the minister's wife facing the yard with a shotgun pressed against her shoulder. Dani went to the window, peeked through the curtains and saw Beau Morgan striding down the dirt trail parting the grass. With his hat pulled low and his duster flapping, he stirred the blades like gusting wind.

"Hold up, stranger!" Adie called.

He stopped and raised his hands over his head. Dani pressed her temple against the wall so she could see the front of the doorway. The shotgun barrel pointed steady and true.

Adie's finger rested on the trigger. "Who are you, mister?"

Laughter rumbled from Beau Morgan's chest. It struck Dani as sinister, but Adie lowered the gun.

"I don't believe my eyes," the woman said.

"Hello, Adie."

"Beau Morgan? Is that really you?"

"It sure is." Beneath the brim of his hat, his mouth widened into a roguish grin. "Are you gonna shoot me or ask me to supper?"

"What do *you* think?"

Gripping the curtain, Dani watched in shock as Adelaide Blue ran to Beau Morgan and hugged him like a long-lost brother.

Beau had thought of Josh and Adie Blue as family ever since he'd stumbled into the church Josh had started in a Denver saloon. The Blues had taught him a simple truth. Even the mangiest of dogs liked good cooking and a clean bed. A few kind words and the meanest cur lost his growl. Add a little love—a good scratch, a woman's laughter—and that dog turned worthless. That's why Beau avoided good cooking and clean sheets. Until he brought Clay Johnson to justice, he had to keep his edge.

He stepped back from Adie. "You're as pretty as ever."

She smiled. "And you're just as ornery."

"Where's Josh?"

"Looking for Miss Baxter." Adie put her hands on her hips. "Would you care to tell me why that girl's running from you like a scared rabbit?"

"I don't know."

"Then you're blind." She looked him up and down. "You need a bath and that's the least of it."

"I haven't had a chance."

"It's more than your looks that frightened her," Adie said. "What's got you in a twist?"

Beau lost his smile. "I got word that Clay Johnson's in the area. I'm still hunting for him."

"Oh, Beau."

"I was closing in when I stopped to see Patrick." Beau shook his head. "I ended up with a farm and a bunch of cows."

"And three little girls."

Adie's voice held a lilt. Beau appreciated her kindness but feared the glint in her eyes. Orphaned at the age of twelve, she'd suffered frightful abuses before settling with Josh and their adopted son. She treasured her family and wanted everyone to have the same joy. Until Lucy's death, Beau had felt the same way.

Adie cut into his thoughts. "Those girls need a home. What are you going to do about it?"

"I'm not sure yet."

"You could stay here and raise them."

"Forget it. I've got a call on my life and I'm following it."

Adie's face hardened. "You're talking about Johnson."

"Of course."

"Oh, Beau."

"What?"

Her eyes misted. "You've got to set that burden down."

How could she say such a thing? She'd laid out Lucy's body in the house he'd rented because his wife had liked the porch swing. That morning, Lucy had tossed up her breakfast and had gone to the doctor. Later Beau learned she'd been carrying their child. She'd put on the pink dress—his favorite—to tell him the news. Behind Adie, he saw Miss Baxter in her pink dress peeking through the red curtains. The colors turned his stomach.

Adie wrinkled her nose, then playfully fanned the air. "Go take a bath. You smell like a bear in April."

Beau grinned. "That good?"

"Worse!"

He appreciated the change in tone. "I've got business in town. I'll be back in an hour."

"Keep an eye out for Josh," she added.

Beau wanted to see his old friend but feared what the Reverend would say. The man dug deep, pulling up weeds by the roots and laying them bare for a man to see for himself. Adie had a different way. She planted seeds and expected flowers. If a man was thirsty, she gave him sweet tea. If he was hungry, she filled his belly. Beau had never known a more generous woman…or a more dangerous one. Watching Adie love the whole wretched world made him want a garden of his own.

Beau tipped his hat to her, saw that Miss Baxter had left her post at the window, turned and headed to town. As he trudged along the path, he thought of his early years in Denver. He'd been a deputy sheriff when Joshua Blue had ridden into town with a Bible and an attitude. Before he knew it, Beau had been sitting in a saloon that doubled for a church on Sunday mornings. A year later, he'd met Lucy and married her. After her passing, Adie had fed him meals until he couldn't stand another bite and had lit out of town.

He wanted to leave now but couldn't. Patrick's girls needed him and so did Miss Baxter. What drove a woman to travel a thousand miles to marry a stranger? Beau didn't know, but he knew how it felt to hurt.

As he stepped onto the boardwalk, he caught a whiff of himself. Adie was right about that bath, but first he had to visit the Silver River Saloon. With a little luck, he'd pick up news about Clay Johnson. Beau disliked visiting saloons, but it had to be done. Men like Johnson didn't hang out at the general store, nor did they go to church on Sundays, or to socials where men and women rubbed elbows and made friends. Neither did Beau.

With his duster flapping, he strode to Scott's office to fetch the wagon, then drove back down the street, crossed the railroad tracks and found the saloon between a second mining office and a gunsmith. He stepped inside and surveyed the dimly lit room. Empty stools lined the bar. A poker table sat in the corner with a battered deck of cards but no players. He had the place to himself, so he stepped to the bar where a man with graying hair was wiping the counter.

"What'll it be?" the barkeep asked.

"Coffee."

The man set down a mug. Numb to the bitterness, Beau took a long drag of the overcooked brew. It splashed in his belly but didn't give him the usual jolt, a sign he was more tired than he knew. Grimacing, he set down the half-empty cup.

"You're a stranger here," the barkeep said.

"Sure enough."

"In town on business?"

"Just passing through." Lonely men liked to talk. Beau hoped this man was one of them.

The barkeep lifted a shot glass out of a tub and dried it with his apron. "If you need work, the mines are hiring."

"I'm looking for someone."

"Oh, yeah?"

"His name's Clay Johnson. He's about six feet with dark hair and a crooked nose." Beau wished he'd been the one to break it.

When the man raised a brow, Beau slid a coin across the counter. The barkeep slipped it into his pocket. "I've seen that fellow."

"In town?"

"About two weeks ago."

Before Patrick's death. "Any idea where he was headed?"

"None. He bought five bottles of whiskey, opened one here and walked out with the rest. I haven't seen him since."

"Anyone with him?"

"Two men."

"What did they look like?"

"I didn't pay much attention. I noticed Johnson because of his nose." The barkeep set down the glass and held out his hand. "I'm Wallace O'Day. I run a clean business."

Beau shook the man's hand. "Beau Morgan."

"Bounty hunter?"

"I'm not in it for the money."

Wallace picked up another glass. "This Johnson fellow. Is he wanted?"

"Yes." By Beau for Lucy's murder and the U.S. government for stealing horses. Of the two, the government would be kinder.

The barkeep glanced at the dregs in Beau's cup. "Want some more?"

"No, thanks." Beau slapped down a sawbuck. "If you hear anything about Johnson, remember it."

Wallace folded the money. "How do I find you?"

"I'll be back."

Beau left the saloon with thoughts of Johnson rattling like broken glass. He saw Lucy again, felt the wetness of her bodice and smelled the blood. He blinked the picture away, but the rage stayed in his blood, swimming like a thousand fish. Needing to get rid of the slithering, he walked two blocks to an emporium where he bought fresh clothes, then headed back to the bathhouse across from the Silver River.

As he neared the splintery building, one of the oldest in Castle Rock, he smelled steam, soap and dirt. The mix reminded him of a simple truth. He could get clean on the outside, but the inside was another matter. Until Clay Johnson met his end, Beau's hate would grow with every breath he took.

Weary to the bone, he stepped into a drafty building with a high ceiling. He paid a Chinese man to fill a tub, then undressed and slipped into the hot water. As he dunked his head, Beau thought about Clay Johnson. They'd been playing this game for a long time now. At first, Clay had run hard and far. Beau had nearly trapped him in Durango, but he'd fled to the Colorado Plateau and into the desert. Beau had picked up the man's trail later in Raton but had lost him near Cimarron. A year had passed before he'd gotten word of an outlaw gang raiding ranches in Wyoming.

Beau had taken a train to Laramie. He'd arrived in time for a trial that didn't include Johnson. In exchange for prison in place of the gallows, one of Clay's cohorts had told the authorities where to find him. Beau had ridden out that day, but Clay had already vanished into the mountains.

With the memory haunting him, Beau raised his head out of the water and wiped his face. He'd been so close. A day sooner and his search would have ended. Instead, Clay had gotten word of Beau's presence and left him a message at the local saloon.

It should have been you, Sheriff. You know it. Leave me alone.

Beau had that note in his saddlebag. He had other things, too. A bullet etched with an *M* for Morgan, presumably from Johnson's gun belt. Other notes. Other tokens. Every time Beau got close, the outlaw taunted him but didn't stand and fight.

Beau wondered why.

What stopped Johnson from setting up an ambush? For five years, Beau had slept with one eye open and for good reason. In a game of cat and mouse, no man liked being the mouse. Someday Johnson would be sick of the chase and become the cat. The man would show himself and Beau would be ready. Dunking back into the scalding water, he hoped that day would come soon.

Chapter Four

"How do you know our uncle?" Ellie asked.

Dani and the girls were sitting in Adie Blue's kitchen. After insisting Dani call her by her given name, the pastor's wife had given the girls snickerdoodles and made Dani a cup of hot tea, lacing it with enough sugar to stop her hands from shaking.

With the girls staring at her, Adie sat down with a cup of her own. "Pastor Josh and I know your uncle from Denver. He used to be a sheriff."

"Where's his badge?" Ellie asked.

Adie paused. "I don't know. Maybe he left it in Denver."

"Why?" Emma hadn't touched her cookie. Of the three girls, she was most aware of their uncertain future and needed reassurance for herself and her sisters.

Dani wanted answers, too. And not just from Adie. Why had God filled her heart with love for Patrick and snatched him away? Even more troublesome, why had He left three little girls in the care of a dangerous man? Dani watched as Adie stirred her tea in slow circles, as if this were an ordinary day. But it wasn't ordinary. Each plink of the spoon sent tremors down Dani's spine.

Adie finally set her spoon in the saucer and looked at Emma. "Your Uncle Beau was married to a woman named Lucy. Something bad happened and he didn't want to be a sheriff anymore."

A wife… Dani didn't know what to think. Beau Morgan had loved a woman and been loved in return. She didn't want to feel his pain but she did.

Ellie's eyes filled with concern. "What happened?"

"It's hard to talk about, sweetie."

Emma glared at the pastor's wife. "As hard as losing Pa?"

"I'm afraid so."

Adie's eyes had the fragility of etched glass. Whatever Beau Morgan had suffered, it had been tragic, maybe violent. The girls needed to feel safe, so Dani stepped in. "I hear you have kittens," she said to Adie.

"I sure do."

Esther jumped up. Cookie crumbs bounced on the table. "I want to see them!"

Ellie caught the excitement. "Is Stephen home?"

Adie glanced at Dani to explain. "Stephen's our son. He and Ellie are the same age."

"We're best friends," Ellie added.

Dani almost smiled. It figured Ellie the tomboy would be friends with the pastor's son.

Adie looked at Ellie. "Stephen's staying at Jake Roddy's house until Sunday."

"Oh."

"But you can still play with the kittens," Adie said. "They're in the stable."

Esther ran for the door.

Adie looked at Emma. "I need to speak to Miss Dani. Would you take your sisters to the stable?"

Emma scowled. "But—"

"I know, sweetie." Adie motioned for Emma to lean closer. "You're old enough to know the facts, but Esther isn't. We need your help."

"Will you tell me later?" Emma asked.

Dani nodded. "I promise."

The girls left through the back door. Adie went to the stove where she lifted an enamel kettle and refilled their cups. "I wish Josh were here."

"Where is he?" Dani asked.

"Looking for you. He must have missed your train."

Dani squared her shoulders. "I'm glad he did. It gave me a chance to meet Mr. Morgan."

"That's not the real Beau." Adie put down the kettle. "Let's sit on the porch. I'll tell you his story, but I need to see the sky when I do."

"Why?"

"To remember that Lucy's in Heaven. Considering how she died, it's the only comfort we have." With her cup and saucer in hand, Adie led the way to the porch and indicated the hodgepodge of chairs. "Take the rocker. It's soothing."

Balancing her teacup, Dani dropped onto the chair and instantly felt the cradlelike rocking. It matched the beat of her heart, calming her thoughts as the hot tea had settled her nerves. Adie said nothing as a man in a black preacher's coat rode into the yard on a dapple gray.

"That's Josh." She set her cup on the table, then went down the stairs to meet him.

At the sight of his wife, Reverend Blue's face turned from stone to living flesh. He slid out of the saddle, slipped his arm around her waist and pulled her into a gentle hug. After lowering his chin, he whispered something in her ear. Dani ached with envy. A husband… A partner and friend. Marriage meant starting a family. It meant belonging to a person and making a home. Dani had lived in Walker County her entire life, but she'd never fitted in. She'd felt that oneness with Patrick and now he was gone.

Why, Lord?

It was a question for Reverend Blue, but the man looked nothing like the minister Dani had expected. When she dreamed of the wedding, she'd pictured him as a twin of her pastor in Wisconsin, an elderly man with kind eyes. Pastor Schmidt had called Jesus the Lamb of God. He'd taught his flock to turn the other cheek.

Reverend Blue had a mane of dark hair, hawkish eyes and a chin that looked as if it could take a punch. For a good cause, Dani suspected he'd welcome it. Would he find her cause worthy? The Blues considered Beau a friend, but they didn't know about the pistols on the porch or the secrecy in town. Dani had to convince them to help her keep the girls.

Reverend Blue guided his wife up the stairs. As Adie sat, he took off his hat and faced Dani. "I'm sorry about Patrick, Miss Baxter. It had to be a shock."

"Yes." Her throat closed.

He dropped into the chair on her right and turned it so they were seated at an angle. "Whatever you need, Adie and I will help. Train fare—"

"I'm not leaving." Dani had to make her case and she had to do it now. "I want to adopt the girls."

The Reverend's eyes stayed kind, but he lowered his chin. "I don't think—"

"I *have* to!" Dani's voice trembled. "I promised Patrick."

The Reverend traded a look with his wife. They had an entire conversation without saying a word. Jealousy raged in Dani's middle. She was mad at everyone right now—the Reverend, Adie, Beau Morgan, Patrick for leaving her, and especially God.

Adie spoke to her husband in a murmur. "I saw Beau."

"How is he?" The Reverend sounded grim.

"He looks terrible," Adie replied.

Dani jumped in. "The girls are terrified of him. Frankly, so am I."

"Of Beau?" The Reverend sounded incredulous.

"Yes." Dani pressed her point. "I don't know what he was like in Denver, but he's not fit to raise three girls. I don't care what Patrick's will says. I have letters. He'd want me to raise his daughters."

"Miss Baxter—"

"I can prove it."

Reverend Blue held her gaze. "Maybe so, but does it matter?"

"Of course, it matters!"

"Why?"

"They prove what Patrick intended."

The Reverend's eyes filled with sympathy. "God might have other plans. Patrick left a will, but—"

Her throat hurt. "The letter is more recent."

Reverend Blue sealed his lips. Dani didn't like his expression at all. He looked like a man keeping a secret. Had Beau already spoken to the Blues? Did they know about sending the girls to school?

She had to make her case. "You can't let him do it."

"Do what?" Adie asked.

"Send the girls away."

The Blues traded another look. Adie turned up her palms in confusion. "I spoke to Beau for less than a minute. I don't know what he's planning."

"I do," Dani said. "He wants to send the girls away to school. I can't let him do it. They need to be in their own home."

Adie's mouth tensed. "They certainly do."

"That's why I want to adopt them," Dani continued. "I grew up on the biggest dairy farm in Walker County. I know the business. I can run the farm and the girls can stay together. It's what Patrick would have wanted."

The Reverend said nothing. Why the silence? If he wouldn't speak, how could she convince him to support the adoption? She didn't know what to think of this hard, silent man, but she liked Adie. She turned to the preacher's wife. "Will you help me?"

"Hold on, ladies." Reverend Blue sounded like Moses about to deliver the Ten Commandments. "Things aren't that simple."

Dani frowned. "Why not?"

"Patrick's will gives Beau authority. He's a blood relative."

"He's also dirty and dangerous!" Dani didn't like her tone, but she felt overwhelmed by emotions. Sadness. Fear. An anger that needed a target. She stared hard at Reverend Blue.

He stared back. "What has Beau done to offend you?"

Dani related Emma's story about the guns, then described the trip to town. Her skin crawled at the recollection of Beau Morgan behind the window, the way his eyes had narrowed to her face. The more she relived the escape, the more deeply she disliked the man who had made it necessary. She took a breath. "I know you and Mrs. Blue consider Mr. Morgan a friend, but people change. He's not the man you once knew."

The Reverend drummed his fingers on the armrest. "Has Beau harmed you in any way?"

"No."

"Has he been harsh with the girls?"

Dani thought of the blankets in the wagon and felt petty. She recalled his smelly clothes and knew he'd worked hard. He'd sounded threatening, but his actions had been courteous, even caring. "He's been a perfect gentleman."

"That's what I'd expect." The Reverend looked her in the eye. "Let me tell you about Beau Morgan, Miss Baxter. He was the bravest, most dedicated lawman Denver ever had. He sang in the church choir. He pounded half the nails in my first church and served as a deacon. He put Bibles in jail cells for men who spat on him."

Dani didn't want Beau Morgan to be human, someone with a conscience who'd fight her for the girls. "That was five years ago. It's a long time."

"So is five minutes," he said. "That's how long it took for Beau's life to change."

Adie touched Dani's arm. "This is a horrible story, but you need to understand."

Dani's insides spun. "What happened?"

The Reverend's gaze shifted to the mountains rising in the west. "It started with a gang of horse thieves. Randall Johnson was the leader. I knew him. I knew Clay, too. They were brothers with Randall being the elder."

"How did you meet them?" Dani couldn't see the connection between the outlaws and this man of the cloth.

The Reverend's lips quirked upward. "Same way I met

a lot of outlaws back then. I rode into their camp and introduced the Father, Son and Holy Ghost. That was a few months before the horse thieving started."

Dani sighed. "I guess the message didn't take."

"We don't know," the Reverend said. "But I *do* know what happened that day in October. The Johnson gang raided Cobbie Miller's place. They burned the outbuildings and made off with a dozen good horses. They also abused Cobbie's two daughters."

Dani felt both ill and furious.

The Reverend leaned back in his chair. "Cobbie stormed into town with the girls in the wagon, wrapped in blankets and looking pale. He went straight to the sheriff's office. Beau put together a posse. Three days later, he shot Randall Johnson in a fair fight. I know, because I saw it."

Dani let out her breath. "Justice was done."

"Not in Clay Johnson's mind. His brother was dead and he wanted revenge. He got it by murdering Beau's wife."

Dani gasped.

Reverend Blue stared into the distance, but his gaze lacked focus as he traveled to that bitter day in Denver. "It happened a week after Beau shot Randall. Clay sneaked into town and positioned himself on the building across from the sheriff's office. He must have been up there for hours, but Beau never made rounds that morning. Of all the stupid things, he'd busted his big toe chopping wood."

Dani blinked and saw Beau Morgan's sock with his toe poking through the hole. Five years ago, his wife would have darned it. She'd have knit him new ones. Dani didn't want to ache for him, but she did.

Adie touched her arm. "It's a hard story to hear."

"And hard to tell," said the Reverend.

"Go on," Dani urged. "I need to know."

Reverend Blue raised his chin in defiance of what he had to relive. "I know what happened because Beau told me. He's gone over that moment a thousand times. Maybe more."

Dani thought of Emma standing at the window, recalling Patrick's riderless horse and the smell of burned flesh. She heard Beau Morgan telling the child not to talk. He'd been trying to protect her from a heartache that rivaled his own. Dani had judged him as hard, yet he'd been acting with compassion.

Reverend Blue took a deep breath. "Beau was sitting at his desk with his foot on a stool when he saw Lucy pass by the window with a picnic basket. She'd been to the doctor that morning and had come to surprise him."

Her heart squeezed. A healthy young woman went to the doctor for just one reason. The picnic basket…a surprise for her husband. Tears welled in Dani's eyes.

Reverend Blue cleared his throat. "In spite of his bad toe, Beau got up to help her. When he opened the door, Johnson fired. Lucy died in Beau's arms."

In Wisconsin, Dani could look at a tulip and see God in the petals. She could catch a snowflake and see the divine beauty. Staring at the rippling grass, she saw nothing but Lucy Morgan's blood and Patrick's riderless horse. "Where was God?" she said in a whisper.

"Same place He is right now," said the Reverend.

"I don't feel Him."

"I think you do, Miss Baxter." She felt the Reverend's gaze on the side of her face. "I see tears in your eyes. Our Lord's weeping, too. For Beau. For you. For those three little girls. Bad things happen. It's a fact. But the Lord will see you through."

"I know that's true," Dani murmured. "It *has* to be true."

Yet she couldn't shake the niggling fear that she'd left God in Wisconsin. She looked to the Reverend for comfort but didn't find it. His eyes were on his wife, blazing with a protectiveness that tore Dani's heart in two. With Patrick's death, she could only dream of a man looking at her that way.

The Reverend's throat twitched with emotion.

Adie's eyes misted.

Dani's throat hurt. It tightened even more when the girls spilled out of the stable door. Emma had a blanket draped over her arm. Ellie had the box of kittens and Esther's little legs pumped as she tried to keep up with her sisters. Dani raised her chin. God had denied her a husband, but she could still be a mother.

The Reverend broke into her thoughts. "I spoke at Lucy's funeral." He bit off the last word, as if he could barely say it. "I'm a man of God, Miss Baxter. I believe in Heaven and Hell and living well in between, but I could barely say a word that day."

Adie interrupted. "I'll tell the rest. I'm the one who cooked Beau his last meal."

"It was roast beef," the Reverend said.

"And raspberry pie. I'd given Lucy the recipe."

Dani bit her lip to fight the dread.

Adie laced her fingers together. "I'll never forget that last night on the porch. Lucy had been gone a month when Beau said he was leaving town. As cold as death, he said, 'I'm going to hunt down Clay Johnson and kill him.'"

"I believed him," said the Reverend.

"I still do," Adie replied.

Dani shivered. "That's why he's been so protective, isn't it? Clay Johnson…is he in the area?"

"Beau thinks so," Adie said.

Fear, danger and dirt. Beau Morgan had brought all three into the lives of three little girls. Dani's heart broke for his loss, but she feared for Patrick's daughters. She turned to Adie. "I have a favor to ask."

"Anything."

"Could the girls and I stay with you a few days?"

Adie tilted her head. "Are you still afraid of Beau?"

"No," Dani replied. "But I *am* afraid of Clay Johnson. What if he comes to the farm?"

Adie looked at Josh. "Dani has a point."

"I'll speak to Beau," said Reverend Blue. "He'll know best."

Dani thought of the ride through town. Surely Beau would want to keep them safe. "Thank you."

Adie touched her shoulder. "You must be exhausted. Would you like to rest a bit?"

Dani shook her head. "If I close my eyes, I'll see Patrick."

"A walk might be nice," Adie said kindly.

"I think I will. Is the church open?"

"Always," said the Reverend.

As she pushed to her feet, Dani looked at the tin steeple. The sun had dropped in the sky, turning it from silver to gray. The edges no longer seemed so sharp. Maybe she'd go inside. Maybe she wouldn't. Mostly she wanted to cry and she wanted to do it alone. She looked across the yard and saw the girls. They seemed content, but in the distance she saw the stirring of dust from a wagon and recognized Beau Morgan holding the reins. He had her future in his hands, as well. She had to convince him she could handle the girls and the farm. That would be hard to do if they stayed with the Blues, but neither did she like the idea of an outlaw stalking them.

Patrick? Are you watching? What should I do?

Silence.

With her heart aching, Dani headed for the cemetery.

Beau steered the wagon into the yard and stopped. The chairs on the porch sent him back in time to Denver, where Josh and Adie had lived in a mansion named Swan's Nest. Beau and another deputy had taken to visiting on Wednesday nights. During the third visit, Josh had opened his Bible and read scriptures from Proverbs, the funny ones about fools and carping women. Their little group had turned into the Wednesday Ruckus, a men's Bible study that didn't mince words. That's how Beau got roped into church on Sunday… How he'd met Lucy.

As he climbed down from the seat, he saw Josh come out of the parsonage. The man looked harder than ever. Rail thin and tall, he resembled a chimney pipe. Beau wasn't in the mood for Josh's kind of fire, but he was glad to see his old friend.

"Hello, Reverend."

"Reverend?" The preacher faked a scowl. "You used to call me Josh."

Beau offered his hand to shake, but Josh pulled him into a bear hug and thumped him hard between the shoulder blades. Beau pounded back. In Denver he'd enjoyed having friends, men who'd told jokes when times were bright and stayed quiet when they weren't. He missed them. He missed a lot of things. He stepped back. "It's been a long time."

"Five years, friend." Josh's eyes burned like coal. "Where in the world have you been?"

"I think you know."

"Only what you told Adie." Josh put his hands on his hips, pulling back the flaps of his coat. "You and I need to talk."

"No, we don't." Beau's voice dropped to a growl. He didn't want to hear about forgiving his enemies. He wanted an eye for an eye. He wanted Clay Johnson to swing from a rope.

Josh aimed his chin at the girls. "You have three children in your care."

"I know that."

"And Miss Baxter, too."

"Only because she's too stubborn to go home." Beau looked at the red curtains in the window. He half expected to see Miss Baxter spying on him, but the gingham hung straight. "Where is she?"

"Taking a walk. I'm sorry about Patrick."

"Me, too," Beau said. "Those girls are suffering."

"So's Miss Baxter."

Beau didn't need to be reminded of the woman's tears. He'd been the one to deliver the bad news. He'd felt the same pain when Lucy died. "I know all about it."

"Yes, you do."

Beau appreciated Josh's plain tone. He hated pity, but he hated Clay Johnson even more. A bitter rage burned in Beau's soul. "Johnson's close, Josh. I can smell him."

"Is he a threat?"

"I don't know."

Beau told Josh about the trinkets Johnson had left him,

the taunting letters. "I don't know what he'll do next. He could run, or he could turn the tables and come after me."

Josh folded his arms again. "You know what I'm going to say."

"I don't want to hear it." Beau thought back to Lucy's funeral. To Josh's credit, he hadn't said a word about forgiveness. He'd saved that speech for the day Beau rode out of Denver.

Bitterness will eat you alive, my friend. Vengeance belongs to the Lord.

Fine, but Beau wanted to be the man to put the noose around Johnson's neck. As soon as he took care of his nieces, he'd get back to the business of revenge. As for the bothersome Baxter woman, she'd be better off in Wisconsin with her family.

Josh's expression stayed hard. "Adie tells me you scared the daylights out of Miss Baxter. That was a fool thing to do."

Beau grunted. "She's as green as grass."

"Not from what I can see."

"Then you haven't seen much."

"I've seen plenty." Josh looked Beau up and down. "Looks like you found time for a bath."

Beau wished he'd worn his duster over his new clothes. The blue shirt made him feel like a dandy, and so did the brown leather vest. The gun belt still hugged his hip, but he'd slicked back his hair and his jaw had a shine. Beau scowled. "Adie shamed me into it."

"Adie's wise."

She was also a good cook. Beau smelled supper on the stove. His mouth watered, but he refused to be hungry.

Josh eyed him thoughtfully. "Thanks to your bad manners, Miss Baxter wants to stay here with the girls."

Beau toyed with the idea but rejected it. "The woman can do whatever she wants, but I want the girls on the farm."

"Is it safe?" Josh asked.

"As safe as I can make it." His nieces shared his name. Beau wanted them where he could see them. He didn't expect Johnson to ride into town, but the outlaw had a sick mind.

"Can I give you some advice?" Josh asked.

"Can I stop you?"

"No, so here it is. The girls think of Miss Baxter as their new mother. They think of you as an intruder. They trust her. No matter what you decide, things will be easier if she's on your side."

"That won't happen."

"Why not?"

"She made a promise to Patrick. She wants to adopt the girls."

"I know." Josh lowered his voice. "I know something else."

"What?"

"I can't share it with you."

Beau thought of Emma standing at the farmhouse window. *He went to see Pastor Josh. He was in a hurry.* Had Patrick gotten cold feet? Beau remembered the day before he'd married Lucy. He'd been crazy about her, but his knees had turned to jelly before the wedding. If Patrick had changed his mind, Miss Baxter's promise to adopt the girls meant nothing. She'd be free to go home to Wisconsin.

Beau hated secrets, but he trusted Josh. "You know best."

"I hope so."

No matter what troubled the minister, Beau knew he'd

wield the sword of truth with discretion. Before coming to Colorado, Joshua Blue had been a high-and-mighty preacher in Boston. He'd suffered for his misplaced words and knew the power of a loose tongue.

So did Beau. He'd spoken too quickly when he'd asked Daniela Baxter to stay at the farm. His belly had been growling and he hadn't given the situation enough thought. The girls were already too attached to her. With each day, that tie would grow stronger and they'd all end up heartbroken. With Harriet Lange in the picture, Beau hoped the situation would be resolved in a matter of days, a few weeks at the most. He could live on pancakes until then.

As for Daniela Baxter, she'd be better off with the Blues. Once the shock of Patrick's death wore off, Beau felt sure she'd head home to Wisconsin.

"Where is she?" he asked. "I need to speak with her."

"Look in the church."

His stomach lurched. No way would he go inside that building. He turned to ask Josh to fetch her, but the minister had already slipped into the house. Beau turned back to the building and scowled at it. He'd gone to church twice after Lucy's death. With a groaning deeper than words, he'd hit his knees. "The Lord is my shepherd, I shall not want…"

That day, Beau had wanted Lucy so bad he couldn't catch his breath. He no longer felt the freshness of the first cut of loss, but he remembered those days bitterly… and the nights, too. He'd slept with his face buried in Lucy's nightgown, breathing in her lilac scent. He'd pressed her pillow to his belly and curled around it.

Surely goodness and mercy... What goodness? Mercy for whom?

Yea, though I walk through the Valley of the Shadow of Death... A valley so long it never ended. A shadow so dark it mocked the night.

I shall fear no evil...

At least that much of the Psalm was true. Nothing scared Beau, least of all death. For five years, he'd been living in a fog of misery so thick it blinded him worse than night. Standing in the yard, he took in the church. The front steps numbered four and were as wide as the double doors. Brass knobs, lit by the sun, waited to be turned. The building, Beau realized, was a twin of the one Josh had built in Denver. Tall windows would line the sides, and the pulpit would be adorned with a soaring eagle.

Annoyed, he climbed the stairs and gripped the doorknob. The brass warmed his palm, but his blood ran cold. Where was God when Lucy died? Where was God now? Beau couldn't stand the thought of going inside the church. As he turned away, he heard someone weeping in the garden. It had to be the Baxter woman. When Lucy died, Beau had been embraced by friends. She had no one. He considered leaving, but he had to speak with her. He also knew exactly how she felt. With his throat tight, he headed for the garden. At the gate, he plucked a lily.

Too late, he realized the flowers marked a cemetery. In the far corner he saw the woman sitting on a bench. He took in her pink dress, the pink roses climbing on the rock wall, the pinkish hue of the grave markers. He couldn't stand all that rosiness, but neither could he walk away. With the lily in hand, Beau went to offer the comfort he'd yet to find for himself.

Chapter Five

The markers in the cemetery were unlike anything Dani had ever seen. They were made from rhyolite, a pinkish-gray stone that made her think of blood mixed with ash. In particular she noticed the stone cross in front of the bench. The crossbars ended in scallops that resembled open hands. The grass had been trampled and someone had left a single rose, now shriveled, at the foot of the marker. Tears welled in Dani's eyes. She'd miss Patrick forever, but God willing, she'd find comfort in raising his daughters and offer it in return. It all depended on Beau Morgan.

Dani bowed her head. *Are You there, Lord?*

Silence.

I need Your help and so do the girls. With her stomach quivering, Dani poured out her heart to the cross. Surely God had a plan for her life, a purpose. She *had* to believe that. She couldn't bear the thought of going back to Wisconsin and intruding on her brother. Apart from her tattered pride, she had no hope of a future in Walker County.

Please, Lord, make my path straight. Show me Your will.

"Amen," she said out loud.

A man cleared his throat.

She opened her eyes and saw a shadow across the grave. Expecting to see Reverend Blue, she looked up. Instead of the minister, she saw Beau Morgan with his hat in one hand and a lily in the other. He'd bathed and bought new clothes. The blue shirt turned his eyes a truer green, and his brown trousers still had a crease. He'd been to the barber, too. Dani took in his clean-shaven jaw and the dip in his upper lip. Without the grit and the dust, Beau Morgan was a handsome man. Even more handsome than Patrick. Dani felt disloyal, but she had to tell the truth. She also had to convince him she could care for the girls and run the farm.

He offered her the lily. "This is in honor of Patrick."

"Thank you."

She held the white trumpet by the stem. Missing Patrick's funeral had denied her a line in the sand, a place that marked before and after. She'd found it today in the cemetery.

Beau glanced at the lily, then stared into her eyes. "It's hard saying goodbye, even harder with things unsaid."

Dani's heart ached. "You understand."

"I do."

She didn't want any deception between them. "Adie told me about your wife. I'm sorry for your loss."

He gave a curt nod. "It was a long time ago."

"But you still miss her."

"Of course."

Dani didn't want to bring up painful memories, but she had to put the girls first. "I don't mean to pry, Mr. Morgan. But the Blues told me about Clay Johnson."

"What about him?"

"Are the girls in danger?"

"That's my concern." He put his Stetson back on his head and pulled it low. The sun lit up half his face, leaving the other side in the shadow of the brim. In a cemetery, the gesture smacked of disrespect.

Dani stood up from the bench and faced him. "The girls are my concern, too. The Blues are willing to take us in. I think that would be wise."

"You're free to accept," he said. "But the girls are staying with me."

"If there's danger—"

"There's *always* danger."

Bitterness spilled from his skin. Dani couldn't stand the thought of leaving the girls in his care. She looked him hard in the eye. "I have to know, Mr. Morgan. Is it safe to be around you?"

As soon as Dani said the words, she regretted them. His wife had taken a bullet meant for him. Being around Beau Morgan wasn't safe at all.

He sneered at her. "Let's put it this way. It's as safe to be around me as it is to be on a horse in a thunderstorm."

Dani blinked and recalled the charred pine. This morning she'd expected Patrick to greet her train. Now she was at the mercy of this bitter man. If he wouldn't let the girls stay with the Blues, Dani would have to stay with them. "You have a point," she said mildly. "We'll be fine on the farm."

The man rocked back on his heels. "I won't be needing your help after all. The situation's changed."

Dani stiffened. "How so?"

"Scott's located another relative, a great-aunt in Minnesota."

He told her about Harriet Lange's offer to take Emma, his concern about the woman's finances and his offer to provide a monthly allowance if she'd take all three girls. Dani searched her memory, but Patrick had written nothing about the girls' grandparents or cousins. She had asked about Elizabeth's family, but he'd ignored her question. She'd figured his first marriage was too personal to share in writing and hadn't pushed.

Beau Morgan shifted his weight. His gun belt creaked. "If things go as I expect, the girls will be leaving for Minnesota in a week or two."

"You can't do that!" Dani cried.

"Yes, I can."

"But this is their home!"

He said nothing.

She gestured to the town. "The girls have friends here, people who know them."

"It's for the best."

"Who says?"

"I do." He sounded kind. The tone threw Dani off balance, as did the regret in his eyes. "If I could, I'd bring Patrick back to life. I'd do a lot of things, Miss Baxter. But I don't have that power. If Harriet Lange's willing to raise my nieces, I'm going to let her."

Dani felt close to panic. "Let me do it."

"No."

"Why not?"

His brow furrowed with impatience. "Where would you live?"

"On the farm, of course."

"I mean no disrespect, Miss Baxter. But do you have any idea how much work it is to run a dairy?"

If a man could be judged by his hands, so could a woman. Dani tugged off her gloves a finger at a time. She put them in her pocket, then held out her hands palm up. “What do you see, Mr. Morgan?”

His eyes softened. “Calluses.”

“What else?”

“You’ve got long fingers.”

“Would you care to guess how many times I’ve milked a cow?”

“Quite a few.”

Dani lowered her hands. “My father owned the biggest dairy in Walker County. He grew it from five cows to fifty. I know the business and I’m not afraid of hard work. We’d have to hire help for the busy times, but—”

“No.”

Her words came faster. “Did you see the lumber by the barn?”

“What about it?”

“It’s for a silo. My father built one six years ago. It’ll hold enough feed for the entire winter. I sent Patrick the plans before I left.”

He spread his boots in the dirt and crossed his arms. “That’s all well and good, but—”

“The cows should have been bred a few weeks ago. Did you check his records?”

He stared in disbelief.

Dani had no time to be shy about nature’s ways. “If a bull didn’t visit, we’re in trouble. Without calves, the cows won’t have milk.”

Mr. Morgan looked amused. “Is that a fact?”

“Of course.” Dani didn’t see the humor. “A second cheese factory is opening. Have you gotten prices?”

He said nothing.

"Denver's booming. With a daily train, we can sell twice as much dairy as we do now." Dani saw boundless opportunity, but Beau Morgan looked like a man with a headache.

He put his hands on his hips. "You're obviously knowledgeable, Miss Baxter. But my answer is still no."

"Why?"

"Who's going to do the heavy lifting?"

"I'll do what has to be done."

"That's foolish."

She wanted to quote Proverbs, the verses about the woman who bought land and sold it, fed her family and worked tirelessly into the night, but Beau Morgan had made it clear that he didn't feel close to God. Quoting scripture would serve no purpose, but neither would she apologize for telling the truth. After years in the dairy business, she knew how to bargain. "I'll make you a deal, Mr. Morgan."

"What's that?"

"The way I see it, you have a problem. You have three little girls in your care, and you don't know the first thing about children."

"That's true."

"You're an honorable man. You want to provide for their future."

"Right again."

Dani's heart pounded. "The problem is your demeanor. You showed up looking like a grizzly bear, then you scared the daylights out of them by sitting on the porch with your guns. They don't like you, but they like me."

"What's your point?"

"I *know* I can run a dairy farm. Give me two weeks. If you're not convinced that it's best for the girls to stay with me in Castle Rock, I'll take them to Minnesota myself."

Beau Morgan shook his head. "I can't allow it."

"Why not?"

"Like I said, the girls will get attached to you."

"They already are."

He rubbed the back of his neck, a sign of frustration.

Dani decided to press. "I know my way around a kitchen, Mr. Morgan. Just think…fried chicken and biscuits as light as air."

He glared at her. "That's not fair."

"I thought you said Emma was a good cook." Dani knew from the child's letters that her biscuits were rock hard. Even Patrick had complained. *Emma tries, but she doesn't have a knack for cooking.*

Beau's grimace showed he held the same opinion, but his eyes twinkled. "I lied and you know it."

She smiled. "There's a peach tree on the side of the house. Do you like cobbler, Mr. Morgan?"

He looked ravenous but said nothing.

"How about peach jam?"

Laughing out loud, he pushed back his hat. The shadow dividing his face disappeared, leaving only light. "You win. But on one condition."

"What's that?"

"I like raspberry pie."

Dani thought of Adie's story about Beau's last meal in Denver. "I'd be glad to make it for you."

"In that case, we have a deal. You have two weeks to prove yourself and my word that I'll be fair."

"I never doubted that you would be."

Dani held out her hand. Beau glanced down, then gripped her fingers, engulfing them in his. The handshake sealed the deal, but the future was far from certain. She didn't doubt Beau's integrity or her ability to run the farm, but today had taught Dani a lesson. Anything could happen to anyone at any time.

She looked into Beau's eyes and saw the same uncertainty. Earlier Dani had prayed for God to make her path straight. For reasons she didn't understand, that path now involved this hard, troubled man. She didn't understand why. She only knew she liked him. He cared about his nieces. He worked hard. A long time ago, he'd loved his wife with the devotion commanded by God. As for Clay Johnson and Beau's search for justice, Dani prayed he'd find peace.

He broke off the handshake and stepped back. "It's time to go, Miss Baxter."

"Please, call me Dani."

His eyes darkened. "We're not friends. We're business partners."

"Whatever you'd like," she replied gently. "I was thinking of the girls. They might like you better if you seem less…distant."

"I like distance." He jerked his chin toward the gate. "Let's go."

With the lily in hand, Dani brushed by him. She caught a whiff of shaving soap and thought about the odd way of appearances. Beau Morgan had cleaned up on the outside, but his soul was still full of grit. She didn't care for his bad manners, but she could tolerate them. As long as he gave her a chance to prove herself, she could put up with just about anything.

* * *

As they left the cemetery, Beau called himself a fool. Raspberry pie? What had he been thinking? No good could come from letting Dani Baxter stay at the farm. He didn't believe for a minute she could handle the cows and the crops alone, but he couldn't back out now. When they reached the parsonage, he caught a whiff of pot roast, thought about fried chicken and scolded himself for thinking with his belly instead of his brain.

Adie met them on the steps. "You're staying for supper, aren't you?"

"Yes, thank you," Dani answered.

Almost drooling, Beau followed the women like a hungry puppy and took a seat at the maple table he remembered from Denver. His nieces filled the chairs at his sides, Josh sat at the head, and Dani sat across from him and near Adie and the kitchen. It was the most company he'd had in a long time. To his embarrassment, he became the guest of honor.

Your Uncle Beau caught a bank robber.

Your Uncle Beau helped us build our church.

The chatter lasted through supper and into dessert. With his plate clean and his coffee cup empty, Beau felt both satisfied and empty. Esther slid out of her chair and climbed on Dani's lap. Ellie smiled at him. Even Emma seemed at ease. If it hadn't been for Clay Johnson, this would have been his life. He and Lucy would have raised a family.

Beau drained the last of his coffee, a brew far better than the muck at the saloon, then set down the cup. His gaze landed on Dani with Esther wiggling in her lap. Like himself, she looked wistful. Clay Johnson had robbed

Beau of a family. A lightning bolt had robbed Dani of the same pleasure. God, it seemed, had turned His back on them both.

Seething inside, Beau pushed to his feet. "It's time to go. The cows won't wait."

"Of course," Dani said.

Esther jumped down from her lap. "We have to say goodbye to the kittens."

Beau opened his mouth to say no, but Adie took the child's hand. "Let's go, girls. I have something special for you."

Dani stood. "I'll start the dishes."

"No, you won't." Josh had used his preaching voice, the one that boomed. "You've got enough to do with those girls. I'll give Adie a hand."

Beau grinned. He couldn't help it. He remembered Josh and Adie teasing each other in the kitchen during a church potluck. Every bachelor had been envious. That night, Beau had decided to marry Lucy. Before his gaze could slide to Dani, he turned his back and walked into the front room where he saw a stone hearth. Tonight Josh would build a fire. Adie would sew and he'd read his Bible.

Beau had spent a thousand nights under open sky, sitting by fires he'd built for himself and no one else. He craved that solitude now, but he had four females in his care and a pasture full of cows who'd be bawling up a storm if they didn't get home soon. Dani had passed him and was putting on her hat. He turned to tell her to hurry up but stopped without saying a word.

She'd bent her neck and raised her arms to stick in a pin. Tendrils of blond hair fell across her nape, brushing the collar of her pink dress. Beau couldn't stand the sight of her, but neither could he turn away. How long had it been since he'd seen a woman put on a hat? How long would it be before it happened again? Weeks, months, maybe years…whatever it took to bring Johnson to justice. Never mind the lonely ache in his chest. He owed it to Lucy to hunt down the man who'd robbed them of a future. God had blinked that day, but Beau had seen every drop of her blood. He wanted vengeance, no matter the cost.

Daniela Baxter was a distraction he couldn't afford. He made his voice hard. "Are you ready?"

"I am now," she replied.

Beau strode forward. Josh cut in front of him and opened the door, motioning her to pass as if she were a queen. When she smiled her thanks, Beau wanted to slug Josh. His reaction made no sense. Josh had been raised in Boston, the son of a shipping tycoon, and he had the manners to prove it. He was also a minister, a shepherd guiding a lost lamb.

Why hadn't God provided that protection for Lucy? Seeing Josh and Adie, sharing a meal, Dani and her hat… Beau couldn't take the reminders of what he'd lost. He wanted to get home, milk the blasted cows and sit alone in the dark. Pulling his hat low, he followed Dani to the wagon where Adie and the girls were huddled at the tailgate.

Beau smelled trouble. He'd have gone for his gun, but the suspects were three little girls and a preacher's wife. Striding forward, he tried to sound casual. "What are you ladies looking at?"

Emma hunched over something in her arms. Ellie gave him a pleading look. Esther was bouncing on her feet like a rabbit thumping its back leg. He looked to Dani for an explanation and saw a chin as hard as his own.

"Miss Adie gave the girls a kitten," she said. "Isn't that nice?"

Beau couldn't believe his ears. What was the woman thinking? As soon as he could make arrangements, the girls would be headed to Minnesota. What if Harriet Lange didn't like cats? What if she was allergic? If she didn't take the girls, he'd be sending them to school. They'd suffer another heartbreak, one that could have been avoided.

Beau glared at Adie. "You should have asked me."

"Maybe," she said. "But it's done now."

Emma straightened her shoulders, revealing a black-and-white kitten with blue eyes and a pink tongue. It yawned, then snuggled in the crook of her elbow. As hard as he'd become, even Beau couldn't tell the girls to give the cat back. Feeling like a fool, he worried about where the kitten would sleep. Tonight the little fellow would cry for his mama and brothers.

Dani scratched the kitten's neck. "A boy or a girl?"

"A boy," said Adie.

"He'll be a fine mouser," Josh added.

The kitten stretched, revealing three white paws and one black one. He looked as if he'd lost a shoe.

Beau gave up. "We best get going."

After hugs and promises for Sunday, the girls scrambled into the wagon. Beau closed the tailgate, then approached Dani and Adie who were jabbering like magpies. Beau felt an old stirring. In Denver, Lucy had taken forever to leave church because she'd had so many friends. Beau would stand at her side, grinning like a fool.

Josh shot him a look of male commiseration, but Beau

wasn't grinning now. He cleared his throat. "Miss Baxter?"

Dani glanced at him. "I'm ready."

She hugged Adie, then turned to the wagon. Before Josh could step forward, Beau gave her a hand up to the seat. The minister wasn't the only man with manners. Beau's just needed a little polishing. He tipped his hat to Adie, shook Josh's hand and climbed onto the seat. After pulling on his gloves, he took the reins and headed home.

Home.

The word caught in his mind like barbed wire. He didn't have a home and he didn't want one. The giggles coming from the bed of the wagon gave him a headache. So did the sun setting over the blue cut of the mountains and the streak of pink in the sky. Dusk usually calmed him. It meant the end of a day, solitude and the peace of sleep. Today the fading sun pressed him to hurry. The cows needed milking. The girls needed their beds.

"Beau?"

Dani's voice matched the dusk. He hadn't invited her to use his given name, but it sounded natural.

"What is it?" he asked.

"Supper was nice. When we first met, I didn't know you were a lawman."

He grunted. "Josh talks too much."

From the corner of his eye, he saw Dani lace her fingers in her lap. "They like you."

Beau said nothing. The man they'd known in Denver had died with Lucy.

"I don't mean to pry." Her voice dipped low. "But you were good at your work. Do you miss it?"

"I never gave it up."

"You mean Clay Johnson."

"And others." Beau shifted his weight. "Johnson rides in and out of my life. Sometimes I get close and he runs. Sometimes he comes after me, makes a threat and runs again. It can take months to pick up his trail."

"What do you do in between?"

"I check Wanted posters."

"How do you choose?" Dani asked.

Mostly Beau got a feeling. "I pick the man with the deadest eyes."

He heard the soft rush of her breath. "You're a bounty hunter."

Beau frowned. "I don't do it for the money. I do it for—"

"Lucy."

He doubted his wife would approve. "I was going to say justice."

Dani stared straight ahead. "The Blues respect you. I want you to know. I do, too."

A woman's praise shouldn't have made Beau square his shoulders, but it did. Aside from earning a living, he found satisfaction in his work. He brought peace to widows and orphans. He helped people who couldn't help themselves. Most of the time, he felt content with his cause, but tonight he missed the things he'd given up.

With dusk settling, he wished he'd never set eyes on Daniela Baxter and her pink dress, his nieces with their blond hair, even the kitten. Parted from its mother and brothers, the poor thing was meowing its heart out. Beau knew how it felt. If the girls weren't careful, it would bite and scratch out of frustration.

Emma's voice carried over the rattle of the wagon. "We have to decide on a name."

"I like Fluffy," said Esther.

Beau winced. No male deserved a handle like Fluffy. He felt offended on the cat's behalf but didn't say anything.

"He's a boy," Ellie said, sounding superior. "Let's call him Prince."

Beau clenched his teeth. Prince beat out Fluffy, but not by much. The kitten was destined to lose all dignity.

Dani turned to the girls. "How about Boots?"

It fit, but Beau didn't like it.

"It's kind of plain," Emma said.

The females batted around names, each one as unmanly as the last. After a mile, Beau had heard enough. "Name him Fred."

"Fred?" the females cried out in a horrified chorus.

"Or Hank or Sam," he said. "Anything but Fluffy."

He'd stunned the girls into silence. Beau reveled in the quiet until Esther spoke up. "Uncle Beau?"

Until now, no one had called him by that name. His belly flipped. "What is it?"

"What name do *you* like?" asked the child.

He thought for a minute. "I'd call him T.C. for Tom Cat."

"I like it," Emma said.

"Me, too," Ellie added.

Dani hummed her approval. "T.C.'s an excellent name."

Beau turned in her direction and saw a shine in her eyes, a longing that matched the pull in his gut. Children…laughter…hope. When she turned to the kitten and smiled, he saw it as an act of defiance. Dani Baxter would grab the rope of happiness, no matter how frayed, and hold on. His belly burned. If Harriet Lange took his offer, that rope would be yanked from her hands. Beau knew how that felt. Her flesh would tear and bleed. He wanted to tell her to let go now, to forget the kitten and the little girls, but he knew she wouldn't do it.

She must have sensed his gaze, because she turned to him. When her lips tipped into a smile, a sad one but honest, Beau felt it like his own. He jerked his eyes back to the road. T.C. meowed hungrily. Dani stared straight ahead. "We'll give him milk as soon as we get home."

Fool that he was, Beau felt happy for the cat.

Clay Johnson lifted the rope from his saddle, made a noose and slipped it around his horse's neck. It pained him to put her down, but Ricochet had stepped in a prairie dog hole and busted her leg.

He'd ridden a thousand miles on the mare, maybe more. Unlike other females, she didn't recoil when he came near. She'd nuzzle his hand and look for apples. Sometimes he thought she liked him. Clay had nothing to give but a quick death, so he unholstered his pistol, pressed the barrel between the mare's eyes and pulled the trigger.

Clay would have said a prayer if he'd thought God was listening, but he had no such illusions. No one could forgive a man who'd done as much harm as Clay. He'd hated. He'd stolen. He'd cursed. He'd even murdered a woman.

He'd never forget shooting Lucy Morgan. He'd been aiming for her husband when she'd rushed into the man's arms. The bullet had hit her square in the back. Clay could still see Morgan's eyes, going wide and then searching the roof across the street. He'd seen the puff of smoke and spotted Clay lowering the rifle. Clay knew he'd signed his own death warrant. A wife trumped a brother in any man's book, including Clay's. He hadn't been ready to die, so he'd run.

He still wasn't ready, though at times like this, with Ricochet gone and Morgan dogging him, he thought about eternity and wondered if the stories about Heaven were true. He remembered his ma's Bible and a picture of Noah's ark. Did animals go to Heaven? Clay hoped so. As he looked back at Ricochet's remains, he coughed to hide the lump in his throat. Holstering the weapon, he looked uphill for his partners. Before putting Ricochet down, he'd transferred his saddle to his packhorse. To keep the other animals from spooking, his partners, Goose and Andy, had led them up the trail.

Clay called out to them. "It's done. Bring my horse."

"Sure thing, boss," Andy shouted.

Clay watched as Andy led the gelding down the hill. With his red hair and freckles, he looked more like a kid than the con man he was. Goose, short for Augusto, watched him from the top of the trail. Mounted on a mustang, he took off his hat and wiped his brow, revealing white teeth and the blue-black hair brushing his shoulders. Goose liked guns and money, in that order.

Clay had met the pair in Laramie. Like himself, they were horse thieves by trade. For the past six months, the trio had been raiding ranches near the Rockies, staying a step ahead of Beau Morgan and the law. Clay didn't mind posses on his tail, but Morgan had gotten on his last nerve. The man wouldn't quit. Deep down, Clay didn't blame him. Was there a greater sin than killing a man's wife? Clay didn't think so.

Andy arrived with the gelding. "Too bad about Ricochet. She was a good animal."

"The best," Clay said.

Andy turned his pony, a quarter horse with a pretty face and big rump, and spurred it up the trail.

As Clay mounted the gelding, he missed Ricochet even more. The packhorse had a swayback and no spirit. When Clay nudged it with his heels, the animal laid back its ears. He kicked it hard. The beast bucked forward, throwing him off balance.

Andy cackled.

"Shut up," Clay bellowed.

The kid hooted like a coyote.

Clay tasted venom. "I said *shut up*."

When Andy hooted again, Goose chuckled with him. "Face it, boss. That horse is a cut *below* a mule."

Clay pulled up next to his partners. Goose's mustang had sure feet. Andy's pony could outsprint anything with legs. Ricochet could have bested them both. Clay missed her so much he felt the press of tears. No animal could replace her, but he needed a better mount than the gelding. The problem was finding one. He couldn't go into Castle Rock and buy a horse. The last time Clay had gotten wind of Morgan, he'd been in Denver. The man was closing in.

Mounted on a nag, Clay wouldn't have a chance if Morgan caught up to him. He and his partners had been headed south to the San Juan Mountains. That course still seemed wise. They needed to move as quick as they could. As soon they reached a town, Clay would buy a horse or steal one.

As he neared his partners, Clay saw Andy's stupid grin and Goose's mocking eyes. "Let's get moving," he said.

Goose rested his hands on the saddle horn. "Hold up, boss. Andy and I have a plan."

"What?"

Goose's lips thinned to a sneer. "The Rocking J's twenty miles back."

Clay had heard of the place, but he'd never seen it. The Rocking J, owned by John Baylor, raised the finest quarter horses in Colorado.

"What's your point?" Clay asked, though he suspected he knew.

"I say we make a raid," Goose answered.

Andy rested his hands on the saddle horn. "So do I."

"Think about it," Goose said. "We take as many horses as we can manage and head for the mountains. We get money in our pockets, and you get a decent horse."

Clay saw the logic. If it weren't for Morgan, he'd have been eager. Sticking around Douglas County didn't appeal to him, but neither did getting caught on a swaybacked gelding.

He turned to Goose. "I'm listening. How's the place laid out?"

"Open. Unprotected. The man has three daughters—"

"Whoo-hooo!" shouted Andy.

Clay wished he'd left the fool in Wyoming. "Shut up. We're talking about horses, not women."

"That's right," Goose said.

"How many head?" Clay asked.

"Twenty, maybe more."

Clay liked the idea of making money and the lay of the land worked in their favor. The canyons twisted like gnarled fingers attached to a hand. A man could move south or hide, depending on his mood. Clay saw one drawback. "If we raid the Rocking J, Morgan'll come after us for sure."

"So what?" Goose said.

Clay stayed silent. Sometimes he felt compelled to

draw Morgan out. He half hoped the man would catch up to him and end the misery. Other times, Clay felt so guilty for killing the man's wife he wanted to die himself. He hadn't meant to shoot Lucy, though he doubted God or Beau Morgan would believe him.

Andy read Clay's frown for cowardice and made chicken sounds.

Clay slapped him with the back of his hand, cursing him for more than a fool. "You don't know a blasted thing about me and Morgan."

Goose squared his shoulders. "I know you've been playing stupid games. Why not stand and fight?"

Clay had asked himself that same question. At first he'd run because he wanted to live. Then he'd run because he was afraid to die. The guilt would hit anew and he'd do something foolish, like leave Morgan a note or a trinket that would inflame his rage. The nights were the hardest. In his dreams he saw Lucy Morgan wearing a bloody pink dress, picking wildflowers in an endless meadow of rich grass. She'd turn and stare into his eyes. "Give up," she'd whisper. The dream would shift and he'd see his mother in her Sunday best, walking in the same meadow. He couldn't see her face and didn't want to. He felt sure she'd be weeping for what he'd become. Clay could barely live with himself these days. He didn't dare share his thoughts with Goose and Andy. If he lost their respect he'd be a laughingstock.

The gelding shifted under Clay's weight, reminding him of Ricochet lying dead in a patch of grass. Clay almost envied her the peace. No dreams. No guilt. Maybe Goose had a point. Maybe the time had come to stop running. If they raided a ranch, Morgan would get whiff of

Clay's trail and resume the chase. One way or another, the men would come face-to-face.

Clay looked hard at Goose. "Let's do it."

Andy did his coyote hoot.

Goose merely smiled. "If Morgan follows us, I promise you, he'll die."

Chapter Six

Dani startled awake. She'd left the bedroom window open, so nothing stood between her and the shriek of an animal. Her stomach turned to acid when she thought of T.C. A week had passed since they'd brought him home, and last night he'd been officially moved to the barn.

The shriek turned to silence. If the kitten had left the barn, he'd met his end. Dani had no illusions about saving him, but she had to know the facts before the girls woke up. She threw off the quilt and pushed to her feet. Fumbling in the dark, she grabbed her day dress from the hook on the door. When she'd arrived, the hook had held a shirt belonging to Patrick. She couldn't bear the thought of the girls suffering another loss.

Please, Lord. Protect T.C.

Even as she thought the words, Dani felt a surge of anger. So far, God had been slow to answer her prayers. In spite of her best effort, Beau hadn't changed his mind about sending the girls away. Every night Dani prayed for peace, but she mourned Patrick with every breath. The girls were just as raw. Esther sucked her thumb all the time. Ellie wouldn't wear anything but her coveralls, and Emma worried about everything. If something happened to T.C., Dani feared they'd slide beyond her reach.

She stepped into the slippers she'd brought from home and hurried to the barn. Moonlight shone on her path, warning her of ruts and throwing her shadow a step ahead of her. The silence held an eerie stillness. Dani thought every day about Clay Johnson. Beau no longer sat on the porch at night, but she knew he was on guard. Unable to sleep herself, twice she'd looked out the bedroom window and seen him sitting in a chair outside the barn. He'd had a rifle at his side and a hard gleam in his eyes. God pity the man who crossed his path.

Dani glanced at the bunk room door but didn't see Beau. Either he was asleep or he'd gone to investigate the shriek. Maybe he'd heard something else… Maybe Clay Johnson was lurking down the road. Or more likely, Dani thought, her imagination had taken flight. Telling herself to stay calm, she lifted the latch on the barn door, stepped inside and lit the lantern hanging on a post. It flared to life, revealing the hard eyes of a man just two feet away.

She shrieked, then burst out laughing. Beau had beaten her to the barn and had T.C. tucked against his chest. With his tousled hair and sleepy eyes, he looked boyish and relaxed. Dani's heart rose to her throat again, and not because she was afraid. When T.C. yawned and rolled tight against Beau's shirt, she felt as cozy as the kitten.

Startled by her peaceful thoughts, she looked at Beau's face. The man had the audacity to grin at her.

"You scared me," she said.

"I didn't mean to." He glanced at the door. "You must have heard that scream."

"It sounded like a rabbit, but I couldn't be sure."

"Me, neither."

Dani glanced at the kitten. The barn had been pitch-black when she'd entered. "How did you find him in the dark?"

"He found me." Beau told about hearing an animal scream. Like Dani, he'd worried about the cat for the sake of the girls. "I came to take a look. When I opened the door, T.C. ran up to my leg."

Beau absently stroked the cat. Dani's heart warmed with hope. Until now, he'd avoided T.C. at all costs. He'd avoided her, too. How could she convince him she could run the farm if he wouldn't speak to her? Dani saw an opportunity and decided to take it.

"I don't know about you," she said. "But I'm not going back to sleep. Would you like breakfast?"

"Don't mind if I do."

"Bring T.C. I bet he's hungry, too."

As Beau looked up from the kitten, Dani became aware of his eyes taking in her day dress, a blue calico she'd worn for years, and then her hair. She usually wore it in a braid coiled around her head. At night she let the braid fall down her back. Sleep had pulled the strands into wisps that framed her face. Self-conscious, she tucked a curl behind her ear. What did a woman say to a man in the middle of the night? She had no experience in such matters, but she knew what she wanted to say to Beau. She had plans for the farm and he needed to hear about them.

"Let's go inside," she said.

She paced across the yard with Beau in her wake. When they reached the porch, he passed her and opened the door. She led the way to the kitchen, lit the lamp and stove, then shook out the match. She turned and saw Beau sitting in a chair, angled so he could stretch his legs. He still had T.C. on his chest and was stroking the kitten with his large hand. Beau looked as relaxed as the cat.

Dani opened the icebox and filled a saucer from a pitcher. When she put it on the floor, the cat leaped off Beau and ran for the food.

As Beau straightened, Dani met his gaze. "I've got something to show you."

"What?"

"I'll be right back."

She hurried to Patrick's bedroom, her room now, and opened the desk drawer. She removed three drawings, walked back to the kitchen and handed them to Beau. "Take a look."

He held the first drawing a foot from his face, studying the lines as if they made no sense. "What is it?"

"It's the silo I told you about."

"For feed storage."

"That's right."

He looked at it dead-on. "Why is it round?"

"It's easier to clean." Dani pulled eggs and ham out of the icebox. She heard the drawings rustle, glanced back and saw Beau spreading the papers on the table.

"Patrick must have liked the idea. He bought the wood."

"I suppose." She'd mentioned the idea in a letter and sent the drawings, describing how to dig a hole and build the structure over it. She and Patrick had never talked about it. Looking back, there were a lot of things he hadn't said. Dani felt her throat tighten. She should have been cooking breakfast for her new husband.

Beau looked up. "How'd you come up with the plans?"

"My father built one of the first silos in Wisconsin." She told him how successful it had been.

Beau stacked the papers. "It's a good idea."

"I have others."

"Like what?"

Dani cut a slice of ham. Her future depended on convincing Beau she could run the farm, but she didn't want to step on his toes. She kept her voice mild. "I already told you about the second cheese factory."

"I recall."

Dani cracked an egg into the pan. "We could sell twice as much milk, maybe three times."

Beau frowned. "You'd need more cows."

"Patrick kept the four heifers. Next year we'll have more."

"More cows mean more work."

"*And* more profit." She tried to sound confident, but her body tensed. She'd caught Beau's skeptical tone. Needing time to think, she placed a ham steak in the fry pan, then spooned butter over Beau's eggs. He liked them over-easy. He also liked toast with jam. She put four slices on a rack in the oven and set the butter crock on the table.

"Coffee's ready," she said brightly.

"I'll pour my own."

Beau lifted two cups from a shelf, took a hot pad from the drawer, then lifted the pot from the back of the stove. The hot pad in his hand had come from her trunk. She'd made it during her engagement to Virgil. Dani's heart pounded. Going home to Wisconsin would mean years of loneliness. She had to convince Beau to let her adopt the girls.

As he filled the cups, she dished up their breakfast. She handed Beau his plate, then filled hers with half as much. They sat at the same time, staring at each other.

Dani folded her hands in her lap. "I'm serious, you know."

"Miss Baxter—"

"Call me Dani." As long as he considered her "Miss Baxter," he'd see her as the woman who'd arrived in a fancy dress, not a woman accustomed to work. She could feel the wall between them and had to break it down.

Beau took a bite of ham, chewed to avoid speaking, then shook his head. "I just can't see it."

"Why not?"

He shook his head. "Running this place is hard work."

"We have ten cows," she said. "My brother has fifty."

"And hired help, I'd guess."

"Three men," she countered. "I could run this place with one. Do you known Howie Dawes?"

Beau frowned. "I know Tom Dawes. He's the sheriff."

"Howie's his son. Patrick hired him to help now and then. I could do the same."

She watched as Beau slathered butter on a slice of toast. "Dairying's not for the lazy, that's for sure."

"I love it," Dani declared. "And I'm good at it."

She felt all the hope she'd had with Patrick. She missed him, but her dream of a new life could still come true. She just had to convince Beau she could do the job. But how? She could talk all day, but he needed to see her in action to believe. Nibbling her breakfast, she flashed back to mornings in Wisconsin, teasing her brother and racing him to the barn. He hadn't been able to resist a dare. If Beau had the same taste for a challenge, Dani had her answer. She set her napkin on the table. "I have an offer for you."

"What?"

"We have a contest for the farm."

His eyes twinkled. "You want to arm wrestle?"

"No. You'd win." She'd seen him haul fifty-pound sacks as if they held feathers. "I was thinking of something else."

He set his napkin on the table and sat back in the chair. He hadn't agreed but she'd earned his attention. "What do you have in mind?"

"You milk half the cows and I do the other. We'll see who gets the most milk the fastest."

"What's the prize?"

"If I win, you admit I can run this place."

"And if *I* win?"

She searched her mind for something that mattered, but he already had complete power over her future. She tried to sound brave. "I don't have anything you want."

He leaned back in his chair and looked at her with mirth in his eyes. "Yes, you do."

Dani had no idea. "What is it?"

"Raspberry pie."

She'd made one three days ago from Adie's recipe. Beau had eaten a third of it and gone to the barn, but not before Dani saw a wistfulness in his eyes. If he wanted more raspberry pie, she'd be glad to bake one.

She smiled at him. "Just to make things clear… If I win the milking contest, you'll admit I can run this place."

"That's right."

"And if you win, I make a raspberry pie?"

"Exactly."

"It doesn't seem fair." She wanted the contest to matter.

"It's not about pie," Beau said. "If I win, I expect you

to take the girls to Minnesota, then go home to Wisconsin. The pie's just because I want one."

Dani raised her chin. "You're pretty confident."

"Very."

"So am I."

He looked her in the eye. She saw no malice, only the twinkle she'd seen earlier. "It's a deal."

Dani stood to clear the table. Her stomach lurched. She *had* to win this competition. After a last swig of coffee, Beau carried his plate to the counter, bent to pet T.C., then winked at her. "Get ready, Miss Baxter. We square off at dawn."

A half hour later, Beau had his backside planted on a milking stool and an empty bucket between his feet. Earlier, he and Dani had met at the pasture gate. Being a gentleman, he'd given her first pick of the cows. She'd looped a rope around the closest one, Buttercup, and led the animal to the barn where he'd cleaned a second spot for today's milking.

Beau's first cow, a stubborn thing named Sweetness, had run from him. She wasn't cooperating any better in the barn.

"Come on, old woman," he muttered.

Reminding himself to be gentle, he looped his thumb and index finger around the Jersey's teat, curled the rest of his fingers and pulled. He'd been milking the cows for more than a week. The first time had been tedious, but he'd taken Emma's advice and tried singing hymns while he worked. He wasn't about to do that with Dani working next to him.

She, on the other hand, had no such reluctance. He'd already heard three choruses of "Shall We Gather by the

River," each verse accompanied by the hiss of milk hitting the bucket. They'd been working for five minutes, and she'd already emptied a pail into one of the metal cans by the door. Each one was numbered and waiting for Webb, the old man who picked up for the cheese factory.

Beau tugged again on the Jersey's teat. It didn't help his concentration to recall Dani hurrying across the yard with a determined look in her eyes. She'd put her hair up, but he'd recalled the tendrils loose around her face. She'd looked lovely, a fact that filled Beau with memories of Lucy and a deep regret for what he'd lost. After watching Dani with the girls and eating her cooking, having all the buttons on his shirts and his socks mended, he couldn't help but like her. She had a good heart. If ever a female needed a family to love, it was Daniela Baxter.

He even liked her name. Dani-ay-la. It felt nice on his tongue, sweet like the pie. Dani suited her, too. He could imagine her as a tomboy shoveling hay from the loft, riding horses and daring her brother to best her at contests like this one.

Sighing, Beau counted his reaction as another reason to win the milking contest. He was dead sure that stepping into the life she'd imagined would limit her future. It took a brave man to marry a woman with three children in her care. If Dani took on the farm and the girls, she might never find a husband. On her own, a pretty blonde in a town full of ranchers, she'd be married within a year. Beau had known the joy of marriage for only a short time, but he remembered the goodness, especially with Dani singing to the blasted cow who was giving more milk than it ever had for Beau. She was on her second bucket and nearly finished with the first cow.

Beau didn't want to listen to the hymns, but he couldn't

cover his ears and milk at the same time. As Dani's soprano filled the barn with the words to "Blessed Assurance" and its promise of Heaven, Beau tasted bile.

Irked, he tugged too hard on the Jersey's teat. The bovine stomped her foot. He muttered an oath, then straightened his back and glared at Dani. "Do you have to sing?"

"The cows like it." The milk hissed into her bucket. "I'm not hearing anything from your side of the barn. You might try it."

He chuffed.

She stood and lifted the bucket, grinning as she turned to the milk can with a swing of her hip. "By the time you and Sweetness make peace, I'll be done."

Beau saw nothing "sweet" about Sweetness. All the cows had names. Sweetness and Light were sisters. Martha, Dolley and Mary Todd were named for former first ladies. The last five, known as the "flower girls" were Buttercup, Rose, Daisy, Lily and Daffodil. Beau watched as Dani neared the milk cans. She set down the bucket, used her long apron to get a better grip on the handle, then hoisted it and poured the milk into the can, not spilling a drop. Beau knew how much the bucket weighed. As slender as she was, Dani had strong arms and a strong back.

She covered the can with a clean towel, then went to fetch another cow. She came back with Lily. After getting the cow settled, she scratched its ears and even kissed its nose.

Sweetness swung her head around, stared at Beau, then bellowed.

Laughing, Dani sat on the stool. Five seconds later, Lily let down her milk. Dani looked over her shoulder. "Sweetness wants you to sing. There's no getting around it."

No way would Beau sing a hymn, but both his pride and his common sense told him he had to do something. He gave the old cow a pat on the leg, realigned the bucket and broke into "Camptown Races." By the second "doo-dah," Sweetness let down her milk. White streams hissed into the bucket in perfect time to the song.

Dani's laughter pealed through the air. Beau had never heard anything quite like the mix of the silly song, her laughter and the beat of the milk. The high ceiling caught the music and bounced it back and around, filling his ears with harmonies he'd never heard. He'd become accustomed to silence, men grunting in saloons, the rush of wind and rivers and the rustling of dried leaves. Today he heard unity, oneness, especially when Dani switched from laughing to singing the "doo-dahs" in "Camptown Races."

Before Beau knew it, his bucket was close to full. He stood, patted Sweetness and strode to the can assigned to him. Dani hurried up behind him and added another bucket to her can.

He had some serious catching up to do. Lowering his chin, he eyed her. "I wouldn't get cocky if I were you. It's not over yet."

She smiled back. "We'll see about that."

She turned so fast her apron flapped. Beau went back to Sweetness, finished the milking and led her to the pasture. He came back with Light and saw Dani filling a new milk can.

He couldn't let her win. Being a man of his word, he'd have to give serious consideration to allowing her to stay with the girls. Beau found the idea both appealing and irksome. As long as Dani and the girls were in Castle Rock, he'd have something akin to a home. Pushing the thought aside, he positioned the bucket under Light and went back to work, singing whatever tune popped into his head.

Thirty minutes later, Dani had milked Rose, Lily and Daisy. Beau had finished with Sweetness and Light. Martha, the oldest of the cows and named for Mrs. Washington, didn't appreciate "Camp Town Races," so he switched to "Pop Goes the Weasel." Martha didn't care for it and neither did Beau.

An old favorite came into Beau's head. Without thinking, he sang the opening line of "The Battle Hymn of the Republic," the verse about a man's eyes seeing the glory of the coming of the Lord. It lifted Beau up. So did the next verse, the one about grapes of wrath. He'd sung the song in church in Denver. It called to his blood and his cause. Beau understood wrath. When he dreamed of finding Clay, the images weren't pretty. He'd shake off the pictures when he awoke, but the bitterness never left.

Except right now, he felt good. Martha liked the song and let down her milk with the ease that made her the best producer. In minutes she'd given all her milk and he'd caught up with Dani. After hauling the bucket to the milk can, he fetched his fourth cow, a sweet thing named Dolley. Dani's fourth cow was named Daffodil. Dolley had a sweet nature and gave generously. Daff was the most stubborn of the ladies, the cow who'd stepped on his foot and inspired his one use of profanity. Beau smelled victory.

As he pulled up the stool, he glanced at Dani, who was coaxing Daff with clucking sounds as she worked the teats. Nothing happened. The lines tightened around her eyes.

"Come on, girl," she said. "What's bothering you?"

Beau had a feeling he knew. He and Daff didn't get along, but he knew she liked being scratched between her eyes. He'd gained on Dani and almost had the lead. If he said nothing, he'd win, but he felt like a heel. He sat straight on the stool. "Give her a scratch between the eyes. It works every time."

"Thanks." She pushed to her feet, gave Daff a long scratch that made Beau think of his own itchy back, then sat on the stool. Milk squirted into the pail.

Without breaking the rhythm, Dani turned her head. "That was nice of you."

"It beats hearing 'Camptown Races' again."

She smiled. "I enjoyed it. You have a fine voice."

He said nothing.

"Do you like to sing?"

His voice choked, but he answered. "Back in Denver, I sang in the church choir."

"That's nice."

He blew air through his nose. Lucy had sung alto. Choir practice had been on Thursday evenings. They'd eaten supper out, and… Beau groaned out loud.

Dani stopped milking. "Are you all right?"

"I'm fine."

But he wasn't. She'd used his given name before, but today he liked the sound of it. His chest swelled with breath, with life. The barn had a window high in the wall. It cast a beam of gold light to the floor between them, catching dust motes and making a gossamer wall between himself and Dani. If he wanted, he could pass through that dust and be her friend, maybe more. But to what end? He had a call on his life. She had a broken heart. She needed the kind of life he couldn't give.

Can't or won't?

Pushing aside the whisper of his conscience, Beau focused on the milk filling the bucket. A little scratching and some sweet talk and the cows gave generously. He thought of Dani's good cooking and the girls playing checkers on the porch. If he didn't watch himself, he'd react as generously as Martha. He'd give his all for this little family.

The barn door creaked open. Along with the hiss of the milk, Beau heard the pad of little-girl feet. He'd never heard that particular scuff until he'd arrived at the farm. Men took long, thumping steps. Boys ran. Little girls scampered, even when they were sad and missing their daddies.

"Who's there?" Dani called from the stall.

"It's me."

Beau recognized Ellie's voice and looked up. She'd reached Dolley and had stopped to scratch her. Dressed in coveralls as always, she reminded Beau of Patrick at that age. They'd grown up in Indiana on a farm similar to this one, half brothers with Beau the elder by three years. Patrick had been the baby of the family, their mother's favorite and his father's pride. Beau's own father, a man he didn't recall, had died in a wagon accident. Beau had toughened up early in life. Losing a father forced a boy to grow up.

Ellie rubbed the side of Martha's head. "I used to help Pa with the milking."

What did a man say to a hurting little girl? Did he talk about Heaven? Beau had rebelled every time some well-meaning fool told him Lucy was in a better place. What could have been better than sharing his bed, his home, meals at the table he'd built with children in mind.

His gaze slid to Dani. She had already straightened

and was looking at him with the same sad expression he'd seen in the cemetery. Then and there, Beau lost the milking contest. Dani needed these children. She needed the farm, a home of her own, and he could give them to her.

He rose from the stool and called to Ellie. "Want to finish with Dolley?"

The child's eyes showed all the chaos in her heart. He wasn't her father, but he looked enough like Patrick to stir up memories. Just for now, he could fill the hole in her life.

"I don't know," Ellie said.

Beau kept his expression gentle. "Dolley misses your pa, too. She'd like it if you'd help."

Ellie's eyes widened and her lips parted as if she wanted to speak. Beau recognized the signs of knowledge dawning on her face. Her father was gone, but life would go on. He'd felt that way when he'd eaten Dani's raspberry pie.

Ellie stroked Martha's nose, then looked at Beau. "I can finish. My pa taught me everything."

As she took his place, Beau stepped into the aisle. He heard the hiss-hiss of Dani milking Daffodil. As he turned, she met his gaze with a question in her eyes. *What about the contest?*

Beau had no doubt about the outcome. Even if he'd edged Dani by a pound or two, she'd bested him in spirit. She knew about breeding, milk prices, feed crops, even confounded things called silos. Even more important, she loved the animals like children. Never again would he hear "Camptown Races" without thinking of this day.

Beau spoke softly. "You won, Dani." He'd used her given name. It tasted sweet, like the berries.

She blushed. "Does that mean…"

She was asking about adopting the girls. “I don’t know yet, but you’re closer.”

He still had concerns. What would happen if Dani lost her heart to a man with his own ambitions? Grief-stricken women made foolish choices. They married too soon and lived with regrets. Before he handed her the responsibility of the farm, he had to be sure she knew the facts. That meant having a long, private talk. Maybe tonight… Beau bristled at the thought. He didn’t want to see Dani in the moonlight. He’d have to find another time.

She’d filled a bucket, so he lifted it and carried it to the milk can. When he brought it back, he took Ellie’s pail and did the same thing. When the last cow was milked, Dani carried the buckets to the well for scrubbing. Beau lifted a shovel and headed for the horse stalls. Ellie picked up a smaller shovel and followed him.

“Uncle Beau?”

“Yes?”

“Do you like to fish?”

“Sure.”

A graybeard in Wyoming had taught him to fly-fish on the Snake River. Beau liked it quite a bit. If he kept his eyes on the water, the current caught his thoughts and carried them away.

Ellie dumped a load of dirty straw into the wheelbarrow. “I like it, too. Pa used to take me.”

Beau felt the itch as if it were his own. “Where’d he take you?”

“To a stream that’s near the mountains. It’s pretty far, but I bet it’s running fast.”

“Trout?” Beau asked.

“Big ones.”

Beau thought for a minute. Planting season was coming to a close. He had to get the alfalfa in the ground, and he wanted to build Dani's silo. Fishing sounded like pure pleasure, but he couldn't say yes. He looked at Ellie, intending to change the subject. Her blue eyes were alive with hope, a bit of sunshine that melted Beau's heart. He'd plant tomorrow. Today had needs of a different kind. Ellie needed new memories, plus he could speak to Dani in private while the girls caught tadpoles.

He braced the shovel on the floor and put his boot on the blade. "How'd you like to go fishing right now?"

"I'd like that."

"Me, too," Beau said.

Ellie smiled. "Can I tell my sisters?"

"Let's check with Miss Dani first."

They went back to shoveling, working even faster than before. When Dani brought the clean buckets into the barn, Ellie blurted the question about fishing.

Dani smiled. "That sounds like fun."

"We can have a picnic," Ellie added.

Dani looked at Beau, saying with her eyes that he'd made her proud. Peace washed over him. Just for today, he belonged on the banks of that stream, listening to the water, the wind, the chatter of three little girls and a pretty woman. As Dani turned to leave, he watched the sway of her skirt, a deep blue that matched her eyes. The light from the window caught in the crown of her braid and glinted gold.

Beau pitched another forkful of straw. Before he knew it, he was humming "Camptown Races."

Chapter Seven

Dani watched Beau's hands as he wielded his pocketknife against an apple, removing the red peel in a single strand. When she'd first laid eyes on him, she'd taken his measure by his hands and doubted his character. Today she saw a man capable of a gentle touch and great patience.

The picnic had been relaxing except for Emma's fussing. Back at the farm, she'd been uninterested in packing the food and had worried about the long wagon ride to Sparrow Creek. She'd also been rude to Beau, who'd endured the girl's sass without a single harsh word. While he and Ellie caught trout, Emma had followed Esther like a shadow, warning her about rocks and ruts and everything in between.

With the sun high in the sky, the five of them were seated on a blanket Dani had spread beneath a cottonwood. She'd passed out sandwiches and apples and was enjoying the sunshine. Beau sat across from her with his back against the tree, his legs bent and his forearms resting on his knees while he peeled the apple. Ellie had positioned herself at his elbow, and Esther had curled up in Dani's lap. Emma was seated between Dani and Ellie.

Beau held up the peeled apple. "Who's first?"

"Me!" Ellie took the fruit and bit into it.

A drop of juice shot in Emma's direction. The older girl jerked back as if Ellie had spit on her. "Cut it out!"

Dani didn't know what to do about Emma's foul mood. She was hurting, but hurting others wouldn't bring her father back. Dani touched her stiff shoulder. "It was an accident, sweetie."

Emma's mouth trembled. "I know."

Beau had a second apple in hand. He finished peeling it and offered it to Emma. "This one's for you."

She took the apple and heaved it as far as she could. "I don't want it."

Dani gasped. "Emma!"

Beau shot Dani a look, the one that belonged to the lawman who'd broken up fights in Denver. *I'll handle this.* Dani welcomed his help. She understood the cause of Emma's anger but didn't know how to handle it. When Dani felt melancholy, she wanted to be left alone. When she cried, she did it in private. She didn't understand Emma, but she suspected Beau did.

He handed Emma a third apple. "If it makes you feel better, throw this one, too."

Tears flooded the girl's eyes. "*Nothing* makes me feel better."

Beau worked his knife around the fruit. This time the peel broke. "It can't be fixed, but it's still an apple and it tastes good." He held the fruit out to Emma.

The child shot daggers with her eyes. "What's going to happen to us?"

Dani wanted to know, as well, but she'd hoped to discuss the matter with Beau in private. He'd conceded the milking contest, but did that mean he'd approve the adoption? Neither of them had told the girls about Harriet Lange. Until now, his nieces had been too afraid of Beau to ask about the future. When they approached Dani, she'd told the truth. Their Uncle Beau had legal authority and was still deciding.

Emma's outburst made the waiting seem cruel. Dani looked pointedly at Beau. "I'd like to know, too."

"I see three possibilities," he replied.

Esther paid no attention, but Ellie stopped chewing the bite of apple.

Emma tensed. "What are they?"

"You're not going to like the first one." Beau kept his gaze on Emma. "I asked Mr. Scott to find a boarding school."

"No!" she cried.

Beau held up one hand. "Hold on. That's not likely to happen."

"It better not." Emma raised her chin. "I won't leave my sisters."

"Fair enough," Beau said. "The second option concerns your Aunt Harriet."

Ellie turned to her big sister. "Who's she?"

"She's a witch!"

"Emma!" Dani cried.

"She's mean," the child declared. "We visited her when I was little. She's mama's great-aunt. She's old and ugly and she slapped my hand for touching one of her stupid little teacups."

Dani felt outraged but cautioned herself. *Judge not.* "That was a long time ago."

"I don't care," Emma said. "If she liked children, she'd have some of her own."

"Not necessarily." Dani's back stiffened. Maybe, like

herself, Harriet Lange hadn't found the right man. Dani had jilted Virgil Griggs and ended up the town pariah. Perhaps Miss Lange had a similar story.

Beau's voice broke into Dani's thoughts. "We don't know what Miss Lange is like."

Emma frowned. "I know she doesn't like *me*."

Dani weighed Emma's comments and worried. Harriet Lange had asked for Emma only, not the younger girls. Beau, thinking money was a problem, had offered to pay an allowance for all three girls. If Harriet Lange took the offer, how would they know she'd done it out of love? Judging by Beau's frown, he'd gone down the same road.

Ellie had her half-eaten apple in her hand. "Uncle Beau?"

"Yes?"

"Why can't *you* stay with us?"

"I've got business elsewhere," he said simply.

Ellie hugged her knees. "If you stayed, you could marry Dani."

No one said a word, not even Emma.

Ellie's voice sped up. "She's pretty and she can cook. Emma and I can do most of the chores. Esther's too little, but she's fun. That counts for something, doesn't it?"

Dani's heart broke in two. Not for Ellie, who looked desperate. And not for Emma, who looked helpless. But for Beau, whose eyes had taken on the color of grass stirring helplessly in a breeze. Across the blanket, she saw the man who'd loved Lucy and married her, the sheriff who'd sung in the church choir in the tenor she'd heard bouncing in the cavernous barn.

Her heart raced with feelings she couldn't name. She loved Patrick. She always would, yet she'd come to know Beau in a way she'd never known his brother. She and

Patrick had traded dozens of letters, but he'd never shared his secrets. Dani had his photograph in her box of keepsakes, but she'd never seen his eyes change with emotion the way Beau's were changing now. The dark glint had turned into a twinkle that matched the grass. He looked at Dani with a wry smile, silently sharing the humor of Ellie's naive remark.

She smiled back.

Beau's eyes lingered on hers, but then he blinked. The twinkle faded, leaving behind the man who'd called himself Cain. Looking away, he hurled the half-peeled apple into the stream. It bobbed once and raced away.

Beau kept his eyes on the apple. "It's not possible, Ellie."

"Why not?" the child asked.

Dani felt sorry for them all. "Your Uncle Beau and I are friends, but we don't love each other."

Esther wiggled in Dani's lap. She hadn't sucked her thumb since they'd left the house, but she had it in her mouth now.

"Why not?" she mumbled through her fingers. "You could be our mama and he could be like Pa."

Dani blushed. "It's not that simple."

Esther pressed even closer. "I want you to stay."

"Me, too." Emma glared at Beau. "My pa wrote to Dani every week. He said *you* disappeared."

Dani knew why, but Emma didn't. Someday the girls would learn more about their Aunt Lucy and Beau's loss but not this minute. "Emma, there are things you don't understand."

"Then tell me," the child demanded.

Beau's expression stayed blank. "My name's on the will. That's all that matters."

"But it's not right," Emma insisted. "Dani knows us. She knows about cows, too. A *lot* more than you do. *And* they like her!"

Beau shifted his gaze to Dani. His expression shot her back to her mother's kitchen and the times her parents traded looks she hadn't understood. Those moments usually involved her brother getting into trouble. Beau, she realized, wanted her to understand him in a way the girls couldn't. They were two adults—equals—addressing a problem.

He made his voice formal. "Birthing season's a tough time of year. Tell me, Miss Baxter. Can you handle it?"

"Yes." She'd helped her father.

His brows lifted with surprise. "Can you build that silo you're planning?"

"I'd hire someone."

"What about the alfalfa?" he asked. "Can you handle the planting, harvesting *and* the baling?"

"If I have to." Dani held his gaze. "The seed should have been in the ground two weeks ago. If you can't finish it in the next day or two, we should hire help."

Emma chimed in. "Howie Dawes will do it. Pa hires him every harvest. We all help. We can help Dani, too."

Ellie sat straighter. "I can do a lot."

"Me, too," Esther said.

Beau drummed his fingers on his knee. "I'll be straight with you, girls. The third option is to leave Dani in charge and get back to my work, but I can't. I have to do what's best, not what's easy."

Emma frowned. "This *is* best."

"Hear me out." Beau held up his hand. "You girls have lost too much already. I know that. I want to see you safe and settled. *How* that happens is my decision."

The suck-suck of Esther's thumb beat with Dani's heart.

Beau looked at the child, then at Emma. "I'd like to speak to Dani in private. Can you watch out for your sisters?"

Emma stared at Beau with the haughtiness of a little girl playing dress-up. "Of course, I can."

"Good." Beau focused on Dani. "Let's take a walk."

When she nodded yes, he pushed to his feet. Dani slid Esther off her lap, tried to stand and wobbled. Her leg had fallen asleep. Before she could steady herself, Beau grasped her elbow. Blood rushed to her toes. They tingled, but not as much as her elbow. She thought of Beau milking cows and peeling the apples. He had strong hands, steady hands. She'd come to trust him…except where it came to the girls. Dani knew best about the adoption. She had to prove it to him.

As soon as she steadied herself, he let go of her elbow. "Let's go upstream."

With the grass twisting around her boots, she cut across the slope to the bank of the stream. She saw prints where Beau had cast his line and caught tonight's supper. Ellie's smaller feet marked the ground next to his. In the distance she spotted a cluster of boulders surrounded by lupines, poppies and tiny pink flowers she didn't recognize.

"That's a good spot," she said. They could see the girls, but the stream would cover their voices.

Beau nodded. "I want privacy."

When they reached the boulders, Dani smoothed her skirt and sat on a slab of granite. She expected Beau to sit at her side. Instead he stood in front of her with his hands behind his back. She felt like a witness in a court of law and didn't like it.

Before she could stand, Beau looked into her eyes. "I have just one question, Miss Baxter."

So she'd stopped being Dani. If he thought formality would give him an edge, he was wrong. "What is it?"

"You traveled a thousand miles to marry a man you'd never met. I want to know why."

She'd been expecting Beau to challenge her skills, not her motives. What could she say? That she'd been courted by every man in Walker County and was impressed by none? That she'd been engaged twice and had jilted Virgil Griggs a week before the wedding? Dani still cringed when she thought of Virgil trying to kiss her. She hadn't loved him, not even a little. He'd smelled like bad onions, and she'd turned her head in revulsion. When she'd broken the engagement, Dani had sealed her future as a spinster.

That Dani Baxter, she's as fickle as they come!

Dani didn't have a fickle bone in her body. She'd been lonely and had made a mistake when she'd said yes to Virgil, but the town had other ideas.

Beau crossed his arms over his chest. The longer she waited to reply, the darker his eyes became.

"Does it matter?" she finally asked.

"Yes, it does."

"Why?"

His voice went low. "There's only one reason a woman leaves her home for a man she's never met."

Dani stiffened. "What's that?"

"She's running from something."

He'd struck dangerously close to home. She'd been

running from loneliness but saw no reason to admit it. "You're wrong."

"Am I?"

"I wasn't running *from* anything," she insisted. "I was running *to* Patrick."

Beau dropped down next to her. Their knees brushed. They both pulled back, but he didn't seem to notice. "I don't believe you, Dani."

He'd used her given name. It made her feel soft inside, but she kept her back straight. "It's true."

"You didn't even know him."

"We wrote letters."

Beau shook his head. "It's been years since I've seen Patrick, but leopards don't change their spots."

Dani's heart pounded. "What do you mean?"

"When we were kids, Patrick had a way of avoiding the facts. He saw things as he wanted them to be, not as they were. He was the youngest. Our ma spoiled him."

Dani bristled. "That was a long time ago."

"Maybe, but I have to wonder… Why did Patrick write to *you?* Why not find a wife in Castle Rock?"

Dani had asked herself the same question. Sometimes it haunted her, especially since she had no one to ask. "I don't know."

"I don't, either." Regret salted his voice. "I *do* know one thing and it's this. If you adopt my nieces, you'll have a harder time finding a husband."

"I'm not looking for a husband. Not anymore."

"Why not?"

"I'm grieving Patrick."

"I know how that is," Beau murmured. "I also know that the pain eases with time. One day you'll wake up and be ready to breathe again."

"Did that happen to you?"

"In a way." He stared across the meadow. "I miss Lucy, but I know she's gone. It's the hate for Johnson that keeps me on the road. I promised myself I'd bring him to justice. I'm going to keep my word."

Dani saw a link. "I made a promise, too."

"To Patrick?"

"Yes."

"He wouldn't expect you to keep it."

"But I want to." Without the girls, she had nothing. For all Beau's talk of husbands, Dani had no reason to believe things would be different for her in Castle Rock. Except for Patrick, she'd never been in love. She pushed to her feet and faced Beau. "I love the girls. I want to be their mother."

"You also want a husband."

Dani was tired of being pushed. "Not if he's as bossy as you are."

"Bossy?" Beau chuffed.

"Yes!" Dani glared at him. "You act like you know what I'm thinking, but you don't. You have no idea what happened in Wisconsin. If you did—" Too late, she sealed her lips.

Beau's eyes glinted. "So you *do* have a secret."

"If you must know, I was engaged twice. Both times, I called off the wedding. Once at the last minute." She blushed. "Virgil Griggs didn't appreciate my change of heart."

"Why'd you break it off?"

Dani's cheeks turned red. "He smelled like onions."

Beau burst out laughing.

"It wasn't funny at the time," she said. "I earned a

reputation for being fickle. I'm not. It's just that…" She shrugged. "I can't explain it."

"You don't have to. I understand."

How could he? She didn't understand it herself. She was about to ask what he meant when he focused his gaze on her face. "I have a bit of wisdom for you."

"What's that?"

His eyes twinkled. "Not all men smell like onions."

Her father had smelled like leather. Her brother used bay rum when he shaved. Dani had no idea how Patrick would have struck her nose, but she knew the scent of Beau's shaving soap. As they'd walked to the rocks, she'd smelled apples.

The thought rocked Dani to her marrow. For all his bluster, she liked Beau and his bossy ways. Her feelings made no sense. She was grieving Patrick. She had no business noticing the mischief in Beau's eyes. He had a glint of male superiority, as if he knew something she didn't.

Dani bristled. "Are you going to let me adopt the girls or not?"

"I haven't decided yet."

"Why not?"

Silence.

Dani wanted to scream. "You *know* I can run the farm."

"There's no doubt about it."

"Then what's the problem?"

His eyes locked on to hers. "I like you, Dani. I want you to be happy."

"Then give me the girls."

His gaze hardened. "Under one condition."

"What is it?"

"Look me in the eye."

She did what he asked.

"Now tell me you don't want a husband."

If she rushed her words, he'd sense her desperation. But the longer she thought, the more her heart pounded with the truth. Of course she wanted a husband, someone to love and cherish. She wanted everything God intended for a husband and wife. She wanted her belly to swell with child. She wanted to laugh in the dark and snuggle at dawn. She'd also made a promise and believed God wanted her to keep it. Why else would he bring her to this moment? As painful as this week had been, she felt needed. She had a purpose. She didn't understand God's logic, but she felt His love.

She took a breath to steady herself, then faced Beau. "I can't say that."

He raised his chin. "That's honest."

"There's more," she said. "I've dreamed of children all my life. I expected to get married and have my own. Instead God sent me here."

Beau's jaw tensed. "Leave God out of it."

"I can't," she said. "I don't know why He took Patrick home, but I know what I promised. I want to adopt the girls."

"Dani—"

"Say yes," she pleaded. "You know it's right."

Barring a miracle, she'd never have a husband. As Beau had said, only an exceptional man would marry a woman with three children. Dani's courtship days were over. For whatever reason, God had made her a widow without ever being a wife. She raised her chin. Someday she'd come face-to-face with the King of Kings. She'd sit at His feet and feel His love. At that glorious moment, she wouldn't recall her earthly loneliness. The thought made her strong.

Beau stood up, putting them eye to eye. "It's a big decision. You don't have to decide now."

"Yes, I do."

"Why?"

"The girls need an answer." So did Dani. "I *know* what I want." She wanted to be a mother. She also wanted to weep for what she'd never have. A husband of her own, a child growing in her belly… She stared harder at Beau.

His expression softened. "If you're sure—"

"I'm positive." She took a breath. "When shall we tell the girls?"

"Now's fine. I'll go to town early in the morning to tell Scott to wire Harriet Lange. As of today, my offer to give her the girls is off the table. They're yours, Dani."

He pulled his hat low, hiding his eyes. Before she could thank him, he walked away.

Chapter Eight

Beau wasn't fond of cleaning fish, but today he welcomed the chore. Not even Ellie wanted to stick around. She'd gone inside with her sisters, leaving Beau to prepare the trout with T.C. meowing at the base of the worktable behind the barn. The racket didn't bother Beau at all. After listening to female chatter all the way back from the stream, he'd felt a lot like T.C. Beau could see the life he wanted, but it glittered like gold at the bottom of a deep pond.

When he and Dani had told the girls about his decision, they'd hugged her hard. She'd made a point of saying Beau cared about them and had made the decision out of love. She'd been right and the girls had sensed it. Esther and Ellie had hugged him. Emma had called him Uncle Beau and apologized for flinging the apple. He'd felt their blood ties in his marrow. If he'd been Emma, he'd have thrown things, too. He'd told her so and she'd smiled. Today had been the best day of his life since Lucy's murder, but it couldn't be repeated. As long as Johnson drew breath, Beau had a call on his life.

He also had three girls and a woman waiting for supper. He lifted the fish from the bucket, slit it open and removed the bones. He didn't care for the sight of fish guts, but a man did what he had to do. Beau set the fish pieces on a plate, then wiped the mess into a bucket he'd dump in the garden later.

As he lifted the second fish, T.C. meowed in outrage.

"You'll get yours," Beau said to the cat.

As he worked the knife, he wondered if he could say the same for himself. After five years, he was no closer to Clay Johnson than he'd been the day he left Denver. The man had a knack for goading Beau and then disappearing. Why wouldn't Johnson stand and fight? Beau didn't understand. If the outlaw wanted to hide, he could have traveled east and lost himself in a big city. Instead he'd started a game of tag by leaving Beau messages. Why? Beau saw only one answer. Clay Johnson had the mind of a snake. The sooner he met his end, the sooner Beau could settle down.

For the first time since Denver, he liked the idea. He'd grown fond of sleeping in a bed and even fonder of Dani's cooking. When he finished cleaning the fish, he'd milk the cows. He'd clean up and go inside the cozy house. He'd sit at the head of the table, passing platters of food and listening to female prattle. As he filleted another fish, Beau muttered an oath. He had to track down Johnson and kill him. Why was he torturing himself with thoughts of Dani and the girls?

T.C. wove around his ankles, meowing with the desperation befitting an annoyed feline. Beau tossed him a bite of fish. "Now scat."

The cat swallowed the tidbit, sat and stared at Beau. He wanted more. He wanted it all.

So did Beau. Looking at the kitten, he faced a sad

truth. Dani and his nieces would live in his heart forever. He'd never forget them. Maybe he'd visit once a year, at Christmas when snow made the days bright. He'd bring toys for the girls and something nice for Dani. Maybe cloth for a dress or a fancy hat. Maybe a necklace made of gold. She liked pretty things. Who knew what the future held? Maybe someday, after Clay Johnson had been caught, Beau would call the farm home.

The thought made his belly roll. Once he finished with Johnson, he'd be a free man. He could marry Dani… He liked the idea quite a bit, but he couldn't expect her to wait for him. In spite of adopting Patrick's girls, Beau figured she'd be married within a year. Only a fool would let her get away.

Sighing, he picked up another fish.

"Nice-looking trout."

Beau turned and saw Josh. "There's plenty. Can you stay for supper?"

"No, thanks. Dani already asked."

"You're missing out."

"This isn't a social call."

Josh rarely sounded grim. When he did, he had a reason. Beau lowered the knife. "What brings you out here?"

"The Rocking J had some trouble."

"What kind?"

"Horse thieves made off with some prize stock."

The local ranch had the finest quarter horses in Colorado. Clay Johnson had an eye for good horseflesh. Beau's nerves prickled. "Any witnesses?"

"Baylor's wife saw three men."

Beau forgot the fish. "Last I heard, Johnson had two partners. What else did she see?"

"Not much. They were wearing masks."

"What about their mounts?" Johnson had ridden the same horse, a buckskin mare with black stockings, for five years.

"One of them rides a pinto," Josh answered. "Another had a nag."

"Anyone on a buckskin?"

Josh shook his head.

The facts didn't point to Johnson, but neither did they point away. The outlaw had been riding with two other men. Beau had been closing in on them when he'd stopped to visit Patrick. Every instinct told him Johnson had raided the Rocking J. He stabbed the knife into the table. "It's Johnson. It has to be."

With the blade twanging, he looked at Josh in his black coat. The man kept a Bible in the front pocket and a pistol at his side. Truth and justice. Heaven and Hell. Josh would have added mercy and forgiveness. Beau didn't care. He wanted vengeance.

The Reverend kept his voice low. "Sheriff Dawes is riding out tomorrow with a couple of men. He wants you to join them."

Beau wanted to leave so badly his calves twitched. His weapons were clean and loaded. If he saddled his roan, he'd be ready to ride. Instead he muttered a curse. "I can't go."

"Why not?"

"Because I've got ten cows to milk, alfalfa to plant and a silo to build for a know-it-all woman!"

Josh raised an eyebrow. "Dani seems capable to me."

"She is."

"So why not go?"

If he didn't finish the planting, Dani would be left to wrestle with a mule and a plow. He couldn't stand the thought. "It's my job," he said. "If the alfalfa doesn't get planted, she won't have winter feed."

Josh arched a brow. "I thought you were selling the farm."

"Not anymore. Dani's staying."

"Are you?" Josh asked.

"Not a chance." Beau explained the adoption and why he'd made the choice. "I'll ask Scott to file papers next trip to town."

The Reverend didn't say a word.

Josh never lied, but neither did his silence ring true. Beau looked him in the eye. "What's wrong?"

"It doesn't concern you."

Beau hated secrets. "Does it concern Dani?"

"In a way."

"Then I have a right to know."

"No, you don't." Josh crossed his arms. "This is between me and God. If something needs to be said, I'll say it. As things stand, you're the girls' legal guardian and using your best judgment. From what I can see, Dani's promise to Patrick hasn't affected your decision."

"Not really," Beau said. "The woman knows cows and loves the girls. That's what made me change my mind."

That, and the fact he liked her. Josh didn't need that information.

The minister nodded. "That's all I need to know."

Beau wanted to know what had led to Josh's concern, but he knew his friend wouldn't break a confidence. He'd proven himself in Denver. Late at night, when Beau had spilled his guts, Josh had kept their talk private. Beau had a feeling he'd done the same for Patrick. If his brother had been having second thoughts about marriage, Beau didn't much care. Dani loved the girls. That was enough.

He'd filleted five trout for supper. That was enough, too. So was five years of chasing Clay Johnson, but Beau couldn't rest until the man swung from a rope.

He snatched the last fish from the bucket and slit the belly. "Tell me about Dawes. Is he any good?"

"Average."

"Can he take Johnson?"

"Not alone."

Beau lowered the knife. "I've been after Clay Johnson for five years. He could be in shouting distance and I can't finish the job. It's not right."

"Maybe it's not your job to finish," Josh said. "'Vengeance is Mine—'"

"'—saith the Lord.' I know." Beau jerked the bones from the trout's flesh and flung them into the bucket. He glared at Josh. "Where was God when Lucy bled to death?"

The Reverend's gaze stayed steady. "The same place He was when His son died on the cross."

Beau wiped the knife on a rag. The table stank of fish and death and blood. Clay Johnson was riding free and the Baylor family was left to struggle with loss and violation. For the second time, Beau stabbed the knife into the wood. "Don't give me that talk."

"What talk?"

"That God knows what I'm feeling. Johnson killed my *wife*."

"I know, I was there."

"I want him dead!"

"I know you do, Beau. It's just that—"

"Just *what*?"

Josh held Beau's gaze. "The bitterness is eating you alive. You know the cure. 'Father forgive them—'"

"Don't you *dare* say it."

They know not what they do. Clay Johnson had carried a loaded rifle to a rooftop. He'd known full well what he intended to do. At best, he'd been sniping for Beau. At worst, he'd shot an innocent woman in the back.

Beau lashed out at Josh. "Don't you *dare* tell me to forgive that piece of human filth!"

"I wasn't going to," Josh said. "That's between you and God."

"That's right."

"I'd say the same thing to Clay. He's going to Hell, my friend. Unless he squares things with the Almighty, he's going to suffer more than you can imagine."

"He has it coming."

Josh raised his chin. "We all do."

Beau felt the words like fire, mostly because Josh counted himself in the same camp as men like Clay Johnson. Fallen short. Weak-minded. A lost soul except for the blood of Christ. Beau knew Josh's story. A long time ago, he'd been a holier-than-thou preacher. He blamed himself for his sister's death and still carried the guilt.

Beau had no illusions of holiness. He sinned as much as any man and he knew it. He was sinning right now… "Love one another as I have loved you." No way could he bring himself to "love" Clay Johnson. Not now. Not ever. Right now, he didn't think much of Josh, either. He wanted the man to leave.

Beau picked up the plate of fish in one hand and the scrap bucket in the other. He looked pointedly at Josh. "Anything else?"

"Any advice for Dawes?"

"Shoot to kill."

Beau strode past Josh. The pastor followed him around

the barn and into the yard where he'd left his horse tied to a post. Josh loosed the reins and climbed into the saddle. "See you Sunday."

"Not in church."

Like last Sunday, Beau would leave Dani and the girls at the foot of the steps, then head into town.

Josh looked down from the saddle. "I didn't expect so, but I'll see you in the afternoon."

"What for?"

"A church picnic."

Beau wanted to spit. "Did Adie plan it?"

"Of course."

Back in Denver, Adie had been every bachelor's hero. She'd organized picnics, dances and Saturday suppers that forced even the shyest men to rub elbows with the ladies in town. Beau had rubbed a lot of elbows before he'd clapped eyes on Lucy. He'd enjoyed those spirited times. He wanted Dani to have fun, too.

Or did he? The thought of her sharing a meal with another man—even one with marriage on his mind—made Beau grit his teeth. He didn't know which annoyed him more, not riding with Dawes or keeping his eye on Dani in a crowd of single men. All in pursuit…full of hope and dreams and things Beau couldn't have.

Josh tipped his hat. "See you Sunday."

The Reverend rode out of the yard, leaving Beau with a bellyache. As if to rub Beau's nose in his helplessness, Josh pushed his gray into a gallop, racing past the charred pine and fields of lush grass. With each stride, the horse and rider grew smaller until the minister was a black dot on a dusty road. Stinking of fish and hate, Beau tensed with frustration. He should have been leaving with Josh, not holding a reeking bucket while ten cows told him what to do.

Beau couldn't stand being in the dark. Had Johnson led the raid on the Rocking J as Beau suspected? Was he still in the area? Beau's nerves twanged like the knife. With horses to sell, the outlaw would head for the mountains, where a maze of canyons twisted through the foothills below the Rockies. Johnson could hide for days, raiding ranches until he'd bled the area dry. He had two partners, both unidentified. Either one could slip into town, catch the gossip and stay a step ahead of the law.

And a step ahead of Beau…

If Johnson stayed true to form, he'd want Beau to know he was close. He'd leave a message at the Silver River Saloon. A taunt. A threat. Did the outlaw have a bead on Beau? On Dani and the girls? Beau blinked and saw pink. If Johnson had left him a message, he had to know. Dani needed him to plant the alfalfa, but she could do without him for tonight. With the stolen horses in his care and the law on his tail, Johnson would stay hidden in the canyons. She'd be safe.

Beau strode to the garden, left the bucket and headed for the back door to the house. Emma saw him coming and opened it. He handed her the plate of fish.

She smiled at him. "Thank you, Uncle Beau." She meant for everything—the day, the meal, especially for Dani.

His belly rumbled with hunger. If he ate supper with the females, he'd sit at the head of the table. He'd share smiles with Dani and eat like a king. Longing stabbed through him, but he pushed it back. "Tell Dani I'm not eating supper."

"Why not?"

"It's none of your business."

Emma lost her smile.

Beau felt like dirt. He'd hurt the child's feelings, but he didn't dare apologize, not when he could smell biscuits and pie. Instead he barked an order. "I left the fish waste in the garden. Someone needs to bury it."

"I'll do it after supper."

"The milking—"

"I can do that, too."

"Good."

Emma raised her chin. "We don't need you to run this place. You can leave and never come back!"

Beau heard the defiance, but he didn't see it in her expression. Tears pooled in her eyes and he knew why. Emma wanted a father. He couldn't be that man, not until Clay Johnson lay dead in a ditch.

He pulled the door shut, then strode across the yard to the bunk room where he'd stowed his things under the cot. Some of them were practical. Some were sacred. Beau dropped to his knees, reached under the bed and pulled out a box that held Lucy's ring, their wedding picture and a ladies' handkerchief, one of two Lucy had embroidered with flowers.

The linen no longer held her scent, but he recognized the pink roses. Beau had carried a similar hankie in his pocket until he'd come across a young mother in a rundown café. She'd had a small child in her lap, a boy with a cough and a nose as red as fire. Knowing Lucy would approve, Beau had given her the hankie. He'd let go of his grief that day, but not the rage. Today, Beau realized, that rage had flickered and almost died. He'd had a good day. For a few hours, he'd forgotten about Clay Johnson.

Furious with himself, he slipped Lucy's handkerchief

into his pocket and pushed to his feet. He strapped on his gun belt, cloaked it with his duster, then saddled his horse and led it into the yard. With dusk turning the sky to pewter, Beau swung into the saddle.

Dani hurried out the front door. Her eyes asked questions he didn't want to answer, so he dug his heels into the horse's side. Josh had left the yard at a gallop. Beau left at a dead run. He barely noticed the rise and fall of the road, the change in the sky from blue to orange, then purplish-black. His thoughts tumbled like rocks in a can, clattering against each other until he arrived in town.

Businesses had closed for the day, but upstairs apartments were alive with families having supper. As he rode toward the Silver River, he heard an argument about a boy eating his peas. Did the mother know how precious this moment could be? Anything could happen. The child could catch a fever and die. A wagon accident could take his life. Tonight could be her last memory.

Beau thought of the handkerchief in his pocket. A week before Lucy died, he'd watched her working a crochet hook. The yarn had been baby blue. He'd wondered, but she'd only smiled and said it was too soon to be sure.

Fiddle music pulled Beau's attention to the saloon. He steered to the wailing notes, hitched his horse to the railing and went inside. Pausing at the door, he surveyed a small crowd of locals, mostly businessmen ending their day with the amber cure. Beau headed for the counter.

Wallace set down the glass he was wiping. "Coffee?"

"And information." Beau slapped down a greenback.

The barkeep put it in his pocket, sent a waitress to the kitchen for the coffee, then looked at Beau. "What can I do for you?"

"Anyone leave anything for me?"

Wallace shrugged. "Not a thing. That man I saw, he hasn't come back."

Beau was glad Johnson hadn't left a vile threat, but he didn't want to lose him, either. He turned his attention to the facts at hand. "What's the word on the Rocking J?"

Wallace summarized what Beau had heard from Josh, then leaned forward. "Rumor has it they did more than steal the horses."

Beau tensed. "What are you saying?"

"Baylor's daughter…"

Beau held in a curse. A tender girl had been brutalized. Where was God?

Wallace wiped another glass with his apron. "Her brother stopped the attack before too much happened, but she's pretty shook up."

Beau wouldn't bother the girl, but he wondered about the brother. "Did he see the man's face?"

"They all had masks."

The waitress brought Beau's coffee. He took a swig, weighing the evidence as the liquid scalded his tongue. His instincts told him Johnson was behind the raid, but he needed hard facts, something peculiar to Clay. If no one had seen the horse thieves, he'd have to find another way to tie Johnson to the theft.

"What else have you heard?" he said to Wallace.

The barkeep shrugged. "A geezer found a dead horse about ten miles south of here. It could be why someone raided the Rocking J."

Beau set down the cup. If the dead horse matched Clay's buckskin mare, Beau would have the clue he needed. "Tell me more."

The barkeep aimed his chin at the back of the room. "That's the fella who saw it. Ask him."

Beau pushed to his feet and turned. In the dim light, he saw an old man with a ragged white beard and the stooped shoulders of a prospector. He was seated at a round table in the corner, hunched over a bowl of chili. As Beau approached, the man looked up with rheumy eyes. He pointed at an empty chair with his spoon. "Have a seat."

Beau dropped down but stayed on guard. "I hear you came across a dead horse a while ago."

"That I did."

"I'm looking for someone. It could have been his mount. What color was it?"

The old man stopped with the spoon an inch from his mouth. "What's it worth to you?"

Beau slapped a silver dollar on the table.

The old man snickered. "That's not enough."

Beau didn't like being taken, but he'd have given every cent he had to find Clay Johnson. He opened his billfold, took out a five-dollar bill and laid it next to the silver.

The prospector snorted, then looked at Beau. "What else do you have?"

Beau slapped down a sawbuck.

The old man laughed out loud.

Beau added greenbacks to the pile one at a time, watching the man's eyes for signs of greed. When he hit twenty-five dollars, he stopped. "You're a thief."

"No, I'm not." The prospector nudged the money back at Beau. "I'll tell you about that horse for free. I just wanted to see how far you'd go."

Beau looked into the man's eyes and saw a sympathy he hadn't expected. It shook him to the core. "What for?"

"I sold my soul to greed," said the old man. "I had a wife, a family. I left them to search for gold and found nothing but mud. I had everything. Now I've got nothing."

"Thanks a lot," Beau drawled. "But I don't need a sermon."

"I think you do."

"I'm not after gold."

"No," he said. "But you're after something. What is it?"

Beau said nothing.

The old man raised a brow. "Only three things make a man crazy enough to throw away his life. Women, money and revenge. You don't need the money. As for the woman—"

Beau saw a flash of pink. "Mind your own business."

"That leaves vengeance."

"Shut up!"

The graybeard hunched forward. Beau saw madness gleaming in his eyes and smelled the heat of the chili. The man's beard twitched as he spoke. "Don't make the same mistake I did, young fella. Go home before it's too late."

"I don't have one." Except his mind flashed to Dani and the girls around the kitchen table.

The old man grinned, revealing a row of rotten teeth. Beau's stomach turned. He didn't want to end up alone and bent, an old man stinking of sweat and onions. He felt cursed. Trapped. He wanted to be free from that fate. That day would come when he brought Johnson to justice.

Beau gripped the old man's collar. "Tell me about the horse."

"You're lost, son."

His fist tightened. "What color was it?"

"A buckskin."

"What else?"

"It had four black stockings, the high kind."

The description matched Clay's horse to the letter. Beau loosened his grip. "Thanks, old man."

The prospector looked at him with stark pity. "You won't thank me when you're as old and rotten as me."

Beau's belly burned. So did his eyes from the stink of the onions. He looked down at the money on the table, then up at the prospector. With one finger, as if it were filthy, he nudged it toward the old man. "Keep it. Go see your wife."

"She went west."

"So find her."

The miner shook his head. "She married my best friend. Doesn't that beat all? I hear they have grandbabies…"

Beau turned his back and left the saloon. He had enough regrets of his own without listening to a bitter old man. He needed air and he needed it now.

Chapter Nine

Dani touched Daff's udder and winced. The hot spot she'd noticed before supper, when she'd done the milking because Beau had taken off, had changed from the size of a penny to a half-dollar. Concerned, she had left Daff in the barn for the night. Now she knew why the cow had been fussy. She had a condition called mastitis and it hurt. Left untreated, it could damage her udder for life.

"You poor thing," Dani crooned.

The cow sidestepped.

Although Daff had fidgeted during the milking, Dani hadn't been alarmed. Cows were sensitive creatures, and Beau's departure had left tension in the air. She didn't mind doing the evening chores. What she minded was worrying about Beau. She knew Pastor Josh had spoken to him behind the barn. She didn't know what the Reverend had said, but she doubted an invitation to a church picnic had sent Beau racing to town. When she'd glimpsed his face, she'd seen the man who'd called himself Cain.

Dani stood and scratched Daff's head. She whispered a prayer for Beau, then stepped out of the stall and surveyed the barn for a cabinet holding liniment and herbs. She hoped Patrick kept camphorated oil. Her father had used it in Wisconsin. She scanned the shelves by the door but saw only cans of nails and what-not. Looking deeper into the barn, she spotted a door. It led to the back room, a likely place for the oil and where Beau spent the night. Dani had no desire to invade his privacy, but she had to help Daff. She lifted the lantern from the wall, walked to door and opened it.

Cool air touched her face, bringing with it the scents of gunpowder and shaving soap. Raising the lantern, she saw shirts hanging from hooks, trousers draped over a chair and a pair of work boots. A set of saddlebags lay jumbled on the floor, open and unbuckled, as if Beau had rummaged for something. What she didn't see was his gun belt.

Her gaze strayed to a cot neatly made with a pillow and wool blanket. The tidiness surprised her. So did the wooden box lying open on the bed. Looking closer, she saw beveled corners and etched roses. It was the kind of thing a woman would own.

Dani had no business looking at the contents. She had a similar box of her own. It had belonged to her grandmother, then her mother. When she'd turned sixteen, her father had given it to her with his blessing and told her to fill it with wisdom before she passed it on to a daughter of her own. Dani's box held memories of her mother, Patrick's letters and keepsakes from home. She knew the meaning of such things. The contents of the box on Beau's cot would reveal his deepest feelings.

With trembling fingers, she lifted a photograph and saw a man and woman dressed for a wedding. Lucy Morgan had the serious expression befitting a formal occasion, but her eyes glowed with happiness. Beau looked ten years younger, not the five that had passed since his wife's death. In the photograph, Dani saw the man who peeled apples and sang to cows. Her pulse raced. She cared about Beau…deeply. How could she not? He'd given her the girls. He respected her abilities. He'd understood why she'd jilted Virgil Griggs. He understood *her*.

With trembling hands, she set the picture on the bed, then looked at the rest of Beau's treasures. She saw a woman's gold ring, a silver badge and a gray rock. A pink ribbon curled around a watch fob engraved with a date, presumably the day of his wedding to Lucy.

"And the two shall become one flesh…"

Beau had known that joy. Dani never would. Tears pushed into her eyes. She had no doubts about adopting the girls, but deep down she wanted more… She wanted a photograph like the one in Beau's box. She wanted a husband.

With her eyes on the photograph, Dani barely heard the slide of metal against leather. She whirled to the door and saw Beau. He holstered the Colt, then pinned her in place with his eyes.

"I'm sorry," she said. "I didn't mean to pry."

"What are you doing in here?"

"It's Daff."

"What about her?"

His gaze bordered on murderous. Dani didn't blame him for being angry. She'd overstepped, but she'd had a good reason. "She has a hot spot on her udder. I was looking for camphorated oil."

Beau stepped inside the room, opened a cabinet and handed her a brown bottle. "Here."

She wanted to flee, but he was blocking the door.

In his duster and hat, he seemed huge. His shoulders spanned the doorway, and the shadow he cast into the barn made him even taller. Heat spilled from the canvas coat. The man she'd seen in the photograph was dead and buried. This one was very much alive. His gaze darted to the picture on the cot, lingered, then slid to Dani. "That's Lucy and me."

"I know."

"She was a good woman."

She swallowed a lump. "I didn't mean to look at your things. The box was open and I saw—"

"I know what you saw." His eyes burned even brighter. "Now you know why I have to kill Johnson."

"I do," she murmured. "But it's not right."

"Who are you to judge?"

"No one. I just know what I see. You're dead inside."

"Far from it." Hate burned in his eyes.

Beau tossed his duster on the chair. Next he unhooked the gun belt and draped it over the back. Without the coat and the gun, he looked like himself…almost.

"Go on," he said. "Get out of here."

Dani stepped to the door. "I'll be with Daff."

Beau blocked her way. "I'll take care of her. Give me the oil."

"No."

His eyes blazed. "I don't want you here. Go inside."

"I can't." She gave him her sternest look. "You're upset. If you go near Daff, she'll feel it. She needs kindness tonight."

"She's a cow!"

"She has feelings!"

So did Beau. He looked mad enough to pound the wall, but behind the rage Dani saw the ragged edges of his heart. Josh's visit had upset him. His trip to town had made him even angrier. She wanted to know what had happened, but she'd invaded his privacy enough for one day.

"Please," she murmured. "Let me by."

She could see Beau fighting with himself. He didn't want her in the barn, but he knew she was right.

Finally, he stepped back. "Suit yourself."

Dani left with the lantern, plunging the room into darkness. Every instinct told her to turn around with the light, but Daff needed her as much as Beau. She could see the cow fidgeting. As she drew close, Daff let out a bellow that shook the rafters.

"It's okay, girl. I'm here."

Dani pulled up a stool, poured oil into her cupped palm, then rubbed her hands together to warm it. Leaning forward, she rubbed the smelly mixture onto Daff's udder. Over and over, she massaged the cow as she'd done on her father's farm. Losing a few pounds of milk would cost money. Losing Daff altogether would be a disaster. The cow, just three years old, had a lot of good years ahead of her.

Prayer filled Dani's mind. She asked God to heal Daff, then thanked Him for giving her the farm and three daughters to raise. She'd never understand the lightning bolt that took Patrick, but she could see God's healing in the aftermath. She prayed for Beau, too. The words came in a rush. *Set him free, Lord. Heal his heart.* Tears pushed into her eyes. She felt his suffering as if it were her own and welcomed it. If her tears would save him a moment's grief, she'd gladly cry for him. This feeling, she realized, was a gift from God, a shadow of how deeply the Lord loved His children.

Love... Dani's hand went still on Daff's udder. With her heart pounding, she thought about apples and raspberry pie, "Camptown Races" and Beau's broad shoulders spanning the doorway. She thought of his hands, too. Strong. Sure. Gentle. Her heart jumped and her eyes opened wide. Had she fallen in love with him? She couldn't have. She loved Patrick…didn't she?

With her stomach churning, she kept on tending Daff. She felt as fickle as Virgil Griggs thought she was, but she couldn't stop the rush of feeling for Beau. He was everything she wanted in a husband, a man who commanded respect but knew when to bend. Beau could make her smile and feel proud. He also had a stubborn streak, cranky moods and a heart full of hate. Somehow those flaws made her love him even more. Dani turned the thought over in her mind. She loved lots of people…the girls, her family and friends in Wisconsin. Her feelings for Beau *had* to be in that vein.

So why was her heart pounding with hope? She wanted to offer him comfort but worried that he'd send her away. Her own feelings shouldn't have mattered, but they did. She'd never felt a pull so strong, a need to give of herself that went beyond friendship, beyond family. The desire to comfort Beau sprang from her very soul.

The door to his room creaked opened, filling the far side of the barn with a dull light. A moment later, his shadow stretched across the floor.

"Dani?"

She didn't dare look up. "The oil stinks, doesn't it?"

"I'm sorry."

He wasn't talking about Daff. He meant for his rudeness. Dani forgave him instantly, but she couldn't bear to look into his eyes. She'd see his suffering and want to hold him in her arms. She thought of reaching for his hand, but the gesture seemed like a confession.

"It's all right," she finally said. "You were upset."

"That's no excuse for my behavior." He let out a breath. "You saw Lucy's picture and the badge. The watch—"

"I figured it was a wedding gift."

"It still keeps time."

He seemed eager to talk, so Dani looked up. "What about the rock?"

"I picked it up the day I asked Lucy to marry me."

"That's very sweet." Dani's heart pinched. "You must have loved her very much."

"I did. I always will, but I know she's gone. God and I aren't close right now, but Lucy's watching from Heaven."

"There's comfort in that thought."

Saying nothing, Beau dropped to a crouch, putting them almost cheek to cheek. He laid his hand on Daff's udder. "Where's the hot spot?"

"Here." She pointed to it.

Beau slid his hand to the place she indicated, then looked into her eyes. "I'd have never found it."

They were so close she could feel his breath on her cheek. He smelled like coffee and leather, nothing like apples. She didn't want to notice his manly ways, but she couldn't help it. She focused on Daff. "She's calmer now."

"You have a way with animals," he said. "Including mules like me."

Dani stared at the glistening oil. "You're not a mule."

"I was tonight. I ran out of here without an explanation. Then I got mean-tempered when you went looking for the oil."

Her heart ached. Only a good man would humble himself. "You caught me being nosy. Anyone would have been angry."

"And anyone would have looked in the box." Beau pushed to his feet. "There's no harm done. In fact, seeing the picture might help you understand where I went tonight."

Dani kept rubbing Daff. "I was worried."

"With good reason." He told her about Josh's visit, the trouble at the Rocking J and his suspicion that Clay Johnson was in the area. "That's why I went to town. If anyone knows what's going on, it's Wallace at the Silver River Saloon."

"What did you find out?"

"A prospector found a dead horse. I'm convinced it belonged to Johnson."

Dani tensed. "So he's in the area."

"I'm sure of it."

"Do you think he'll come after you?"

"I don't know." He pushed a piece of straw with his boot. "Most of the time he runs, but sometimes he leaves messages."

"Like what?"

"Notes telling me I'm going to die. Once he left a pink ribbon."

"That's horrid."

Dani stopped rubbing Daff. The cow stomped her foot, then settled down. Dani looked up and saw Beau scratching the cow's ears. How could a man talk about his wife's murder and soothe a cow at the same time? Sensing her gaze, he looked down. His eyes blazed with the glow she'd seen when he'd looked at the photograph. Only instead of seeing Lucy, he saw her.

Her cheeks turned pink. "I worry about you, Beau."

"Don't."

"I can't help it."

"Johnson can't hurt me any more than he already has."

Not even death scared this man. She ached for him, but she also recalled the gun belt that lived on his hips. Dani quivered with fear. "Maybe he'll take the horses and run."

"That's my guess. Just the same, I want you and the girls to be careful."

"Of course."

She'd answered quickly. Too quickly to hide the shake in her voice. In Wisconsin, her biggest worry had been bad weather. Here the weather was deadly and so were strangers.

Beau pulled up a stool. "Let me take a turn."

Dani barely heard him. She blinked and imagined Clay Johnson lurking in the yard. "I won't sleep knowing that man's around."

"Think of me instead."

His voice had gone low. He'd meant to sound reassuring, but Dani heard a lilt. It matched the beat of her heart and she wondered if she'd ever sleep again. When Beau laid his palm against the small of her back, her breath quickened.

"I'll keep you safe," he said. "I promise."

He'd felt her fear but had misunderstood it. Clay Johnson made her nervous, but it was Beau's touch that scared her. His knee rested an inch from hers. She could feel strength in his forearm and gentleness in his fingers. She wanted to stay in this spot forever. Air rushed from her lungs. She covered the sudden quivering with a yawn.

"You're tired." Beau slid his hand from her back, clasped her fingers and took her hand off Daff's udder.

Dani turned her wrist and matched their palms. The

oil made their fingers slide together. She looked into Beau's eyes, where she saw a fierce light.

"I mean it, Dani. I won't let Johnson get near you."

She wanted to believe him, but Beau wasn't God. He was a man, one who had loved and suffered a loss. She'd loved and lost, too. Both afraid and unwilling to let go of the moment, she squeezed his fingers. "Did you eat supper?"

His eyes darkened. "I lost my appetite in town."

"I could make you a sandwich."

"No, thanks." He let go of her hand. "Go on inside."

Before she could tempt him with pie, Beau went to work on Daff. Feeling dismissed, Dani stood and left the barn.

As she walked through the yard, the night air cooled her face but not her blood. She wiped her oily fingers on her apron, but she still felt the imprint of Beau's hand on her back. She felt all sorts of things…all of them confusing. As soon as the adoption was complete, Beau would leave. Losing her heart to a bitter man, one who'd turned his back on God, was pure foolishness.

Dani hurried up the steps. As she opened the door, the mantel clock chimed twice. As tired as she felt, she knew she wouldn't sleep. She needed to chase Beau's face out of her thoughts, so she went upstairs to check on the girls. With her heart pounding, she looked first at Emma, sleeping alone in the smallest bedroom. The child's hair lay like scattered straw on her pillow. Dani saw a precious gift and thanked God with a silent prayer.

Brimming with love, she stepped across the hall, where Ellie and Emma shared a double bed. The sight of the little girls, curled in opposite directions to make a heart, made her breath catch. If Patrick had lived, they'd be sharing this moment. He'd have held her hand and led her downstairs. They'd have talked about Ed, Ethan and Ebenezer and dreamed of the future.

Desperate to feel close to Patrick—and safe from Beau and his bitterness—Dani went downstairs to her bedroom. She lit the oil lamp, opened her trunk and lifted the stack of letters from Patrick. With her heart aching, she put on her nightgown and brushed out her braid, climbed into bed, and unfolded the first letter she'd received from a dairyman in Colorado.

His descriptions of the girls came alive. When he said he had ten cows, Dani pictured each one. She knew their names, their quirks and how many pounds of milk each one gave. She also knew about the singing, though Patrick didn't mention it. How many other things didn't she know about him? Did he have a deep voice or a high one? Could he sing as well as Beau? Scolding herself for silly comparisons, she skimmed the letters until she reached the one where Patrick had proposed.

I need a wife and you need a change. I believe we'd be a good match. Would you marry me, Daniela?

She'd taken the use of her formal name as a sign of his respect. Tonight it sounded foreign. He'd added a few compliments about her good mind and warm heart. At the time, she'd blushed with his praise. Now it seemed impersonal. He could have been writing to a business partner, someone he was hiring to do chores and care for his children. He'd signed the letter, "With great hope."

Dani stared at the bottom of the page. Not once had Patrick written that he loved her. She'd figured he was saving that special moment for when they met in person, but now, looking at his letters one after another, she wondered if he would have said the words at all. She had to know. Blinking, she thought of Beau's box of memories. They told a love story. Dani needed that story from Patrick. What treasures had he set aside? She knew where to look.

When she'd moved into the bedroom, she'd spotted a cherrywood case on the top shelf of the wardrobe. Dani hadn't opened it, but tonight she needed to see what it held. She climbed out of bed, lifted it off the shelf and set it in the middle of the bed. As she raised the lid, the hinges creaked. Light spilled from the lamp, revealing a package of letters tied with a black ribbon.

Her letters… With her heart fluttering, she touched the paper and realized she'd made a mistake. She'd bought special stationery to write to Patrick, the finest she could find. She'd used a fountain pen because it fit sweetly in her hand. These letters were written on newsprint. Feeling ill, she untied the black ribbon, opened the top letter and saw Patrick's bold hand.

"Dear Beth…"

Her stomach lurched, but she calmed herself. Patrick had written to his wife. Any woman would have treasured such letters and kept them in a special place. With her heart pounding, Dani read on.

Chapter Ten

You've been gone a week, my love. Alone in our bedroom with the lamp trimmed low, I don't think I can survive. You were the best part of me, Beth. The part that could love, the part that knew happiness of the finest kind. Without you I'm a lost man. My soul is drifting on the wind, a spirit parted from the body but nowhere close to Heaven. This is purgatory. I'm among the living dead.

Struggling to make sense of the letter, Dani looked at the date and saw the month and year of Beth's death. Patrick, she realized, had written them at the pinnacle of his grief. He'd loved Beth deeply. Dani admired him for that commitment. The letters held the private feelings she'd expected him to share with her once they were married. Bolstered by that thought, she continued to read.

She finished the first letter, read three more and realized Patrick had written to Beth every Saturday night, each time pouring out his grief and wondering if he wanted to live. By the fourth letter, Dani felt ill.

"Stop reading," she said out loud.

But she couldn't. She needed to know what he'd written about *her.* She skimmed through the stack until she found the first mention of her name.

> Do you remember my cousin Kirstin? She wrote to me about a friend of hers, a girl named Daniela who can't find a husband.

Dani bristled. She'd *found* a husband. She'd found two of them, but neither man had made her feel alive. She didn't like Patrick's comment, but she couldn't blame him for Kirstin's introduction.

> Miss Baxter has invited me to write to her. I hate to do it, Beth. But our girls need a mother. I'm going to write back. If this woman is at all acceptable, I'll think about writing to her again.

Dani's heart plummeted. She wanted to be more than "acceptable." She wanted to be loved. She wanted to be understood. Until now, she'd thought Patrick had been courting her, not judging her usefulness. Had his feeling changed from resignation to hope? Dani had to know, so she read the next letter with her name in it.

> She's educated and seems kind, though you can't know a person from letters alone. She sent a picture. I suppose she's pretty. Blonde, not brunette like you. She's thin, too. Maybe that's why she hasn't found a husband.

Dani gasped with outrage. She'd made a trip to Madison with Kirstin to have that tintype made. She'd spent hours picking her dress and fixing her hair. She'd even let the photographer apply rouge, something that felt foreign and naughty. Now, reading Patrick's comments, she felt like a cow on an auction block.

The letters went on and on. He questioned himself with every stroke of the pen, criticizing Dani to Beth for faults both real and imagined. By the time she opened the last letter, she felt nauseous. She looked at the date, saw it was written the day before Patrick died and knew this letter mattered the most of all.

Dear Beth,
I give up. I can't live another minute with this lie of an engagement. It's too late to tell Daniela to stay home. I figure she's on the train outside of Chicago. Her arrival will be my punishment. After months of letters, she deserves to hear my regrets in person. I don't love her, Beth. I can't marry her.

My dearest wife, every night, I dream of you, of us. When I milk the cows, I remember naming the calves. I remember Martin Dryer bringing the bull and how you talked about the wonder of it all. Do you remember that night? I do. We…

Dani read something so intimate she blushed.

A man can't marry one woman when he loves another. Will I ever find peace without you? If it weren't for our daughters, I'd ride west to escape the memories. I'd ford rivers with the hope of drowning. I'd scale mountains and hope to fall. But I can't do that. Our daughters need a home.

I'll give it to them, but it will be a home without a mother. That's the best I can do.

Forgive me, Beth. I know you'd want me to marry again, but I can't. It wouldn't be fair to that poor, lonely girl who expects to be my wife. As soon as I break the engagement, I'll send her back to her family.

Dani stared at the page. Patrick hadn't loved her. Even worse, he'd lied to Dani and himself. Anger shot through her veins, cauterizing the cuts of grief. Being called a "poor, lonely girl" was the last straw. Still shaking, she forced herself to finish reading the letter.

I'm sure of my decision, Beth. My only worry is for the girls. If something happens to me, they'll need a guardian. Right now, Beau's named in my will. I haven't seen him since Lucy died. We both know he went crazy, but he's a blood relative. That counts for something. Not that it matters… I expect the Lord to torture me with a long life, watching as I miss you more with every passing day.
Your husband for eternity,

Dani stared at Patrick's signature in horror. His final words voided the letter in her trunk. She had no right to adopt his daughters. He'd wanted her to leave.

Numb with shock, she stared out the window. Where was God now? He'd taken Patrick from her, first through his death and then through his lies. He'd taken her pride, her hope and even the right to call Patrick's daughters her own.

Dani searched for a way to keep the girls and found a

solution that made her cheeks redden with shame. If she burned the letters in the stove, no one would ever know about Patrick's change of heart. Beau had already agreed to the adoption. What difference did the letters make now? She looked at the sheets of newsprint scattered on the bed. One by one, she put them in a pile. She had to light the stove for breakfast. One stick of wood and the letters would be gone.

She *had* to keep the girls. They needed her as much as she needed them. Burning the letters was wrong, but showing them to Beau meant risking everything. He'd changed his mind about the adoption because of her abilities, but he also lived by a code of honor. Patrick's final request would matter to him. With her stomach churning, she put on her day dress and shoes. She glanced in the mirror but didn't braid her hair. Instead she tied it back with a ribbon, then stared hard at her own face.

Not once had she willfully done something as dishonest as destroying the letters. Beau deserved to know the truth, but showing him Patrick's final words meant casting herself fully on God's and Beau's good graces. She thought of his hand on her back and how strong he'd felt. She'd sensed kindness in his touch, but she'd also seen his face when he'd found her in his room. Beau didn't compromise. He saw black-and-white. Dani saw shades of gray.

"Now we see through a glass darkly."

The scripture came from her memory. She felt trapped in a mist, confused by circumstances and unsure of God's mercy. She couldn't bear to think about losing the girls. What if Beau shipped them off to Harriet Lange? Closing her eyes, she imagined a hawkish old woman ordering Emma to bring her tea. She saw Esther crying and

Ellie unhappy in starched ruffles. Dani could spare them that misery, but it meant compromising her integrity. If she burned the letters, she'd be turning her back on God, Beau and everything she believed.

Are You there, Lord?

Silence.

Confused and trembling, she carried the letters into the kitchen. The mantel clock chimed four times. Soon Beau would come to the house for breakfast. She opened the stove's firebox and peered inside. With the rush of air, the embers flared. If she added the letters, they'd be gone in seconds. Orange light burned through the gray ash. In that flare of heat and light, Dani saw her own soul.

She'd been looking at the ash of her circumstances. The charred ruins of her engagement and Patrick's deception. But below the surface—through that glass darkly—a simple truth burned as bright as the embers. God hadn't left her to cope alone. She knew right from wrong, the difference between truth and a lie. Someday she'd see the Lord face-to-face and she'd know why she'd come to this place. Until then, she had her faith to see her through.

With the letters safe on the table, Dani lifted newspaper from the kindling box, crumpled it into a ball and added it to the coals. As it caught fire, she closed the stove door. When Beau came for breakfast, she'd show him the letters. Weak in the knees, she sat at the table where the sheets lay in a pile, a monument to lies and lost dreams. Bowing her head, she wept so hard her shoulders quaked. She tasted the salt of her own tears and felt them stinging her cheeks.

"I'm scared, Lord Jesus," she said out loud. "Without the girls, I have nothing."

Nothing but me.

The voice was in her head, but the hand on her shoulder belonged to a flesh-and-blood man.

"Dani?"

She looked up and saw Beau. With her thoughts in a jumble, she blurted the truth. "He didn't love me."

"Who didn't?"

"Patrick."

Beau's eyes narrowed. "What brought this on?"

She nudged the letters with her fingertip. "I found those." She sniffed, then wiped her eyes with her sleeve.

Keeping one hand on her shoulder, Beau reached into his pocket and pulled out a ladies handkerchief. "Use this."

Dani opened the square and saw roses. The hankie, she realized, had belonged to Lucy. With more tears welling, she looked into Beau's eyes and saw a glow akin to the embers in the stove. Beneath the ash, he was very much alive. Judging by his expression, he wasn't happy.

He dropped into the chair next to hers. "What's in the letters?"

"The last one says it all."

He picked up the letter, read every word, then looked into her eyes. "I'm sorry."

Her heart pounded with dread. "I found them a few hours ago. I was upset, so I looked through Patrick's things. I wanted to feel…"

She hung her head to hide her eyes. Had she wanted to feel close to Patrick or separate from Beau? Right now, she felt the opposite. She'd never cry for Patrick again, but she felt closer to Beau than she'd ever felt to another human being. Lucy's handkerchief was more personal than a touch. Gripping the linen, she waited for him to decide her future.

With their gazes locked, he crumpled Patrick's letter into a ball. "If you don't burn this trash, I will."

Dani's mouth gaped. "Really?"

"My brother was a fool." Beau's voice shook with anger. "I'm sorry to speak ill of the dead, but he was a two-faced mama's boy who whined about everything. You're better off without him."

She clutched the hankie. "I can keep the girls?"

"Of course."

He picked up the letters, walked to the stove and shoved them in the firebox. The newsprint caught with a whoosh. He latched the door and faced Dani. "If Patrick were alive, I'd haul him behind the woodshed. Of all the foolish drivel…"

She couldn't find her tongue.

Beau gave her a firm look. "Don't you dare doubt yourself."

"But I do." She hung her head.

"You shouldn't." He crossed back to the table. "You're a beautiful woman, Dani. If it weren't for Clay Johnson, I'd—" He sealed his lips.

She looked up. "You're being kind."

"No, I'm not."

"I know pity when I hear it." She faked a smile. "Thank you for trying, Beau. But I need to face the facts."

He looked baffled. "What facts?"

"I've been engaged three times now. I'm just not fit for marriage."

"That's flat-out stupid." His tone, warm like milk, softened the words but not the look in his eyes. "You're so full of goodness it shames me."

"Thank you for the compliment, but I have to be realistic." She shrugged. "There's something wrong with me. I've never felt what I thought I'd feel."

His gaze lingered on her face, studying her, reading her thoughts in the flush of her cheeks until his eyes glinted with understanding. "You mean the 'wanting' part."

Her cheeks flamed even brighter. "I don't know."

Beau stopped breathing. So did she. Ever so gently, he tipped up her chin with his fingers, then oh-so-tenderly, he kissed her on the lips.

Her knees went weak. Her first kiss…and Beau didn't even know it. He raised his head and looked at her with that glow in his eyes. Dani felt both naive and amazed. A kiss…the start of what God allowed between a man and wife. "And the two shall become one flesh." One life, one hope. A couple joined in body, mind and soul. Dani wanted that joy, and she wanted it with Beau. With her eyes wide, she watched his expression change from kindly to confident.

The man looked downright pleased with himself. "You're an amazing woman, Dani. Don't ever doubt it."

With a look that bordered on proud, he went out the back door, leaving her confused but sure of one thing. Not all men were as fickle as Patrick. And not all men smelled like bad onions. Dani may have been engaged to three men, but this was the first time she'd truly been in love.

Beau wasn't the least bit sorry he'd kissed Dani. Patrick had shattered her confidence. With that brush of their lips, Beau had given it back to her. He'd go back later for breakfast and pretend nothing had happened. It had been a kiss, one so chaste it bordered on brotherly…

except for the way it made him feel. Alive. Strong. Privy to secrets she didn't understand.

As he crossed the yard to the barn, he fought the urge to whoop like a fool. He'd given Dani something to think about, that was for sure. He hadn't felt this good in years, maybe never. Lucy would have been glad he'd given Dani the handkerchief. Beau had put it in his pocket as a reminder, but he was in no danger of forgetting Clay Johnson.

Last night, when he'd seen the light in his room, he'd imagined Johnson harming Dani. He'd half expected to find her tied up with the outlaw's pistol pressed to her temple. When he'd drawn his gun, he'd been ready for anything but what he'd found. Dani looking at the treasures he'd neglected to put away.... He'd seen tenderness in her eyes and a caring that linked the past and present. If he stayed in Castle Rock, he could take her for buggy rides and moonlight walks. If their hearts met—and he was certain they would—they'd be free to marry.

As he walked into the barn, Beau raked his hand through his hair. What was wrong with him? He'd made a vow to kill Clay Johnson. Until the outlaw met his eternal destiny, Beau couldn't rest.

He went to Daff, reached down and checked her udder. The hot spot still felt normal. He'd noticed the change earlier. Seeing the glow from the kitchen window, he'd gone inside to share the good news with Dani and found her weeping. He'd never forget the hurt in her eyes. Irritated, Beau stood straight, scratched Daff and headed for his room. With each step, he thought of Patrick's insulting words. Beau had meant what he'd said about taking his brother to the woodshed. Hurting or not, a man had to take responsibility. Beau understood about missing Beth. He knew about mistakes, too. What he didn't understand was not loving Dani.

The wanting… He felt it now. Not in the way of bodily lust but in his soul, the place in his heart that wanted to protect Dani from all harm and provide for her. As he walked into his room, he thought of the saddlebags stowed under the cot. He lit the lamp and saw the scratchy bedroll where he'd sleep alone. At the sight of his gun belt on the chair, he almost asked the Almighty to help him catch Clay Johnson. Once the outlaw paid for Lucy's death, Beau would be free. He could stay in Castle Rock and court Dani. He'd be Uncle Beau, not a bounty hunter cursed to work alone.

His jaw tensed. He thought of Josh preaching to the men at the Wednesday Ruckus. *Don't pretty it up, men. Speak your heart. God can handle a cuss word or two. Even more if that's all you can manage.*

"God—" Beau clamped his jaw shut.

The room seemed to press in on him, so he stepped back into the barn and blew out a breath. The thoughts in his mind were ugly but honest. Beau felt sure the Lord understood every cursed word. He was just as sure the Almighty didn't care. Beau tipped his face up to the rafters. He heard hymns bouncing and closed his eyes, then he murmured what might have been a prayer.

"Let me kill him, Lord."

"Vengeance is Mine…"

Beau muttered a foul word. He wanted to love and laugh and make Dani his wife. One bullet and Johnson would be dead. Justice would be served and Beau would be free. With his eyes shut tight and his hands knotted, he listened for God's voice.

Daff mooed.

A horse snorted.

But the rafters stayed silent. Heaving a sigh, Beau went back to his room. God might have heard his prayers, but He hadn't answered them.

"Now's the time, boss," Andy said to Clay. "I heard about it in town. Morgan's living on a dairy farm with three kids and a pretty blonde. I say *we* go after *him*."

The three men were sitting around a fire. Two days had passed since they'd raided the Rocking J. They'd ridden deep into a canyon with so many twists Clay wondered if he could find his way out. Last night they'd camped in a cave. Rain had washed away their tracks, so they'd decided to rest a day while Clay picked a horse. Goose had picked the spot well. The gorge narrowed, limiting the number of ways a posse could approach. If the law—or Beau Morgan—came after them, they'd have the edge.

Clay stubbed out his cigar. "Why are you worried about Morgan? He's my problem."

Goose shrugged. "He's trouble for all of us."

Andy played with his knife. "Right now, he's a sitting duck."

Clay didn't trust the kid's judgment. Before raiding the Rocking J, he'd sent Andy to town to listen for talk at the Silver River. The kid had spent two nights and come back late Monday. "How do you know about Morgan and the farm?"

"I went to church."

"You *what*?"

Andy grinned. "That fool pastor shook my hand and invited me back."

"That was flat-out stupid." Clay tossed the stub into

the fire. "We wore masks at the Rocking J, but you could still be recognized. The Baylors are church folk."

Andy's expression turned wicked. "Don't worry, boss. I pulled it off."

"Who does the minister think you are?" Goose asked.

With a blink, Andy's face turned from leering to boyish. "I'm a lost soul looking for work and Jesus. I tell you, church is the best place for talk. Women gab, and the young ones look at a fella like he's special."

Clay knew Reverend Blue. Several months before Randall's gang started raiding ranches near Denver, the minister had ridden into their camp and asked for coffee. He'd said grace over their supper of beans and entertained them with a story about a man-eating fish. A kid named Chet had accepted Jesus that night. A week later, he'd left the gang.

Clay didn't know what had become of Chet, but he knew where *he* stood with God. He'd killed a woman. That crime put him beyond forgiveness. When the time came, Clay expected to meet up with his brother in Hell. Sometimes the thought made him nervous. Other times he didn't care. Lately he'd felt so bad about Lucy Morgan that he couldn't stop thinking about a person's final moments.

Goose stretched his legs. "Maybe Andy's right."

Clay didn't like Goose, but the man had good instincts. "Why do you say that?"

"If the woman's going to church, you can bet Morgan's sleeping alone in the barn. We could hit the ranch late at night and string him up before anyone knew what happened. You'd be rid of him."

Andy howled like a dog. "I've got first call on the blonde."

Goose threw hot coffee at him. "Settle down. We're doing this for Clay."

Clay stared into the fire. When he'd told Goose and Andy about killing Morgan's wife, he'd talked tough, as if he'd sniped her to pay for Zeke and had no regrets. They'd believed him, but it wasn't true. Her death had been a mistake, one that filled him with profound regret. Sometimes he thought about what Joshua Blue had said about that giant fish. A man named Jonah had lived in its belly for three days. He'd come out alive and told the story. The Reverend said a man named Jesus had done the same thing. He'd died on the cross and risen from the grave. The Reverend said men could make that death their own. He'd told Clay he could die to his sins and be reborn. He didn't have to be a murderer and a thief. He could be washed in the blood of the Lamb and be made brand-new.

Clay had thought about that talk for five years. He was still thinking about it. Sometimes he felt so bad about Lucy Morgan he wanted to die. If he prayed Reverend Blue's prayer, what would happen? He was afraid to find out. Guilt made a man do foolish things, and Clay had enough guilt to build a castle.

"What'll it be, boss?" Goose asked.

Clay's mind turned to Beau Morgan holding his dying wife. He couldn't stand the thought of putting another woman, let alone three little girls, in harm's way, but he'd had all he could take of the chase. He wanted it to end, but on his terms. Face-to-face. Man-to-man. But then what? Clay didn't know exactly. He just knew he had business with Beau Morgan.

"We're staying put," Clay said. "This time I want Morgan to come to me."

"But, boss—" Andy whined.

"Shut up," Clay ordered.

The kid winked at him. "Can I at least go back to church?"

"Sure, just don't do anything stupid." Clay wished he could go himself. He liked the story about the whale.

Chapter Eleven

Supper was over and Dani had put the girls to bed. Needing to think, she lifted her shawl off a hook and went out to the porch. With the moon shining bright, she sat in the rocker closest to the side railing. Pushing with her feet, she wondered if she'd ever feel like her old self.

Two days had passed since Beau had kissed her. Everything about the man was rough, but his lips had been rose-petal soft. When he'd come to breakfast, he'd acted as if nothing had happened. He hadn't mentioned the letters and neither had she, though after he'd finished breakfast, Dani had fetched the letters she'd written to Patrick and burned those, too.

With the picnic on Sunday, she had a decision to make. She'd told Pastor Josh she wouldn't be bringing a basket for the auction, but Beau's kiss had given her second thoughts. The caress had been brotherly, but she'd seen a glint in his eyes that went beyond kindness. Considering how her own feelings had exploded into raw hope, she wanted to know what Beau felt for her. She felt certain he'd come to the picnic if only to keep an eye on her and girls. If he bought her basket, they'd be eating together. It would mean the kiss had meant as much to him as it had to her.

Rocking gently, she closed her eyes and pictured Beau sitting with her on a blanket under a tree, sharing a meal and trading sweet looks. The answer to her deepest prayers glimmered just out of reach. She knew how he felt about Clay Johnson, but she believed in a big God, one Who'd overcome hate with love through the gift of His son. Beau and God weren't on speaking terms, but Dani had hope.

Closing her eyes, she asked the Lord to heal Beau's heart. The words tumbled through her mind, mixing with her dreams until she heard Beau's boots scuff the dirt. She opened her eyes and saw him awash in moonlight, standing with one foot braced on the bottom step and his hand on the post supporting the overhang.

"A penny for your thoughts?" he asked.

She managed a smile. "They're worth more than a penny."

"Tell me."

Not in a million years. She hunted for another subject. "The girls are excited about the picnic."

Beau grunted.

Dani thought the sound was charming, a sure sign she'd lost her heart. She smiled at him. "What does *that* mean?"

"I'm not fond of church picnics."

"Why not?"

Frowning, Beau climbed up the steps and sat next to her. Her rocker squeaked and thumped. His stayed still. "Is Adie doing a box lunch auction?"

"Yes, she is."

"That's how I met Lucy."

Dani thought of the hankie in her pocket. Was it Beau's love for Lucy that made him carry it, or was it a reminder of his hate for Clay Johnson? Dani understood grief. Time brought healing. Someday Beau would love again and she wanted to be that woman. Hate was different. It ate a man alive, feeding on his soul until there was nothing left. The only cure was forgiveness, a pardon that came from compassion.

Dani wasn't about to preach forgiveness to Beau. She didn't have that right, but she knew about love. So did Beau. Hoping to see the man who'd sung in the church choir, she turned the conversation to the past. "Did you buy Lucy's basket?"

A smile lifted the corners of his mouth. "No, but I arrested the man who did."

"What did he do?"

"I knew this so-called gentleman carried a whiskey flask, so I kept an eye on him. Sure enough, he got drunk and caused a stir."

"And you stepped in."

"I sure did."

Dani hummed softly. "I bet Lucy fell for you that very minute."

"Nope." He grinned. "It took six months of courting, mostly because she was enjoying herself."

Dani envied Lucy with every fiber, yet she wasn't jealous. They'd have been good friends. "She was blessed to have you."

"I was the blessed one."

She studied the square cut of his jaw, the arrow of his nose pointing west. He looked at peace in a distant way. "You liked being married," she said matter-of-factly.

"Very much."

"My parents were happy. So's my brother." She gave a light laugh. "Maybe there's hope for me after all."

Beau gave her a sideways glance. "There's hope, all right."

With you? If it weren't for Clay Johnson, would you stay? She couldn't ask the question without revealing her heart, but she could do a little fishing. "I think I'll make a basket for the auction."

Beau's eyes narrowed. "What for?"

"For one thing, it's a fundraiser for the Baylor family."

He said nothing.

"For another, it might be fun." Dani paused, then jiggled the bait. "Maybe I'll meet someone."

With a bend of his knee, Beau put the rocking chair in motion. "Like who?"

"Whoever buys my basket."

"That could be anyone."

"It's just a picnic," she replied. "But that's how things get started, isn't it? A sunny day, sitting in the shade..."

Their chairs thumped in perfect time until Beau's creaked to a stop. "If that's what you want, bring fried chicken."

She'd made a batch two days ago. "You liked it?"

"It's the best I've tasted."

Dani took his interest in the menu as a good sign. Blushing with pleasure, she smiled. "What about raspberry pie? Should I bring that, too?"

"Sure." He drummed his fingers on the armrest. "There are some good men in town."

He sounded matter-of-fact, as if he were discussing cattle. Dani's heart sank until she realized Beau had put his rocker back in motion. Again, the rhythm matched hers. He was fighting his feelings. She was sure of it.

He stopped the rocker with a thud. "Sometimes I wish for things, Dani. But it can't be."

Her throat tightened. "The past hurts, I know. But the future—"

"Is out of my hands."

But it wasn't. He had a choice. Dani wanted to fight for him, but the set of his jaw brooked no argument. His eyes, though, glimmered with a longing for love, a family, peaceful nights and a full belly. He also wanted to avenge Lucy. He'd made his choice, but that didn't mean he couldn't change his mind. Dani didn't know everything about Beau, but she knew he liked fried chicken.

She went back to rocking. "I'm definitely bringing a basket for the auction."

"Good idea."

"It's going to have that chicken you like, fresh apples, slaw and sweet tea."

Beau raised his chin. "Don't forget raspberry pie."

"I won't."

Dani kept rocking. Slowly, Beau matched the pace of his chair to hers, giving her hope that he'd bid on her basket. The conversation drifted to the cows, names for the new calves, the girls, the silo and the weather. Not once did their chairs lose their matching rhythms. She hoped it was a sign of things to come.

"There's a problem with the adoption."

Beau was seated across from Trevor Scott in the attorney's office. The meeting hadn't been planned. Twenty minutes ago, when Beau had dropped Dani and the girls at church, Adie had slipped a piece of stationery into his palm. The note had been from the attorney and had read, "Urgent. Come to my office during the morning service."

Beau had the note in his pocket now. "What happened?"

"Harriet Lange wants all three girls and she's prepared to fight for them."

"That's ridiculous."

"Don't be too quick to judge, Mr. Morgan." Scott leaned back in his chair. "I received a letter from her attorney."

"What does it say?"

"Miss Lange is appalled at the thought of Miss Baxter adopting the girls. To quote her attorney, she believes 'blood is thicker than water.'"

Beau had to grit his teeth. "Dani loves those girls."

"I believe you, but that doesn't change the facts. Unfortunately, my second letter stirred up a hornet's nest."

"In what way?"

"Miss Lange has enlisted the aid of other family members. They've pledged financial support for all three girls with Miss Lange acting as legal guardian."

Beau frowned. He'd made a promise to Dani and intended to keep it. "I won't agree to it."

"You may not have a choice."

"Why not?"

"Miss Lange is questioning your character."

Since hearing Emma's story about being slapped, Beau had regretted contacting Harriet Lange. He had his faults, but so did she. "What's she saying?"

"That you're a drinker."

"That's a flat-out lie."

"Is it?" Scott asked. "The family hired a Pinkerton's detective. He saw you in the Silver River Saloon."

"Did he tell Miss Lange I ordered *coffee*?"

"Apparently not."

"She knows you're a former lawman, but the detective was quick to note your more recent profession. Bounty hunting—"

"That's not the whole story." Beau didn't track killers for the money. He did it for the sake of justice.

"But you've lived that life."

"I'm after one man in particular," Beau said. "It's like fishing. A few others took the bait and got caught."

"That may be true, Mr. Morgan. But from what I understand, your profession has made you a wealthy man."

Beau didn't feel wealthy. Losing his wife had made him the poorest man on earth. "It depends what you call rich."

Scott laced his fingers over his chest. "Nonetheless, the money is evidence of your lifestyle."

"It's evidence of hard work."

The attorney eyed him thoughtfully. "Why do you go to the Silver River?"

"For coffee."

"You need to be straight with me, Mr. Morgan."

Beau didn't want to talk, but Scott needed the whole truth to do his job. "I go for information. The man I'm chasing is Clay Johnson. Rumor has it he raided the Rocking J."

Scott's features hardened. "Are you a target, Mr. Morgan?"

"Possibly."

"Are the girls in danger?"

Beau didn't know what Clay would do next, only what he'd done in the past. No one knew what tomorrow held. Beau looked Scott in the eye. "They're in as much danger as Patrick was riding home in a storm."

The attorney's gaze hardened. "You're telling me you're being pursued by a killer and you have children in your care."

"It's not like that."

"Maybe," Scott said. "But that's what the Lange family sees. Even the *appearance* of danger will work against you. I suggest you stop visiting the saloon."

Irritated, Beau walked to the window. He didn't want to give up his trips to the Silver River. They were his link to Clay, but Scott had a point. "I'll think about it."

"Good."

Beau drummed his fingers on the sill. Time wasn't on his side. "How long will it be?"

"A few weeks. Judge Hall is overworked these days. If there's no protest, he'll sign the documents and I'll file them in the Douglas County Hall of Records."

"Any way to speed things up?"

"I don't think so."

"Then get it rolling."

He looked at the pendulum clock on the wall. Church had ended ten minutes ago. He blinked and imagined Dani milling with the crowd, surrounded by single men looking for a wife. Beau had no intention of bidding on her basket, but he planned to watch every man who did. He knew exactly which basket she'd brought. She'd tied a bright blue ribbon on the handle and had asked him to carry it to the surrey. He'd put it in the back, but she'd moved it up front where the smell of chicken had wafted to his nose. It would be a small torture to watch her share that meal with another man, but Beau saw no alternative.

He lifted his hat off the hook, walked downstairs to the surrey and drove to the church where Josh was already auctioning boxes.

* * *

Dani scanned the crowd outside the church but didn't see Beau. Instead her gaze landed on the cowboy who'd sat behind her in church. Before the service, he'd introduced himself as Andy. Wearing a shy smile, he'd inquired about her picnic basket. Dani had no interest in sharing the meal with him, so she'd given him a vague answer. As the auction began, she searched the crowd for Beau but didn't see him. If Andy bought her basket, she'd have to be polite.

She glanced down the road to town, then shifted her gaze to the children playing "Mother May I?" She spotted the girls, giggling as Stephen, Josh and Adie's son, chased after Ellie. No matter who bought Dani's box, the girls would be sharing the meal. She looked back to the front of the church, where Adie had arranged the baskets on a table at the top of the steps. If Josh took the suppers in order, hers would be the seventh to go. Nervous and hopeful, Dani watched as Reverend Blue whistled for attention.

"Listen up, gentlemen. We have fourteen baskets today. Bid fast and bid high. The money's going to the Baylor family."

As the crowd clapped, Dani searched again for Beau.

"Howdy there, Miss Baxter."

Without turning, she recognized Andy's voice. Not only had they spoken before the service, he'd sung "What a Friend We Have in Jesus" as if he'd meant it, except he'd sung it loud like Mr. Rayburn in Wisconsin, whom everyone knew made trips to Madison for less than noble purposes. Dani didn't want to turn to Andy, but she saw no choice. Without smiling, she said, "Hello."

He winked at her. "Which basket is yours?"

"You'll have to guess." Dani looked straight ahead.

Andy leaned closer, crowding her to the point of discomfort as he made his voice low. "If you won't tell me which it is, I'll just look for the prettiest one."

Dani sidestepped. "I have children with me. I better check on them."

"I'll go with you."

"That's not necessary."

Andy's smile might have been friendly, but the glint in his eyes held a trace of anger. Dani wanted to call for help, but what could she say? He hadn't done anything except stand a little too close. She stayed where she was, in front of the steps where she could see Adie and the baskets. When Adie made eye contact, Dani waved. Ignoring Andy, she turned to check on the girls. Emma, seeing the auction had begun, rounded up Ellie and Esther and hurried in Dani's direction.

Andy grinned. "Cute kids."

"Yes." Dani willed Emma to go back to "Mother May I." She didn't want the girls near Andy, but she had no way to signal them to stay with their friends. They reached her side as Pastor Josh lifted the third basket. Andy tipped his hat to Emma, then smiled at the younger girls. "You three must be sisters."

"We are," Ellie said.

"How did you ladies meet Miss Baxter?"

No way did Dani want to share her business with this man. "It's a long story. One I won't bore you with Mr.—"

"Andy."

Dani ignored the familiarity. Turning, she scanned the crowd again for Beau. Pastor Josh handed the fourth basket to a gray-haired man who'd bought his wife's supper, probably for the thirtieth time in thirty years.

Andy stayed at Dani's side, making small talk with the girls about the town.

Pastor Josh held up another picnic supper, a large basket decorated with ribbons and red gingham. "What do I hear for an opening bid?"

"Six bits!" said a man in the back.

A few bids followed, but everyone knew Tim Landers would spend his last nickel for his fiancée's supper. When the bidding stopped, Dani looked down the road and saw Beau. Pastor Josh lifted the sixth basket. As he started the bidding, Beau walked from the surrey to the edge of the crowd, where he spoke with Sheriff Dawes. A young man won the basket, picked up the supper and smiled boldly at a girl who'd struck Dani as shy.

Pastor Josh lifted Dani's basket next. "I smell fried chicken, gentlemen. What do I hear for an opening bid?"

"That's ours!" Esther announced.

Dani wanted to put her hand over the child's mouth.

Andy raised his hand. "Two dollars."

Dani cringed. The other baskets had gone for a dollar and change. She sought Beau with her eyes, praying silently that he'd bid on her basket. Instead of signaling a bid, he crossed his arms over his chest. He hadn't looked at her once.

A man in a suit raised his arm. "Three dollars!"

Dani recognized the banker. He glanced at her and smiled.

Andy upped the bidding to three dollars and change. The banker raised it to five. A rancher in a paisley vest bid six.

"Seven!" Andy shouted.

The rancher smiled at her but tipped his hat in defeat. The banker raised his hand. "Ten!"

"Do I hear eleven?" Josh looked straight at Beau.

"Twelve!" The bid came from Andy.

Dani's heart shriveled. Beau hadn't bid at all.

"That's once," Pastor Josh said. "Twice."

"Twenty dollars." The voice belonged to Beau, and it rang with an authority that stunned the crowd into silence.

Looking at him from across the yard, Dani didn't know what to think. He'd just spent twenty dollars for her fried chicken, but he looked far from pleased.

Chapter Twelve

Beau strode to the front of the church, paid for Dani's basket and headed in her direction. His gaze snapped to the red-haired man at her side. During the auction, he'd spoken to Sheriff Dawes and learned the fellow was a stranger in town. Under any circumstances, Beau would have sidled up to the kid and asked questions. With Dani in the picture, he felt even more wary.

With the basket in hand, Beau approached Dani and the girls. The stranger locked eyes with him, then turned to Dani. "I'd say you're spoken for, Miss Baxter." He tipped his hat and walked away.

"Wait up!" Beau called.

Red kept going. Beau wanted to drop the basket and haul him to the sheriff's office for a little talk, but he had no evidence of wrongdoing, just a feeling in his gut and those weren't always right. Neither could he leave Dani and the girls. Red had raised Beau's hackles, but so had his talk with Trevor Scott. Beau didn't like being watched by a Pinkerton's detective. Heading to the church from Scott's office, he'd decided to bore the detective to tears by playing horseshoes and watching Dani from afar.

Now she was at his side, looking worried while they headed for the shade of a cottonwood. The girls ran ahead. Emma flapped the blanket, giggling as it settled into a crooked square. As the girls plopped down, Beau set the basket on a corner. Smiling nervously, Dani dished up his plate. He bit into the fried chicken, holding in a groan of pleasure as he chewed. The supper had been worth every penny, but he didn't compliment Dani. Instead he got down to business. "Who was that fellow?"

"Someone named Andy," she replied.

"Where's he from?"

"I don't know."

Emma wrinkled her nose. "He sat behind us in church."

The younger girls had been in Adie's Sunday school class and were more interested in dessert than talk. Beau wanted details from Dani, but she was wiping crumbs from Esther's face. With her shoulders angled and her chin dipped, she seemed almost shy.

Beau didn't understand. During the auction, he'd watched her from the corner of his eye and seen her agitation. He'd expected her to thank him for chasing away Andy. Instead she seemed anxious. Looking at her flushed cheeks, Beau worried that he'd made her angry.

He set his plate on the blanket. "Sorry I had to buy your basket. I know you're looking to meet people." He couldn't bring himself to say "men."

Dani's gaze snapped to his. "You're *sorry*?"

"I wrecked your plans, but that Andy fellow—I couldn't let him have supper with you."

"Why not?"

"I didn't like his looks."

She looked at him with a mix of hope and concern. "Was that all?"

He scowled. "What else would it be?"

Dani turned back to Esther. "I see."

The girls finished eating, then went to play with their friends. Dani stacked the dirty plates with a clatter and set them by the basket. Beau didn't know a lot about women, but he knew a snit when he saw one. He gentled his voice. "What's wrong?"

She slapped her own plate on to the pile. "I'm sorry you wasted your money."

"What?"

"The basket… You didn't want it."

Oh yes, I did. He couldn't answer truthfully without muddying the waters, so he shrugged. "It had to be done."

"No, it didn't."

In his better years, he'd have flirted with Dani until she smiled. Instead he set down his plate, leaving the pie unfinished. "Tell me about this Andy character."

"He's not your concern."

"Oh yes, he is," Beau said, grumbling. "He just cost me twenty dollars."

Dani's lips tightened. "You didn't *have* to buy the basket."

"What was I supposed to do? Let him eat with you?"

"Why not?"

Because you're mine... Because I want you for myself. Beau's thoughts stopped in the back of his throat, but his irritation leaked from his lips. "You're raising my nieces, that's why."

"Is that all?"

No, but it was enough. "You and the girls are in *my* care. Before a man comes courting, he's going to earn my approval."

Dani raised her chin. "You're leaving. What happens then?"

Beau couldn't say. Looking at Dani, all fierce and defiant, he felt a force he hadn't felt in a long time. He wanted to protect this woman and provide for her. What would it be like to make her his wife? They'd fight, that was certain. They'd make up, too. With kisses and forgiveness and the supple bending of their wills. All he had to do was set down his hate for Clay Johnson. He simply couldn't do it.

He picked up the glass of tea but didn't drink. He had to think of Dani, not himself. She deserved a husband. He couldn't be that man, but others today had shown interest. He drummed his fingers on the cup. "I'd be glad to see you married, but only to a good man."

She lowered her eyes. "Like who?"

"The rancher looked like a decent sort. So did the fellow in the suit. Anyone but that cowboy."

Dani grimaced. "To tell the truth, I didn't like him at all."

"Me, neither."

She looked at Beau with a sad smile. "Thank you for buying my basket. I appreciated it."

"It was nothing." Never mind that he wanted it to lead to everything. He drained the tea. It tasted sweet but splashed in his belly like acid. He had to stay focused on the business of finding Clay Johnson.

Beau lowered his glass. "What else happened with that Andy fellow?"

She described how he'd sat behind her in church and quizzed her about the basket. With each word, she looked more nervous.

Beau wanted to chase down Andy and slap him. "I don't want to upset you, Dani. But you have be careful."

"I know."

"Andy could be running with Johnson. They could be scouting out the next ranch to raid."

"Or looking for you."

"Yes."

He plucked a blade of grass and rolled it in his fingers. He wanted to crush Johnson with the same ease.

"Hey, Morgan!"

He turned and saw Wallace hurrying in their direction. When the barkeep reached the blanket, Beau made a hurried introduction, then motioned for the man to sit. "What's up?"

Wallace stayed on his feet. "Do you remember about Johnson coming in for whiskey?"

"Of course."

"He had two men with him that night. One of them just came back."

Beau had already stood. "What did he look like?"

"Young with red hair."

Just as he suspected, Andy had been up to no good. Beau thought of the surrey he'd driven to town and groaned. He couldn't go after the kid without a good horse, nor did he want to approach Clay without his long guns. The pistol on his hip was fine for a Sunday picnic but not the battle he felt coming. Andy had been the spotter. Clay Johnson was ready to strike.

Beau sensed Dani's gaze and turned. "You'll have to stay with Josh and Adie."

Her eyes clouded. "The cows—"

He'd never felt so tied up in his life. He wanted to go

after Clay, but he couldn't leave Dani and his nieces unprotected on the farm. "I'll think of something."

Wallace interrupted. "We need to find Dawes."

Beau scanned the picnickers. By a tree he saw a crowd of children, his nieces among them, skipping rope. He spotted the sheriff eating with his wife and son. With Wallace in his wake, Beau strode through the crowd.

Dawes saw Beau and stood. "What's up, Sheriff?"

Beau respected the use of his old title. What Dawes lacked in talent, he made up for in decency. "That red-haired kid, did you see him?"

"I sure did."

"Wallace saw him with Clay Johnson."

The barkeep described Andy's visit to the saloon. The kid had knocked on the back door, bought six bottles of whiskey and left. "That was twenty minutes ago. You can still catch him."

Beau's legs itched for a fast ride, but Andy had caught him unprepared. No horse. No guns. Nothing but fury and the knowledge that Dani had become a target.

The sheriff motioned to his son. "Come here, Howie."

Beau hadn't met the boy, but he knew Howie from the girls' stories. Emma, he guessed, had a crush on the sixteen-year-old. Beau looked him up and down. He had height, some muscle and seemed responsible.

Howie joined his father. "What happened?"

"Get Teddy and Ace. Tell them we have a lead on Johnson."

Howie's eyes glinted. "I want to go."

"Sorry, son."

"But—"

"You're too young."

Beau felt for the kid. He also saw an answer to his

problem. He stuck out his hand, greeting Howie like a man. "I'm Beau Morgan."

Howie shook. "You're Emma's uncle."

"I'm riding out with your pa. Miss Baxter and my nieces are staying in town. Can I trust you to see to things at the farm?"

Howie looked at his father. "I'd rather go with you."

When Dawes gripped his son's shoulder, Beau's mind tripped down a dangerous road. What would it be like to have a son with Dani's eyes?

The sheriff spoke in a low tone. "We need your help, son."

Beau understood young men. Howie wanted respect, and Beau knew how to show it. "I'll pay you." He named an amount that matched the importance of the job.

Howie stood tall. "I'll do it."

"Here's the plan." Beau laid out the details. He'd borrow a horse from Dawes and ride hard to the farm. He'd get the tools of his trade—his own horse, guns, ammo, irons and a rope—and join the sheriff and his men. Howie would take the surrey to the farm and stay. Dani and the girls would go home with Josh and Adie. Beau had to speak to the Blues, but he felt certain they'd help.

The Reverend must have seen the men talking, because he walked up to them. "What happened?"

Beau told him about Andy.

Josh's face hardened. "I saw him bird-dogging Dani. If you hadn't bought that basket, Adie and I would have joined them for supper."

When a man didn't trust God, he needed friends. Beau had Josh. "I need a favor."

"Anything."

"Can Dani and the girls stay at the parsonage?"

"Sure. Stephen'll enjoy the company. What about your stock?"

Howie spoke up. "I'm headed out there now."

Dawes looked at his son with pride. "Stay alert."

"I will, Pa."

"It's settled," Dawes said. "We'll meet at the office."

As the sheriff left, Josh clapped Beau on the back. "Go with God, my friend."

Beau's mouth hardened. "He's welcome to ride along, but I doubt He's interested."

Josh didn't say a word. He simply looked at Beau with the same eyes that had wept with him for Lucy, then he left to find Adie.

Beau strode back to the blanket where Dani was neatening up. At the sight of him, she pushed to her feet. She'd worn pink today. Until now, he hadn't noticed. Beau stopped three feet away. He could still smell the chicken. "I'm riding out with Dawes."

"Of course."

He hated himself for the quaver in her voice. He wanted to keep her safe, not cause her worry. He wanted other things, too. Things he couldn't have until Clay Johnson paid for Lucy's murder. To keep from touching her, he crossed his arms. "I spoke to Josh. You and the girls are staying with them."

Her brows snapped together. "What about the milking?"

"Howie's handling it."

"I see."

Beau had expected a fight. Instead Dani's expression melted into womanly concern. His stomach knotted with thoughts he couldn't afford. Beau couldn't bring himself to pray to the God who'd let Lucy die, but he wanted to.

In the distance he saw the cemetery with its stone markers. He heard children skipping rope and the muffled voices of men and the women who'd fed them. Wordless, he turned to go.

Dani grasped his arm. "I have something for you."

His eyes followed her hand to the pocket of her pink dress. She reached inside and withdrew Lucy's handkerchief. "This is yours."

"Keep it."

"But—"

"I want you to have it."

Neither of them had spoken of their feelings, but he could see Dani's heart welling in her eyes. She cared about him…maybe she even loved him. Beau expected to come back in one piece, but bullets, like lightning, struck without warning. He couldn't leave without showing Dani how he felt, so he kissed her cheek.

She tipped up her face, putting them just inches apart. "Be careful."

"I will."

With his throat tight, he left to borrow a horse from Sheriff Dawes. The sooner Clay Johnson dangled from a rope, the sooner Beau could come home.

Dani and the girls sat huddled on the divan in the parsonage. Stephen had built a fort on the floor out of books and had lined up soldiers for a war. Adie was still in the kitchen, but Pastor Josh had started a story. He'd picked Noah's ark, a fitting choice with rain pounding the roof and thunder rumbling down the mountains.

Any child would have been frightened, but for these girls, Emma in particular, the storm evoked memories of Patrick's horse racing into the yard. Lightning flashed again, filling the room with a blue light. As the girls grabbed for each other, thunder shook the house. Dani whispered a prayer for Beau.

She'd learned from Josh that he'd left with Sheriff Dawes and two deputies. No one had seen Andy leave town, but Sparrow Canyon, a maze of gorges running north and south at the base of the Rockies, offered good grass and places to hide. Knowing Johnson, Beau had felt confident he'd be in those canyons and had led the men in that direction.

Dani prayed he was right. Her cheek still tingled from the brush of his lips. He'd bought the picnic basket to protect her from Andy, but the kiss had been a confession. He cared about her. The hankie, folded in her pocket, told her just how deep his feelings ran.

Adie came out of the kitchen with a lantern. "That's quite a storm."

Emma trembled. "I wish God would stop the thunder."

"Me, too," Ellie said. "Uncle Beau's out there."

No one said a word.

Dani's mind raced through possibilities. Patrick had died on a night like this one. Lightning could strike. A flash flood could rip away the sides of a canyon and carry a man and his horse to their doom. In His wrath, God had flooded the earth and cleansed it of iniquity. In His mercy He'd promised to never do it again. He'd given Noah a rainbow and a dove. Dani prayed Beau would find that peace.

Pastor Josh bowed his head. "Let's pray."

Stephen copied his father. Dani and the girls held hands. Adie sat next to her husband and reached for his hand.

"Lord Jesus, we come to You in faith." Josh spoke in

a normal tone, but Dani felt it like thunder. His words soared on the wings of Noah's dove, rising higher and growing stronger.

"Beau Morgan, our friend and uncle, needs Your grace. His heart is weary, Lord. We ask You to sustain him in this troubled time. We pray he'll be guided by Your wisdom and protected by angels. We pray for the healing of his heart, Lord. Beau lost a wife and he wants revenge. You lost a son and offered mercy to the whole human race. We praise You for that gift. We thank You for the promise of Heaven, a place where there's no pain and no wrongdoing, where justice is complete and love abounds. May Beau have that assurance. Amen."

Six voices echoed Pastor Josh, making a choir of sorts. The thunder hadn't lessened nor had the lightning dimmed, but Dani felt calmer.

Esther, who hadn't sucked her thumb in spite of the storm, looked up at her. "My pa's in Heaven, isn't he?"

"That's right."

"I'll see him again."

"You sure will," Josh said.

Adie joined in. "And your mother, too."

Someday Dani would see her own parents again. Beau, she believed, would greet Lucy. And Patrick…he'd gone home to be with Beth, the woman he'd loved to the point of misery on earth. Christ had torn the veil between time and eternity. She knew Beau had that faith. She prayed he'd find the peace to go with it, and that he'd find it soon.

Thunder rolled again, more distant now.

Josh cleared his throat. "Let's finish Noah's ark."

Stephen chimed in. "I like the animals. Did Noah bring horses?"

"Sure," Josh answered. "He brought two of everything—bears, horses, all the pretty birds we see."

By the time the Reverend finished the tale, the animals had names and personalities and the storm had passed. The girls, even Emma, were giggling about the messy ark. When the dove came back with the olive branch, Adie sent Stephen upstairs to bed, then offered to tuck the girls into bed in the guest room. Josh went with his son, leaving Dani alone.

She lifted her shawl off the hook by the door and went out to the porch. The rain had washed the air clean and left a million stars. Hugging herself, she looked up and wondered if Beau saw the same beauty.

The door creaked behind her. Adie came to stand at her side. "You love him, don't you?"

She meant Beau. Dani knew her feelings, but she feared Adie's opinion. She didn't want to appear fickle. "It's not that simple."

"Why not?"

"Things just don't make sense."

Adie's voice dipped. "I know you loved Patrick, but that doesn't mean you can't love again."

Dani almost laughed. "It's not Patrick."

"Then what?"

Clutching her shawl, she told Adie about Patrick's letters to Beth and his intention to send her home. In the middle of the story, she sat in the chair she'd used her first day in Castle Rock. That day she'd been afraid of Beau. Now she feared for him. If he didn't come back—she couldn't stand the thought.

Adie sat next to her. "Does Beau know about the letters?"

"Yes." Dani started to rock. "He burned them. I was

crying. He gave me a handkerchief, then he…" *Kissed me.* She couldn't say the words. "He was so kind, so strong. I felt… I don't know what I felt."

"Safe?"

Dani nodded.

"Cared for?"

"And more." For that moment, they'd had one heart.

Adie hummed softly. "I know about the 'more.'"

"I like it."

"Me, too." Adie smiled. "Does Beau know how you feel?"

"I haven't told him."

"So you're waiting for him to speak first."

"Mostly I'm afraid."

The moon had turned the yard into streaks of silver and black velvet. Dani saw beauty yet knew a deeper truth. If she stepped off the porch, she'd be up to her ankles in mud. Her feelings for Beau glistened like the water, but she didn't know what lay below the surface. If she told him how she felt, would they walk on the water or sink in the mud? She pulled the shawl closer. "I care for Beau, but he won't rest until he catches Clay Johnson."

"How do you know?"

"He told me."

Adie rocked gently. "Maybe they'll catch him tonight."

"I hope so." But would it be enough? Dani flashed on the pistols she'd seen in Beau's room. "He's hated Johnson for so long, I wonder if he can stop."

"A man can change."

"If he wants to."

"God has a way of making that happen."

Dani stared at the puddles. They were growing smaller

by the minute. "Maybe, but right now Beau's out in the storm."

"It's what men do. They fight for the people they love."

"You mean Lucy."

"No, I mean you." Adie's voice turned light. "I saw Beau's face when he bid on your basket. He'd have paid double for it."

Dani smiled. "He likes fried chicken."

"He likes *you* even more." Adie sat straighter in her chair. "There's just one thing for you decide."

"What's that?"

"Do you love him enough to fight for him?"

Her chest ached. "I do. But how?"

"Put arms on the love of God. Show him what he's missing. For some reason, the Lord dropped Beau into the middle of a good life. He brought you to the same place at the same time. I have to believe there's a reason."

"I can see it."

"It's a matter of courage," Adie said. "Can you trust God to finish what He started?"

Dani looked across the yard where the last puddle reflected the moon and stars. Someday she'd come face-to-face with her Lord and the past weeks would make sense. Until then, she had a choice. Believe God for the best or protect herself from the worst. Dani's heart swelled with longing. She wanted everything God had for her future. She wanted Beau and would fight for him with her best weapons.

A good meal.

Children at the table.

Listening when he talked. Staying silent when he didn't.

Warm to her toes, she smiled at Adie. "Of course, I'll fight. I love him."

"He's a blessed man."

Dani looked at the distant hills. She needed Adie's wisdom. "What should I do?"

The pastor's wife got a look in her eyes that made Dani think of Adam, Eve and the apple. "There's a dance next Saturday. It's to honor the church's third anniversary."

"I like to dance."

"So does Beau."

Dani's mind drifted to the dresses hanging in her wardrobe. She'd brought something special for her wedding, an ivory gown that had belonged to her mother. She wanted to wear it for Beau, but not yet. The rest of her gowns held memories of Wisconsin. "I wish I had a new dress."

Adie grinned. "We'll go shopping tomorrow."

Dani felt embarrassed. "I don't have much money."

"I'll raid the cookie jar."

"But—"

"No 'buts'!" Adie said. "I know just the dress. It's blue like your eyes. It'll be worth every cent to see Beau's face at the dance."

Dani imagined fiddles and guitars and whirling in Beau's arms. Worrying about a man was a trial, but courting promised a world of wonder. Shivering, she looked at the stars and prayed Beau would feel the same way.

Chapter Thirteen

Two days had passed since Beau had left Dani at the picnic. Every minute had been a torture. He missed her. He missed the girls and even the blasted cows. To add to his irritation, Dawes and his two deputies had as much grit as goose feathers. Beau bristled at their whining, but they had reason to be disgruntled.

A storm had destroyed whatever tracks Andy had left. A packhorse had gone lame, forcing them to visit a local ranch. Dawes had accepted the offer to spend the night, so they'd lost time. To add to Beau's misery, the youngest of the two deputies, a kid named Teddy, whined like a buzz saw. He'd gotten stung by a hornet and was still fussing. The other deputy called himself Ace and claimed to be "a real wild card." Dressed in a bowler and purple vest, Ace talked about poker and not much else.

Beau didn't give a hoot about cards and bee stings. He wanted to end his fight with Clay Johnson and he wanted to do it now. He blinked and saw Dani in her pink dress. She'd looked so pretty, so fresh and young and full of hope. His mind flashed to Ellie being a tomboy in the barn. Esther had stopped sucking her thumb and he didn't want her to start up again. Emma, for all her anger, maybe because of it, was the closest thing he had to a daughter.

Daughters.

Sons.

A wife... Beau had paid twenty dollars for Dani's basket. He'd have paid a hundred for it, but he couldn't give her what she most wanted...the next fifty years, every day of his life. He had to end his business with Johnson before he could think of Dani as more than a friend. If he'd been a praying man, Beau would have begged the Almighty to bring Johnson to justice, both on earth and for eternity, but the words stuck in his throat. Two fruitless days on the trail had rubbed him raw. Looking up at the sky, he blamed God for the rain, the injured horse, bees, poker and everything else that had gone wrong.

Even Dawes had been a thorn. The lawman had gotten confused and led them five miles into a box canyon, forcing Beau to hold in a snort. No outlaw would shelter in a canyon with one opening. Never mind the good grazing and fresh water. The spot didn't suit Johnson and Beau knew it.

But Sparrow Canyon did... Talking over jerky and beans last night, Beau had surmised from Dawes that Sparrow Canyon had three openings. The ravine lay within a day's ride of Castle Rock. A gorge ran west and led into the Rockies, and an easy trail stretched to the south. Sparrow Creek, the stream where Beau had caught fish with Dani and the girls, marked the way.

They were miles past that peaceful point, but Beau kept the memories of that day tucked in his heart. He hadn't stopped hating Johnson, but somewhere in the past few weeks, he'd started caring about Dani and his nieces. Josh had once told Beau that darkness and light couldn't fill a room at the same time. The light, he'd said, would always win. Beau hoped that was true.

"How much farther?" Teddy's whine cut into Beau's thoughts.

Dawes answered over his shoulder. "Just around the next bend."

They couldn't arrive soon enough for Beau. Aware of the pistol on his hip and the long gun in the scabbard, he urged his horse forward and followed Dawes out of a ravine. What he saw made the hairs on his neck prickle. The canyon had lush grass, a stream and good cover. Beau inspected the rocky slopes and spotted a cave. From a distance, it looked black, narrow and deep.

"That's the spot," he said to Dawes. "That's where Johnson would hole up."

The four of them stopped short of the cave. Taking charge, Beau turned to Ace and Teddy. "You two cover me from the trees." He looked at Dawes. "Go north and watch from the other side."

Beau motioned for the men to take position, dismounted, then walked along the creek where willows shielded him from view. As he neared the cave, he looked for tracks but saw none. He listened for horses but heard only a rustle in the trees. With his weapon drawn, he stared at the opening in the rocks. His gut told him Johnson had fled, but he fired one shot to be sure. Bats burst out of the cave, a sure sign no one was inside. Even so, he approached with caution. When he reached the side, he turned the corner with his gun drawn.

The empty cave stared back at him. Lowering his Colt, Beau took in tin cans, empty whiskey bottles and something he recognized…the tiny stub of a cigar. No one but

Clay smoked them that low. More than a few wanted men had used the cave for shelter. Beau felt certain Johnson had been one of them.

He shouted for Dawes, Teddy and Ace, then squatted next to a fire pit and took a pinch of ash. It couldn't have been colder. He let it go and watched it vanish into thin air.

Dawes walked into the cave. "Looks like we missed them."

Beau said nothing. If they hadn't dawdled at the ranch and gone down a box canyon, they might have found Clay.

The sheriff crossed his arms. "What do you want to do, Morgan?"

"Forge ahead."

Teddy and Ace walked up together. Teddy pouted like a little girl. "Johnson's gone. I say we go home."

"Me, too." Ace slouched against the opening. "There's a game at the Silver River tomorrow. If we hurry, I can make it."

Beau clenched his jaw. "We're not done."

Teddy frowned. "My bee sting hurts."

Beau pushed to his feet, faced Teddy and squared his shoulders. "Look, kid. I'm sorry about your *bee sting*, but you need to toughen up." He directed his gaze to Ace. "So do you."

Dawes frowned. "Now, Morgan—"

"I'm plenty tough," Ace said to Beau. "If anyone needs to wise up, it's you. Any *fool* can see Johnson's gone."

Teddy stood taller. "We're going home."

"Hold up," Dawes said. "I'll make that decision."

"Johnson made it for us." Ace waved his arm. "Look around. He's gone."

The sheriff rubbed his moustache, then turned to Beau with a pitiable lack of leadership. Beau understood lawmen like Dawes. He was a peacemaker at heart. He valued justice but didn't hunger for it. Beau wouldn't find peace until justice had been served, but he had to face facts. Being quick to compromise, Dawes would take a vote. Beau would lose three to one. He didn't like the lawman's methods, but he respected the badge.

He also had an ache in his gut that hurt as much as Teddy's bee sting. He missed Dani. She'd be worried about him. So would his nieces. Riding on alone, without a goodbye and finalizing the adoption, should have tempted him, but he couldn't stand the thought of leaving Dani in the lurch. Beau cursed God for His cruelty and Dawes for his incompetence. If they'd come to Sparrow Canyon first, they might have caught Johnson.

He kicked the ashes. "Let's go home."

He followed Dawes and his deputies out of the cave, but paused to stare up the canyon. It meandered for miles, an outlaw's paradise with jagged turns and places to hide. The meadow rippled with thick grass for stolen horses and the stream flowed fast with melted snow. Best of all, the trail veered south and west, giving a man on the run two routes of escape.

Beau couldn't shake the feeling that Clay was just a mile or two away, up the canyon and watching them, snickering at their lack of will. Beau itched to keep going, but he had a responsibility to Dani and his nieces. Johnson would have to wait. So would his feelings for Dani. Of the two delays, he didn't know which annoyed him more.

Clay lay on his back, staring at the night sky. A week had passed since they'd raided the Rocking J. The horses, grazing in the moonlight, whickered to each other like old friends. Goose and Andy had shuffled a deck of cards and were gambling for swigs of whiskey. Clay had expected Morgan to find them by now. Instead the lawman had come within a stone's throw and turned around.

Clay knew Morgan had come into Sparrow Canyon because of yesterday's ride. He'd gone after a stray mare, seen tracks near the cave and had gone inside. Someone had kicked the fire pit in a fit of temper. Clay felt sure it was Morgan. The man usually rode alone, but Clay had counted three more sets of boot prints. He didn't think for an instant Morgan had turned back by choice. Clay suspected he'd been with the local sheriff, a man known to be weak.

Looking at the stars, Clay called himself a fool for staying near Castle Rock. With Morgan stuck on a farm with a woman and three girls, Clay could have lost him, maybe for good. He'd had his fill of Goose and Andy, too. If they'd gone south, he could have given them a cut, said goodbye and gone east. He could have been free.

So why hadn't he done it?

Clay didn't know. He'd been irked by Andy's chicken sounds, but more than pride kept him in this canyon. Was it regret? Guilt? He wanted to think he was beyond such feelings—that he was beyond feeling anything at all—but his gut had been churning ever since he'd put down Ricochet. He couldn't stop thinking about death, Heaven and Reverend Blue's stories about Jesus.

"For God so loved the world, He gave His only begotten son…"

Clay snorted through his nose. No one—except Beau Morgan for the wrong reasons—cared whether he lived or died. The shedding of blood for sin? Someone dying in his place so he could be free? Clay knew nonsense when he heard it, yet somehow he felt a yearning for such goodness. He wanted to believe in Jesus, but he was afraid to pray the prayer Reverend Blue had said with Chet. Clay didn't know what would happen, but he doubted it would be good. Not even God could forgive a man like Clay.

"You awake, boss?"

Clay glanced across the fire and saw Goose staring through the flames. He grunted. "I am now."

"I've been thinking."

"About what?"

"Morgan," Goose said. "He should have found us by now. I say we smoke him out."

Clay couldn't sleep, so he decided to listen. "Got any ideas?"

"I say we hit another ranch. We send Andy down the canyon with the horses. You and I set up an ambush. When Morgan comes through, he's dead."

Clay saw the logic, but the plan left a bad taste. Killing Morgan in cold blood would solve one problem, but what about Clay's guilty conscience? He wanted to sleep at night, not lie awake feeling like pond scum. He already felt so bad that sometimes he wanted to die. Killing Morgan in cold blood wouldn't make the pain go away.

"I don't like it," he said to Goose.

"Why not?"

Clay wasn't about to bare his soul to Goose, so he looked for another excuse. "What about Dawes?"

"He's weak. He'll give up."

"I still don't like it."

Goose's face went hard. "There's another possibility."

"What's that?"

"We bring the fight to Morgan."

Clay wished he hadn't opened his eyes. The thought of putting children in harm's way made him ill. "I won't do that."

"Why not?"

"Because I won't."

"It would be easy," Goose said. "I'll go to the Silver River. Someone'll tell me where the farm is. We pay a midnight call and just like that—" he snapped his fingers "—Morgan's hanging from a tree."

For three little girls to find…for the woman to cut down and bury. Even worse, what would happen if the woman ran to Morgan's rescue? They'd have to hurt her. Clay muttered a curse. "It's too risky."

Andy rolled over. "I say we visit the farm."

"No."

"The woman's pretty. She smells good, too."

"Shut up," Clay growled.

Andy dropped flat and sighed.

Goose stared hard through the fire. "You're acting like a whipped dog."

Clay's pride flared, but he said nothing.

Andy clucked like a hen. He'd been drinking and was sloppy drunk. Clay hated sloppy drunks. His father had been one. He'd either laughed himself silly or beat his wife and sons. Clay's own father had broken his nose twice. Every time he looked in the mirror, he saw the crookedness and hated it. He pushed to his feet, walked past the fire and kicked Andy in the gut.

The kid curled into a ball. "What was that for?"

"For being you."

Clay was sick to death of these two clowns. Going east sounded better than ever. He had a cousin in St. Louis. He hadn't seen the fellow in years, but last he'd heard, he ran a dry goods store. The two of them had been boyhood pals, kicking each other in church while the minister droned.

Goose broke into his thoughts. "What'll it be, boss?"

Clay was still in the St. Louis dry goods store, thinking about his cousin and the Bible stories he'd heard as a boy. He'd had enough of running. Enough of the guilt. But Morgan would never stop.

Goose gave him a stare that challenged more than Clay's pride. It gave him a choice. Fight like a man or put up with Andy's chicken sounds. The only feeling in Clay's life stronger than guilt was a yearning for peace. He couldn't explain that feeling to Goose or Andy. They were young men intent on leaving their mark. Clay had seen more than forty years of life, and the last few had been tiresome to say the least. He'd had enough. One way or another, he wouldn't leave this canyon until he settled the score with Morgan.

But settle it how? With a confession? *I'm sorry... I didn't mean to shoot her.* Or with bloodshed and a quick trip to Heaven or Hell? Looking at the sky, Clay didn't think Beau Morgan would care that he was sorry. He doubted God would, either. Clay thought hard about his choice. Another raid would satisfy his men and add to their bankroll, but it would also draw out the law. He didn't want to deal with Dawes and a posse. He just wanted to settle things with Morgan. That meant sending the man a message.

Clay looked at Goose. "Andy can't go to town, but you can."

"What do you have in mind?"

Clay went back to his bedroll, dropped to a crouch and slipped a single bullet from his gun belt. He handed it to

Goose. "Leave this at the Silver River. Tell the barkeep to give it to Morgan."

Goose palmed the casing. "How will he know it's from you?"

"It's the same caliber that killed his wife."

Goose laughed.

Clay felt sick.

Andy rolled over in his bedroll. "Let me take it. There's a social on Saturday. I want to go."

Andy, Clay decided, was an idiot. "You're the one they followed down this canyon."

"For no reason." Andy pouted. "I was nice to that girl."

"You're staying put." Clay turned to Goose. "Leave the bullet with the barkeep at the Silver River but skip the dance."

Goose pinched the brass casing, turning it to catch the light of the fire. The bullet glowed orange, reminding Clay of a setting sun. Weary, he slid into his bedroll, put his head on the ground and closed his eyes. Unless Morgan had lost his instincts, it wouldn't be long before he came all the way down the canyon.

Chapter Fourteen

Back in Denver, Beau had enjoyed church socials. He'd liked flirting with pretty women and he didn't mind dancing. Once Lucy had come into his life, dancing had been more than fun. They'd found the rhythms unique to them. Beau wanted to find that rhythm with Dani, but nothing had changed since he'd ridden out of Sparrow Canyon. When he'd reached Castle Rock, he'd stopped at Scott's office and told the man to push hard for the adoption. As soon as the papers were signed, Beau intended to go after Johnson. One way or another, the chase would end.

After seeing the attorney, he'd ridden to the parsonage. He'd greeted Dani with a tip of his hat, not the embrace he'd wanted, but the girls had all hugged him. Now, standing in the Castle Rock schoolhouse, dressed up for the dance and holding a cup of punch, he could still feel their skinny arms around his middle.

For the third time in ten minutes, Beau looked at his pocket watch. He wanted to visit the Silver River for news, but he couldn't leave Dani. He didn't know where she'd gotten the dress, a royal blue gown that matched her eyes, but it fit her to perfection. Riding next to her in the surrey, he'd stared at the dirt road to keep from noticing her dainty shoes and the way she'd tapped her toes to an imaginary waltz.

She'd volunteered at the punch bowl, a place where every man in town would have a reason to talk to her. Dani didn't know it, but Beau was standing five feet behind her, keeping a watchful eye.

A few bars into the opening polka, the first man dared to approach her. Beau recognized the rancher from the picnic. While riding with Dawes, he'd quizzed the sheriff about every man in Castle Rock. The rancher, a recent widower, had a little boy. He never missed church, paid his hands well, didn't gamble or drink and was the first to show up when a neighbor needed help.

His only fault was bad taste in vests, but Beau counted that reason enough to dislike him. As the man approached Dani, Beau crossed his arms and stared. Unaware he was being watched, the man turned on the charm. Dani gave him a cup of punch. As he lifted it to his lips, Beau lowered his chin. The motion caught the rancher's attention. So did Beau's hardest stare. The poor fellow nearly choked. With a stiff nod, he set down the cup, walked away and asked another woman to dance.

Good, Beau thought. Dani didn't need a goody-two-shoes rancher for a husband. She needed a man who understood her. Beau watched as she squared her shoulders. The blue silk puffed at her shoulders, then narrowed to fit her arms. He thought of her hands. She was wearing white gloves, dainty things trimmed in lace with pearl buttons at the wrist. Beau thought the gloves were nice but unnecessary. He liked Dani's hands just fine.

Another man approached. Beau didn't know him from Adam and didn't care to. The fool hadn't bothered to shine his shoes. He took a cup of punch, saw Beau and left without a word. Dani followed him with her eyes. When he asked another woman to dance, she sagged a bit but not for long.

Looking at her back, he imagined the smile pasted to her face and felt bad. Then again, if a man couldn't meet Beau's stare, he didn't deserve to dance with the prettiest woman in the room. Dani didn't need a weakling for a husband. She needed a man who knew how to fight and love. A man who could be tender with children and cows but fierce with everything else. A man like… He clenched his jaw.

Five more men wandered to the refreshment table. All five looked at Dani, saw Beau and turned a pasty white. They each asked other women to dance, leaving Dani alone at the punch bowl with her shoulders as stiff as those of a stone angel. Beau's gaze drifted to the dance floor where he saw Josh and Adie gazing into each other's eyes. They'd been married for years, but they danced like newlyweds. As the couple turned with the music, Josh spotted Beau. He said something to Adie. They stopped dancing and walked toward Beau.

To hide the fact he'd been watching Dani, Beau went to greet them. "Nice social," he said as they met at the punch bowl.

Josh grinned. "It would be nicer if you were dancing."

Adie leaned close to Dani and pretended to whisper in her ear. "I hear Beau's light on his feet."

Dani's cheeks turned pink. They both knew Josh and Adie were playing matchmaker. The effort irked Beau to no end. He didn't need any prodding to ask Dani to dance. He'd been fighting the urge all night.

Still blushing, Dani gave Adie a cup of punch. "You must be thirsty after all that dancing."

She sounded wistful. Beau felt bad about chasing away her dance partners, but no one had measured up.

Josh and Adie traded a look. Without a glance at Beau, Josh offered his hand to Dani. "May I have this dance?"

Dani turned pinker. "I don't think—"

"Go on," Adie insisted.

Josh swept Dani into the crowd. Adie said something friendly, but Beau didn't hear the words. His eyes were glued to Dani, who looked happy for the first time all night. The fiddler played a fancy scale. The guitarist joined in, followed by the bellow of the accordion playing the first bars of a polka.

Dancers crowded the floor, but Beau had eyes only for Dani in her blue dress, whirling with Josh, who'd said something that made her smile. Four bars into the song, Beau spotted three men closing in on Josh, intending to cut in. Not caring that Adie was in midsentence, he strode onto the dance floor, beating out the other men, including the rancher who'd been ahead of him.

He tapped Josh on the shoulder. "I'm cutting in."

No small talk. No smiles. Just an order to hand Dani over and do it now.

Josh had the bad manners to chuckle. "Of course," he said, making a slight bow to Dani.

The next thing Beau knew, they were spinning and whirling and he'd never felt so sure of the rightness of having this woman in his life. Nor had he felt such conflict. He wanted to make Dani his wife, but first he had to finish with Johnson. One dance, Beau told himself. Just for now, he'd enjoy the smile he'd put on her face. He'd let the scent of her hair drift into his nose. He'd look at the gold waves and imagine them free from pins and ribbons, cascading down her shoulders. Just for now, he'd let himself feel the blessing of two hearts beating as one.

When the song ended, Dani looked into his eyes. Short of breath and flushed, she smiled. "That was a surprise."

Without the shelter of the music, Beau felt the bleakness of the future. He had to leave. Now. Before the band struck up a waltz or reel. It didn't matter what the musicians played. He had to resist.

Beau hooked his arm around her waist and aimed for the door. "It's time to go home."

"What?"

"It's late."

"But we haven't cut the cake."

"Forget the cake. I want to leave."

She gave him a look that tore him to shreds. He didn't know if she was angry, hurt or both. Before he could decide, the musicians played the opening chords of "Camptown Races." The music tripped him like a rope.

Dance with her... Just one more.

He saw the interest in her eyes, a curiosity that reminded him of her innocence and her tender heart. She wanted a husband. She wanted a family of her own and to be loved for herself. Beau wanted to give her those things.

But he couldn't. Not now.

"Beau?" Her eyes clouded. "Are you all right?"

He sobered instantly. He couldn't let Dani see his feelings. He'd already crossed the line by kissing her in the kitchen and again at the picnic. Brotherly caresses, he told himself. Except her feelings, he suspected, were growing as fast as his. He couldn't risk hurting her. He had to be her friend, nothing more.

Beau schooled his features. "Sorry," he said in a level voice. "If you want cake, we'll stay."

She touched his arm. His bicep bunched, a reflex he couldn't stop.

Dani looked into his eyes. "I'd like to dance some more."

"I can't."

Her voice dropped to a murmur. "Because of Lucy?"

Beau fought the urge to lie. If he claimed to be grief stricken, Dani would let him off the hook. If he told the truth—that he loved her and it hurt too much to hold her—she'd fight for him. He didn't think he could resist, so he thinned his lips to a line. "It's got nothing to do with Lucy."

"Then why?"

He didn't want to hurt her, but he had to make her leave. "Mind your own business."

Dani blinked in disbelief. "I don't deserve that."

She was right, but Beau couldn't apologize. They'd be dancing to a waltz and finding that rhythm he wanted. He couldn't let that happen, at least not yet, so he said nothing.

Dani's mouth tightened. "Excuse me. I'm going to help with the cake." She brushed by him.

Instead of going to the refreshment table, she raced out the door. Beau held in a curse. He couldn't let her walk alone in the dark, so he followed her, pausing on the steps to let his eyes adjust to the night. As his vision cleared, he scanned the landscape. To the west he saw a stand of pines, pale grass and nothing else. He looked east and saw an empty meadow. He hadn't seen anyone suspicious tonight, but that didn't mean a thing. Back in

Denver, he hadn't seen Clay Johnson on the roof. With his heart pounding, he shouted Dani's name.

Holding her skirt and fighting tears, Dani hurried away from the schoolhouse. She feared Adie had seen her spat with Beau and would come after her, so she ran for the cover of a group of pines. When she reached the farthest tree, she circled away from the schoolhouse and slumped against the rough bark. She could hear the music coming from the open windows, but the shadows made her invisible.

That's how she'd felt at the punch bowl. Not a single man had asked her to dance. The rejection had reminded her of embarrassing times in Wisconsin. After she'd broken the engagement to Virgil, she'd become a wallflower. A pariah. Unloved and unwanted by anyone. She hadn't been bothered when the rancher left her alone. She wanted only Beau, but after the third man walked away looking pinched, she'd faced a hard truth. She didn't measure up.

Dani didn't understand. She tried to be kind. She had a good mind and pitched in wherever she could. The blue dress fit perfectly and flattered her figure. She'd seen Beau's eyes when he'd helped her into the surrey and silently thanked Adie for being a tad bit bold. Riding to town, she'd imagined dancing with Beau but not the way it had happened. He'd cut in on Pastor Josh because he'd been worried about someone like Andy, not because he wanted to move with her to the music.

He cared about her, but he cared more about killing Clay Johnson. That was the sad, hard truth.

"Dani!"

His voice roared over the music. She felt bad for hiding but didn't want to be found sniffling like a child. She reached in her pocket for a handkerchief, felt Lucy's embroidery and burst into tears.

"Dani!"

He sounded close to panic. Hurt or not, Dani couldn't let him suffer. Hoping the darkness would hide her puffy eyes, she raised her voice. "I'm over here."

Beau walked through the pines, stirring the needles as he peered into the shadows until he found her against the tree. "Why are you out here?"

"I'll go back in a minute." Her voice quivered.

"What's wrong?"

"Nothing."

"Then why did you leave?"

"I needed air. That's all."

She could smell the starch of his shirt, the bay rum he'd splashed on his jaw. Even blind in the dark, she felt Beau's nearness. So much remained unsaid. Unfinished business. Unspoken promises. With the moon turning the meadow a pale green, Dani flashed on Patrick's failure to share his true feelings. He'd left her with a mountain of doubt. She wouldn't do the same to Beau. He deserved to know how she felt.

Before she could find her tongue, he aimed his chin at the schoolhouse. "I'll walk you back."

"Not yet."

"It's not safe out here."

I love you. The words were strangling her, but Beau's eyes stopped her from saying them. Bitterness glinted in his dilated pupils. She could hear the tension in his voice. She'd felt it in his hands when they'd danced. She longed to spill her heart, but not with Beau on the verge of a rant. She turned on her heel and fled.

He grasped her arm. "Dani—"

She sidestepped to avoid him, then left the shelter of the pines. A full moon lit the meadow, turning the grass into shimmering blades. The next thing she knew, Beau had his hand on her shoulder. Without a word, he spun her around. Their gazes collided in the dim light that revealed her tearstained cheeks.

"You've been crying," he said. "Tell me why."

"No."

"I didn't mean to hurt your feelings."

She didn't know what to do. She couldn't tell Beau that she loved him, but neither did she want to turn away. She settled for the easiest truth. "Tonight reminded me of the dances in Wisconsin."

"Why?"

She gave a rueful smile. "After the fiasco with Virgil, no one ever asked me to dance."

Beau hesitated. "Josh asked you tonight."

"He's a minister!" Dani couldn't believe her ears. "It was like dancing with my father."

"I cut in, didn't I?"

She huffed. "*That* was like dancing with my brother." It hadn't been, but that's how she saw it now.

His eyes stayed locked on hers. "Is that how you felt?"

"No." Her voice squeaked. "But no one else asked. Josh danced with me out of pity. You did it out of worry."

"You're wrong."

She could at least be honest. "I know what I saw."

"I know what you *didn't* see." He was still holding her arm, lightly, but she felt the warmth of his grip. "I was standing right behind you. If a man didn't measure up, I gave him the evil eye."

"You *what*?"

"I chased the men off—all of them."

"You don't have that right!" Not even her brother had been so high-handed. "Why did you do it?"

"I care about you."

Her breath hitched. "You mean as a friend."

"I mean—" He sealed his lips, then slipped his arms around her middle and held her gently against his chest. His lips brushed her hair, her temple. When she tilted her face up to his, he kissed her lips. The caress held all the restraint he'd shown in the kitchen, but this time his arms were around her. She felt…wanted.

Beau raised his face from hers, then tucked her head under his chin where she heard the pounding of his heart.

"You're beautiful, Dani. Any man—"

"I don't want any man." The truth had to be told. "I want you, Beau. I love you."

"Don't."

He'd spoken firmly but hadn't let her go. Dani took it as a confession. "Why not?"

"I can't love you back. At least not yet."

He kissed the top of her head, then released her. Warmth filled Dani from top to bottom. Beau hadn't denied his feelings for her. He'd gone to war with them. It was a battle he had to win for himself, but Dani intended to fight at his side. She looked into his eyes. "It's because of Clay Johnson, isn't it?"

"Yes."

"There are other ways to find him," she said. "You could hire a detective."

He shook his head.

"What about the law? Sheriff Dawes—"

"Isn't much of a lawman."

Dani's heart sank. "The U.S. marshals?"

"They don't care like I do." Beau turned his back on her. "I don't expect you to understand. What I feel goes beyond reason. Bringing Johnson to justice is something I have to do."

"For Lucy," she said.

Beau shook his head. "She'd call me a fool."

"Then why keep going?"

"If I give up now, I've wasted five years."

"You could waste five more."

"I know that, but I can't rest until Johnson's dead."

Dani felt as if she'd stumbled into a grave waiting for a body. The hole was deep and dark with slick slides. She didn't know how to climb out. Beau hadn't said he loved her, but his kiss had given her hope. She braided that hope with love and faith, then prayed silently that God would be merciful to this man who'd lost so much.

"What are you going to do?" she asked.

"Same thing as before. As soon as the adoption's final, I'm leaving. You'll have a farm and three little girls."

Dani's heart squeezed with loneliness. "You were right, you know."

"About what?"

"I want more. I want a husband."

He turned around but didn't come closer. "I care for you, Dani. I won't say how much because there's no point. I'm leaving."

"But you'll come back."

Beau shook his head. "It could be months, even years. I won't ask you to wait for me. There are some good men here. Find one who'll love you and the girls."

Beau meant well, but she'd had it with his domineering ways. "Isn't that for me to decide?"

"No."

Dani's temper flared. "It's not for *you* to decide, either."

"All right," he said. "We'll toss a coin. Heads you marry the rancher. Tails you waste the next five years of your life waiting for a man who's so filled with hate he's not worth knowing. Is that what you want?"

"You're not filled with hate. You love the girls." *Do you love me, too?* She didn't need to voice the question. Beau could see it in her eyes. In his, she saw the answer but knew he wouldn't say it.

He angled his chin at the schoolhouse. "Go dance with the rancher."

She refused to budge. "Do you know what I think?"

"What?"

"You're tired of the chase but too stubborn to admit it."

"You bet I'm tired." His voice shook with fury. "I want this fight to be over, but it's not. That *almighty* God of yours let a killer get away."

"I could be angry, too." She'd lost Patrick, yet that suffering had brought her into Beau's world and given her a new life. "We don't always understand why things happen the way they do, but we can still trust God to know our needs."

"That's rubbish."

"It's true." She set down her pride. "The letters from Patrick, do you know what I realized?"

"What?"

"He's been reunited with Beth. He's happy now."

Beau sneered. "Tell that to the girls."

"They've suffered," Dani admitted. "But it's just for now. They'll see their parents in Heaven. I can't explain the in-between times, but I know that love matters."

Beau crossed his arms. "You don't know squat."

"I know you're living in the past." Dani could scarcely believe her boldness, but Beau needed to hear what she had to say. "Lucy would be ashamed of you. She'd want you to live a good life."

Beau stared at her with burning eyes. Dani ached to reach for his hand but resisted. She loved him and wanted to help him, but only God could soften his heart. Until he made peace with the past, the future glimmered beyond their reach. They were trapped in the present between hate and love. Dani didn't like the tension between them. Believing love would win, she held out her gloved hand. "I'm sorry we argued."

Beau looked at her fingers, cotton-white in the dark, then took her hand and squeezed. "I am, too. Let's go inside."

"I'd like that."

She didn't expect to dance again, but she could stand at Beau's side. At least that's what she hoped until they reached the front of the schoolhouse, where he stopped in the yard. "Go on," he said. "I have an errand to run."

"Where are you going?"

"The Silver River."

"Oh." If he left, the rancher and others would ask her to dance. She didn't want to dance with anyone but Beau. She squeezed his hand. "Could we go home instead?"

"I have to see Wallace."

Before she could tempt him with cake, the doors to the schoolhouse opened and the crowd spilled into the yard. Ellie spotted Beau and ran up to him. "The fireworks are starting! Let's get a good spot." The child gripped her uncle's hand and tugged.

Dani looked at Beau. His expression changed from

a mulelike stubbornness to the way T.C. looked with a ball of string.

"Sounds like fun," he said to the child. He turned to Dani, who'd been joined by Emma and Esther. "We'll stay for the fireworks."

With the girls clutching their hands, they walked to the field behind the schoolhouse, the one where they'd kissed in the pines. Someone launched a rocket that exploded into a giant star. It lit up the sky then faded to nothing. Beau reached for Dani's hand and squeezed. The show lasted for ten minutes, with each burst of light soaring into the dark and filling the night with hope. The girls clapped and cheered. Even Beau had an air of joy as the manmade stars filled the sky with sulfur and smoke.

When it was over, Esther yawned.

Dani looked at Beau. "Do you still want to go to the Silver River?"

He glanced at Esther, then ruffled her hair. "The girls are tired. We'll head home."

Dani smiled her approval.

For tonight, Beau had put love ahead of hate. He made a good uncle. He'd be an even better father. She didn't know what tomorrow held, but God did. Silently she prayed for a future with Beau, one full of stars and sleepy children.

Chapter Fifteen

When Beau saw Trevor Scott driving his buggy into the yard, he knew the man had bad news. Tomorrow at twelve noon, he and Dani were supposed to sign the adoption papers in the presence of a judge. Something must have gone wrong to pull the attorney away from his desk. Dressed in a suit and a bowler hat, he'd come on a formal call.

Beau had been questioning the choice he'd made, to chase Clay rather than stay in Castle Rock, with every waking breath. Aside from his feelings for Dani, he'd lost more of his heart to the girls. He wanted to be a part of their everyday lives, not a favorite uncle who showed up once a year with presents. They needed a man who'd be a father to them. Someone who'd teach them things and chase away boys when the time came.

Once the judge signed the papers, Beau would be free to leave. Howie had agreed to work for the rest of the summer, and Josh had offered to help Dani with any hiring she had to do. The alfalfa had sprouted, and Beau had finished the silo. Two days from now, he expected to be riding into the heart of Sparrow Canyon.

"Hello, Morgan," Scott called. "I'm glad you're here."

"What happened?"

"I'd like to speak in private. Is there a place—"

"This way."

Beau led the attorney to the side of the barn where he sat when he couldn't sleep. Dani wouldn't see them. Earlier she'd lugged the washtub into the backyard and asked for his dirty clothes. Confident he and Scott would be alone, Beau indicated the only chair. "Have a seat."

Scott stayed on his feet. "I received a letter from Harriet Lange's attorney. She's fighting for custody. Judge Hall put a hold on the adoption."

Beau couldn't believe his ears. "On what grounds?"

"She claims you're unfit to be guardian."

"That's ridiculous."

Beau didn't drink, rarely cussed and treated women with the utmost respect. In Denver he'd upheld his badge with an integrity that still made him proud. Harriet Lange had slapped Emma for touching a teacup. The woman had a fight on her hands and it wasn't with a little girl. Beau tucked away his temper and focused on Scott. "What's she saying?"

"The things I mentioned before."

"The Silver River?"

Scott nodded.

"I haven't been since we spoke." But he'd wanted to go. Badly. Not visiting Wallace after the dance had left Beau twisting in the wind. Late at night, he imagined Johnson watching, waiting for him. Only his concern for Dani had kept him from making a late-night ride.

"There's more," Scott said. "Miss Lange doesn't believe Miss Baxter will provide a secure home for the children."

Beau fought to stay calm. "That's ridiculous."

"Is it?" Scott asked. "Miss Baxter is young and single. What will happen to the girls if she marries?"

"Dani loves them. That won't change."

"But surely you can see the concern."

Beau had shared it. He still did but for different reasons. He wanted to marry her himself. "Like I said, Dani's loyal."

"That may be true," Scott said. "But what matters is the judge's perception. As things stand, Miss Lange and Miss Baxter are both single women. Miss Lange is a blood relative, has a small but stable income and family members who'll provide moral and financial support. Miss Baxter is young, unemployed—"

Beau frowned. "She runs this place."

"Again, Mr. Morgan. I'm talking about *perceptions*."

The attorney spoke as if he were in court, planting seeds that would grow into thoughts. Beau had used that trick, too. "What are you getting at?"

"If you and Miss Baxter were to marry—"

"Marry?"

The attorney held up one hand. "Hear me out, Mr. Morgan."

Beau didn't know whether to cover his ears or hang on to every word the man said. Marry Dani? But what about Clay Johnson? Beau had spent too many years to give up now.

Scott laced his hands behind his back. "As I was saying, if you and Miss Baxter were to marry, Miss Lange's case would be significantly weakened. The girls would have a mother *and* a father." The attorney looked Beau in the eye. "What happens after the legalities is no one's business but yours. An annulment—"

"I know what you're saying." Beau had taken vows. He knew what made a marriage real. "When do we have to decide?"

"The sooner, the better."

"I'll let you know."

The attorney tipped his hat and walked back to the buggy, leaving Beau alone behind the barn. His mind spun with the possibilities. If he and Dani took vows, the adoption would be settled. He'd be free to leave, but Dani wouldn't be free at all. She'd be tied to him until he came back or she had the marriage annulled. They wouldn't consummate the union. He wouldn't even kiss her again.

Once he found Johnson, he'd come home. He'd be free to make the marriage everything Dani dreamed it would be. Cozy talks and morning coffee. Children of their own… Beau stopped himself from going down that road. If he thought too long about loving Dani, he'd go to her and drop to one knee. He'd ask her to marry him for real, then regret it every time he saw the color pink. Tonight he'd tell Dani about Scott's suggestion. If she agreed, he'd make arrangements for the ceremony. A judge would marry them without questions, but Beau wanted Josh to do it. This would be a marriage in name only until he caught Clay, but the vows mattered to him.

Before he spoke to Dani, he wanted to clear the plan with Josh. He headed for the barn to saddle his horse. T.C., well fed from milk and hunting mice, lay asleep in a pile of straw. Beau envied the cat to the point of sinfulness. The feline had a soft bed, food in his belly and four females who scratched his ears. Beau liked living on the farm. He had a reason to get up in the morning and went to bed satisfied with a day's work. What more could a man ask? Nothing…except peace of mind.

He saddled his horse, led it into the yard, then went to find Dani. He didn't like leaving her alone on the farm, but more than a week had passed since he'd ridden with Dawes. He felt certain Johnson had either left to sell the stolen horses or holed up somewhere to plan another raid. Even so, Beau wouldn't be gone long. He'd have a word with Josh, visit Wallace and be home by supper.

He found Dani behind the house, scrubbing the collar of his shirt with a vengeance. The dirt didn't stand a chance. Neither did Beau's heart. With wisps of hair sticking to her neck and her cheeks flushed, she couldn't have been prettier. Beau surveyed the yard and saw Emma hanging a pinafore on the clothesline. In the garden he saw Esther digging in the dirt and Ellie pouring out a bucket of rinse water.

The girl had a sly look in her eyes. Before he could speak, she touched her finger to her lips, signaling him to stay quiet. Being fond of mischief himself, Beau winked at her.

Tiptoeing, Ellie snuck up behind Emma and splashed the dregs of the bucket on her older sister.

Emma cried out in shock.

Ellie dropped the bucket and took cover behind Beau. Showing no fear—a fact that warmed him—Emma grabbed a second bucket, the one at Dani's feet, and charged at them. Ellie had been armed with a cup or so of water. Emma had two gallons and wanted revenge. She got it by dousing Ellie. Beau got caught in the crossfire.

Dripping wet, he laughed. "You're going to regret that, young lady!"

Emma grinned. "Now you don't need a bath!"

"No, but Esther does." Beau indicated the little girl in the garden. "I think she's eating bugs."

Groaning, Ellie and Emma went to fetch their sister. Beau turned to Dani. Her eyes were focused square on his chest. Her expression made his heart pound.

Looking down, she went back to scrubbing the shirt. "You're as wet as I am."

"Almost."

Blotches of water had turned the white apron to a dull gray. Beau looked in the tub where he saw more of his clothes. Dani worked hard. She deserved the best life he could provide. That meant securing the adoption and settling his score with Johnson.

He rested his hand on the edge of the tub. "I have to go to town."

She stopped scrubbing. "Why?"

He didn't want to mention Scott's visit. "I have to see Josh."

She raised her eyes. "Is something wrong?"

"Not a thing," he said. "Do you need anything from town?"

She smiled. "Butterscotch?"

Dani liked sweets. He'd buy a pound of the candy, maybe two. He felt generous these days, as if he couldn't give her enough. He'd be leaving in a few days. That called for gifts for the girls, something special for Dani. They deserved more, but trinkets were the best he could do. After promising to be home for supper, Beau went back to his room to change his shirt, climbed on his horse and rode to the parsonage.

As he neared the house, he saw Josh in front of the church with a brush and a can of paint. Half of the front wall looked new. The other was weathered and worn from the sun.

Beau dismounted and called a greeting.

Josh looked over his shoulder. “Perfect timing. Grab a brush.”

“I can’t stay.”

“So what’s up?” Josh kept painting.

Beau felt like a louse for not helping, but the thought of whitewashing the church left a sour taste. In Denver, he’d pounded nails and hauled lumber. God might have noticed his efforts, but he hadn’t cared enough to save Lucy.

“Come on down,” Beau called.

“You come up.”

Josh could be stubborn. If Beau had to shout, so be it. “Something’s come up with the adoption.” He told the minister about Miss Lange’s concerns about Dani. “I’m sure you can see the problem.”

Beau hoped Josh would put the pieces together and bring up marriage. Instead the minister dragged the brush up and down. To Beau, each stroke felt like a mile. He wanted to arrange the wedding and be on his way. Josh acted as if he had all the time in the world. “How can I help?”

Beau tried to sound matter-of-fact. “We need a marriage certificate.”

Josh stopped the brush at the highest mark, then brought it down with a long swipe. He put it in the bucket, then faced Beau. “That’s an odd way to ask me to marry you and Dani.”

“It’s a marriage in name only.”

“I see.”

“This is the surest way to give Dani and the girls a real home.” Beau heard his pleading tone. He’d begged just once in his life—for God to save Lucy. The answer had been no and he’d never done it again.

Josh ambled across the porch and sat on the top step. "Has Dani agreed?"

"I haven't told her yet."

"I see." Josh's eyes drilled into him.

Beau widened his stance. "Will you help us or not?"

"I have a question for you."

"Go ahead."

"How does a fake marriage give Dani a real home?"

Beau should have seen the fight coming. Josh took marriage seriously, but he'd also been unpredictable. He made some couples wait a year for his blessing. For others he spoke the vows the same day. Beau didn't need Josh's help. He and Dani could go to the courthouse, but he wanted the minister to understand. For Dani's sake, he wanted Josh's approval.

Beau wished he'd picked up the paintbrush. "It's a legal arrangement, nothing more."

"What'll you tell the girls?"

"Nothing."

"What's Dani supposed to say when men come calling?"

"She'll say no." Beau didn't like the thought of other men at all. "We have feelings for each other. I'd stay if I could."

"You can."

"You don't understand."

"I think I do," Josh replied. "You love Dani and the girls. You want to provide for them. Is that right?"

"Yes."

"You also want to see Clay Johnson hang."

Beau nodded.

"You've figured out how to have it all. You tie up the woman you love in an empty marriage, get revenge against Clay, then come home and expect her to be happy about it."

Beau felt sucker punched. He hadn't considered Dani's feelings at all. "If she wants an annulment, I'll give it to her."

"And that will fix things?" Josh looked incredulous.

"It's all I can do."

"It's flat-out stupid."

Beau didn't want to hear a rant, but he'd knocked on the door and Josh had swung it wide. The minister came down the steps, hooked his thumbs in his trousers and got in Beau's face.

"This plan is so selfish I can't believe *you* conjured it up! If you marry Dani in name only, you'll break her heart. Both today and every night she goes to bed alone. You *know* what marriage means. Dani doesn't, not yet. I'm not going to ruin her hopes with a big, fat lie."

"It's not a lie," Beau said. "It's an answer."

"A bad one."

Josh started to pace. "I'm not naive, Beau. People marry for all sorts of reasons. Not everyone's head over heels in love. Sometimes marriage is born out of need and the love comes later. But what's got to be at the foundation—always—is truth."

"I *am* being truthful."

Josh's expression turned mild. "I don't think you are."

"What do you mean?"

"Do you really want to leave?"

"It's necessary."

"Says who?"

Right and wrong seemed plain to Josh. Beau saw gray mist. It didn't matter, though. He lifted the reins from the post. "My mind's made up."

"So change it. Raise your nieces and make Dani your wife. Give her all the things she needs."

Beau thought of the butterscotch he planned to buy. She deserved far more. A husband. A partner. A man who'd sit next to her in church. The smell of whitewash filled his nose to the point of sickness. The church looked brand-new. He wanted that freshness for himself, but paint only covered the marks of time. It didn't remove them. Beau turned to his horse.

Josh gripped his arm. "Stay. Marry Dani, but do it right."

"I can't."

"You won't."

How could Josh say such a thing? He'd buried Lucy. Beau swung onto his horse. "Thanks for nothing."

Josh kept talking. "Clay stole Lucy from you. Don't give him Dani, too."

Beau tasted bile. "I want *justice*."

"Then let God have His way," Josh insisted. "He's far smarter than you."

"He had His chance. It's up to me."

"Is that so?"

Beau frowned. "What are you getting at?"

"You've been chasing Clay Johnson for five years and he's still on the loose. Clay's not that smart. Either you're a lousy lawman or God's keeping him a step ahead of you."

Beau often had the same thought. In five years, he'd caught twenty-two men. Why not Clay? Sometimes he imagined God baiting a hook and jerking it away. The thought made him furious.

He glared at Josh. "If you won't do the ceremony, I'll get a judge."

"Suit yourself." The minister went up the stairs and picked up the brush. "I'll be around if you need me."

Beau clicked to his horse. He still had candy to buy, but he felt pulled to the Silver River. Maybe Wallace had news… Maybe Johnson was close enough to kill. Tasting bile, Beau rode to the wrong side of town. As he neared the saloon, he looked for Harriet Lange's detective. He had no intention of avoiding the man. He wanted to fight and the man who'd been spying on him was a worthy target.

Seeing no one, Beau dismounted and went into the Silver River. He smelled chili and thought of the graybeard with the bad teeth. Beau didn't want to become that man, but he could see the signs. Without Dani and the girls, he had nothing.

Wallace came out of the back room. "It's been a while. Where've you been?"

"Around."

"Coffee?"

Beau nodded, then watched as Wallace poured. The barkeep set the mug in front of Beau, then took something from a drawer. He rested his closed fist on the counter, then opened his fingers to reveal a bullet. "Someone left this for you."

Beau saw the caliber. Lucy's pink dress flashed before his eyes. Only Clay Johnson would leave a bullet for the rifle that had killed Beau's wife. He pinched the casing until his thumb ached. "Who left it?"

"Some fellow with dark hair. I've never seen him before. He said to give it to you, that was all."

"Did you tell Dawes?"

"First thing, but he didn't act concerned. He said bounty hunters brought trouble on themselves."

Beau couldn't believe his ears. "What about the raid at the Rocking J?"

"He thinks the thieves are long gone. He said the bullet was your personal business."

"Fool," Beau muttered.

Wallace wiped a glass. "Do you know who left it?"

"No, but I know what it means." Johnson had sent him a summons. "When did he leave it?"

"Last Saturday."

The night of the social… If Beau had come to the Silver River instead of watching fireworks, he'd have seen the man for himself. With his palm warming the casing, he made a decision. Tonight he'd offer Dani a marriage in name only. Tomorrow they'd take vows in front of a judge. He'd be out of Castle Rock by noon. With a little luck, he'd be home in a week. The other possibility, that he'd be doomed to wander for five more years, made him ill. Either way, Dani and the girls would be secure.

Smoke stung his eyes. He loved Dani, but he hated Clay Johnson even more. The truth shamed him, but as Josh had said, it couldn't be denied.

Beau put the bullet in his pocket, paid for the coffee and walked out of the saloon. At the store he bought three pounds of butterscotch, dolls for the girls and the one thing he'd sworn not to buy. A ring for Dani. He picked a silver band with a pretty blue stone that matched her eyes. Someday he'd put a gold band on her finger. For now, silver and blue would have to do.

Dani worried every minute of Beau's absence. The instant he mentioned Pastor Josh, she'd sensed trouble. When he walked into the house with enough butterscotch for a year and toys for the girls, her worry hardened into fear. Supper didn't ease her heart. She'd expected him to be quiet as usual. Instead he was charming to them all. With the girls giggling and Dani enjoying his praise, the meal couldn't have been more normal.

The girls washed the dishes and went upstairs, leaving Dani alone on the porch. She could see a light in Beau's room and was tempted to knock on his door. Before she could decide, he strode across the yard. He'd shaved, something he usually did in the morning. He'd also put on his best shirt.

"It's a nice night," he said. "Let's take a walk."

"Sure."

As she came down the steps, Dani considered Beau's behavior. He'd gone to town to see Josh. He'd come back with candy, gifts and a secret. Her heart beat with the rhythm of a waltz. Her mind raced to reasons a man spoke in private to a minister.

With the moon lighting the way, Beau hooked his arm around her waist and guided her down the path to the stream behind the pasture. Full of snowmelt, it tumbled over rocks and made deep pools. When they reached the bank, Dani crouched and dipped her hand in the water. Her fingers tingled.

Beau cleared his throat. "I brought you here so we could speak in private."

Dani blushed. "It's a lovely night."

He looked nervous. It charmed her until his eyes glinted with irritation. "I have bad news about the adoption."

The tingle from the stream turned to a burn. Dani pushed to her feet. What a fool she'd been to expect talk of love. Putting aside thoughts of rings and her ivory dress, she faced Beau. "What happened?"

She listened as he described Trevor Scott's visit. With every word, her anger grew. She didn't care about Miss Lange's opinion of *her*, but Beau deserved respect, even kindness. For the sake of his nieces, he'd stayed in Castle Rock. He'd done it for her, too. How much longer would he stay? Afraid to ask, Dani looked upstream and said a silent prayer.

Please, Lord. Show me what's right. Protect the girls and show Beau You love him. You know my heart. You know what's best. Amen.

Beau stepped to her side. "That's the bad news. There's good news, too."

"There is?"

"Scott had a suggestion."

Dani turned her head. Her eyes landed on Beau's shoulder. She saw strength. It made her brave. "What is it?"

He kept his eyes on the stream. "If we got married—"

"Married?"

"In name only, of course."

"I see."

Dani blinked and saw her wedding gown. Earlier she'd imagined it touching her skin. She'd felt a ring on her finger, but Beau hadn't offered that kind of marriage. "I don't know what to say."

"It sounds crazy, but Scott has a point."

Dani huddled in her shawl.

Beau crossed his arms. "If we got married, the adoption would be secure. Harriet Lange couldn't even sneeze at us."

Dani liked the sound of "us," but he didn't mean it the way she did. "What about you?"

"I'm leaving."

"For how long?"

"As long as it takes to find Johnson."

Dani wished she hadn't asked. She turned to the stream and dipped her hand into it. The cold jarred her senses but failed to numb her feelings.

Beau stepped up behind her. "Once the adoption's settled, you can get an annulment."

Not once in her dreams had she even thought that word. She understood the principle. An unconsummated marriage wasn't a marriage at all, but what about her feelings? If he thought she could stop loving him, he'd lost his mind. Dani bit her lip to hold in an angry remark. Lecturing Beau—even telling him she loved him—wouldn't make a whit of difference.

He touched her arm. "I have to say something else."

"Not now."

He leaned closer. "I care for you, Dani. Johnson's close. If things go as I hope, I'll be back in days, not months."

But what then? Would killing Clay bring Beau peace? He thought so, but Dani had her doubts. Beau had been fighting God as much as he'd been battling Clay. Dani loved him, but she feared for the future. She also feared losing the girls.

Sighing, she faced Beau. "When do I have to decide?"

"The sooner, the better."

"So you can leave."

He nodded.

"That's why you went to see Josh," she said. "To arrange the ceremony."

Beau frowned. "He won't do it."

Dani respected the pastor for his choice. She felt the same inclination, but she had to consider the girls. Before she made a decision, she wanted to hear Josh's opinion for herself. She looked at Beau. "I'll give you my answer on Sunday."

He looked peeved. "That's three days."

"I need time. Surely—"

"Fine. Sunday it is."

With her heart breaking, Dani led the way back to the house. Of all the marriage proposals she'd received, this one was by far the saddest.

Chapter Sixteen

Beau drove Dani and the girls to church on Sunday. He'd been on his best behavior after visiting Scott, but he had no intention of stepping inside the building. He had nothing more to say to Josh, and he doubted Adie would take his side. Dani alone controlled the future.

Beau stopped in front of the church, helped Dani down from the seat, then watched as his nieces went to Miss Adie's Sunday school in the parsonage. Dani walked up the steps without looking back. If she had, she'd have seen Mr. Paisley Vest with his son, a young boy who needed a haircut. The kid saw the girls, spoke to his father and scampered off to be with Miss Adie. Beau wondered if she still used puppets to teach Sunday school. He'd helped her once. He'd been a bear named Jed and had hammed it up.

Stifling that memory, he sat in the surrey, waiting for stragglers to pass before he lifted the reins. The last couple went inside the building, but no one closed the door. When the pianist struck the opening chords of "Blessed Assurance," Beau sat paralyzed. The hymn carried him beyond the moment, beyond his hate. When the music ended, a man read a Psalm filled with utter anguish. Beau understood every word. When it ended, the pianist struck a ponderous chord. Beau recognized "A Mighty Fortress Is Our God." He'd always liked that hymn. He found himself mouthing the words until the last note.

In the sudden silence, he heard Josh's deep voice.

> "Who is among you that feareth the Lord, that obeyeth the voice of His servant, that walketh in darkness, and hath no light?"

Beau felt a chill. He'd feared God his entire life. He'd obeyed the Lord's commands, yet here he was…walking in darkness with no light.

Josh kept going.

> "Let him trust in the name of the Lord and stay upon his God."

Beau held in a curse. He'd trusted God and where had it gotten him? In the weeks after Lucy's murder, he'd prayed every day. He'd waited for God to bring justice and received nothing. Beau wanted to leave, but Josh's voice had the same quality as the familiar hymns. It struck chords that rang true. Instead of lifting the reins, Beau stared at the open door.

> "Behold, all ye that kindle a fire, that compass yourselves about with sparks."

How many fires had Beau kindled on the open trail? At least a thousand, maybe more. Alone, he'd stared into the blaze, imagining the moment he'd find Clay Johnson. Those flames had encircled his soul.

Josh deepened his voice.

> "Walk in the light of your fire, and in the sparks that ye have kindled. This shall ye have of Mine hand; ye shall lie down in torment."

Rage poured through Beau's veins. He'd walked by the light of his own fire for five years, but only because God hadn't given him so much as a matchstick to light the way. At night, when Beau had lain devastated on the hard ground, God hadn't done a thing to help him. The stars had winked in the cold sky, reminding him that somewhere Clay Johnson was seeing the sky and Lucy wasn't.

Beau stared at the church. The white boards glistened in the sun, forcing him to squint. Who needed a God that would whitewash a murder? Not Beau. Before Josh could utter another word, Beau picked up the reins. As soon as he married Dani, he'd be riding out. He needed supplies, so he headed for town.

Dani had come to church needing a special touch. For three days, she'd agonized over Beau's proposal. She could justify a marriage in name only in her mind, but she couldn't settle it with her heart. She didn't know what to do, and Heaven had remained silent. God, she believed, was listening. He just wasn't talking.

He seemed to be talking now, though. The instant the organist played "A Mighty Fortress," Dani felt like a child at her father's knee. Her own father had been a man of few words, but he'd loved that hymn. After the music, Pastor Josh opened his Bible and read from Isaiah. His impassioned tone reminded her of the nights her father had read out loud to his family. He finished the verses, closed the Bible and looked right at Dani. "Some of us have hard decisions to make today. We know what we want. We know what other people want. But what does God want?"

Dani sat straighter. Josh had described her situation exactly. She didn't want to be selfish or naive. She wanted to make the right decision no matter the personal cost. As Josh told stories about people in the Bible and the choices they'd made, she hung on to every word. When men trusted God, they triumphed. When they acted on their own, as Moses had when he'd struck the rock, they paid a price. She didn't want to make that mistake.

Pastor Josh locked eyes with her. "How do we know God's will?"

Dani thought of the obvious answers. Prayer. Reading the Bible. But what did a woman do when her choice would put others at risk? A marriage in name only struck Dani as wrong, but it would protect the girls. Saying no to Beau would protect her integrity, but the girls could end up in Minnesota.

The Reverend held her gaze. "God hasn't spoken through a prophet like Isaiah in a lot of years, but He speaks to each of us every day. Sometimes He whispers in our ears. Sometimes He gives words to a friend. I've found when people say God's not talking, most of the time—not all—they're not listening. Why is that? The Creator of the Universe loves us. He sent His son to lead the way to eternity, yet we hold on to our ideas, our plans, as if we know everything. Why do we put faith in ourselves when the Lord knows far more than we do?"

He gave the congregation a minute to think.

"The answer's simple. We're afraid of the dark. We stop trusting God and start our own fires. They give off light but just for a while. They give us heat but only in a tiny circle. Those fires die out, leaving us colder than ever. Sometimes our fires do the opposite. They burn out of control and destroy our lives. Either way, we end up back in the dark."

Josh paced some more. "So what do we do? How do we manage when the night stretches beyond our understanding and we're as scared as children? The answer's both easy and hard. We wait for the Lord to light the way. We walk by faith, not sight. That's what this story is about."

The words settled into Dani's soul. If she married Beau, she'd be doing it out of fear, not faith. Her body tensed with dread. She couldn't marry him, not even for the sake of the girls. God, she had to believe, had a better plan than a deceitful marriage. Her stomach was doing flips, but she had peace about her decision. Tonight she'd tell Beau she couldn't marry him. She didn't think he'd leave without finalizing the adoption, but she couldn't be sure. Refusing his offer could cost her everything, but so could taking it. She wanted a real marriage, not a compromise.

With that thought, the light of her own fire went out completely, plunging her into the dark. She couldn't speak to Beau until the girls were asleep, which meant she had all afternoon to imagine a lonely train ride back to Wisconsin. As the organist played the closing hymn, Dani prayed for strength.

Tired of pacing by the stream, Beau glanced up at the moon. After church, Dani had whispered that she'd reached a decision and would speak to him after the girls went to bed. Ever since, he'd been tense and wary. He almost wished he'd gone inside the church to hear Josh preach. Back in Denver, the man's sermons had been like a match to tinder. Beau's faith had caught fire, but Lucy's death had doused those flames.

Beau didn't know what the Reverend had said today, but Dani had come out with her chin held high. She'd looked ready to fight, but with whom? Beau or Harriet Lange?

He didn't know, but he'd find out soon. Twenty minutes ago, she'd asked him to meet her at the stream. He'd been grateful to walk alone. Every minute he spent with her made him doubt his decision to leave. To stay focused, he kept the bullet in his pocket. He had it now. He also had Dani's ring. If she said yes, he'd give it to her tonight.

Beau sensed movement, turned and saw Dani walking along the fence. The sight of her stole his breath. She had on a pale blue dress, one he'd never seen before. It matched her eyes. She'd taken time with her hair, too. Instead of a coiled braid, she'd pinned it up in a smooth knot. Had she dressed up for the occasion? He hoped so but chastised himself. They were conducting business, not a courtship.

"Hi there," he called.

"Hi."

"Nice night," he said, sounding casual.

Dani didn't seem to hear him. She stopped two feet away and raised her chin. "I've reached a decision. While I appreciate your offer, I can't agree to a marriage in name only."

Beau had been in a lot of fights but never one with so

many players. Dani had Josh on her side, Adie, the girls and Lucy, too. In a bizarre twist of irony, Beau's only ally was Clay Johnson. That fact should have told him something, but he turned a deaf ear to the small voice of his conscience. He couldn't leave until the judge finalized the adoption. He had to make Dani change her mind.

"Why not?" he asked.

She stood ramrod straight. "It would be dishonest."

"It's necessary. Think of the girls."

"I am."

His blood started to burn. "What about Harriet Lange? She's already causing trouble."

"It doesn't matter."

"Of course, it matters!" Beau thought she'd lost her mind.

Dani laced her fingers at her waist. "I have to believe that God has a plan. He knows what's best."

"He doesn't give a hoot!" The only man Beau trusted these days was himself. He didn't want to antagonize Dani, so he tried to sound mild. "I know this is hard for you, but a marriage in name only is the easiest way to settle the adoption."

"Maybe, but it's not the best way."

"Dani—"

"I can't, Beau." Her voice shook. "It would be wrong in so many ways."

"Name one."

"We'd be telling three girls that marriage is nothing but a business arrangement."

"They don't have to know."

"So we'd be lying."

She had a point, but so did he. "This arrangement is no one's business but ours."

"I'd be lying to myself and to the girls." Her voice dropped to a murmur. "I can't do it."

He shook his head in disgust. "Josh must have preached a barn burner of a sermon."

"He made me see the truth."

"What truth?"

"God has a plan for us, and it doesn't include a fake marriage. If we do it *His* way, not ours, He'll see us through."

Beau's jaw tightened. "Like He saw Lucy through?"

"I'm so sorry—"

"*Sorry* doesn't cut butter."

If she told him to set down his hate, he'd walk away. He half hoped she would. He'd have a reason to storm off. Instead she looked at him with heartfelt sympathy, then held out her hand. Beau stared at her fingers. Long and strong, they reminded him of the twigs a bird used to build a nest. She deserved a nest of her own. He wanted to build that home and share it with her, but he couldn't. If he took her hand tonight, he'd never leave.

Dani crossed the two steps between them and cupped his face in her palms. "There's another reason I can't say yes."

"Don't say it."

"I love you, Beau. You know that."

"Dani—"

"I want everything God has for us."

Beau knew what it meant to love a woman, to carry her burdens and share her dreams. He'd have died in Lucy's place. He felt the same way about Dani. He also knew how it felt to be loved. A woman's smile made a man stand tall. It made him stronger and better in ways no man understood. Beau felt that love now. It was time to be a better man—Dani's man—but he couldn't do it without denying his own need for justice.

He jerked away from her touch. "Maybe you're right."

Her eyes filled with hope. He hated himself for what he was about to say, but it couldn't be helped. "You need a husband, a man who won't leave. I'm not that man."

"You could be."

He clenched his teeth. He loved this woman, but he couldn't tell her how he felt. Leaving would be hard enough without an empty promise.

She stepped closer. "I want you to be that man."

Beau breathed in the scent of her hair. If he reached for her, she'd be in his arms. He'd kiss her and tell her he loved her…then where would they be? He had to finish his business with Clay. He reached into his pocket, pinched the bullet and raised it for her to see. "Johnson left this for me."

Her eyes filled with revulsion, then fear. "He wants to kill you."

"The feeling's mutual."

"Stay," Dani pleaded. "We can have a good life. We can—" She bit her tongue, then turned her back and gave a dry laugh. "I've never begged in my life. I'm embarrassed."

Beau touched her shoulder. "Don't be. I'm honored." He wanted to turn her around but settled for looking at every hair on her head. "I have to go, Dani. With a little luck, I'll be back soon and free to say what's in my heart."

Her shoulders quivered. "When are you going?"

"The instant the adoption's final."

"But Harriet Lange—"

"I'll visit Scott tomorrow. Maybe he can speed things up."

"I see."

"No, you don't." He sounded as hoarse as a mule skinner. "I'd stay if I could. I'd do a lot of things."

"I'm sorry," she replied. "I wish I could make things easy for you."

"I feel the same for you."

Either one of them could have ended the standoff, but at what cost? If Dani sacrificed her integrity, she'd stop being the honest woman he loved. Beau could let Clay live, but he'd still be consumed by bitterness. He couldn't change his own heart. He didn't have that ability.

No, but God did. Beau heard the voice in his head. He knew God's ways. He also had Clay Johnson's bullet in his pocket. It promised finality, the only kind Beau trusted. He saw the choice as plain as day. He could put his faith in God or in a brass casing filled with gunpowder. Of the two, gunpowder was more reliable.

"Let's go home," he said to Dani's back.

She squared her shoulders, then gave him a sad smile. "You can always change your mind."

"So can you."

He followed her to the house, walking in the dark because God had hidden the moon.

Chapter Seventeen

"When will we know about the adoption?"

Emma had asked the question, but all three girls looked up at Dani from across the kitchen table. They were making cottage cheese the way Dani had made it a thousand times, the way her mother had taught her. Yesterday she had clabbered the milk. Today she and the girls were squeezing the whey and adding salt to taste. She'd serve it with tonight's supper.

Emma looked at Dani expectantly. The question deserved an answer, but Dani didn't have one. She kept her voice mild. "Mr. Scott's working on papers for the judge."

The girls didn't know anything about Harriet Lange or Beau's marriage proposal. Earlier she and Beau had explained that Mr. Scott had to write up a contract to make the adoption permanent, and that a judge had to approve it. They didn't mention Harriet Lange's threats to fight in court.

Emma squeezed the cheesecloth. Whey dripped into a bowl. "It's taking a long time."

"Too long," Ellie added.

"I think so, too," Dani said. "But it can't be helped."

Had she just lied? Last night she'd refused Beau's offer. They could have been married today if she'd compromised. Dani didn't doubt her decision, but she feared the consequences. Last night, lying in the dark, she imagined Harriet Lange slapping Emma.

"Dani?" Esther sounded older. She hadn't sucked her thumb in days.

"What is it, sweetie?"

"I'm scared the judge will say no."

"Me, too," she answered. "We have to trust the Lord to know what's best."

The girls had grown up with prayers and Bible stories. They knew Jesus for themselves. With time, their faith would grow. Dani hoped to help them down that path. No matter what happened, she wouldn't waver or doubt. Life, she decided, was like the curds she'd spread in a pan. Yesterday they'd been raw milk, but heat and time had turned them into something even better. She was trusting God for the same miracle in her life.

Did I make the right choice, Lord?

She thought of her favorite Psalm and the sparrows that had a nest for themselves. She wanted a nest of her own, a home with children and Beau for a husband. Last night she'd helped him with the milking. Over and over, she'd hummed "Amazing Grace." When they'd finished, Beau had muttered something about grace being wasted on Clay Johnson and had left the barn.

Dani finished covering the tray of curds and set it aside. A knock on the front door startled all four of them. Praying Trevor Scott had come with good news, she wiped her hands on her apron. "I'll get it," she said to the girls.

As she stepped into the front room, she craned her

neck to see through the window into the yard. She saw a horse and buggy with a driver, a well-dressed man she didn't recognize. She thought of calling for Beau, but he and Howie were repairing the fence on the far side of the meadow. Dani opened the door and saw an old woman in a gray traveling suit. She stood five feet tall and had pretty white hair. Dani was a regular at church now and had been invited to join a sewing circle. The woman at her door, with her round face and dainty nose, seemed familiar. Perhaps she'd come with another invitation.

Dani smiled. "May I help you?"

"I believe you can," she said sweetly. "Is this the Morgan farm?"

"Yes, it is."

"I'm Harriet Lange."

Dani had expected the girls' aunt to be a crone. This woman had laugh wrinkles and twinkling eyes. Slightly plump, she had the pillowy softness of a grandmother. Dani felt sick inside. What right did she have to deny this woman her nieces? None, but appearances could be deceiving. Dani glanced at the woman's hands and saw fancy gloves. Did the silk cover fingers capable of a tender touch or a hand that would hurt a child?

"I've taken you by surprise," the woman said gently. "May I come in?"

"Of course." Dani wished she had on a better dress. She opened the door and motioned for Miss Lange to step into the front room. "We were just making cottage cheese. If you'd give me a minute—"

"Of course." The woman scanned the room.

"Please, sit down." Dani motioned to the divan, but Miss Lange walked to the hutch displaying Beth's collection of teacups. The girls, especially Emma, treasured the reminders of their mother.

The older woman picked up a cup with a silver rim. "I gave this to Beth when she married Patrick."

Dani didn't know what to say. "It's lovely."

"So was my niece."

She'd clipped her words. Dani heard a hint of bitterness and wished she knew more about Beth's side of the family.

Miss Lange set the cup back in place. "I'd like to see my nieces."

"I'll get them." Dani hurried to the kitchen where the girls stood by the door, frozen like scared rabbits.

"Your Aunt Harriet is here." She focused on Emma. "Go get Uncle Beau."

Emma ran out the door. With Ellie and Esther hovering at her side, Dani filled the teakettle, smoothed her hair and looked out the window to the spot where Patrick and Beth lay side by side. She no longer loved him, but she wondered what he and Beth would want for their children. Beau had a piece of paper on his side, but Miss Lange seemed genuinely concerned. She'd taken a long train trip, one that had to be expensive and tiring. Dani's own happiness hinged on the adoption, but she couldn't think about herself. Only the girls mattered now.

Aware that Esther had put her thumb in her mouth, Dani said a silent prayer. *You know what's best, Lord. Your will be done.*

She poured two cups of tea, set them on a tray with milk, sugar and a plate of cookies. She picked it up and turned to the girls. "I'll be with you."

Ellie shook her head. "I want to wait for Emma."

"Me, too," said Esther.

Dani saw no reason to force them. She carried the tray into the front room and set it on the table. Miss Lange smiled her thanks, sipped, then looked carefully at the sugar bowl. "That belonged to my mother."

So much history… If Dani kept the girls, the details of their family heritage would be lost. Was adopting them wrong after all? Had God stopped her from marrying Beau because these children belonged in Minnesota, surrounded by their mother's family?

Miss Lange peered through the doorway. "I heard you speaking to my nieces. Where are they?"

"Waiting for Emma."

"Posh!" said Miss Lange. "Girls, come out here this instant. I want to see you."

Dani bristled. She used a gentler tone when she called the cows. Hoping to reassure two frightened children, she made her voice friendly. "It's okay. Come and sit with us."

They walked into the front room side by side. Ellie's pinafore had a blotch of whey from squeezing the curds, but at least she had on a dress instead of coveralls. Esther, wide-eyed and frightened, saw her aunt and jammed her thumb in her mouth.

Miss Lange huffed. "Child, take your *thumb* out of your *mouth* right now. For goodness' sake, you'll give yourself buckteeth!"

Esther whimpered. Ellie put her arm around her sister's shoulder. Holding tight, she looked to Dani for help.

"Miss Lange—"

"That child needs discipline," she said. "If you smack her hand, she'll stop that bad habit. Mark my words, Miss Baxter. Spare the rod and spoil the child."

Beneath Miss Lange's silk gloves, Dani felt sure she'd see gnarled fingers that would slap a child at will. She wanted to throw the woman out of the house, but losing her temper wouldn't help the children. Dani shot Ellie a look that promised she'd fight, then faced Miss Lange. "The girls have had a difficult time."

"That's no excuse for sloppy behavior." Miss Lange sounded almost cheerful. She focused again on her nieces. "Our little thumb-sucker must be Esther. You must be Eleanor."

"I'm Ellie."

"That's a silly name," Miss Lange said. "Eleanor suits you."

It didn't suit the tomboy Dani knew.

Miss Lange looked the child up and down. "Your pinafore has a stain. Perhaps you'd like to go upstairs and change?"

Ellie's eyes glinted. "Yes, ma'am. I would."

"You're excused."

Esther, clinging to her sister's hand, turned to follow Ellie upstairs. Miss Lange huffed. "Esther, you're a big girl now. Let go of your sister's hand."

Esther did as she'd been told, but her lower lip trembled. As Ellie turned to argue, Dani caught her eye and motioned for her to go upstairs alone. She hurried to Esther, hugged her and told her she could sit with the grown-ups and have a cookie.

"Really?" Esther asked.

"You sure can."

No way would Dani allow Miss Lange to pick on a frightened five-year-old. She led Esther to the divan and gave her the treat. Dani didn't believe in bribing children for good behavior, but Esther needed a distraction. When they sat, Esther climbed on Dani's lap. The child's weight numbed her legs, but she let her cuddle.

Harriet Lange arched her brows. They looked like gray worms. "Miss Baxter, you're spoiling these girls."

"I disagree."

The woman harrumphed. "Of course, you do. You're a child yourself."

"I'm twenty-two."

"You're barely older than Emma."

Dani had heard enough. "Why are you here, Miss Lange?"

"To take custody. You have no claim to these children. As for Mr. Morgan, he's not fit to raise them."

"You don't know him," Dani countered. "You don't know *me*, either."

"I know that children need a firm hand."

Ellie's footsteps pounded down the stairs. She walked into the front room wearing coveralls and boots.

Miss Lange gasped. Before Dani realized what she intended to do, the woman marched up to Ellie and raised her hand. "Why, you disrespectful—"

"Stop!" Dani plopped Esther on the divan and ran to Ellie, who had already jumped back.

Miss Lange stayed still.

Gripping Ellie's shoulders, Dani glared at the older woman. "You can't have these children, Miss Lange. You're not fit to raise them."

The old lady turned and arched one brow at Dani. "And *you* are?"

"Yes."

"You're no more qualified than I am, Miss Baxter. You're a single woman. So am I. I have the wisdom that comes with age. What do *you* have?"

Dani had what mattered most. She had a heart full of love and the faith to believe God would see them through this hard time. She flashed on the girls seated at the supper table, smiling and feeling safe. She saw herself at one end, loving them as her daughters. She also saw an empty chair at the head of the table, Beau's place if he chose to fill it. Dani would do anything—give up her dreams, live with that empty chair—to protect the girls from Harriet Lange. Her heart ached with the sacrifice she was about to make, but it had to be done.

She raised her chin. "I can give the girls a real home. Mr. Morgan and I are getting married."

Ellie gasped. "Really?"

"Yes." Dani smoothed the child's hair. She and Beau would be married in the eyes of the law and Harriet Lange. Someday, if he made peace with himself and Clay Johnson, they'd be married in the eyes of God.

Miss Lange narrowed her eyes. "When is the wedding?"

"As soon as we can arrange it."

"This is rather sudden, isn't it?"

Dani said nothing.

The woman's eyes glimmered with suspicion. "Is this marriage legitimate, Miss Baxter? Or is it a scheme to hold on to the life you expected from Patrick?"

Dani's cheeks flushed red. She couldn't lie, but neither would she hand this woman a weapon to be used against her. She sealed her lips.

"I see," said Miss Lange.

The back door opened and slammed shut. Dani looked down the hallway, where she saw Beau pacing like a man on fire. His gaze shifted from Harriet Lange to Ellie and finally to Dani. "What's going on?"

"I told Miss Lange about our engagement."

Beau put the pieces together in an instant. He'd already seen the buggy and the Pinkerton's agent. Miss Lange, it seemed, had come to make threats and Dani had protected the girls with the only weapon she had. She'd sacrificed herself, her dreams and her hope for a real marriage. Her goodness shamed him. Spoiling for a fight, he looked at Harriet Lange. She seemed mild enough in her gray frock, but he didn't like the set of her mouth. The lawman in him sensed trouble.

"Good afternoon, Miss Lange. I'm Beau Morgan."

"I know who you are, sir."

"Why are you here?"

"To take my nieces, of course."

"I have custody."

Her cheeks turned pinker. "May I remind you, Mr. Morgan. Your attorney approached *me*. He made it clear that you wished to return to your *business* as soon as possible. He offered me money—a goodly sum—if I'd take all three girls."

Beau regretted that offer more than he could say. He also wished Emma, Ellie and Esther had never heard it. The three of them had clustered on the divan and were hanging on to every word. They needed to know he'd keep them safe, so he looked at them one by one, then said, "That offer was a mistake. It's off the table." He turned back to Miss Lange. "I'm keeping custody."

"Forgive me, Mr. Morgan, if I'm not convinced of your sincerity. Your engagement to Miss Baxter seems rather fortuitous."

The woman smiled like a grandma but hissed like a snake. Beau crossed his arms. "Our plans are none of your business."

Her expression turned smug. "I'll ask you the same

question I asked Miss Baxter. When are you getting married?"

"Soon." Beau didn't know what Dani had said. If he contradicted her, Miss Lange would use the confusion against them.

"In church?"

Beau answered by crossing his arms. "It's none of your concern."

"I'll be blunt, Mr. Morgan. I don't believe for a minute that you intend to provide a home for my nieces. My detective tells me you've been a bounty hunter for five years, and that you make a good living. I suspect Miss Baxter has charmed you into giving her what she wants."

The irony left Beau speechless. Instead of making Dani's dreams come true, he'd denied her what she desired most—a family, a husband, a home.

Miss Lange's expression turned smug. "When it's settled, you'll go back to bounty hunting. Is that correct?"

How could the truth be so right and wrong at the same time? Beau couldn't deny the facts, but he had the power to change them. He could stay in Castle Rock. He could marry Dani. The thought burned like fire, but so did his hate for Clay Johnson. He had to send Lucy's killer to eternity and he had to do it now. Not in a month or a year, but by Sunday so he could take Dani to church. To protect the girls, he had to marry her. To protect Dani, the marriage had to be real. That meant bringing Clay to justice and coming home for good.

Beau's next words were for Harriet Lange, but his eyes stayed on Dani. "If Miss Baxter will have me, we'll get married this Sunday."

"In church?" Dani asked.

Beau nodded.

Questions burned in her eyes. He had to explain his plan, which meant getting rid of Harriet Lange. He turned to the gray-haired witch. "Are you satisfied?"

"I suppose."

"Miss Lange?" Dani had spoken.

"Yes?"

"I love your nieces. I'll take good care of them."

To Beau's surprise, the old lady looked at the girls with misty eyes. If they hadn't exchanged words, he'd have thought she was kind. She even smiled at Dani. "Just remember what I said. 'Spare the rod and spoil the child.'"

Not in Beau's book. Judging by Dani's expression, something ugly had happened. Emma's mouth tightened and Ellie's eyes burned with venom. Esther whimpered, then jerked her thumb out of her mouth. The sooner this woman left the house, the better off they'd be.

"That settles it," he said.

Miss Lange smiled as if nothing had happened. "Of course I'll be attending the wedding."

Beau wanted to tell her to stay away, but he couldn't stop her from attending church.

Dani squared her shoulders. "Of course."

Miss Lange looked at the girls with something close to tenderness. "I know I seem harsh, but I want what's best for you." She eyed Esther, who was still cowering, then looked Ellie up and down. She sighed at the sight of Emma, then faced Beau. "If there's no wedding, you'll hear from me."

"I'd expect so."

Eager to be rid of her, Beau opened the door. She went to the buggy, where the detective helped her onto the seat, then lifted the reins. Not once did the old woman look back. That told Beau everything he needed to know about

Harriet Lange. She had the discipline of a general. She'd keep her word about attending the wedding.

He closed the door and turned to Dani. Before he could speak, his nieces ran to him and hugged his waist. Beau dropped to a crouch so he could reach Esther. Her skinny arms twisted around his neck and he picked her up. He tousled Ellie's hair and kissed the top of Emma's head. He'd slain a dragon for them. Now he had to slay one for Dani and himself.

He set Esther down. "I need to speak with Dani. How about checking on T.C.?"

As obedient as lambs, the girls went outside. Dani looked weak in the knees, but she stayed on her feet. "What just happened?"

"Let's sit down."

He guided her to the divan. On the table he saw a cold pot of tea, the only evidence Harriet Lange had turned their world upside down. Beau dropped down next to Dani, then touched her back. "Are you all right?"

"I don't know."

His throat felt like gravel. "I meant what I said about Sunday."

"But how? Josh won't marry us."

"He will if my heart's right." Beau hurried his words. "Clay's waiting, Dani. I can feel it. I'm going to hunt him down and be done with it."

"Oh, Beau."

"No matter what, I'll be back by Sunday."

When she closed her eyes, he imagined her thinking a prayer and dreaded what she'd say next. When she raised her face, he saw the woman who'd told him no at the stream.

"What if you don't come back?" she asked.

"I will. I promise."

Patrick had once said the same thing and they both knew it. She stood and walked to the window. "I want to believe you, Beau. But how can I? Anything could happen."

He stayed silent.

Dani stared through the glass at the rutted yard. "We have to consider the girls."

"I am."

"Then stay." She turned to him. "You weren't here when Harriet Lange made Esther cry. She almost slapped Ellie. How can you leave, knowing she'd take them away?"

Her voice cracked. Beau wanted to throw the blasted teacups against the wall.

"Stay," she said gently. "Let the authorities worry about Johnson."

"I can't."

Her eyes burned with defiance. "I'm not sure I want to marry you."

"Why not?"

"Because you hate Clay Johnson more than you love me."

Beau pushed to his feet. He loved Dani. He'd just asked her to marry him, but he'd done a poor a job of it. He'd been so choked with hate for Clay that he hadn't told her that he loved her. He wanted to say the words now, but he knew they'd sound hollow.

His throat hurt. "You and Clay… It's apples and oranges."

"It's still a choice."

She went to the door and opened it wide. "Go on, Beau. Leave. Do what you have to do."

"All right," he said. "Get your things."

"What do you mean?"

"I'm taking you and the girls to town. You can stay with Josh and Adie."

"Absolutely not!"

"It's not a choice."

"Oh yes, it is! I'm staying right here."

Beau raked his hand through his hair. "I can't leave you and girls unprotected. Clay could be watching right now."

She raised her chin. "If you're that worried, stay."

"Six days," he insisted. "That's all I'm asking. Even if I don't find Johnson, I'll be back."

"Then what?" she demanded.

"We'll cross that bridge when we get to it."

Dani had a gleam in her eyes, the one he remembered from the day of the milking contest. It filled his mind with harmonies and the rhythm they'd found at the dance. He couldn't stop himself from loving her, nor could he hold back a need as profound as air.

Protect this woman, Lord. Be with her. I'm a low-down cur bent on revenge. She deserves a man with a clean heart. Keep her safe, Lord. Give her joy.

With that silent prayer, Beau crossed a line. He wasn't willing to listen to God, but he hoped God would listen to him. He wanted to quit hating Clay Johnson but didn't know how. Dani had become an obstacle, one he had to shatter.

"Get packed," he said with a growl.

Before she could argue, he stormed out of the house. He had to get ready for Johnson, so he strode into his room, where he kept his guns, ammunition, ropes and irons. He lugged his things into the barn, saddled his horse and tied down the tools of his trade. In the past, he'd have touched Lucy's handkerchief and recalled her goodness. He couldn't do that today. Dani had the hankie. In its place Beau carried the bullet from the Silver River. He touched the casing but found no comfort, only warm metal and a reminder of the ring he'd bought for Dani. He'd grown accustomed to carrying something that linked him to what he knew to be good, so he went back to his room, fetched the ring and put it in his pocket. Lucy's hankie had reminded him of what he'd lost. The ring stood for what he hoped to gain.

He had six days to hunt down Clay Johnson. On the seventh, Beau would be in church with Dani. God willing, he'd find peace at last.

Chapter Eighteen

Dani called the girls inside, told them Beau had to take a short trip and explained they'd all be staying with Pastor Josh and Adie. They went upstairs to pack a few clothes, leaving Dani to finish the cottage cheese. She packed it in a crock to take to the parsonage, made sandwiches for Howie who'd be tending the cows alone, then put a change of clothing for herself in the satchel she'd carried on the train.

Her decision to stay with Josh and Adie had nothing to do with Beau's order. Dani needed to sort her thoughts, and Adie would listen all night if that's what it took to understand why Beau couldn't set down his hate for Clay Johnson. If Dani understood, maybe she could forgive him for leaving. As things were now, she felt wounded and alone. Earlier, she'd put Lucy's hankie in her memory box. She took it out, pressed it in her Bible and added both things to the satchel. She carried it to the front porch where she saw Beau's horse. A looped rope hung from the saddle, a leather scabbard held a rifle and the saddlebags bulged with provisions. Beau came out of the barn, leading the horse and surrey. Dressed in his duster and the faded clothes he'd worn the day they'd met, he looked like Cain.

As he lifted Esther into the surrey, Dani strode across the yard. Saying nothing, he helped her on to the seat. She took the reins, watching as he swung his tall body into the saddle, pulled his hat low and clicked to his horse. He might have been clicking to her, too, but Dani paid no attention. She had to see Adie and Josh.

When they arrived at the parsonage, Adie, as always, opened her home to them. Josh saw Beau and led him to the stable for a private talk. Ten minutes later, with Dani watching from the window, the men came out of the building. Josh headed to the parsonage. Beau rode west without a goodbye.

She hated parting company with unkind words between them, but she had nothing more to say. She'd begged Beau once and wouldn't do it again. He knew the stakes, yet he'd chosen to go his own way. Dani stood at the window, watching him grow smaller with every stride of his horse. When he turned to a speck against the mountain, she let the curtain flutter back into place.

Pastor Josh opened the door. "How are you?"

"Angry. Afraid."

"Let's sit outside."

Dani followed him out the door and took the chair facing the church, the same one she'd used her first day in Castle Rock. She'd been grieving, confused and doubtful of God's plan in her life. Now she felt sure of the Almighty's hand but feared for everyone she loved.

Josh walked past her to the railing and crossed his arms. "Beau's an arrogant fool, but I understand why he's going after Clay."

"You do?"

"If someone harmed Adie, I'd be hard-pressed to practice what I preach."

Dani wanted an ally. "But we have to forgive."

"True." Josh sat next to her. "But we're not made that way. We need God's mercy. It's knowing we're forgiven that gives us the grace to forgive others."

"Beau will never forgive Clay Johnson."

"Maybe, but God already has."

Dani understood the cross. Christ had died to set men free. Ever since, human beings had battled between their sinful desires and the goodness of God. As the soul prospered, the flesh died. Until a man surrendered, he lived with constant conflict. A lump pushed into her throat. "Beau's at war with himself, isn't he?"

"And with God."

She thought of Josh's sermon about a man walking by the light of his own fire. He'd described Beau that day. She didn't want to be that kind of woman. "I have to stay strong."

"You will." Josh sounded confident.

"It's a matter of faith."

"And knowing God loves Beau even more than you do."

Dani almost smiled. "Loving him can be a trial, that's for sure."

Josh looked pleased. "Most men are. Beau's stubborn and willful, just the way God made him. The Lord knows how we feel."

"Beau wants justice."

"So does the Lord."

"It's hard." Dani's voice quavered.

"We have a hard God," Josh replied. "He loved us enough to sacrifice His own son. I don't know what

Beau's going to face in that canyon, but I know with certainty he's not riding alone."

The minister's faith gave Dani comfort, but she had to face the facts. Beau had gone to war. Soldiers died.

Dani's stomach clenched. "I feel so helpless."

"We're not. We can pray."

Before they could bow their heads, Adie opened the front door. "Josh? We need you. The girls are frightened."

Dani pushed to her feet. "Where are they?"

"In the front room," Adie replied. "I'm hoping Josh will tell us a story."

"Sure," he answered.

Dani followed Adie into the house, with Josh ushering both women through the door. She saw the girls on the divan. Stephen had gone to a friend's house, but Adie had set up his checkerboard. It sat untouched on the table. As Dani settled next to Emma, Josh and Adie took their usual chairs. They traded a look that made Dani ache.

"Adie thinks we need a story," Josh said to the girls. "What'll it be?"

Ellie spoke up. "The one Dani told us."

"About Daniel and the lions," Emma explained.

"Good choice," Josh said. "Who knows how it starts?"

"I do," Ellie said. "The king put Daniel in a cave."

"Was he alone?"

"There were lions," Esther said. "*Hungry* ones."

"They roared," said Ellie.

"That's right." Josh sounded serious. "Was Daniel afraid?"

The girls said nothing. Dani took the lead. "I know he was, because I'm scared right now."

"Me, too." Emma's voice trembled. "What if Uncle Beau doesn't come back?"

Josh looked at the girls one at a time, then focused on Emma. "Your uncle isn't in a cave with a real lion, but he's locked up with something just as big."

"What?" Ellie asked.

Josh looked to Dani for help. The girls had heard about their Aunt Lucy, but they didn't know she'd been murdered. How did an adult explain hate to a child? Dani didn't know, but she understood love. She wanted the girls to understand that part of Beau. "Do you remember about your Uncle Beau being married?"

The girls nodded.

"Your Aunt Lucy died because of a bad man in Denver." Dani skipped the details. "The bad man got away. Your Uncle Beau wants to put him in jail."

Esther looked puzzled. "Is he in a cave with the bad man?"

"Sort of," Dani answered. "He can't stop being angry. That feeling roars all the time, just like a real lion."

Josh chimed in. "Who knows what happened to Daniel?"

"I do," said Emma. "God put the lions to sleep."

"He kept Daniel safe," Josh said. "I'm praying the bad things around your uncle go to sleep just like the lions."

"Me, too," Dani said.

Josh looked at Adie. "Feed our guests, but I won't be having supper tonight."

"Why not?" Ellie asked.

"We can pray in all different ways," he said. "We can talk to God out loud or think in our heads. Tonight I'm praying with my whole body. Every time my belly growls, I'll be saying a prayer for your uncle."

Dani looked at Adie. "I won't be eating, either."

"That's three of us," Adie said. "We'll spend the evening on our knees."

"Four," Emma said. "I can pray, too."

"Five," said Ellie.

"Seven!" cried Esther.

Emma frowned at her. "You mean six."

"No, I mean seven. I'm counting Jesus."

Dani's eyes misted. How could God not honor the faith of a child?

Beau rode down the same trail he'd traveled with Dawes, only farther. Pressing his roan, he went past the cave where he'd seen the ash and straight down the throat of Sparrow Canyon.

He'd been riding for three days now, almost four. If he turned around this instant, he'd get back Saturday afternoon. He'd have time to clean up and have a word with Dani before they took the vows Beau now feared he wouldn't be able to keep. He loved her. He'd be faithful to her in body and mind, but his soul would still be hunting Clay.

Clay… When had Beau started thinking of the outlaw by his given name? He tried to pinpoint the moment but couldn't. Neither could he decide whether to go forward or turn around. He had a few more hours of daylight. The ride back, all downhill, would be quicker than the ride up the canyon, but he had to consider the weather. The afternoon had turned sultry. The still air promised a storm, anything from a drizzle to a downpour.

Beau looked carefully at the sides of the ravine. The trail cut deep into the mountain about ten feet above the streambed. Boulders secured the base. Even if the stream flooded, a distinct possibility if it stormed, Beau felt certain he'd be secure. Looking ahead he saw a bend around a ridge. He knew from Dawes that Sparrow Canyon opened up beyond that spot. A meadow would offer grass and fresh water, the perfect place for Johnson to linger. One more mile… Beau couldn't turn back now. He nudged the roan up the trail.

A hundred yards later, he heard thunder. Clouds boiled over the mountains and turned the sky gray. A drop of rain hit his hat. Another landed on his gloved hand. Ten feet below him, Sparrow Creek rushed past the boulders like an animal on the run.

Common sense told Beau to go home, but he ignored the nudge. He had to see around the next bend.

Lightning flashed across the sky. Thunder rolled through Beau like an erratic heartbeat. One minute it pounded; the next it stopped with a hint of death. Rain fell in buckets. He flashed on Emma dousing him in the garden, but he kept going. Below him, Sparrow Creek had picked up speed. A new roar filled Beau's ears. Unlike the thunder, it came from the earth itself. Suddenly skittish, his horse backpedaled. Beau looked up the ravine and saw a wall of water, six feet high and rolling over itself, rushing down Sparrow Canyon.

He had considered the possibility of a flash flood, but he'd expected two or three feet at the most. He'd never seen anything as high and deep and wide as the water coming straight at him. He believed the trail would hold, but his horse didn't have the same hope. The animal balked. At the same instant, a boulder the size of a melon tumbled down the mountain. It caught the roan's back leg and knocked the animal half off the trail. To give the horse a chance, Beau rolled out of the saddle. He smacked facedown in the mud and lost his wind.

The roan's churning legs cut away at the mountain. Beau started to slide. The horse found purchase and heaved itself to safety, but Beau couldn't get a toehold in the mud. He slid a foot, then another. Water filled his boots. The current sucked at his knees.

He lost his gloves and clawed with his bare hands. When he found a stringy root, he gripped it. No thicker than a pencil, it bore his weight. He found a second root, thicker this time, and pulled his legs out of the water. A boulder tumbled past his head. He looked up, saw another ready to fall and slithered on his belly until he reached a stable part of the trail.

With his sides heaving, Beau pictured red apples, little girls with pink cheeks and Dani in a white dress. He heard milk hissing into a bucket and imagined her rose-petal lips. Rocking with the rhythm of their one dance, he called himself a fool. He had business to do with God and he knew it, but movement up the canyon caught his eye.

Peering into the rain, fading now, Beau saw a man on a gray horse. He hadn't seen Clay Johnson in five years, but he knew the slope of his shoulders. When the outlaw went for his rifle, Beau cursed the weapon that had killed Lucy.

Johnson raised the Winchester to his shoulder.

Beau went for his Colt.

Clay squinted down the barrel.

Beau took aim and pulled the trigger.

Nothing happened. No recoil. No smoke. Only the empty click of a misfire. Beau cursed himself for a fool. Mud and rain had dampened the gunpowder.

Looking at Clay now, he expected to die. If the rifle shot didn't kill him, the ride to Castle Rock would. He'd grieve Dani and the girls. He'd die without telling her that he loved her. She'd go back to a lonely life in Wisconsin, and the girls would be doomed to tea parties with Harriet Lange. This moment, Beau realized, had been born of his own arrogance. Life and death—only God could make the call. Beau knew that now.

Have mercy on me, Lord.

He saw the next two seconds the way he'd seen Lucy die. Every detail came alive. Water dripped from Clay's hat and splashed on his glove. His oilskin poncho turned from black to silver and cast a bluish light on his hollow cheeks. His eyes, black and empty, couldn't have been more lifeless. Beau could have choked on the irony. He'd spent five years chasing a man who was already dead, at least on the inside.

He steeled himself for the bullet, but it didn't come. No blast. No smoke. Only the rush of the stream as Clay lowered the weapon. Wordless, the outlaw turned his horse and disappeared into the mist, leaving Beau to wonder what in the world had just happened.

A hundred yards up the canyon, Clay slid off his horse, dropped to his knees and threw up. When he'd seen Morgan crawling in the mud, he'd instinctively aimed his rifle. He'd told himself to fire, but his finger hadn't pulled the trigger. Not even when Morgan shot first had Clay been able to do the deed. Why not?

With mud soaking his knees, he thought about Goose and Andy driving him crazy with their taunts. Spring had filled the canyon with pink flowers, and Lucy Morgan had haunted his dreams every night. This morning when a horse went missing, Clay had ridden down the canyon alone to search for it. The gray had good instincts, but he'd missed Ricochet so much he'd cried. All morning, he'd wondered if horses went to Heaven.

Chilled to the bone, he hung his head. If Morgan's gun had fired, he'd have made the trip to eternity himself. He'd have been worm food. Dry bones. Maybe something worse… A man being eaten alive for all time in the belly of Reverend Blue's whale. But Clay hadn't died. Neither had he killed Beau Morgan. He'd done something right. How could that be?

Blinking, he thought of his mother reading him Bible stories. He could see her brown hair piled on her head. He smelled bread and candles and recalled one night in particular.

Jesus loves you, little boy. I do, too. But I have to leave.

Why, Mama? Where are you going?

She'd coughed until she was breathless. She'd done that a lot in those days. He recalled the handkerchief she kept tucked in her sleeve, a cotton square dotted with blood. A month after that talk about Jesus, she'd died of consumption. Recalling her stories now, Clay knew she'd gone to be with the Lord. Blinking, he recalled asking her a question.

Can I go with you?

Not now, but someday.

She'd prayed with him. He'd been a mere boy, but he'd understood that Jesus loved him. After his mother's death, for a time he'd gone to church with his cousin, but that had changed when Clay got his height and muscle. He'd been an angry young man and life's temptations had called to him. He'd put his boyhood prayer out of his mind, but then Ricochet died. Now he couldn't stop thinking about eternity.

"Help me, Lord."

As he bowed his head, he expected to feel the whack of his father's fist breaking his nose. Clay had done terrible things. He'd stolen. He'd maimed. He'd killed six men. Worst of all, he'd shot Lucy Morgan in the back. He didn't deserve to live, yet here he was…breathing in gray mist when Beau Morgan's bullet should have sent him to eternity.

Someone had spared his life and it hadn't been Beau Morgan. Startled, he opened his eyes. Where did a man look for God? In the sky with its promise of Heaven? In a meadow full of pink flowers? Clay didn't know, but he understood a simple truth. God had been in the canyon. For reasons Clay couldn't grasp, the Almighty had spared his life. He'd spared Morgan, too. The men had made a trade of sorts. An eye for an eye…a life for a life. As a boy, Clay had learned about another trade. Jesus had died for Clay's sins. But what about now? How did a man wash a woman's blood from his hands? The answer came in a whisper.

A man told the truth.

He paid a price.

If need be, he faced the gallows. Jesus had paid for Clay's sin for the sake of eternity, but Beau Morgan had a right to justice in the here and now. Clay had the power—the need—to give it to him. Feeling as if he'd set down a fifty-pound stone, he climbed on the gray. Rain had washed the dust from the canyon. Grass glistened as if covered with morning dew. Not even the smell of mud filled his nose as he neared camp, where Goose and Andy were splitting a pint of whiskey.

Goose saw him and frowned. "Where have you been?"

Clay ignored him. "I'm leaving."

"You're *what*?" Goose said.

"We're splitting up."

"Why?" Andy asked.

"I'm done."

Goose looked him up and down, taking in his muddy hands and the stains on his knees. "Did you fall and hit your head?"

"I'm sick of it," Clay said. "I've had enough."

Andy chimed in. "What about the horses? We agreed to a three-way split."

"I'll buy you two out."

Clay wasn't worried about going to jail for stealing horses. He figured he'd hang for Lucy Morgan's murder. Returning the horses was a matter of pride. It made him feel like a man.

Andy knocked back a slug of whiskey, then wiped his mouth on his sleeve. "How much?"

Clay named the amount of cash he had in his saddlebag.

"We'd get more in Durango," Goose said.

"You don't know what you'd get," Clay said mildly. "This is a sure thing."

Goose wrinkled his brow. "I don't get it. What are you going to do with the horses?"

"Give 'em back."

Andy knocked his head as if he had wax in his ears. "What'd you say?"

"I'm taking them back." Clay didn't want his partners to think he'd gone soft. A man had his pride. "I've got a plan. I just saw Morgan."

"Did you kill him?" Andy asked.

"I had a misfire." Not the gun. Clay's finger had failed.

"If I were you, I'd head south. This fight is mine." So was the surrender.

Goose grunted. "I'm sick to death of this canyon."

"Me, too," said Andy.

Clay crouched by the fire and poured himself a cup of hot coffee. It tasted good. He hadn't enjoyed coffee in a long time. Feeling generous, he looked at his former partners. "I'm giving you two a chance for a clean start. Take it."

"What about you?" Goose asked.

Clay smiled. "I'm going to church."

Andy smirked. "You're going after Morgan."

"That's right."

Only Clay knew he'd be going unarmed. He knew from Andy that Morgan would bring the woman and the girls to church, but that he wouldn't stay. Clay planned to slip into a back pew, listen to Reverend Blue and even sing a hymn or two. When the service ended, he'd turn himself in for Lucy Morgan's murder. It didn't matter if he hanged or went to prison. He'd found peace.

Chapter Nineteen

Beau had been gone for six days when Dani heard a knock on the parsonage door. She opened it with a prayer on her lips. *Please, God... Let it be him.*

Instead of Beau's broad shoulders, she saw Howie Dawes with mussed hair and windburned cheeks. His horse stood behind him, glistening from a fast ride.

"What's wrong?" she asked.

"It's Daff. Her udder's hot."

"Come inside."

As she held the door, Adie came out of the kitchen. "What happened?"

"It's one of the cows." Dani explained Daff's history. "We could lose her. I have to go."

More than Daff's milk was at stake. Dani had spent hours with Adie, praying and trying not to worry about Beau. What if he didn't come back? She'd been with the Blues for six days. Tomorrow would be the seventh. Without Beau there would be no wedding. Without a wedding, she'd lose the girls. Dani would fight for them, but it would take a miracle for a judge to rule in her favor. If she lost a cow now, she wouldn't stand a chance against Harriet Lange.

Dani hoped Adie would understand. "The girls and I need to go home."

Her brow creased. "What about Beau?"

"He knows where to find us." Dani turned to Howie. "Would you hitch up the surrey?"

"Sure."

As the boy walked to the stable, Adie touched Dani's arm. "Will we see you in church tomorrow?"

"I'll be in church, but I won't be getting married."

"Don't give up," Adie said.

"I already have."

She'd spent six days worrying about Beau and praying for him. She'd begged God to keep him safe and give him the peace he couldn't find on his own. She'd prayed for the girls, too. They needed protection, the kind she couldn't give alone. Beau had let them down, but Dani had her faith. The future belonged to God, not Beau Morgan.

"There's still time," Adie said. "If he—"

"It's too late."

Dani went to the backyard to fetch the girls. When she told them they were going home, no one said a word. They said goodbye to Stephen, then went to the guest room to gather their things. The girls understood the impact of Beau's absence as well as Dani. Harriet Lange loomed like a specter.

Dani had more than a few harsh words for the man who'd put them in this position. Even if he made it back in time for a wedding, she had doubts about the marriage. Beau had chosen Clay over her. His decision hung like a cloud, but so did Harriet Lange and her threats. With two bad choices—marrying Beau in spite of her resentment or saying no and fighting Harriet Lange—Dani thought of Josh's sermon about a man walking by the light of his own fire. Right now, she had no light at all.

As she guided the girls into the yard, Howie drove up in the surrey. "Are you ready, Miss Baxter?"

"Yes. Thank you."

He climbed down from the seat and took off his hat. "Would it be okay if I went to see my ma?"

At the sight of Howie's eager expression, Dani felt her heart crack with longing. She wanted children who'd call her mama and be eager to see her. "Of course. In fact, you can stay home until Monday."

"Thanks!" The boy climbed on his horse and rode off.

Adie hugged Dani. "Stay strong, honey. Beau's a mere man, but the Lord won't let you down."

The girls said goodbye to Adie and climbed into the surrey. Dani steered for home. The future loomed like a long night, but she wouldn't be facing it alone. Even in the dark, the Lord was at her side.

Beau stopped to rest his horse, but he didn't indulge in real sleep or eat more than jerky. At the spot where he'd gone fishing with the girls, he washed the mud from his face and arms. His clothes were caked with it, but he didn't bother to change. He had to get home to Dani. He had amends to make and he knew it.

What he *didn't* know concerned Clay Johnson. Why hadn't the man fired his rifle? Beau didn't know and the lack of understanding troubled him. Johnson had shown him the ultimate mercy. He'd spared Beau's life. Beau wouldn't have been so kind. All the way down the trail, he'd thought about the look in Johnson's eyes. If it hadn't been for his promise to Dani, he would have followed Clay into the canyon.

But for what purpose? Beau didn't know what to think. Was he supposed to be grateful to Clay for sparing his life? He wouldn't have been there if Clay hadn't killed Lucy in the first place. It added up to one big tangle. Beau intended to marry Dani and stay with her, but a piece of his soul had ridden into the mist with Clay. He didn't feel at peace with God, either. The Almighty had saved his life twice, but Beau still hadn't hit his knees. Had justice been served? God had spared Clay, too. Beau wanted finality. Instead he had more loose ends than ever.

Riding into Castle Rock, he tasted his old bitterness. Johnson and his men were still wanted for raiding the Rocking J, so Beau rode to Dawes's office and went inside. Instead of the sheriff, he saw Ace at the desk with his feet up. The deputy saw Beau and smirked. "You're a mess."

Beau ignored the barb. "I found Johnson."

"Where?" Ace slammed his feet to the floor.

"Deep in Sparrow Canyon."

"Did you get him?"

Beau grunted. "My weapon misfired. He got away."

"Tough luck," said the deputy. "Though it might explain Baylor's horses."

"What about them?"

"They showed up at the ranch. All of them except a gray."

Beau knew the horse and who was on it, but he didn't know why Clay and his partners had turned the horses loose. He'd expected them to ride south. It didn't make sense. Beau didn't think Clay would come after him, but he couldn't be sure. That moment in the canyon had been crazy, even unreal. For three days, Beau had struggled to make sense of it. Maybe Clay had done the same thing. Maybe he'd changed his mind about killing Beau. Maybe he liked the chase and had let Beau live just to torture him.

"Where's Dawes?" he asked.

"Having supper." Ace stood and reached for his hat. "He needs to know what you saw. I'll take you to his house."

"You tell him." Beau headed for the door.

He had to get to Dani. He didn't expect Johnson to go after her, but neither could he rule it out. With the sun hovering above the hills, he urged the roan to the parsonage. Expecting to stay for supper, he led the horse into the stable, where he saw Josh's rigs but not the surrey. Beau could think of only one reason for the surrey to be missing and he didn't like it. Dani had gone home. Leaving his horse saddled, he strode to the parsonage.

Josh stepped through the front door. Crossing his arms, he looked Beau up and down. "Did you crawl out of a grave or dig one?"

"Both."

"I take it Clay's dead."

Beau chuffed. "Not hardly. Where's Dani?"

"At the farm."

"I told her to wait here."

"One of the cows had a problem. She went to tend it."

Beau worried about Daff. As he turned to leave, Josh kicked a chair away from the wall. "Sit down."

The minister wasn't prone to foul moods, but he was in one now. Beau raised one brow. "Is that an order?"

"Only if you want to get married in *my* church."

"It's God's church."

"And he put me in charge."

Thanks to Harriet Lange's interference, Beau needed Josh's approval. He feared for Dani's safety, but the odds of Clay beating him to the farm were slim. Beau had ridden hard. The Rocking J lay on the opposite side of Castle Rock. Beau strode up the steps and sat. "Make it quick."

"What happened?" Josh stayed on his feet.

Beau told his friend about the flood, the mud and the misfire. "He could have killed me, but he didn't."

"What do you think stopped him?"

"I don't know."

Josh lowered his voice. "It was a long time ago, but I planted seeds in Clay's life. He knows about God's grace. Maybe those seeds finally sprouted."

Beau flashed on Clay lowering the gun. Josh's explanation made as much sense as Beau's belief that Clay had gone crazy. Either way, the outlaw had lost his mind. For good or for evil? It remained to be seen.

"You know the parable," Josh said. "Some seeds fall on good soil and grow. Others break through but die when the weather turns bad. Some don't grow at all. Frankly, Clay struck me as hard soil, but dirt changes with time and bad weather. So does a man."

Beau thought of the storm in the canyon. Rain had softened the earth to mud. Water had moved boulders and ripped away trees, changing the course of the stream and its very nature. The rain had blurred Clay, as well. Even with his gun in hand, he'd seemed as formless as his name.

Josh's voice dipped low. "Be careful, Beau. I hope Clay's changed, but we can't know for sure. Nothing's more dangerous than a man who sees the light and then turns his back."

Beau had made that choice when he'd left Dani. She'd offered the light of love. He'd chosen the darkness of his hate and had almost destroyed their future. He'd never make that mistake again. Before this night ended, he'd have that overdue talk with the Lord. In the meantime, he needed Josh's help.

"I know about turning my back on the light," Beau said. "I'm home to stay."

"That's good news."

"It'll be even better if you'll agree to marry Dani and me."

Josh looked at Beau with an expression befitting the seriousness of the question. "Do you love her?"

"I do."

"Will you raise your nieces as your own?"

"You bet I will."

"I have another question," Josh said. "A hard one."

"Ask it."

"Do you love them enough to forget Clay Johnson?"

Beau hadn't seen the question coming. "I won't lie, Josh. I'm not done with it. I don't understand what happened in that canyon, but I know one thing. Dani matters more than Clay."

"You need to tell her."

"I will," Beau answered. "Will you do the ceremony?"

"When?"

"Tomorrow."

Josh's eyes twinkled. "I'll do it, but I'm not the one you have to convince."

Beau pushed to his feet. "Say a prayer. I have some apologizing to do."

"It's good practice." Josh chuckled, but Beau barely heard it. He'd already gone down the stairs.

He didn't have to push his tired horse. When they reached the road to the farm, the roan went into a lope. As they passed the charred pine, Beau thought of his brother. This journey had begun with his passing, but it wouldn't end in sorrow. Silently he promised Patrick that he'd love Emma, Ellie and Esther like his own children. He didn't mention Dani. She was Beau's alone.

He rode into the yard and swung down from his horse. The front room and kitchen were dark. So was Dani's window. Beau looked up to the second floor where he saw a lamp burning in the girls' bedroom. He pictured Dani reading them a story. Someday she'd read to a child carrying his blood.

That is, if she'd have him.

Needing to care for his horse, Beau headed for the barn. As he gripped the reins, his gaze landed on a gold triangle stretching from the open door. A shadow—Dani's shadow—inched into the light. He took in the length of her body, her crossed arms, the tilt of her chin as she spotted his horse. She stopped at the threshold. "You're back."

Beau stopped, too. "I kept my promise."

"I see."

"If you'll have me, Josh will marry us tomorrow."

Dani didn't know what to say. Six days ago, Beau had left the farm as Cain, a man doomed to wander without God. He'd come back for the sake of the children, but had he come back for *her*? Even more important, had he come back with the piece of his soul he'd given to Clay Johnson? Looking at him in the moonlight, she couldn't tell. He'd pulled his hat low, hiding his eyes but not his ragged jaw. His duster, blotched with mud, looked as stiff as his spine.

She wiped her hands on her apron. "I'm still milking."

"I'll help."

"It's not necessary. Buttercup's the last one."

Beau's brow creased. "Josh said a cow was sick. Is it Daff?"

"She's fine." As soon as Dani had arrived at the farm, she'd checked the fussy cow and found nothing. Daff, she decided, had missed her family. Looking at Beau, she wondered if he felt the same way.

He pushed back his hat. "I'm glad Daff's okay."

His concern riled Dani beyond reason. If he thought he could waltz home and she'd fall at his feet, he had some more thinking to do. Dani went back in the barn, sat on the stool and went to work on Buttercup. She had her back to the door, but she heard the clop of hooves as Beau led his horse to its stall. He set the saddle on a rack with a thud, then brushed his horse and gave it a measure of oats.

Dani lifted the milk bucket and carried it to the can. While she poured, Beau took the cow to the pasture. She covered the milk cans, then went outside to wash the bucket. She finished the chore, turned and saw Beau in the doorway, blocking her from putting the pail away. She wasn't in the mood for his high-handed ways.

She marched up to the barn. When he didn't move, she planted her shoes across from his muddy boots. "I need to get by."

"No, you don't." He lifted the bucket from her hand, set it inside the door and snuffed out the lamp, plunging them into darkness. Beau touched her jaw. "I love you, Dani. Marry me."

He'd said he loved her, but he reeked of mud, maybe death. He'd left his duster in the barn, but she could still smell the rot. She jerked away. Before she let down her guard, she needed answers. "Did you find Clay?"

"He found me."

"What happened?"

"It's a long story. Right now, only one thing matters. I'm back. I spoke with Josh. He's willing to marry us."

The girls would be safe.

He'd said that he loved her.

Two stars glimmered in Dani's mind, shedding divine light but not enough to show her the way. Had Beau really changed? Had he made peace with God and himself? She smelled the mud and wondered. "I have to know what happened."

With a crescent moon shedding the dimmest light, he told her about the canyon, the flood and the misfire. Her blood chilled with the knowledge that he'd almost died, then warmed with gratitude for God's mercy. The Lord had been with Beau in Sparrow Canyon. Judging by his eyes, he knew it. Two more stars pierced the dark around Dani's heart, but she worried when his lips thinned to a line.

"I won't lie to you," he said. "I'd be glad to see Johnson hang. He spared my life, but I don't know why. I still hate him, Dani. I always will."

She wanted Beau's whole heart, not most of it. What would he do if he caught wind of Johnson in a month or a year? Could she trust him to stay? Promises could be broken as easily as they were made. She watched as he reached into his pocket, then opened his palm to reveal the bullet Clay had left for him. He closed his fingers again, hauled back and threw it as hard as he could into the night.

"That takes care of Clay," he said. "Now for us."

He reached into his pocket a second time. When he opened his fingers, she saw a silver ring with a blue stone. It made a perfect circle. Endless. Complete. She imagined him taking her work-roughened hand, seeing the calluses and the broken nails, the imperfections that came with being human. That's when she knew she'd say yes to Beau in spite of her fear that he'd go after Clay Johnson. She wasn't a perfect woman. She made mistakes every day. Beau would make them, too. Big or small. It didn't matter. Love, as complete as the circle, covered their failings.

He clasped her fingers. "I love you, Dani. No matter what happens, I'll never leave again."

Her heart pounded. "I love you, too."

"Will you marry me?"

"Yes, I will."

He slid the ring into place. Expecting a kiss, she tilted her face to his. Beau answered with a lazy smile. "I want a son. A boy with your blue eyes."

Dani's heart hummed. "I want that, too."

"And another girl." He grinned.

She grinned back.

He kissed her then, a tender brush that made her see stars. A thousand of them—each as bright as the sun—burned away the rest of the darkness, leaving her warm in Beau's embrace. Tomorrow, she decided, would be the happiest day of her life.

Chapter Twenty

Beau walked Dani to the house, kissed her again, then headed alone to the creek. He washed off every speck of mud from the canyon, put on clean clothes, shaved, then sat on a rock. He'd promised to do business with the Almighty and that time had come. With his head bowed, he confessed his arrogance, praised God for His mercy, then looked up and counted the stars. With each one, he thanked the Lord for a different blessing until he reached the one gift he couldn't understand.

Why had Clay spared his life?

Beau had no desire to go after the man, but neither did he have as much peace as he wanted. He'd hated Clay for five years. It would take more than five days to break the habit. Tonight, when he'd touched the bullet, the hate had burned as bright as ever. Even now, with Dani's kiss fresh on his lips, he could feel the old resentment.

A month ago, he'd have raised his fist at the heavens. Tonight he bowed his head. "I want peace, Lord. What do I have to do?"

Beau knew the answer in his gut. He had to forgive Clay Johnson.

"Not in a million years," he said out loud.

The silent nudge to his heart turned into pain, but he could only groan. The Lord was asking too much. Beau wouldn't go after Clay, but neither could he forgive the man for what he'd done. Beau knew he had a problem. His hate for Clay had the potential to stand between himself and Dani. It also made it hard for Beau to see past the stars to the God who'd made them. "I can't forgive him," he said out loud. "If You want me to forgive that scum, I need help."

Irked, Beau gathered his dirty clothes, the bar of soap and his shaving kit. He'd cleaned up as best as he could, but he still felt the grit of his trip. He'd said no when Dani asked him into the kitchen for supper, but he couldn't deny his need for sleep. Exhausted in every way, he headed back to the barn, where he slept until the sun spilled through the window. As if he'd never left the farm, he awoke the next morning and milked the cows. It felt good to do chores and even better to walk into the kitchen, where he saw Dani at the stove.

She smiled shyly.

Beau wanted to kiss her but didn't. They couldn't honor the tradition of the groom not seeing the bride before the wedding, but he wanted everything else to be perfect. Nothing else mattered, least of all his turmoil concerning Clay Johnson.

He eyed the bacon. "Smells good."

She blushed.

Before he could tease her, Emma walked into the room. She saw Beau and gasped. Ellie came up behind her, shrieked and ran to hug him. Esther charged at his knees. Beau looked at Dani and grinned.

She nodded, a silent signal to tell the girls their news.

Just like Josh and Adie, he and his wife-to-be could trade thoughts without a word.

Beau sat down, putting him level with girls. "Dani and I have something to tell you."

All three straightened. Emma looked wary. Children who'd lost a parent learned to be cautious. Beau intended to erase that fear. "We're getting married today."

The younger girls squealed, but Emma stayed serious. "Are you staying for good?"

"I am."

She turned to Dani. "Is it true?"

"It better be." She smiled at him. "I stayed up half the night pressing my dress."

"Can I see it?" Ellie asked.

"Sure," Dani answered. "After breakfast."

As if this were an ordinary day, they sat at the table and ate. While the females chattered, Beau took in the blush of Dani's cheeks, the awe in Emma's eyes and the sight of Ellie and Esther eating oatmeal as if it tasted like ice cream. As a man who'd once lost everything, he knew the value of a single moment. He and Dani would remember this day forever. Every minute counted; every gesture meant more because of the vows they'd take. Nothing would spoil this day. Beau wouldn't allow it.

When they finished eating, the girls cleared the table. He went to his room, where he shaved a second time, put on a suit and fancy tie, then hitched up the surrey and pulled it into the yard. Ellie, dressed for church with a red ribbon in her hair, waved to him. Emma and Esther came out the door, followed by Dani, who had a satchel in hand. She'd done up her hair with white ribbons but hadn't put on her wedding dress. She had it in the bag and would change at the parsonage. He met her on the steps, took the satchel and stowed it in the back of the surrey.

The girls climbed in on their own, but Dani waited for him. When he offered his hand, she took it and squeezed. "This is the best day of my life."

"Mine, too."

He helped her onto the seat, then took the reins. As they pulled out of the yard, Beau felt a mix of joy and tension. Five years had passed since he'd been inside a church. The last time had been in Denver and he'd walked out in the middle of a hymn. He wanted to erase that memory, so he winked at Dani and started to hum.

She heard the first notes of "Camptown Races" and laughed.

The girls laughed, too.

That's how they arrived at the parsonage, a family sharing a moment they'd never forget. Beau halted the surrey at the foot of the steps. As his nieces climbed down, he took Dani's hand. A man didn't kiss his bride before the wedding, but his wife-to-be had a look that made him think about it. Feeling mischievous, he leaned a bit closer. Her eyes gleamed with a dare. Beau moved another inch. So did she.

Their lips were inches apart when Adie opened the parsonage door. "Beau Morgan! Don't you *dare* kiss the bride. At least not yet!"

Laughing, Dani drew back and hopped down from the seat. After fetching the satchel, she ran up the steps, stopped at the open door and blew him a kiss.

Adie hugged Dani, then approached Beau. "I'm glad to see her happy."

"Me, too."

"What about you, Beau?" she asked. "How are you feeling?"

"Good."

"Just good?"

He grinned. "More than good. I'm a happy man, Adie."

"Josh told me about Clay. It's a strange story."

Beau wished she hadn't mentioned it. Just hearing Clay's name stirred up old feelings. He had to put them aside, especially today. When Dani came down the aisle, she'd see love in his eyes. Nothing else.

He forced his jaw to unclench. "That story will have to wait."

"Of course." Adie stepped back. "Go find Josh. He wants a word before the ceremony."

Beau nodded, but he had no intention of speaking with his friend. If Josh mentioned Clay, Beau would be hard-pressed to keep his composure.

He clicked to the horses, then steered to the field where farmers would leave their rigs. He'd brought Dani early so she could dress, but he had a need of his own. It had been a long time since he'd been in God's house, and he wanted a moment alone. He tied the horse, then ambled to the front of the church where he saw the brass knobs shining in the sun.

A sudden dread turned Beau's feet to sand. He'd made his peace with God last night, but he had the terrible feeling his anger was about to erupt again. A month ago, Beau could have left in a snit. Today he *had* to go inside. He'd promised Dani a perfect day and he intended to give it to her. With his hat in hand, he walked into the church.

The building matched the one he'd known in Denver. Seven windows, the width of a man's shoulders and as tall, lined the two longest walls. Sunshine poured in through the glass, casting beams that met on the floor and made a row of diamonds. Two sets of pews waited to be filled and Josh's podium, the same one he'd used in Denver, displayed an elaborate etching of an eagle.

Peace settled around Beau like the blanket Dani had spread for their first picnic. It opened, fluttered down and landed in a perfect square. Beau blinked and tasted apples. He felt God's mercy in the cool air. Divine love abounded in the light. Beau had come home.

Thank You, Lord.

With the prayer on his lips, he raised his eyes to the front wall of the church. In Denver, he'd have seen a wooden cross. What he saw now turned the picnic blanket into a bloody pink dress. Stones of pink rhyolite, the finest he'd ever seen, formed a cross in the center of a gray wall. Someone had polished the rocks to a shine, bringing out veins of red and black.

Bitterness gripped him from the inside and squeezed. He didn't want these feelings. Not now. Not with Dani about to become his wife. He wanted to be rid of them forever, but he couldn't control his reaction. Hate lived in his blood. It pumped from the very core of his being. A horse couldn't change its color. Neither could Beau stop the hatred burning in his gut.

He wanted to walk out of the church and never come back.

He wanted to see Clay Johnson die.

He wanted God to end the pain. A stifled groan tore at Beau's throat. He wanted to fight. He wanted to weep. More than anything, he wanted to be free from his own stupid thoughts. "Help me," he whispered.

The stones stayed silent. Beau spun on his heel and walked out the door. He'd marry Dani in spite of the shiny pink cross, but his heart had gone dark. Struggling to stay calm, he paced to the far end of the porch, as far as he could get from the people arriving for the service. In spite of Beau's scowl, men called out to him and women smiled.

Trevor Scott walked the length of the porch to offer congratulations. Beau shook his hand but said nothing.

Sheriff Dawes said hello.

John Baylor tipped his hat. "Thanks, Morgan."

Harriet Lange saw him and offered a gracious dip of her chin, a sign of surrender. After today, the girls would never have to worry about stupid teacups.

Beau was close to breathing normally when Josh came out of the church. "There you are."

Beau grunted.

Josh's smile died. "Are you as nervous as you look?"

"I'm fine."

"You don't look fine."

"I just need a minute."

Josh lowered his voice. "Memories?"

Beau shook his head.

"Second thoughts?"

"Not a one." His voice rasped. "It's Johnson. He's got me by the throat."

"No, he doesn't." Josh's expression turned as hard as flint. "You're the one who won't let go."

Beau scowled. "I don't need a lecture."

"I don't want to give one," Josh said. "Considering what Johnson did to you, I don't have that right. But there's someone who does.

"'For God so loved the world, He gave His only begotten son… Forgive your enemies as I have forgiven you.'"

Beau's jaw tensed. "I don't want to hear it."

"You think forgiving Johnson's impossible, don't you?"

"It is."

"Not for God." Josh stepped closer. "Are you willing, Beau? That's all that counts. The Lord does the rest."

Before Beau could tell Josh to drop dead, Adie opened the parsonage door and waved.

"That's our signal," the minister said. "Your bride's waiting."

Nothing would stop Beau from making this day perfect for Dani. Not Clay Johnson and not a pink cross. He pushed by Josh. "Let's go."

With the minister in his wake, Beau walked down the aisle to the front row, where he sat alone. The pianist struck the chords to a lively hymn. When the music ended, Josh stepped to the podium.

"Ladies and gentlemen, I have a surprise. Most of you have met Daniela Baxter. I'm pleased to announce that she and Beau Morgan are getting married this morning."

Applause broke out.

Josh signaled to him. "Come up here."

Beau stood and turned to the congregation. Josh signaled to the pianist, who played "Blessed Assurance," Dani's favorite hymn. Someone closed the door. Any minute it would open again and the wedding would begin. Dani would enter in a cloud of white. Thoughts of her calmed Beau's nerves. When the knob turned, his heart soared. Someone cracked open the door, but just a foot. Instead of Dani, he saw a man. And not just any man… Clay Johnson had come to church.

Expecting Dani, the congregation turned to look. No one paid attention as Clay slipped into the back pew. Dawes had never seen him. Wallace didn't attend church.

John Baylor had seen three men in masks. He didn't know Clay Johnson from Adam, but Beau did. So did Josh. The minister gripped Beau's shoulder but didn't speak. The decision to confront Johnson now or stay silent belonged to Beau alone.

Instinctively, he sized up the situation. If Clay had something ugly in mind, the people in the pews were lambs waiting for slaughter. Beau had a two-shot pistol in his boot, but he hadn't worn his gun belt. Dawes carried a revolver, but the man had no instincts.

With Beau watching, Clay squeezed between a matron with a feathered hat and the blacksmith, a man twice his size. He had on a worn shirt and trousers. No hat to hide his face. No coat to hide weapons. When the matron smiled, Clay smiled back as though he meant it. Beau didn't know why the outlaw had come to church, but he felt certain it wasn't for the wrong reasons. As long as he stayed in the pew, Beau could endure the confusion pulsing through him. This was Dani's day. Nothing else mattered.

Unaware of the drama, Adie opened the door wide. The pianist pounded the keys with a new vigor. Esther, holding a bouquet of roses, walked down the aisle with surprising dignity. Ellie followed and Emma came next. The three of them lined up opposite Beau. He didn't know where to look—at Clay or the door where Dani would appear.

The pianist struck the opening notes of a bridal march. The music soared to the rafters, bounced off the walls and filled Beau's head with memories of singing hymns in the barn. He had a new life…a good life. He loved Dani more than he could say. God had saved Beau's soul, but she'd saved him from his hate. No way would he give

Clay Johnson this precious moment. Without a whit of hesitation, he focused on the spot where he'd see his bride for the first time.

Just as he imagined, Dani came through the door in a cloud of ivory and gold. A veil hid her eyes but not her smile. Her dress, a mix of lace and silk, made him think of snow melting in the sun. When she'd first arrived at the farm, he'd complained of too much purity and light. Now he cherished it. When Dani reached his side, he touched her elbow and smiled. Together they faced Josh.

When he saw the minister's scowl, Beau remembered Clay Johnson. "It's okay," he whispered. "Do the ceremony."

Dani didn't understand. Why would Beau tell Josh to go ahead with their vows? Had Harriet Lange threatened to protest the wedding? Dani glanced at Beau and saw nothing but confidence. It settled her nerves until she saw Josh peering over Beau's shoulder. She wanted to turn but couldn't. Every eye in the room was focused on her back.

The minister cleared his throat. "Dearly Beloved, we're gathered here today to witness the joining of Daniela Baxter and Beau Morgan in holy matrimony. Marriage is a sacred bond, one that unites a man and woman for the rest of their lives."

Josh sounded steadier, but he glanced again to the back corner of the church. His eyes hardened. She'd seen him use that look once before. Harold Day had been harsh with his wife and Josh had escorted him outside for a talk.

Was he looking at Harriet Lange? Who else would disrupt the wedding? Dani didn't know, but she'd go toe-to-toe with anyone who'd question her love for Beau.

Apparently sensing her unrest, he gripped her elbow. Josh opened his Bible, looked from Dani to Beau, then focused on the congregation. "I know Beau and Dani well. They've overcome loss, heartache and challenges to their faith. It's a privilege to lead them in their vows."

Dani breathed a sigh of relief. In a moment she and Beau would be joined forever.

Josh looked first to Dani. "Face Beau and repeat after me. 'I,' then say your name."

Dani looked into Beau's eyes. "I, Daniela Sarah Baxter."

"Take you, Beaumont Christopher Morgan."

"Take you, Beaumont Christopher Morgan—"

"To be my wedded husband."

"To be my—"

Footsteps pounded up the stairs. Startled, Dani turned and saw a balding man in a white apron charge into the church. "I gotta talk to Beau!"

Beau looked mad enough to spit. "Not now, Wallace."

"But I saw Clay Johnson!"

"I *said*—"

"But he's here," said the barkeep. "I saw him ride into town."

Sheriff Dawes pushed to his feet. John Baylor followed. The room broke into a tumult. Johnson and his gang spelled danger for everyone but something even more sinister for Dani. Beau's greatest temptation lay within his grasp. Today he would choose between love and hate.

She looked up at his face, but his eyes were skimming the congregation. She started to lower her flowers, a surrender to the inevitable, but he clasped her fingers under the bouquet and kept it level. He raised his other hand to signal the crowd.

"Hold up!" he shouted.

The room went still.

"Sit down. All of you."

They sat…except for a ragged-looking man in the back pew. Needing to see clearly, Dani lifted her veil. She'd seen the stranger slip into the church just before her entrance. She hadn't given him a thought. Looking at him now, she put the pieces together. Clay Johnson had come to church.

The outlaw glanced at Dani. "I'm sorry, miss. I didn't mean to spoil your day."

Dani didn't need the wedding hoopla, but she feared desperately for Beau.

He still had his hand on hers. "What do you want, Johnson?"

"What happened in Denver…" His voice quavered. "I didn't mean to kill your wife. It wasn't exactly an accident. I was aiming for you, but that seemed fair at the time. When she fell, I…" His eyes rose to the pink cross, lingered on the stones, then focused on Josh. "I can't live with what I did. My mama was a God-fearing woman. She'd be ashamed of me."

Josh met his gaze. "You're not alone, Clay."

"I know, Reverend. You told me about the whale."

Dani didn't know anything about whales, but she saw a broken man. Was Beau's quest for justice finally over? With a prayer on her lips, she turned to read his expression. She saw wonder in his eyes, even awe.

He looked at Clay without rancor. "You came to turn yourself in, didn't you?"

"That's right."

"In the canyon," he said. "You could have killed me, but you didn't."

"I have a bullet coming. You don't."

Beau squeezed Dani's hand so hard she felt the tension in her wrists. "I'm no better than you, Clay." With a shine in his eyes, Beau faced Dani. "As sure as Clay took Lucy's life, I almost destroyed our future. I put the girls at risk, and I left you to suffer the consequences of my stupidity. I will *never* make that mistake again."

He'd make others and so would she, but today promised a new beginning.

Beau turned back to Clay. "I chased you for five years with more hate than a man should feel. I'd have done anything to see you dead. I wanted vengeance, but only God can make that call. Today you've given Lucy justice. I think it's time for mercy for us both."

Clay took a deep breath. "I expect to hang for what I did."

"We'll leave it up to a judge," Beau answered.

Dawes pushed to his feet. So did John Baylor. "You got my gray?" the rancher asked.

"Yes, sir."

"I want it back."

Clay looked proud. "It's out front."

Dawes maneuvered past the people in the pew. "You're under arrest, Johnson. For Lucy Morgan's murder and raiding the Rocking J."

Clay stepped into the aisle. Dawes jerked the outlaw's hands behind his back and herded him out the door. Beau's chase had come to an end. Dani touched his arm. "Are you all right?"

His eyes twinkled. "I'll be better after I kiss the bride."

She smiled. "That sounds good to me."

Josh spoke in a low tone. “I can finish up or—”

“Finish up,” they said in unison.

Josh signaled the congregation for quiet. “Ladies and gentlemen, we have a marriage to witness.”

As the crowd settled, Dani and Beau laced their fingers together. She glanced at the girls, wide-eyed but unafraid, dressed in white with red ribbons in their yellow hair. Her gaze rose to the pink cross, then shifted to Beau’s meadow-green eyes. The ring on her finger sparkled with silver and blue.

In that blending of all colors—the fullness of perfect light—Dani and Beau took the vows that made them man and wife. One flesh, one life, one hope. Forever and ever. Amen.

* * * * *

A popular and highly acclaimed author in the Christian market, **Sara Mitchell**'s aim is to depict the struggle between the challenges of everyday life and the values to which our faith would have us aspire. She is the author of contemporary, historical suspense and historical novels, and her work has been published by many inspirational book publishers.

Having lived in diverse locations from Georgia to California to Great Britain, her extensive travel experience helps her create authentic settings for her books. A lifelong music lover, Sara has also written several musical dramas and has long been active in the music ministries of the churches wherever she and her husband, a retired career air force officer, have lived. The parents of two daughters, Sara and her husband now live in Virginia.

Books by Sara Mitchell

Love Inspired Historical

Legacy of Secrets
The Widow's Secret
Mistletoe Courtship
A Most Unusual Match

Love Inspired

Night Music
Shelter of His Arms

Visit the Author Profile page
at Harlequin.com for more titles.

LEGACY OF SECRETS

Sara Mitchell

Jesus wept.

—*John* 11:35

For I am convinced that neither death nor life,
neither angels nor demons, neither the present nor
the future, nor any powers, neither height nor depth,
nor anything else in all creation, will be able to
separate us from the love of God that is in
Christ Jesus our Lord.

—*Romans* 8:38

For B.K. and Barry—neighbors and dear friends who not only walk the extra mile, but provide new shoes, food for the journey and umbrellas for all the storms of life battering our family these past few years.

Thanks for being there.

Acknowledgments

Many thanks to:

Dr. Robert S. Conte, historian at the Greenbrier at White Sulpher Springs, for his hospitality, help and endless patience with all my questions. Any historical inaccuracies fall solely on my shoulders!

Melissa Endlich, my editor, whose enthusiasm and insight warm the heart and energize the creative soul.

Janet Kobobel Gant, my long-suffering agent, whose belief in me never falters.

Prologue

Richmond, Virginia
September 1862

On a humid, chilly evening in late September, the boy finally reached his goal. His journey had lasted three terrifying nights and four equally terrifying days; except for the first night, when he'd stowed away on a northbound freight train, he was forced to evade swarms of soldiers, rebel and bluecoats alike. They roamed the countryside and main roads like the biblical plague of locusts his grandmother talked about, the ones inflicted upon the Egyptians.

For two of those nights the boy hid shivering in fear under cover of a forest, in a thicket of wild rhododendron, his nose filled with the ripe odors of leaves and wet earth while a hundred yards away the awful sounds of bloodcurdling battle rent the air. The thought of killing a human being twisted his insides. When he could no longer bear the cold and fear and uncertainty, he clapped his hands over his ears, choking on tears wept in desperate silence.

Swallowing hard against the memory, he focused on his present surroundings—a narrow alley on a busy street. Tall brick buildings engulfed him instead of trees; a cluster of wooden crates shielded him instead of bushes. Instead of the noise of battle, the sounds of a city filled his ears. Buggies and wagons rattled past in the street. Crowds of people choked the walkways. As the moments passed, gradually he crept onto the sidewalk and huddled in the shadow of the doorway to some kind of store. Directly across the street, a fancy hotel rose in lofty grandeur between two nondescript brick buildings. Inside that hotel, the man he had traveled over a hundred miles to see dined with his family, oblivious to the existence of the scrawny thirteen-year-old boy who was his nephew.

Time passed while he tried to decide what to do. He could feel his heartbeat clear up inside his ears. Dusk settled in, and he watched the lamplighter's progress along the street, lighting up the tall streetlights. Several times shiny carriages stopped in front of the hotel, collected and discharged men in top hats and expensive-looking suits, along with women in their hooped skirts wide enough for a flock of chickens to hide under. A colored man clad in a hideous purple uniform guarded the hotel entrance, nodding to arriving guests as he held open the door.

Several passersby glanced askance at the boy, and one frowning man in a greatcoat actually stopped, asked him what he was about, loitering on the walk.

"I'm waiting for my uncle."

"And where might your uncle be, boy, that he left you here on the street after dark?"

Sweat gathered on his palms and at the small of his back. "Oh, he'll be out in a few moments. He had to leave a message for someone in the hotel."

"Hmm. Well—" his voice turned brisk "—that's all right, then, I expect. How old are you, son?"

He stood straight, keeping his gaze open and earnest upon the gentleman. "Thirteen. You don't need to worry about me, sir. I'm perfectly fine." The cultured drawl of his proud North Carolina grandmother rolled easily off his lips, and he watched smugly as the lingering suspicion faded from the man's face.

"Very well." He touched two fingers to his top hat. "But you be careful, son. There's a war going on, and it's drawing closer to Richmond every day. I'd hate to see you conscripted into the army, though you've one foot in adulthood." Some emotion flickered in his eyes. "War's horrific enough for grown men. Don't believe anyone who claims otherwise, or fills your head with stories of the glory of battle. You tell your uncle to take better care of you, in the future."

"Yessir."

The man patted his shoulder, then walked on.

The longing boiled up, fast and ferocious, as it always did. He watched the stranger stride down the street, wishing so fiercely it made his teeth hurt that he had a father who cared whether or not he loitered alone on a city street. Who tried to shield him from the brutality of war. Before the fear could take hold again, he darted across the street and ducked inside the hotel while the doorman was busy handing some ladies down out of a dark green brougham.

The lobby was a maze of gleaming oak columns and red-cushioned chairs scattered between huge urns of potted plants. Mindful that his clothes were rumpled and dirt stained, he slipped from urn to urn, behind columns, making his way toward the dining room. The scullery maid at his uncle's imposing town house on Grace Avenue had been easily persuaded to provide directions to the hotel; ever since he'd been a toddler he'd perfected the art of pleasing females.

Heart thumping, as a large grandfather clock dolefully bonged nine times, he slipped inside the dining room—and saw them. Even when seated, his uncle was a commanding presence in his swallow-tail coat and blinding-white shirt, where a diamond stickpin winked with every motion he made. Next to him sat a pretty plump woman dressed in a deep red gown. Jet earrings and necklace decorated her ears and throat. That would be his aunt, and the two little boys dandified up in revolting little suits his cousins.

Everybody was smiling and talking, including the boys. He watched, still and silent as one of the wooden columns, while his uncle leaned over to hear something his wife was saying, a tender expression on his face the boy had never witnessed on another man's countenance, not in his entire thirteen years.

The longing intensified until it was a monster, biting into him in chunks of indescribable jealousy and pain.

Suddenly one of the sons, the one barely a toddler, knocked over a glass. His older brother laughed.

Across the room, the boy tensed, not breathing, while he waited for the father to reprimand his son, to perhaps even backhand him. Waited for the mother to deliver a shrill scolding, to lecture the hapless child on proper deportment.

Instead, the father calmly signaled for the waiter, righted the glass himself. Then he ruffled his son's hair, the expression of indulgence on his face visible all the way across the room.

Something snapped inside the boy.

That little boy should be him. He should have been part of a well-to-do family who dined in fancy hotels. *His* mother should be dressed in fancy lace and velvet, seated next to her husband. His father. His home should be the immense stone town house with the neatly manicured yard.

For years his mother and grandmother had filled his head with stories and promises of a grand Mission that someday he would undertake, to right a Grievous Wrong. Now, unnoticed and invisible to the family that should have been his, he made a vow of his own.

Chapter One

Charlottesville, Virginia Spring 1889

The funeral service was over, the mourners dispersed. A light breeze carried the faint scent of spring hyacinths, and the sound of the church bell, tolling its doleful message. Six blocks away, Neala Shaw followed her brother Adrian up the front steps, into a house devoid of light and life. Silently they hung coat and cloak on the hall tree, then just as silently wandered into the parlor. Unable to bear the shadowed gloom, Neala made her way to the windows to pull back the curtains before confronting her brother.

"Adrian…what you said, about leaving?" The silken threads of the tassels holding the curtains were tangled; she concentrated on combing through each strand with her fingers. "Tell me you didn't mean it."

"I did mean it. Every word." He tugged at his tie, yanking it off with quick, jerky movements. The stiff shirt collar followed. "Mother and Father are gone. Even if I wanted to, there's no reason to stay here."

Neala dropped the tassel and turned to stare blindly out

the window, wishing just once her temperament would allow her the satisfaction of retaliating with equally hurtful words. How could Adrian behave so, when less than an hour earlier they had buried both parents?

She could still hear the sound of the shovels, still see the clumps of dirt pouring onto the coffins, signaling with brutal finality that, while Edward and Cora Shaw's souls were with God, their lifeless bodies were forever consigned to the earth. Until she herself died, Neala would never see them again, never hear their voices, never inhale the scent of Mother's honeysuckle toilet water or Father's sandalwood hair tonic. Never feel the warmth of their hugs.

All because of an accident. A tragic, deadly accident that shocked the community and devastated the few members left in the Neal Shaw family.

"Adrian, this is our home. I don't—"

"*Was* our home. The house and all its contents go on the auction block tomorrow, remember? Father may have been a respected university professor, but he knew as much about providing for his family as a squirrel finding nuts in a snowstorm."

Neala winced. "Where will you go?"

He shrugged, abruptly looking much younger than his twenty years. "I bought a train ticket for Newport News yesterday. Always wanted to see the ocean."

Curiosity overpowered caution. "Adrian, how on earth did you pay for the ticket?"

He avoided her gaze. "Sold Father's watch," he muttered after a minute. "I didn't have anything else." His voice rose in the face of Neala's silence. "It's not as though Father's here to care one way or the other. Besides, it's his fault we're in this mess. You could always sell Grandfather's legacy. I doubt if it's worth more than a few dollars, but that's more than Father left."

He could have slapped her face and not wounded her so deeply. "I will never part with the clan crest badge. Perhaps that's why Grandfather left it to *me*, instead of you." Neala watched her brother's face close up, but she was beyond placating him. "That crest has been part of the Shaw family for over three hundred years. Now it's the only legacy we have left. It's a shame I'm the only one who appreciates it."

"What did you expect? They named you after him, not me. He left the crest badge to you, not me. Not his only surviving grandson."

Silence gathered in the room, hanging like a damp fog. "I need to finish packing," Adrian finally muttered. "You'll be all right, won't you, sis? With the auction, I mean?"

"I'll manage just fine, Adrian."

"Um…do you know what you're going to do? Where will you live? The Johnsons'?"

"No, they don't really have room, especially with Hannah in the family way."

"Oh. What about the Marsdens?"

"Mr. Marsden suffers from sciatica. They're moving to Thomasville, Georgia, this fall."

Adrian hunched his shoulders, his expression sheepish but defiant. "Well, what about one of the boardinghouses where some of the teachers live?"

Neala folded her handkerchief into a neat square to give herself time to collect her sluggish thoughts. "Too expensive, I'm afraid, my dear." She managed with Herculean effort to produce a matter-of-fact smile. "Mrs. Hobbs told me about a school for women," she shared, the words dragging. "It's farther north, somewhere up in the Blue Ridge Mountains, I believe. She suggested I apply for residency there. I hadn't considered it because you were here, and this school is apparently only for women who have lost all their family connections. Mrs. Hobbs says tuition is paid through donations or trusts or something, since the only applicants accepted are those who find themselves without any resources." Carefully she kept her voice stripped of any hint of censure, but Adrian's cheeks turned a dusky red.

"Then you have nothing to worry about," he snapped. "This time tomorrow I'll be long gone. Tell everyone I'm dead, too. The way things have gone over the past few years in our family, I may as well be."

He stormed out of the parlor, and a moment later Neala heard the front door slam.

Philadelphia

The odors in the squalid alley would suffocate a buffalo. How could a human being survive, much less breathe here, Grayson Faulkner wondered as he and his partner picked their way down what seemed like a tunnel into perdition. A pack of snarling, slobbering dogs fought over the bloody carcass of another animal; Gray averted his gaze and breathed shallowly to keep his gorge at the low end of his throat. Rotting garbage, putrid food scraps and rusted tins formed piles higher than their heads. If he'd known what teaming up with a bounty hunter entailed, he'd never have let Marty Scruggs talk him into it.

When this job was finished, his old friend would have to hornswoggle a new partner. Seeking adventure all over the earth had been a satisfying way to explore life.

But even Gray's years as a deputy marshal out in Wyoming Territory, where he'd seen plenty of depravity in the wild cattle towns, hadn't prepared him for the likes of a city slum.

Beside him, Marty gagged, then cheerfully cursed the dogs, the place, and the man they were looking for.

"I agree," Gray said. "So I hate to break it to you now, but after this job, my friend, I'm through."

"You and me both. But you lasted longer than I thought, seeing as unlike me, you're a gent born with a whole place setting of silver spoons in his mouth."

They passed a pile of steaming garbage, the stench so rank Gray's eyes watered. When he finished this job, he'd take a long-needed vacation, he promised himself. Somewhere green and fresh, where the air sparkled and he could hear birdsong. Somewhere nobody knew or cared about his prowess with a gun, or his family. Surely some little corner of this vast country could provide relief for a man on the verge of destroying whatever passed for his soul.

"Isn't this the one?" Marty hissed.

"Looks like it," Gray agreed after a moment.

They climbed several flights of creaking stairs lit only by a single bulb hanging from a long wire in the wretched foyer; the higher they climbed, the darker and more stale the air grew. Through thin, decrepit doors they heard voices arguing, babies wailing, smelled the stomach-turning odors of urine, sweat and mildew along with rancid food. Gray opened one flap of his shapeless sack coat, curling his fingers around the holstered Smith & Wesson revolver. It was a new hammerless model that had replaced his trusty Peacemaker; Gray was as proud of the New Departure model as a parent with a precocious child.

"I'm right glad you're along." Marty grinned slyly. "Still the best marksman east of the Mississippi, I hear."

Gray felt heat burn his ears and cheeks. "I don't know what you've heard, or read, but likely it's tommyrot."

They reached the top floor; in wordless accord they approached the door on the end, and Marty knocked twice. The churning in Gray's belly stilled, and an almost eerie calm descended—the falcon, poised to swoop upon its prey.

The door opened a crack, just enough for the two men to see a woman's pitted face and suspicious eyes. "Don't know ye," she snapped. "Go 'way."

Marty planted his foot in the door. "We're here to collar Kevin Hackbone. Please step aside, ma'am. We know he's in here, and we know there's no way out except through this door."

Gray watched a multitude of expressions streak across her face, unable to completely divorce himself from an uprising of pity. If she'd had a chance, a decent place to live and a man who took care of her... He stepped closer, crowding the doorway until reluctantly the woman stepped back. "He won't go easy," she said, jerking her chin toward a narrow hall.

"His choice," Gray returned quietly.

"If you help us, it'll be better for you," Marty added. He exchanged glances with Gray, then tugged out a pair of handcuffs and headed down the hall, to a closed door. "Come on out, Kevin," he called. "You're under arrest back in New York City, for robbery, assault and battery, and too many other crimes to waste more breath on."

"Come and get me, ya boot-kissing son of a sewer rat!" a nasal voice yelled through the flimsy panel.

"Now, Kevin, there's two of us out here." He shot

Gray a quick glance, winked. "One of us is the Falcon himself. You've heard about him, right? Might wriggle away from me, but *you* know and *I* know you'll never make it past him."

"Got a knife, boyo. And I'll use it, I will."

"I've got a gun," Gray called back, glaring at his irrepressible friend. "And I'll use it."

The door opened. Looking like a mangy ferret, Kevin eyed the cuffs dangling from Marty's hand, then glanced down the hall where Gray waited by the door. After a long moment, Kevin heaved a sigh and held out his hands. "Knew it was just a matter of time," he muttered, all bluster gone.

Going too easy, Gray thought with a prickle of disquiet. He watched, every muscle tensed, waiting for Kevin to make a move as Marty proceeded to handcuff his hands behind his back.

"No!" the woman behind Gray suddenly shrieked, a demented scream ripping from her throat. She dashed down the hall before Gray could stop her, and there was a knife in her hands, a knife she lifted high above her head, a knife aimed for Marty's unprotected back.

It happened too fast. Even as he raced after her, shouting at her, Gray knew he was too late. Too late he screamed somewhere in the deepest recesses of his mind as he lifted the gun and fired but the knife had already plunged into Marty's back. Marty half turned, his eyes wide with disbelief. He shook his head, his gaze finding and holding Gray's even as his hands fell away from Kevin and he dropped to his knees, then crumpled on top of the dead woman—the first woman Gray had ever been forced to kill.

Gray scarcely noticed Kevin's escape. He gathered

Marty in his arms, feeling the blood soaking his hands. "Hold on," he pleaded, pressing against the wound with all his might. "Hold on, Marty. You have to hold on…."

The friendly brown eyes, always so full of humor, full of life, were glazed now, staring vaguely up into Gray's face. Marty's mouth moved, and he coughed, blood trickling down his chin. "Gray…" he whispered, one hand fumbling aimlessly until Gray grabbed it, gripped it tightly. "Glad it wasn't you, Falcon…" The ghost of a smile flickered across his lips. "Would…ruin…your reputation."

His head lolled, and his body went slack.

His friend was gone.

Chapter Two

Isabella Chilton Academy for Single Females
April 1890

Drizzling rain accompanied a week of demanding examinations, but winter session at the Isabella Chilton Academy was finally over. Along with academic and home-management courses, graduates from the Academy were educated in every facet of etiquette and social skills in order to survive a world where a woman's role was no longer as rigidly defined. Since 1866, when Miss Isabella had converted her husband's family estate into a school in order to save it from Yankee carpetbaggers, every student who completed the four-year curriculum acquired either a husband or gainful employment with which to support themselves.

"God's design from the beginning was for marriage between a man and a woman," Miss Isabella liked to remind the students. "Regrettably, the world seldom chooses to abide by God's design."

Neala had spent the better part of the past year learning that painful lesson.

As was the custom, on the first day the capricious April weather cooperated, Miss Isabella treated students to a day trip. Today the destination was a shopping-and-luncheon trip to Berryville, which spawned a giddy atmosphere among all the women except Neala.

Restless, a trifle pensive, Neala had elected to stay behind to assist Miss Crabbe with school paperwork. An Academy fixture for years, Eulalie Crabbe was an excellent secretary, but the high-strung spinster could handle no more than two tasks at any given moment. "But it's not just the paperwork," Neala explained to Abigail Schaffer, one of her new friends at the Academy. "I, well, I need to take a long walk this afternoon. To think about…things."

"I understand." Abby gave a smile that belied the wistful tone.

"Why can't you help Miss Crabbe tomorrow?" Nan Sweeney interrupted from behind Abby. "You told me last week you were hoping to finally purchase a new ready-made wrapper, to replace the dress you ruined in the harness-room fire."

Would anyone ever forget that wretched imbroglio? It had happened over five months ago! All right, she could have perished—but if she hadn't tried to put out a fire she was responsible for starting, she would never have been able to look in a mirror again.

Violet Gleason, a farm girl standing next to Nan, chimed in, "Please do come. It won't be the same without you, Neala…"

"All right, my dears. Her decision's made, and I concur."

With the brisk kindness for which she was famous, the headmistress silenced the rest of the protests with a commanding wave of a gloved hand. Liam Brody, the school's coachman and stableman, handed the women into the coach, then shut the door with such haste he caught the ribboned hem of someone's gown. Muttering what no doubt were Gaelic imprecations, he rectified the mistake, jammed his top hat farther down over his forehead and swung up into the driver's seat.

Neala and Miss Isabella shared a smile. "Don't let Eulalie keep you past two," the headmistress ordered. She pressed her plump heliotrope-scented cheek against Neala's. "And don't forget to carry your whistle when you go for your walk. Mr. Pepperell is planting tomatoes this afternoon. I've told him to keep an ear out."

"I'll be fine."

"Hmm." The older woman idly stroked the side of her nose. "You haven't yet learned your limitations, have you?" A faint frown appeared between her eyes. "Don't let the new girls pester you so you miss your walk."

"They're never a bother," Neala murmured. "If I can help them know they're not alone, it's the least I can do."

"We all help one another here, it's true. But you are neither their mother, nor headmistress of the Isabella Chilton Academy. My students must also learn how to embrace solitude, and endure loneliness."

Heat crept up Neala's cheeks. "I just want to be a friend."

Miss Isabella's face softened. "Ah, Neala. My dear, I do understand. You are indeed a very good friend, to all of us. Even when you're trying to shoulder more than your share." She smoothed the row of ruffles on her basque. "While you go for that walk, remember that you do have a home here. People who care about you—simply because you're you. Think about that as well, hmm?"

* * *

At a little past four o'clock, Neala headed toward the thick forest that screened the Academy from fierce northwestern winds. Today, however, the wind was light, playful; spring bloomed in all its flagrant abandon. Neala loved this season of new birth, with the scents and colors of restored life bursting forth from the earth, reminding all mourners that death was never final.

Some time later she reached the sunlit glade she'd designated her forest chapel. Most of the students found hideaways like this, somewhere on the vast grounds where they could escape for a sip of solitude. Few of them… All right, only Neala and the mysterious widow Tremayne ventured this far into the woods. What *was* her name? Josephine? No—Jocelyn. Jocelyn Tremayne. Several times Neala had invited Jocelyn to join her. Though polite, the widow always refused, saying she needed time to adjust to her new life. If Neala pleaded, Abby occasionally joined her for a hike down to the river. But Abby preferred to spend most of her spare time in the stables, because she loved horses, so Neala tried hard not to be the infernal nag her brother considered her.

She kicked an acorn, then sighed, allowing the tranquil surroundings to purify her restless spirit. She hadn't yet grasped the notion of embracing lifelong solitude, but these walks seemed to help.

She would have made a wonderful explorer, like Lewis and Clark. Or perhaps an Indian. Yes, definitely an Indian squaw with beautiful long black hair. Long, straight hair worn in easy-to-manage braids. Not an infuriating head full of wispy brown curls that refused to obey hairpins no matter how firmly attached.

An hour later, pleasantly winded, mostly at peace,

Neala started back for the school. She was humming a hymn whose words she had forgotten, absently stroking tree trunks as she wound her way back along the faint path her footsteps had created over the past ten months, when the resounding crack of a rifle shot rent the twilight silence.

Simultaneously the bark of the white pine inches from her face exploded outward. Neala leaped back, hands flying to cover her eyes even as realization slammed into her with the same force as the bullet struck the tree.

Some stupid hunter had almost killed her, thinking she was an animal.

She ducked behind the pine even as another bullet zinged past a mere two feet behind her. How stupid of her, to have worn dark mourning clothes for her walk, which made her far more difficult to distinguish from a deer or some other large animal. Neala scanned the direction from which the shot had been fired, but she could detect no sign of movement. She cupped her hands on either side of her mouth to create a makeshift megaphone like a ringmaster at Barnum & Bailey Circus.

"Don't shoot again!" she yelled. "I'm a person, not your supper!" Then, after two seconds of thrumming silence, she added, "And this is private property! One more shot, and I'll see that you're the one being hunted!"

A massive oak with two joined trunks offered more protection than the pine. Neala gathered up her skirts, hunched her shoulders and darted behind a thicket of mountain laurel, then raced for the oak's protection. She hunkered down, frustrated and angry because the oaf out there had spoiled the atmosphere.

Cautiously she peered around the tree. A hand's width from her nose, leaves and dirt exploded almost simultaneously with the echoing crack of a third shot. Stupid, careless hunter, she thought, a lump forming in her throat. If Adrian were here…

Impatient with herself, Neala smacked a fist against her palm. Right now she needed to extricate herself from a potentially dangerous situation, not wallow in maudlin longings. And if she didn't put in an appearance within two minutes of the coach's return, someone—probably an irate Liam—would set out to search for her. If the hunter were still in the vicinity, he might accidentally shoot Liam as well. What a wretched dilemma!

"Did you hear me?" she yelled again.

There was no response. For several vexing moments Neala sat, her mind searching furiously for a solution. Only when she crossed her arms did she remember the whistle dangling around her neck. All students, regardless of the length of time, were required to carry a whistle with them if they were out of sight of the main house. *Neala Shaw, you have nothing but a mess of day-old oatmeal for brains.*

Shaking her head, she lifted the whistle to her lips and blew.

Gray lay sprawled under one of the trees planted years earlier by new students, a charming if somewhat mawkish custom, to his way of thinking. Hands folded to pillow his head, eyes half-closed, he could almost hear Aunt Bella's crisp denouncement of such cynicism. From her perspective the trees were planted so newly orphaned students would have something to nurture, something they could claim, at a place she wanted them to regard as home.

Home.

Gray rolled and sat up, fighting the ever-present discontent with his life. Nothing assuaged the malaise, not women nor drink nor even a couple of shooting competitions where he'd reaped adulation and medals for pretending every shot he fired was aimed at Kevin Hackbone's heart. Sumner—no, it was not Sumner anymore. Now his only refuge from a stifling lifestyle was a school for females. Life was full of bitter irony.

Gray shuddered.

Why did Aunt Bella have to pick this particular day to hare off to Berryville?

He'd arrived an hour earlier, eager for a much-needed visit with the only female left on earth whose presence he could tolerate longer than twenty-four hours. Growing up, Gray spent miserable hours wishing Isabella was his mother, instead of the sweet but overprotective woman who refused to let Gray become a man. Even now, on his visits home, she treated him as though he were a perpetual three-year-old toddler. At fifteen, he finally rebelled and ran. Aunt Bella was the only family member with whom he'd stayed in touch. Understanding soul that she was, she'd waited out a year; when he turned sixteen she calmly told him to take his sorry carcass back home and mend fences, or she'd write his mother herself. And send Gray's two older brothers to fetch him.

A smile tweaked the corner of his mouth, remembering that first reunion. Aunt Bella had been spot on, of course.

He flicked open his watch, to discover only seven minutes had passed since he checked the time. Swearing beneath his breath, Gray stood up, scanned the winding drive again. It was going on five, dusk not far away. Why weren't they back home? He needed to talk, needed to hear her advice, soak up the love offered without chains.

When he heard the faint but piercing sound of a whistle, he whipped around, hand automatically going to the butt of his gun. Across the lawn, Mr. Pepperell had also straightened. He dropped his tools, his head swiveling back and forth as he, too, scanned the estate's southern woods. Gray loped over.

"What is it? Who's ruining the peace and quiet by blowing a blasted whistle?"

"I—oh, my, it most likely is Miss Shaw. She told me she was going for a walk." He paused to wipe a shaking hand across his brow. "I don't know precisely what—that is to say, I hadn't expected..."

"Why is she blowing a whistle?"

The gardener swallowed several times, his Adam's apple bobbing. Instead of a dapper gentleman politely sharing botanical tidbits, now he resembled an old man on the verge of collapse. "Distress." He peered dazedly up at Gray. "It's to be used only as a call for help. A—a safety measure, if you will. All students wear one when out of sight of the main house. They're most of them young women from towns and farms, not used to the country."

Clumsily he began untying his gardener's apron. "I must go. I'm the only one—"

"No, you're not," Gray interrupted. "I'll go see what the problem is. You stay here, alert the household to be prepared with bandages or whatever might be required."

Ignoring the gardener's halfhearted protests, he took off at a run in the general location of the last whistle call. When he reached the woods he paused, rapidly searched and discovered a path of sorts. Good. Jaw set, Gray plunged into the shadowed forest.

Chapter Three

Within two minutes, Gray was forced to slow his pace. Wet shrubs newly leafed slapped his sides; low-hanging branches tried to gouge his face, and he slipped twice on the narrow path that seemed to delight in its number of twists and turns.

After ten minutes he stopped completely. He swiped at his face, then tugged off his jacket and hung it on a dead branch. Irritation boiled through him. This whole day had been nothing but one infernal nuisance after another. And some timid female who couldn't find her way out of a potato sack… Well, this was just what he needed, tearing through unfamiliar woods like some stupid Galahad, only to wind up more lost than the equally stupid female. And she wasn't helping much at all.

"Where are you?" he roared. "Blow the whistle again!"

He waited, yelled again. Nothing. Very well. *Stay lost, then.* A chilly night in dark woods would teach a valuable lesson.

The whistle blew.

Gray ignored the quick tug of relief, turned on his heel, plunged off the narrow path and fought his way through yet another thicket of wet leafy shrubs, only marginally pacified when the whistle continued to blow at regular intervals. The young miss deserved a blistering lecture for getting herself lost—and he deserved to deliver it.

Of course, a remote possibility existed that she actually had hurt herself, along with getting lost. Aunt Bella needed to apply a firmer hand with her students, since these woods doubtless were home to bears, maybe even a wildcat or two. Trespassing hunters…

The skin at the back of his neck tightened. No matter how helpless or irrational a woman behaved, she never deserved to be mistreated. If this one had been harmed in any manner, or even frightened by some wandering weasel, Gray would track the vermin down and teach him a few manners.

He burst into a small clearing, and a feminine voice called loudly, "Halt this instance! You've been shooting at me, not a deer or a…bear!"

What—? Gray swiveled toward the voice, which emanated from behind a large two-trunk oak. "Shooting at you?" he shouted back, marching across the glade. "Stop spouting nonsense and show yourself." With an effort he moderated his tone. "You're safe now. I'm here to guide you back. You've nothing to fear."

He reached the tree, peered around, and barely avoided getting brained with a dead tree limb.

"I don't need a guide. And I don't believe you." A bedraggled moppet with curly brown hair and snapping brown eyes brandished the limb in his face. "Who are you? You're trespassing, and furthermore hunting is forbidden on this land." Her irate gaze fastened on Gray's revolver. The flushed cheeks paled.

Gray propped his shoulder against the tree trunk

and crossed his arms over his chest. Her head scarcely reached his chin; she'd gotten herself lost, and she was alone in the middle of the woods with a man she'd never met. Yet she stood there, taking him to task without a shred of awareness of her helplessness. "Your stick wouldn't deter a tabby cat, much less a man with a gun. Even a man without one," he drawled, palm itching to slip the weapon from its holster to scare a modicum of common sense into her.

For a second the girl stared at him wide-eyed. Then she popped the whistle back in her mouth and blew. The sound at close range shrilled into Gray's unprotected ears, and he covered them in a reflexive action worthy of the greenest tenderfoot.

"Mr. Pepperell will be here any moment," she confidently stated after trying to deafen him. "Also a very husky Irishman. They won't take kindly to a trespassing hunter. You could have killed someone through your carelessness."

Disbelieving, for the first time Gray studied the woman objectively, without the haze of resentment fogging his mind. At first he'd pegged her for one of Isabella's youngest students, too naive to grasp her circumstances. Upon closer examination he realized she had to be in her early twenties, possibly a few years older. The wild tangle of curls and guileless eyes were nothing but a smoke screen.

She might be orphaned now, but he'd wager she'd had siblings at one time, all of them younger, poor saps she ordered about with the same officious superiority his sisters had inflicted upon his own miserable childhood.

"For your information," he finally said, mildly enough considering his mood, "I happen to know that your husky

Irishman is only an inch taller than you, say, five feet six inches? And he's about as husky as a plucked rooster. As for Mr. Pepperell, he's nearing seventy. Had he come hunting you down, by now he would have expired from heart palpitations."

He lowered his head until their faces were mere inches apart. "Did you bother to consider the shock to his heart, the risk he'd face trying to race over a mile of rough terrain, to rescue you? I volunteered instead." He paused. "But turns out you're not lost. Or hurt. You're only supposed to blow that whistle if you're in danger, or dire straits. Ever read the fable about the boy who cried wolf?"

The chit searched his face with nothing but relief showing on hers. "If you know Liam and Mr. Pepperell, you couldn't be the irresponsible hunter, even though you are wearing a gun." She heaved a long, unladylike breath. "Are you one of the sheriff's new deputies?" With a quick flick of her wrist, she tossed aside the stick, then absently tucked wayward curls behind her ears. Her expression remained as bright and friendly as a puppy's.

"No!" Gray ground out, his back teeth snapping together in an effort to keep his temper from exploding full force. "I happen to be Isabella Chilton's nephew. I just arrived for a visit—a much-needed, *peaceful* visit. But my aunt wasn't there. So I didn't have anything better to do than chase through the woods to rescue an idiot girl who doesn't have enough sense to steer clear of an angry male."

"Well, what on earth are *you* angry for? You're not the one who could have been killed by a trigger-happy hunter."

A late-afternoon breeze dislodged more of her hair. Sighing again, she plucked out some hairpins and haphazardly stuffed the loose curls back into a slipping topknot. Despite his extensive travels, Gray had never encountered a woman so indifferent to her appearance. "Since you're not the hunter," she finished, "would you mind scouting the area before we leave? I doubt he's around, since I finally remembered to blow the whistle, but it wouldn't hurt to check."

"Are you seriously suggesting that someone was, ah, shooting at you?" He swept her disheveled form with another raking glance while the memory of Mr. Pepperell's worried eyes and trembling fingers filled his mind. "How about telling me what you're really up to, and save us both from a scene I'll probably regret. I despise liars, especially female ones who never consider the consequences to anyone but themselves."

She blinked, the self-assurance squaring her shoulders and tilting her chin fading. As rapidly as the sun disappeared behind the mountains, she transformed into an uncertain young girl whose aura of wounded dignity pricked Gray's conscience. "It's probably safe enough now," she murmured. "I'm going back this way." She gestured with her hand. "It's longer, but less strenuous." Without another word she headed off, her every step away from Gray a silent reproach.

He fought a losing battle with the nettles pricking his conscience. "Wait," he called, reaching her in half a dozen strides. It was a half-dozen more before he gathered the courage to speak again. "Listen. I apologize. I had no right to speak to you the way I did."

He yanked at his shirt collar, feeling stupid, petty—and a complete churl. Impossible to explain how her innocent query about his being a sheriff's deputy had ripped wide open a wound so painful to his soul he wasn't sure he'd ever heal. But he owed her something. "Will you stop a second, so I can at least offer a proper apology?" he growled.

She hesitated, then glanced up, her expression solemn. "All right."

"I'm sorry." He bit the inside of his cheek, then shrugged. "It's been a long day. I lost my temper. I'm usually not this boorish."

A shy smile flirted at the corner of her mouth. "It's all right. I shouldn't have accused you of being a careless hunter."

Gray still didn't believe her story, but finally had enough presence of mind to keep the thought to himself. "Well, we'd best make haste. By the time we return, Aunt Bella should be back."

"With my 'husky Irishman' driving the coach," the young woman added dryly. "Not to mention all the others, who aren't going to be happy at all with my latest snarlie."

Latest...*snarlie*? Where had Aunt Bella unearthed this creature?

"Well, it's over now," Gray said, and managed what he hoped was a comforting smile. "All is well, hmm?" Ha. His need for peace was unlikely to be satisfied now, and the talk he'd yearned to enjoy with his aunt unfortunately would revolve around someone other than himself.

He started down the path, but the woman didn't budge. "What is it?" Regrettably, he was unable to erase the edge in the words.

For a few seconds more she stood there, her bottom lip caught between her teeth. Then she shrugged. "Yes. You're right. All is well. Thank you for...coming to rescue me." There was a pause, then she added in a wistful tone, "You're nothing at all like your aunt, are you?"

They didn't speak again. Thirty long minutes later, grateful for the excuse, Gray left her at the edge of the woods to return and fetch his jacket. Slanting sunbeams poured across the lawn, bathing Miss Shaw with a golden aura that contrarily enhanced her aloneness. Gray stomped back into the woods, and considered seriously the temptation to find a very large oak tree so he could bang his head against its trunk.

Chapter Four

Rutter, Virginia

Shoulders slumped, Will Crocker trudged down the dirt lane that led to his home. It was dusk, when light and shadow blurred surroundings into indefinable shapes. A man could be invisible at dusk, if he were careful. Will shrugged, vaguely uncomfortable with the thought, and hurried toward the four-room unpainted frame house where he and his mother had lived for the last fifteen years.

The hardscrabble community of Rutter, population 973, boasted few amenities, though one or two families made persistent efforts to achieve a level of civilized comfort—whitewashing the clapboard, planting a flower garden; one family had ordered an entire parlor set of golden oak out of the Sears catalog.

Momma always had a good word to say about their neighbors; she tried as much as she could to thank Will for his efforts to improve their own home, despite the disconsolation that plagued most of her waking moments. Life's unfairness had crushed her spirit; by the time Will reached his twelfth year her hair was completely gray, her eyes sunken in the once pretty face.

When Grandmother died, they had lost everything. Many a night when Will came home, the sound of his mother's bitter weeping seeped like cold fog through the thin bedroom wall. She seldom wept in front of him, and he allowed her to cling to the illusion that he didn't know how often she cried herself to sleep.

Mood bleak, he drew aimless patterns in the dirt with the toe of his shoe. No matter how bitter he might feel during these isolated moments, his mother loved him as much as she was able. Will was her only remaining relative. If he abandoned her, he knew she would die. Twice, in his late twenties, he'd gone so far as to move out. The first time his mother quit eating and almost starved herself to death; the second time she'd almost burned the house down. Will never tried living on his own again.

A vague shiver danced along his spine, one of fear and the longing he never quite knew what to do with because he couldn't remember a time when both emotions hadn't been part of his life, all forty-one years of it. When the Zuckermans' snug little house appeared at the bend in the lane, light glowing through the windows, he gave in to the longing instead of the fear. Silently, imagining himself invisible as a gray field mouse, he slipped up to a side window and peeked through the narrow gap in the curtains. Mrs. Zuckerman had died the previous year, but their oldest daughter, a horse-faced but congenial spinster everyone called Miss Leila, moved in to take care of her father. At the moment they were sitting at a small table, playing some kind of board game. A fire danced merrily in the parlor stove. Pretty crocheted doilies were scattered about on tables and the backs of chairs. Their old hound dog slept beneath the Mr. Zuckerman reached do sentminded scratch behind

The ache in his belly g he'd slipped up to the wi turned a resolute face to he found when he stepped deal with it. He was no longer the boy prone to nightmares, or the scarecrow forced to work repugnant jobs for degrading wages so they wouldn't be thrown out into the streets.

Yet he could still feel the darkness inside, spreading like spilled ink. One day it would blacken him entirely, and he would disappear.

When he reached the door to their house, he paused, flexing his hands in a relaxing motion. Then he gave two brisk knocks and turned the rusting knob.

"Momma? I'm back!" Carefully he hung his bowler hat on the hall tree.

"William!" She rushed from her bedroom, her arms out-flung. "Is it finished, then? Were you successful this time? Do you have it at last?"

He hugged her, savoring the welcome, the warmth that could transform so quickly into anguish…or anger. When he felt her stiffen, he released her instantly. "It's good to be home, Momma. But I'm very tired. Spent the last two days traveling, you know." He tried a laugh. "Had to walk the last fifteen miles."

She drew back, crossing long skeletal arms over her flat chest while her gaze seemed to devour him. "William? You look so tired, baby. And I don't see any excitement on your face." Vague fear swam into the pale brown eyes so like his own. "Something happened, didn't it?

d." Two bright red spots appeared on her lliam, please don't tell me you failed. Not , not again. I've been hoping—praying for you. o close…"

refully Will gripped her shoulders, sat her down er rickety old rocking chair he'd salvaged from the ump on the edge of town. "I promised to take care of us, and I will. Some things take a long time, remember? Listen, why don't we eat, and I'll tell you about the trip," he finished, hoping to divert her. "Let me hang up my coat, and—"

"Don't turn your back to me!" Her hand closed over his forearm, her fingers digging in. "You're lying…" She slapped him hard, right across his mouth.

As abruptly as the rage boiled up, it disappeared. Tears swam into her glittering eyes. "Oh. Oh, William, baby, I'm sorry. So sorry. I can't bear it." She choked on a sob that brought moisture to Will's eyes. "I didn't mean it, you know I didn't mean it. William, forgive me. Please."

With a final anguished, tear-drenched look at Will, she fled to her room and slammed the door. A broken stream of sobs and wails about how horrible a mother she was, about the unfairness of life echoed from the room, washing over Will in a seething flood.

His jaw throbbed from her blow, and he slowly lifted a hand to wipe away the trickle of blood from the corner of his mouth.

The unnerving attacks were becoming more frequent. Yet he didn't blame her. He couldn't. She was his mother. He owed her his life, and to a great extent, his future. But this last attack… He released a long, tired breath. Footsteps heavy, he headed for the stove. The squalor of unwashed dishes and unemptied slops pail, the odor of rotting food and musty ashes revolted his senses.

But on the grease-laden warming plate rested a dish. A neatly folded piece of cloth covered his dinner.

With stoic resignation, Will sat down to eat before he set about cleaning the kitchen.

Chapter Five

Isabella Chilton Academy

The cuckoo clock Mr. Chilton had bought her over forty years earlier on their wedding trip to Europe finished declaring the nine-o'clock hour. Isabella gratefully settled into the cushions of her favorite settee, and allowed a wisp of sweetly painful nostalgia to drift through her mind. *Everett, that clock always did make you smile...*

Unlike his previous visits, this evening Grayson ignored the clock's charming antics of woodcutter and wife chopping while the cuckoo warbled. Instead, as restless as one of the school toms on the prowl, he wandered about her private parlor, his hands idly drifting over the collection of objects given to Isabella by her students. His expression remained aloof, almost grim. She waited without comment for him to speak, though as always the growing hardness that surrounded him like a suit of medieval armor saddened her.

He swiveled suddenly, dropping back onto the game board one of the chess pieces he'd been fiddling with. "Aunt Bella, I need to talk with you about—" A muscle twitched in his jaw; he lifted a hand to tug his earlobe, an endearing boyhood habit he'd never outgrown.

Calmly Isabella laid the piecework in her lap. "Talk to me about what? Perhaps your recent adventures over these past few months? Those, ah, shooting exhibitions? Don't scowl, dear. You had to know your mother would write to me when she read about you in the weeklies. Your father was kind enough to include several of the articles, one with a rather…interesting…photograph of you."

Grayson emitted an ungentlemanly snort. "Ah, yes. The photograph. The one where I was straddled with a foot on the back of two horses while I shot a bull's-eye at the target? Caused the gents to swear and the ladies to swoon. Doubtless Mother's was the only swoon not feigned." His laugh was short and bitter. "When I stopped by home for an overdue visit my 'reckless behavior that shamed the family name' provided fodder for three evening meals."

"I'm sorry your visit home was another difficult one."

He merely shrugged again, and looked away. "Never mind. It's not important."

"Come along, now." Isabella leaned forward. "Talk to me, my dear, about whatever you need to. But since it's after nine, doubtless there'll be a knock or two on the door soon." She paused, then finished matter-of-factly. "Ofttimes in the evenings, after chores, a student comes to me with her burdens, needing to share, or just needing a chat."

"There. That's what I want to talk about with you, Aunt." Her nephew casually scooped up the glass paperweight from the piecrust table and turned it round while he talked, his words increasing in volume along with velocity. "You run a school for orphaned women. But that doesn't mean you're their mother. No matter how many years they live here, they're not family. In truth you know little about them. Yet you take on all the responsibility for their misfortunes, not to mention their futures—and your own."

"My future, and that of my students, rests where it always has. In God's hands."

Isabella was not surprised when Grayson merely arched a brow, looking more cynical than ever. "The truth of what I'm saying doesn't change, especially after today's incident in the woods, with Miss Shaw."

Ah. Here then was the real purpose for this circuitous conversation.

"Now, really, Grayson. Someone shot at her. I think her reaction proved to be remarkably levelheaded."

"Ha! You wouldn't say that if you'd been there." He paused. "What do you really know about her background, Aunt Bella? I don't think you have ever fully appreciated the risk, inviting strange young women without any family connections into your life. I know Uncle Everett's family pretty much washed their hands of you after he died, and you turned Sumner into this school. But I don't think Uncle Ev—"

"Without the Academy's existence, I would have no home at all, Grayson. Not here, at any rate." Not for the world would she admit that his words jabbed, deep inside. "Tell me, are you more concerned about the fact that Sumner is no longer the beautiful Chilton family estate, or are your objections primarily all the 'strange young women,' Neala Shaw in particular?"

"Aunt Bella..." A band of red spread across his deeply tanned cheeks, but his expression revealed little. Somewhere over the years the boy had learned to screen his feelings from even his favorite aunt. "I'm not quite that much of a heartless cad. I'm sorry for her orphaned status—I know life is difficult, especially for…for women like Miss Shaw—but my first concern is you. For your safety and well-being, especially when you insist on maintaining such a small household staff. What if I hadn't been here this afternoon? Your gardener would have expired from the exertion had he been forced to traipse through the woods, after an irresponsible woman old enough to know better than get herself lost, then spin wild tales."

"Neala is neither irresponsible nor given to melodrama. Really, Grayson. Last fall, for example, when she'd been here less than a month, she saved the stables from burning down. She almost died herself because she refused to run away. If you knew her—"

"The point is that you don't *really* know her any better than I do. She could have set that fire herself, Aunt Bella."

"Grayson! What a scandalous observation."

Her nephew shrugged. "Just staying objective. You seem to think letters of introduction from solid citizens, detailed applications, and one personal interview are sufficient to protect you. But I've seen—"

"As they have been," Isabella interrupted. She tapped her foot several times, then forced it to stillness. "I've been operating this school for almost twenty years, my boy. I can count on one hand the students who had to be dismissed for lack of good character."

"All it takes is one," Grayson muttered darkly. "Women have never been the 'weaker' of the species, regardless of how you view them." For a nightmarish second an expression on his face turned him into someone Isabella didn't know at all. "Contrary to your quaint notions about creating godly wives and 'Able Stewards of Society'—isn't that one of your slogans?—a lot of females these days prefer to dump their husbands completely, or marry a lonely old man in hopes he'll die soon after the vows. They'd rather help rob a bank than work in one. Sweet young things with innocent-looking eyes can be ruthless, far more devious than most garden-variety male criminals. Women kill, Aunt Bella. And smile at you while they carry out the deed."

Oh, my dear, my dear. He was still suffering, deeply. "You are referring to your friend's tragic death last fall, I presume."

Grayson had been in a very bad state, Isabella knew. He had written her a brief note explaining about the death of his childhood friend, asked if he could come for a visit—then spent the next months making a spectacle of himself with that dreadful pistol of his. Until the telegram two days earlier letting her know of his pending arrival, Isabella had not heard from him at all since the note.

"'Tragic death.'" He slammed the paperweight down hard enough to scratch the table and send several other knickknacks skittering toward its scalloped edge. "What an insipid description of the deranged woman who plunged a butcher knife in the back of an unarmed man. The partner I was supposed to be protecting. The friend I'd known for most of my life." His eyes glistened as he stared through Isabella, seeing frightful images she could scarcely imagine before he covered his face with his hand.

A knock sounded on the door. "Miss Isabella?" The door opened a fraction. "Can I talk with you for a little while? It's about this afternoon— Oh!"

Neala Shaw froze in the portal, her eyes flooding

with dismay, guilt—and a smattering of outrage. "Mr. Faulkner. I didn't know you'd be in here."

Though her aching knees protested, Isabella managed to rise without betraying the effort it required. "Do come in, my dear. As it happens, my nephew would like to talk about this afternoon, as well."

"Yes. Do join us, Miss Shaw," Grayson echoed so mockingly Isabella almost swatted his arm. The mask was firmly in place again, all emotion smothered beneath the cynicism.

Small wonder that Neala walked across the room with the aura of a condemned convict headed for the gallows. Isabella started to speak, then caught herself as she watched the pair of them size each other up as though they were the only two people in the room. Hmm. She silently thanked the Lord for His nudge, and waited for an appropriate moment to leave.

"Mr. Faulkner, since you're here, I suppose I should apologize for hitting you with a stick."

"Miss Shaw, no apology is needed, since in point of fact, you missed."

"Yes, I did." Two bright spots of color turned her pale complexion the color of broiled salmon. "But it wasn't for lack of trying. Perhaps I should extend an apology anyway, since in God's eyes the intent of the heart, as much as the action, determines one's guilt."

"Spare me your self-righteous homilies. I need them even less than your contrived excuses." He stalked across to stand in front of her, hands fisted at his hips. "My aunt, and Mr. Pepperell—now, they're the ones who deserve your apology. They're the ones who would have worried themselves into early graves if I hadn't been here."

"Your aunt knows I would never—" Neala broke off,

then whirled around to Isabella. "Miss Isabella…are you all right? I thought you looked…fatigued, at supper, but I thought it was from the trip to Berryville. I didn't know, I mean I didn't realize…and I haven't seen Mr. Pepperell since lunch. Is he—is he—"

"Calm yourself, Neala." Isabella slid Grayson a reproving stare as she laid a hand on the girl's rigid shoulder. "Mr. Pepperell and I are both right as rain. You've done nothing wrong, and certainly nothing to cause me worry. Concern, perhaps, because you still tend to assume more responsibility than is appropriate. How fitting, isn't it, that my nephew seems to share that very same trait?"

Grayson made a derisive sound, which Isabella ignored. Keeping her lips pressed together to keep a smile at bay, she squeezed Neala's shoulder a final time, then started for the door. "I'm sure the two of you can talk about me much more freely in my absence, so I'll go take care of a matter and return shortly."

"Aunt Bella…"

"Miss Isabella…"

"I trust both of you to remember what they say about the spoken word? Once allowed to escape, it cannot be recalled."

She closed the door behind her, and let out a soft chuckle. *Well, Lord, You wanted me out of the room. I leave them in Your far more capable hands.*

Gray stared at the closed door in consternation. His aunt had left him alone in the room with Neala Shaw. He didn't know which would provide more relief: tossing the conniving little baggage out the window, or exiting that way himself.

Neala cleared her throat. "Obviously she expects us to come to some sort of accord." Her fingers fluttered at her waist before she twined them together. "Mr. Faulkner, it would help tremendously if you believed me, about someone shooting at me, I mean."

"Why should I, Miss Shaw?"

"Because I'm not a liar!"

"Well, now how would I be knowing that, me darlin'?" he retorted in a perfect mimicry of the Academy's Irish stableman. Her obvious frustration pleased Gray more than was polite, but for some reason he couldn't seem to quit needling her. He folded his arms, rocking a little on his feet while he watched a barrelful of expressions race across her face. "This is only the second time we've met, after all. Why, for all I know your hunter might be lying in wait in my bedroom."

"Well, if he was, at least he'd be close enough to do the job! Oh!" The brown eyes rounded in dismay as her palm flew to belatedly cover her mouth. "I can't believe I said that! I can't believe… I don't know what came over me. I don't talk like that, I don't even *think* like that."

Abruptly she turned her back to him.

Deprived of the entertainment of watching her face, Gray's attention zeroed in on a long strand of curling hair that had escaped the pins to dangle down the back of her neck. She'd managed to stuff the rest of the mass into a twist of some sort; he thought it made her look dowdy, incredibly old-fashioned. Yet his fingers itched to twine that strand around his hand. He wanted to know if her hair felt as soft as it looked, if the curls were as untamable as the fire sparking in her eyes a moment ago.

And he hated the longing almost as much as he hated himself.

"Apparently you've not heard about my reputation," he observed coolly. "Even if you send a man with a gun after me, Miss Shaw, I'm not the one who'll end up in a pine box." When she turned back around, something in the dark brown eyes goaded him to add, "Well? Why don't you go ahead and say what you're thinking—that your headmistress's nephew is a dangerous fellow, and today he tried to shoot you out in the woods?"

She blinked, and the expression disappeared. "Mr. Faulkner," she began, then hesitated. Just as Gray opened his mouth to deliver another jab, she drew herself up and leveled a look upon him worthy of Aunt Bella. "Mr. Faulkner, do you enjoy intimidating people and insulting women innocent of any wrongdoing, or do you merely possess a misogynistic streak?"

"I only enjoy intimidating devious women," he whipped back without missing a beat. "Insults I save for conniving liars. As for an innocent woman, I can't remember the last time I encountered one, age notwithstanding. So you might say my…ah…misogynistic streak developed over years of exposure to various members of your misnamed 'gentler' sex."

This time she stepped back as though he'd just sprayed her with venom, but at least she didn't turn her back on him. "There's no use trying to talk with you, is there?" she whispered, half to herself. "You're just like Adrian…"

Adrian? "Who's Adri—"

"Tell your aunt I wished her a good night," Miss Shaw chirped in a voice women used with toddlers and small children. Without meeting his eyes she scuttled across the room to the door, where she delivered her parting shot. "I'd wish you the same, except I think you've forgotten how to have a good anything, which I find terribly sad."

The door opened and closed with a firm click. Gray stood, her words ringing in his ears. The desolation he'd been fighting for months pressed back around him, squeezing all the air out of his lungs.

Neala Shaw…

He closed his eyes, half lifted his hand as though reaching out for that dangling strand of hair. Eventually, moving as if he were fighting his way through thorns, he returned to the fireplace and sat down in the chair where Aunt Bella had been sitting. The faint scent of his aunt's toilet water wafted through his nostrils.

With a shuddering sigh Gray leaned his head back and tried not to think of anything at all.

Chapter Six

After completing morning chores, Neala grabbed her old corduroy jacket, a small writing tablet and a freshly sharpened pencil. As an afterthought, on the way out she retrieved a small magnifying glass from her desk. It was Saturday, and a brisk southwest wind carried the scent of rain and lilac through the windows. On her way downstairs, she debated whether or not to fetch an umbrella, decided the contraption would only be in the way and darted toward the back entrance off the kitchen, hoping nobody would stop her for a chat.

Grayson Faulkner's scowling image intruded into her mind as she scurried past the entrance to one of the school's informal parlors. What an infuriating man! Rude, unpleasant—a bully, he was. And he had hurt her feelings, which infuriated her even more. How could a saintly soul like Miss Isabella be kin to Mr. Faulkner?

Well, by the end of the day the rude bully of a man would be the recipient of a much-needed lesson. When Neala returned from her outing, she planned to be armed with enough proof of the hunter's presence in the woods yesterday to satisfy an entire room of Pinkerton detectives, much less Miss Isabella's nephew, who thought entirely too much of himself.

A small voice tweaked her conscience. All right, Neala conceded the point. Grayson Faulkner might be rude, unpleasant and arrogant, but last night, in the parlor, she'd sensed an undercurrent of emotion that, for the flicker of an eyelash, had almost prompted her to…feel sorry for him?

"Neala!" Judith Smithfield, her arms full of quilt scraps, interrupted the discomforting revelation. "We're quilting in an hour. Join us this time?"

"Not today, Judith." She waved an arm and grinned. "I'm off on a mission. I'll try to join the fun next Saturday." She ducked into the kitchen, almost tripping over a half-full pail of sudsy water.

"Oops, sorry, Neala!" Deborah McGarey sang out from beneath the huge island in the center of the kitchen. "I'm making pound cakes, but decided to break the eggs on the floor instead of the bowl."

Both of them laughed as Neala carried the pail closer. "Need help?" she asked reluctantly, relieved and guilty when Deborah shooed her on with a wry remark that only the guilty party should clean up smashed eggs.

Now *there* was the manner in which congenial people engaged in conversation, Neala thought, tossing her head. Stride determined, she crossed the grounds toward the forest. Civil people did not assume the worst about perfect strangers. Civil people did not act as though you had just perpetrated a crime of Machiavellian proportions, or accuse you of lying. And certainly a man who rushed to the rescue of a damsel in distress did *not* react like a churl.

The damp breeze swooped down, tugging several pins

from Neala's hastily bundled hair. When a handful of curls blew over her eyes, she glared upward, then stopped long enough to untie a large kerchief from around her neck. In a few ruthless movements she covered her hair and retied the ends beneath her chin. She looked like a gypsy washerwoman—but since there was nobody to see her but birds and other woodland critters, what did it matter how she looked?

What mattered was unearthing evidence of the wayward hunter.

Over an hour later, Neala was ready to concede that the general populace afforded scant appreciation to detectives and officers of the law. Not only could she not find the exact spot where she'd been when the first shot rang out, she could not find the tree she'd ducked behind, from which she'd hoped to extract a bullet, or at least mark as evidence of being struck by a bullet. Thoroughly out of sorts, she finally collapsed beneath a stumpy pine tree, yanked off the kerchief, and rubbed her face with it. The wind had blown the clouds away, leaving behind sunshine and a watery, pale blue sky. Much preferable to a rainstorm when one was playing detective.

And playing detective was all she had accomplished, besides collecting dirt in her shoes and the remains of a spiderweb in her hair. On the other hand, the day had turned pleasantly warm, she was alone in one of God's forest cathedrals, and nobody was clamoring for her attention. All in all, perhaps 'twas best to send both hunter and Mr. Grayson Faulkner the way of the clouds. Neala lifted her sturdy nickel brooch-style watch to check the time, made sure the whistle around her neck was still within instant reach, then with a contented sigh opened her notebook and began to write.

Some time later, a flying pinecone landed smack on top of the notebook in her lap. Neala yelped in surprise and dropped her pencil. The pinecone scattered detritus along with her concentration as it rolled to a stop in the crease of her notebook. Neala gawked at the missile for a bemused moment, then leaned forward to retrieve her pencil. When she straightened, her eyes almost popped out of her head. Mr. Faulkner had materialized between the trees some twenty paces away. He strolled toward her, grinning like a mischievous boy while he tossed a second pinecone in his hand.

"You were so lost in your girlish scribblings I probably could have jumped from behind the tree instead of lobbing a missile before you noticed."

Neala ignored the crack about girlish scribblings. Based on her scant acquaintance with the man, it was not an unexpected remark. "You're fortunate I didn't scream louder than this whistle—" she glanced at his holstered gun "—which I might have if you'd decided to gain my attention by firing a bullet over my head."

The smug look on his face deepened. "But you're already accustomed to dodging bullets, aren't you?" He extended a hand.

Neala allowed him to help her up, but stepped back the instant she gained her feet. She ignored the strange squiggle that shivered through her from the firm warmth of his bare palm, focusing instead on irritation. "Mr. Faulkner, did you follow me just to bait me like you did yesterday?"

The smugness on his face darkened to disapproval. "Absolutely. And for the last ninety-six minutes I followed, you never so much as glanced behind you." One eyebrow lifted in a sardonic arch. "Too busy trying to scout out a likely spot to plant some evidence, I daresay." The forest stilled—no rustling leaves or twittering birds or even a stray breeze, as though nature held its collective breath while Mr. Faulkner scratched his chin and contemplated Neala. "If I wanted to shoot you dead, you'd be stretched out on the ground, with nobody the wiser. Tell me, Miss Shaw, do you enjoy tempting fate, or do you merely have a wish to expire in the woods, like some fairy-tale maiden?"

His phrasing replicated her accusation of the previous day, and the gleam in his eye told her he'd done so deliberately. All right, enough was enough. Neala returned his bold appraisal, though the weapon strapped to his side intimidated by its sheer presence. On the other hand, the bizarre prescience she'd experienced in Miss Isabella's parlor returned in greater force, the one where Mr. Faulkner very much reminded her of Adrian. Her brother also used to cover his unhappy restlessness with hurtful words and a facade of hatefulness. "Mr. Faulkner, it's plain that for some reason you don't like me very much. It's not necessary for me to understand why, but I'd like to. Miss Isabella's fond of saying that a few bruises on an apple don't mean the entire fruit's gone completely bad. It just means that—"

"I'm well acquainted with the concept, and its application." He ran a hand through his hair, took a long breath. A faint glimmer of humor washed through his eyes. "Miss Shaw, you look like a squirrel's nest."

Neala self-consciously lifted a hand to the unruly locks of hair dangling around her face and neck. "My hair has a mind of its own, especially when the humidity is high. But it's rude of you to remark on it, Mr. Faulkner. Didn't your mother teach you better manners?"

"My mother taught me many things, including manners. I've spent the past fifteen years trying to forget every one of her…lessons."

The rancor in his voice sent a chill along Neala's spine. "I better return to the school," she began with forced cheeriness. "Three hours is the limit for Saturday free time on your own, unless you're on the school grounds within sight of the house." She lifted her hand to cup the whistle and took a steadying breath. "I have no idea why you've chosen to think the worst about me, nor do I particularly care to defend myself against someone whose mind is closed to reasoning. But for your information, Mr. Faulkner, I came out here in order to find evidence of that hunter—not to 'plant' it, as you accused me of."

"Didn't find any, did you? I wondered how long you planned to wander around."

"In a war, spying is a hanging offense."

"Then it's a good thing we're not at war, Miss Shaw."

"Aren't we?" Neala retorted quietly. She turned her back and retrieved her notebook and pencil. "I'm going now, Mr. Faulkner. You can either follow along or choose your own path. Either way, you've made your feelings toward me obvious. I'd appreciate it if you'd ignore me in the same manner I plan to ignore you."

He frowned, then abruptly swiveled on his heel and hurled the second pinecone into the trees. "You understand nothing about my feelings, Miss Shaw. Toward you or anything else. If I'm wrong about you, I apologize. If I'm not—" the pause was loaded with thinly veiled threat "—and you cause my aunt or her school any suffering at all, even a moment's concern, you'll not be able to run far enough or long enough. I'll find you, and you'll think my behavior today saintlike by comparison."

"I…see." Neala tapped her pencil against her lips in a vain attempt to hide the smile threatening to burst free. Oh, but the relief flooding her insides was a heady sensation, the urge to reassure Miss Isabella's thunderous nephew impossible to ignore. "Mr. Faulkner, I think you're a lion with the heart of a kitten. Bless you for trying to protect Miss Isabella and the Academy."

She lost the battle with her smile. "At least I finally understand the source of your anger, misguided though it was. After all, yesterday I did try to wallop you with a tree branch. I know you don't believe me, but someone really was shooting out here in the woods yesterday. And when the bullet hits the tree trunk inches from my nose, I have to conclude that—albeit by mistake—they were shooting at me. I'll let the matter drop, however, since it's obvious I've been unable to produce any tangible proof." She shrugged. "You've also helped me realize that my actions might cause Miss Isabella more concern—of course, you know she doesn't 'worry'! I… Well, I've grown very fond of your aunt. Ever since my parents' deaths, I suppose I've come to regard her as—"

She stopped, belatedly aware that the hue of Mr. Faulkner's tanned face had turned a deep shade of red, and a muscle twitched the corner of his mouth. *Ninny*, she scolded herself. Few men were comfortable with sentimentality. "I'll hush," she murmured, then impulsively reached across to lay her hand on his forearm. "Don't worry, Mr. Faulkner. I know God is watching over Miss Isabella every breath of every day."

Mr. Faulkner snarled an ill-tempered curse. Then, without another word, he turned his back and strode rapidly into the woods, disappearing within seconds beneath the trees.

Neala remained a few moments longer, watching until she realized she must look like a moon-eyed girl gazing after her sweetheart. *Rubbish*, she thought. Idiotic, as well, gazing after a man who had just blistered the air with invectives. By the time she found her path back to the school moments later, however, she was forced to admit that loneliness was even harder to bear, after meeting a man like Grayson Faulkner.

Chapter Seven

May, 1890

Two weeks later, after classes on a lazy Thursday afternoon, Neala and Abigail decided to spend their free Saturday hiking down to the Shenandoah River. A picnic on the riverbank would be their reward for the muscle-stretching trek down the steep cliff. To be sure, a well-marked path had been carved out by some Chilton ancestor over a century earlier; more recently Liam had hammered out handholds on some of the steeper sections. The hike posed little danger as long as the hikers exercised due diligence.

"We're all of us adult women," Miss Isabella lectured new students. "Therefore I 'restrict the restrictions' here at the Academy, because I expect each of you to exhibit common sense in all your choices. Since fresh air and healthy exercise offer an excellent venue with which to strengthen our individual godly temples, it is my hope that all of you feel free to explore the five hundred acres surrounding the Academy. Carefully. Good sense is a gift from our Lord. Expend it wisely, my dears, and try to limit your *non*sense to games of croquet, badminton and the like."

"I enjoy Miss Isabella's sense of humor," Abby said around a mouthful of oatmeal cookie. "Did you hear her earlier today, pleading with Mr. Pepperell to stop talking to the tomatoes because she's afraid we'll end up with such a bumper crop the house might slide off the cliff from the weight?"

Neala looked up from the list of supplies she was writing down in her tablet. "'Tis very wry, is it not?" she agreed. "I remember when I first arrived I never knew when she was serious, or merely teasing. Um…shall we take lemonade in our canteens, or sassafras tea?"

"Better stick with tea. I don't believe we have many lemons in the springhouse right now."

Neala dutifully added tea to their list, and they spent several congenial moments discussing other particulars. Then Abby took a deep breath and began fiddling with the eyelet edging of her shirtwaist. "Neala?" she asked, her voice softer. "Are you… I mean, do you still…" She grimaced, her gaze touching on Neala's, then shifting to some place that bespoke of a pain more vast than the universe. "I had another dream last night," she finished in a rush. "It wasn't a nightmare—I don't have those as much anymore. But I was with my family, and it was so real…" Her hand reached out blindly and Neala grabbed it, wrapping reassuring fingers around it. "I didn't want to wake up, Neala. I didn't want to wake up, because then I would have to accept all over again that they're gone, and I'm not. I'm still here, scarred and disfigured and…and alone. I mean, alone because I know I'll never marry."

"Oh, Abby…" Neala swallowed hard, her own throat

tightening against tears. "I understand. Sometimes I still think I need to tell Grandfather, or Mum…" Her voice trailed away. "But I do understand, completely," she finished. "Your heart sort of jerks when all of a sudden you remember they're gone. And it hurts so bad it's hard to breathe."

"At least your brother is still alive, even if you never see him again. Oh—I'm sorry, Neala. I didn't mean that the way it sounded. Truly I didn't."

"I know." Neala squeezed her hand once more and released it. They both sat back in the grass and smiled at each other. "Sometimes I dream that Adrian returns to Charlottesville, buys back our home, then finds me…" She stopped with a deprecatory grimace.

"Perhaps someday he will."

"Not likely." Neala chewed her lip for a moment, then waved a dismissive hand. "I'll always love Adrian, but I know I need to stop weaving fanciful tales that will never happen. Miss Isabella reminds me at least twice a week that I need to learn to accept how people are, instead of trying to nicely bully them into what I think they ought to be. I know she's right, but it's difficult."

She lifted her face toward the sky, soaking up the sunshine. "God planted a yearning in me for everybody in the world to get along, I suppose. But I must have a really hard head underneath all these wretched curls, because I keep trying despite the futility of it. My brother used to get so annoyed with me…"

Abby reached across to tug one of the infernal curling strands that was forever escaping the pins. "I love your hair. I wish mine had all that bounce and shine."

"Well, I've always admired yours because it's straight."

"What about Jocelyn's? Have you ever seen such a beautiful shade of red? She's very private, have you noticed? Even when I compliment her hair, she just gives me this sad smile. I wish she'd share her story."

"I'm sure she will, one day. Perhaps she's been able to follow Miss Isabella's advice better than the rest of us. 'Talking about the past can't redo it. We waste the present, and bore the listener…'"

"'…Because we all have a different past, and must walk a different path to overcome it,'" Abby continued, quoting one of their headmistress's most oft-repeated homilies.

They both laughed. Miss Isabella had a quote for everything—and never hesitated to trot an appropriate one out for a listener.

Neala pulled an annoying curl away from her face and wound it around her finger. "Well, I'll probably never accept that my brother's dead, but I have accepted that he… that he abandoned me." There. She'd finally stated the words aloud. "That's why I was allowed to come here. Miss Isabella decided I was enough of an orphan." She shrugged. "In all but the strictest sense, I am. I've heard nothing from my brother in over a year now."

"We both should remember that all of us here are only orphaned in bloodlines," Abby reminded her gently. "We have a home now, remember. And sisters?"

With a determined wave of her hand, Neala banished the hovering wisps of grief. "Absolutely. And now that I've come to know him, I might claim Liam as an uncle despite him being an Irishman instead of a Scot." They laughed again, and scrambled to their feet. "Come on, let's go inspect the kitchen and make sure our choice of picnic supplies is available."

"Don't forget to post our names on the list so everyone knows where we are. We may never have found your hunter, but when Nan and Alice climbed down to the river last week, they happened onto a pair of day-trippers, and I heard yesterday that someone else spotted either a hiker or a hunter—or was it some kind of animal?—on the edge of the grounds."

They commenced strolling across the grass as they talked. "The view over the river, toward the mountains, is breathtaking. With the Colonial Highway just at the bottom of the hill, I can easily imagine how a weary traveler would decide to break his journey, wander about. Sometimes I think I can almost hear God's voice in the river water, or the wind in the trees before a rain."

Abby only shrugged. Unlike Neala, her friend's faith in a loving God remained cautious, at times indifferent. Neala might not understand completely, but her imagination was vivid enough to realize that anyone's faith might be damaged beyond repair, when God allowed your entire family to burn to death.

Saturday morning dawned clear but chilly. A spring storm had swept through the previous night, followed by a refreshing northwest wind that plunged temperatures back toward February instead of May. Due to the chill, Abby and Neala decided to wear their cloaks, despite the awareness that it would hinder their progress down the cliff.

"But I'd rather watch my step a little more carefully than fall ill with ague," Neala cheerfully stated as she slung the cloak over her shoulders. "Besides, I've had this cloak since I was a child, and it's short enough not to trip me up."

Abby glanced ruefully down. Her own cloak covered all but the tips of her boots. "The pastor's wife gave this one to me several years ago, before I came here. She was taller than I am, but I was grateful to have a cloak at all."

"Hmm. I have an idea," Neala announced, fingers flying as she dumped shoulder satchel and canteen, then proceeded to unbutton her cloak. "We'll switch. I'm taller than you are, so my cloak will fit you better. Yours won't hang down to the ground, so neither one of us will have to worry about tripping."

"Neala, I didn't mean…"

"I know. But I do. So hurry up. We have to be back by three, remember."

Forty minutes later they paused for breath, giggling at each other because a strong wind had forced them to pull the cloaks' hoods over their heads and Neala announced they looked like a pair of phantoms floating down the cliff.

"Does add a bit of drama to our outing, doesn't it?" Abby said, giving a little shiver. "The wind creates all these rustling sounds, but we can't see anything much to the side, or behind us. There might be a bear about to pounce, or a wolf who mistakes one of us for Red Riding Hood."

"We'll wallop 'em with our walking sticks—oh, fiddle-faddle. My shoelace caught on these briars. Here—I'll sit on this rock and untangle it."

"Be careful. Those thorns are vicious. Want me to help?"

"I've got it. Why don't you go on ahead? This is the section where we have to go single file anyway. I'll be along in two shakes of a flea's whisker."

Abby nodded agreeably, and a moment later disappeared around a jutting boulder the size of a house. Neala only faintly heard the sound of her boots scraping over the stones. She hurriedly yanked at the laces, jerked when a thorn stabbed through her glove. Then her fumbling efforts caused the laces to knot. Several moments had evaporated by the time she retied her boots and set off after Abby. Impatient with the delay, Neala had to resist the urge to leap down the cliff like a mountain goat instead of exhibiting the common sense Miss Isabella prized so highly.

"Abby? Here I come!" she called, just as a gust of wind buffeted her back and shoulders. From somewhere above she heard a crunching, grating sound, like stone grinding against stone. Neala tossed her head in a vain effort to clear wisps of hair out of her eyes, at the same time fumbling for one of the handholds Liam had carved. Drat this wind, but it was difficult to see, between her wretched hair and the hood. "This wind is dread—"

An explosion of sound, as if a giant had just wrested one of the cliff boulders loose and hurled it over the side of the mountain, kicked the word back down her throat.

The path! Abby! Neala's heart lurched, pounded in sickening hard beats as she scrambled, slipping and reckless, down the trail, ripping her glove, tearing fingernails as she desperately fought to keep her balance on the steep, rock-infested path.

"Abby! Answer me! *Abby!* Did you see—" Gasping, she skidded to a trembling halt. "Father in heaven… Jesus, blessed Lord, help me." The agonized prayer died as Neala froze, not wanting to believe.

Abby lay sprawled in an unmoving heap on the only level part of the trail, her body completely covered by the rippling folds of Neala's cloak. All around her lay chunks of shattered stone. As though from a great distance Neala heard a faint splash—the remains of the falling boulder hurling itself into the river.

She didn't remember rushing to Abigail's side, didn't remember much of anything but the sound of roaring in her ears as she knelt beside her friend and with shaking hands pulled the cloak away from Abby's head. When Abby stirred, then moaned, breath and sound and color spewed through Neala in a flood tide. She gasped Abby's name, tears leaking from her eyes as she gently, carefully turned her over and stuffed Abby's cloak beneath her head. Sluggish blood oozed from a gash just above the other woman's eyebrow, but after a frantic search Neala found no other signs of blood, no other evidence of injury or a broken bone. Praise be to heaven above, but apparently she'd only suffered a glancing blow.

Abby's hand jerked, and her eyes fluttered open. She blinked several times, then winced. "N-Neala? Did… I… What happened?"

"Shh… You'll be all right. You're alive… Thank You, Lord! Oh, Abby…you're alive." One hiccupping sob escaped before Neala managed to throttle the wild emotion clamoring inside. Tenderly she laid her hand against her friend's chalk-white cheek. "The Lord worked overtime today, dearest. Somewhere above us, a boulder dislodged and fell. Probably loosened from all the rain we've been having." She struggled to catch a breath. "You s-seem to have been in its way. But you're alive. I don't know what I would have done… I couldn't have borne it, Abby… If you'd waited with me instead of going ahead…"

Abby's cold hand crept across to brush Neala's. "Do…

hush," she whispered, her voice clear but weak. "I'm just glad it didn't…squash me like a bug." A faint smile barely lifted the corners of her mouth. "But I think—I think you better…blow the whistle?"

Chapter Eight

The Grand Hotel, Philadelphia

The rowdy bunch playing poker at a nearby table erupted into another argument. Gray and his friends, lounging up at the bar, turned to watch.

"My money's on the gent with a beard." Carl toasted his choice with his half-full glass of ale. "Looks mean enough to settle the fight with fists."

"Nah…too civilized here. We're not in Denver anymore," Dan said. "I'll go for the tall guy with the prissy middle part in his hair and too much pomade. Probably a lawyer. Fork-tongued pettifoggers can talk their way out of a hornet's nest after convincing the hornets to sting the innocent bystanders. Whaddaya think, Falcon?"

Gray clapped a hand on Dan's broad-as-a-barn-door shoulder. "I think I know better than to place bets on anyone about anything. How 'bout having the barkeep send a round to the winner of their… What's this one? The fourth shouting match?"

"Sixth," Carl replied with a sloppy grin. With his carrot-red hair and youthful face, he looked more like a tipsy leprechaun than Gray's old buddy. "It's the sixth altercation," he repeated. "But who's counting? I'll pony up an' send 'em a round, pal, but only if you pick the winner first. I wanna see if your luck's still as bad at wagering as it's good at shootin'."

Gray elbowed him in the ribs, causing Carl to stumble against the man on his other side. Everyone apologized and toasted each other…a companionable assembly of gentlemen enjoying a few after-dinner drinks in a high-quality tavern across the street from a quality hotel. No prickly sensibilities, no irrational reactions, or raucous tempers itching to explode like the ill-mannered foursome playing poker. Why couldn't females understand a man's need to fraternize with other men without feeling guilty about it?

"Quit stalling, Gray," Carl jibed.

With a good-natured snort Gray gestured across the room, toward the saturnine man holding his cards in a white-fisted hand. His unmoving silence presented a stark contrast against his arguing fellow card players. "I'll take the quiet one," Gray said. "Been my experience the ones who make the least noise wind up the most dangerous."

His two friends solemnly nodded. Ten years earlier they'd all signed on as army scouts at the same time, then maintained a deep if largely disconnected friendship after they'd left the army. Periodically they'd meet somewhere between Kansas City and New York—wherever each could travel within a day's time—to catch up on each other's lives. Gray mused with fuzzy sentimentality that he hadn't realized until now how lonely he'd been since Marty's death.

"I think we should consider establishing some kind of business together," he announced, smacking his palm against the bar with a resounding thud. “Settle down in one place. Get respectable.”

“Settle down? Get *respectable*?” Dan swiped a strand of wheat-colored hair off his forehead. “You been letting your aunt sweet-talk you into giving up your sinful ways?”

“Not a chance. Aunt Bella knows better.” Gray spread his arms wide, almost knocking Carl off balance again. “She just welcomes me home like the prodigal son.” Then he scowled, for a brief moment remembering his motive for joining his friends in this saloon. “Sure wish I’d known there’d be a curly-headed little hornet in the jar this visit.” He swore ripely over the subject, not for the first time, causing Carl and Dan to roar with fresh laughter.

“Never known you to react like this to any woman outside your mother,” Carl observed between chuckles. “Some of ’em you treat like they’re another man, and some a foul-tasting tonic you have to imbibe. Never understood why they all still flutter ’round you.”

“Some young ladies seem to thrive on dreams of taming us wild ones.” Dan nodded sagely. “Did I ever tell you about this schoolteacher I saved from a scalping when—”

“Yes!” Gray and Dan chimed in together.

Unabashed, Carl grinned. “So how ’bout when Dan brought his purty little cousin to Richmond, two years ago, wasn’t it? Thought he’d finally found someone to pull the thorn out of Gray’s woman-hating heart.”

“Don’t hate women,” Gray muttered, feeling heat steal up the back of his neck. Not even the one who irritated his memories, with her thick mass of hair he wanted to bury his hands in, whose voice tantalized his thoughts with its soft Southern drawl. Neala Shaw was the only woman in years who didn't cower.

And Gray didn't want any part of her. Or any woman. He could enjoy a woman same as any other man—without allowing her to take over his life. "Just…don't ever want to be tied down to one," he finished, the words delivered almost defiantly. The clinging…the tears…the hurt looks calculated to instill permanent guilt—never again. No, sir, never again. He was a man, not a six-foot little boy, and he did *not* need mothering, or managing.

But he didn't hate all women. Fact was, he wanted to protect them, keep monsters from taking advantage, hurting someone weaker—no. If either of the species were weaker, it had to be the hapless male. Take himself, for instance. All he'd ever wanted was—

"Well, don't fret about Roberta chasing you down." Dan interrupted his sodden musing. "She married a train engineer last October. You're safe from her fluttering eyelashes—and me, having to pound your head, for breaking her heart."

"Ha! *You're* the one who's safe," Carl interrupted with an inebriated guffaw. "'Cuz you'd've been the one getting his head pounded, not our friend here. Good ol' Gray. Best man with a gun, best man with his stropped-razor tongue and falcon's eyes, and best man with his fists."

For some befuddled reason, the turn of conversation pricked Gray on the raw. Deep inside he knew his behavior toward women, and at times men, as well, could be disrespectable, and more often than he cared to admit, ventured perilously close to dissolute. The idealistic boy out to save the world from evil was long dead and buried somewhere west of the Mississippi River, and Gray told himself he didn't mourn over him. But surely at the advanced age of thirty-two Grayson Faulkner had not transformed into a misogynist, as that prissy urchin had accused him of. Surely he retained enough family honor to justify the moniker of gentleman.

When he wasn't three sheets to the wind, that is.

"On second thought," he abruptly announced, "let's call it a night." He waved toward the massive wall clock hanging between the stuffed heads of an elk and a ten-point buck. "It's after eleven. Closing up in less than an hour, anyway. Tomorrow's Sunday, y'know. Can't have drunkards and carousers spoiling the Sabbath, remember."

"When's the last time you sat on a pew for a church service, Gray?" Carl asked.

Before Gray could answer, the quiet poker player across the room shoved away from the table and surged to his feet. "You there!" he called in a flat nasal voice, the tone belligerent. "You there at the bar with your pie-eyed friends. You been staring at me, and I don't like it."

Ignoring the angry blustering of the other men at the table, the man tossed down his cards and started toward the bar.

"Uh-oh." Dan glanced from Gray to the oncoming poker player. "Want us to take care of him for you, buddy?"

"Yeah, we'll settle it," Carl chimed in, slamming his drink down on the bar. "Shame for you to go visit your folks sporting a black eye."

Weary to the bone, eaten up with a bitter sense of shame that would not leave him alone, Gray was tempted to give in.

Pride, and a sense of fair play, wouldn't allow him. "I could go home wearing a blasted three-piece suit from

Paris, with a carnation in the lapel, and the reaction would be the same as if I sported buckskins. And a black eye." As casually as he could manage given his none-too-steady knees, Gray stiffened his back and shifted his stance. "My family condemns me for my actions." Almost as much as he condemned himself.

The poker player stopped a yard away. "Got no use for rude drunks."

"Me either," Gray responded, flexing his hands. "Didn't mean to stare. Sorry to cause offense and all that."

Carl and Dan made a poor job of stifling laughter.

The stranger's face burned brick-red. "Seems ta me you and your drunk friends need someone to teach you a lesson."

"Ah…mm…" Gray struggled to retain a hold on his slippery temper. "Been out of school a while now." He tucked his thumbs into his waistband and propped his elbows on the counter behind him. "I don't want a fight, mister. Why don't you go on back to your table and try to teach *your* friends a lesson. From the looks of it they need schooling more than we do."

The man's head lowered and he took another step forward. "You don't want to make sport of me, you drunken lout."

"Nope," Gray cheerfully agreed. "Matter of fact, we were just leaving, weren't we, boys?"

Grinning like maniacs, Carl and Dan nodded.

"And," Gray repeated more softly, "I don't want a fight. This isn't the West, you know, friend. There are laws against public scenes."

"I ain't your friend. And if you weren't angling for a broken jaw, ya shouldn't have stared at me."

Without warning, the man swung, coming in with a left hook that might in truth have broken Gray's jaw if the blow had connected. But Gray read the action in the man's glittering eyes, and in a few swift moves rendered the astonished fellow immobile, sweating with pain. Both men knew the slightest pressure could break either a wrist or an arm; only Gray knew how thin the thread keeping him from losing control was. He blinked, fighting the tremors and volcanic emotion that stretched his body as taut as a man on a rack.

"When you live around pigs too long, the stench tends to cling." Sucking in a sobering breath, Gray released his victim except for a punishing hold that kept the man's right hand at an angle that ensured his continued compliance. "If you knew me, you'd know better than to provoke a fight I don't want. Now go on back to your poker buddies, and leave me alone." With a contemptuous shove he released him.

Silence hovered throughout the room as the routed card player slunk between tables. Men shifted their gazes as he passed by.

Feeling lower than a snake's belly in a deep pit, Gray muttered a curse beneath his breath. "Let's get out of here. I'm sick of feeding fodder to the Faulkner gristmill."

But as he stalked out, flanked by Carl and Dan, Gray lost the battle against the penetrating voice warning him that he was the perpetrator of the gossip, not the victim of it. For years he'd fought to free himself from suffocating familial chains, only to discover that in his determination to escape he'd trapped himself inside a cell without a door. He might as well wish himself on the North Star as to wish he could repudiate the Faulkner name, or change the person he had become.

Wouldn't it be a fitting cosmic joke if Neala Shaw were right after all? Grayson Faulkner, youngest son of a prestigious family whose honor and philanthropy dated back four generations, *was* a misogynist. And on the way to becoming a public punching bag as well.

Isabella Chilton Academy

Tucked fifteen feet up in the notch of a massive oak, screened by branches and a cluster of leafy maples, a man watched the wiry Irishman and the girl—*who should be dead*—explore the edge of the cliff. Still as a hoot owl, he watched them discover where he'd patiently chipped the base of the boulder until one hard shove sent it over the cliff. Of course he'd been canny enough to wipe away the boot prints, so he wasn't concerned with discovery. They would assume he'd climbed down the cliff and escaped in a boat up the river, or vanished into the forest. People were predictable and seldom thought their way beyond the obvious.

Nonetheless, the unpleasant truth scraped his mind like a hacksaw blade: Neala Shaw was still alive. Instead of preparing for a funeral, someone had decided to investigate. And even a brainless dolt would realize the significance of their findings. Sure enough, moments later he clearly heard the windblown voices, heard them reach the inevitable conclusion. The Irishman—Liam, he heard her call him—vented his spleen in a loud mixture of Gaelic and English.

"...and ye can be sure as St. Patrick's cowl I'll no' be standing back fer that dunderhead of a sheriff. The black-hearted jackanapes who'd be after harming Miss Isabella's girls will be answering to me, see if he don't."

"Liam…"

"Now, missy. You got eyes, and a brain underneath all them curls. You know same as me the way of it, here."

Temptation cascaded through his veins; he wanted to finish her off now, right now, not even caring that he'd have to kill the Irishman as well. He wrapped his arms around the thick tree trunk to keep from giving in to the urge.

Frustration knotted his stomach and set his head to throbbing like a wound. *The boulder hadn't even struck the right girl.* All his careful preparations, every second of his meticulous planning, the dark nights he'd sweated through preparing the site to ensure the supposition of an "accidental" death…and *still* she was alive. She might as well be rubbing his nose in the dirt, gloating over his failure.

How could he have known they'd change cloaks? Why had they done so? It wasn't fair! *It was not to be allowed!*

He closed his eyes and struggled to remember his ultimate goal. Over the past several years he'd experienced other failures, but in the end patience and persistence always yielded success. Neala Shaw would be no different. And this time, the final act of retribution would bring about the final victory.

When he reopened his eyes, Neala and the Irishman had vanished. He could hear nothing but leaves scuffling in the breeze, and his own ragged breathing. Panic raced over his skin, freezing cold, like sleet in January. Then his ear caught the faint sound of voices. Ah. They were returning to the house, then. Not searching the woods or the path down the cliff to the river. He was still undetected, still safe. Still in charge of destiny, theirs as well as his own.

Carefully he climbed down the tree, dropped to the ground, then set off after them. Through binoculars he watched as they crossed the lawn and entered the main house.

Nothing to do now but wait. And maintain the watch.

For the next two days he prowled, a silent onlooker stoking resolve with a blend of righteous anger and bitter frustration. They knew the boulder was deliberate—but was there enough evidence to point to Neala Shaw as his target? The sheriff hadn't put in an appearance, but that might be because the old woman who ran the school didn't want to broadcast such disquieting news: either a student had been singled out for elimination, or the intent had been to kill whoever was on the path at the time.

Every now and then he wanted to laugh. Delicious temptation goaded him to ignite a whispering campaign, for the pleasure of watching all the other students flee like roaches escaping a fire. The hoity-toity Isabella Chilton Academy's reputation would be as smashed to bits as the boulder he'd shoved over the cliff.

By the end of the second day temptation dribbled away. All he truly cared about was Neala's reaction. Would she finally run again? He passed delicious hours hoping so. He was weary of this place, especially since it only served to remind him of his failures to eliminate Neala Shaw. And he'd been sighted at least once, which festered inside, more of a worry than he liked to admit. The longer he lurked about, the greater the likelihood of exposure, questions. Speculations that would force him to have to kill an innocent bystander.

The possibility sickened him. Despite his skill at it, he had never enjoyed taking life. Such an act shouldn't be so easy, like swatting flies or squashing worms. Men who killed for the sport of it, or worse, for money, deserved the hangman's noose.

But when there was no choice, when duty and honor required it, he did what was necessary. Yet the responsibility weighed him down as heavily as the hundredweight sacks of flour he used to have to lift in one of his many jobs.

His job right now was to deprive Neala Shaw of life.

On the morning of the third day, he awoke in his cozy sleeping bag covered by leaves with tears dampening his face. Even peppermint drops could not soothe the sour taste in his stomach. It was with profound relief that shortly after the sun cleared the Blue Ridge he watched Liam-the-Irishman drive the coach up to the house; moments later Neala and the headmistress appeared. What an ugly old woman, he thought, shuddering. He'd hate having to arrange for *her* demise. The Irishman handed Neala inside the coach, then tossed several pieces of baggage and a large trunk into the boot.

At last! Neala had decided to flee. Finally he would depart this cursed school, which in his mind had taken on the personality of a brooding guardian, protecting Neala Shaw and thwarting his every effort.

Now that she was leaving, she would be more vulnerable. Wherever she fled, he would follow, as he had followed her here the previous year. And this time—he would finish the task.

He would not enjoy it, but confidence filled him as he watched the coach slowly clatter down the long winding lane toward the turnpike. This time *he* would emerge the victor instead of the vanquished.

Then he remembered: he had no horse. He did not have

a horse, much less a buggy, or even a wagon. Without transportation he would never be able to track the coach to its destination.

He dropped to his knees, pounding the earth in helpless rage.

Chapter Nine

Like the shrouded boatman carrying departed souls across the river Styx, the night train swayed and rattled its way southwest toward the West Virginia mountains. All its passengers save Neala were asleep, no doubt enjoying blissful dreams of their destinations. Wide awake, hands clenched in her lap, Neala yearned in vain for blissful dreams, rather than the living nightmare of leaving the Academy—of the reason *for* leaving.

Why couldn't Miss Isabella understand that she hadn't wanted to go? She was compelled, by what she considered irrefutable evidence: someone, for some unknown reason, apparently wanted Neala dead.

Restlessly she shifted about on the seat, her mind as jostled as her body. Over the past endless hours of travel she'd forced herself to reexamine all the deaths in the family the past several years. The unhappy conclusion, at least for Neala, could neither be escaped nor ignored: every one of those deaths except for her grandfather's heart seizure could have been carefully arranged to appear as though they'd been accidents. Her uncle's drowning…one cousin struck by a runaway freight wagon, the other in a hotel fire…her parents.

And her own "accidents" at the Academy—the fire in the harness room. The hunter who had "mistaken" her for an animal. Then finally, the boulder that had almost killed Abby, because she'd been wearing Neala's cloak.

A spasm of grief tightened her throat, grief and the ever-present anxiety that now coated every moment. She couldn't stay at the Academy, of course. But what on earth could she have been thinking, scuttling off to hide at a place like White Sulphur Springs?

For over a hundred years the Old White, as it was referred to by long-standing guests, had enjoyed a reputation as one of the world's premier springs resorts. Presidents and politicians mingled with wealthy landowners, European aristocrats and Yankee industrialists. Old South debutantes—"the belles"—those young ladies of impeccable breeding and beauty, flocked to the Old White for the sole purpose of securing a husband and supplying guests and journalists with an unending store of gossip.

Even under the chaperonage of an old family friend, Neala would be a scruffy stray kitten amidst a bevy of pampered Persians. Fiddle-faddle. She huffed out an impatient breath. It didn't matter. She wasn't going to the Old White to fit in, much less cast lures for a husband, regardless of what her chaperone and family friend Mrs. Frances Wilkes might have "arranged" for her.

Neala was going there to hide, in a crowded, respectable setting. Surely the murderer would never consider searching for plain Neala Shaw among the elite guests summering at White Sulphur Springs.

Still, she would always have to be on her guard, not

only for herself, but for everyone around her. She could not bear the thought of bringing danger upon dear Mrs. Wilkes, who had known the Shaws as long as Neala could remember.

An unacceptable lump swelled in her throat. She always found herself longing for something she couldn't have. Losing. Leaving, having to let go. How much time would have to pass to assuage the grief of leaving the Isabella Chilton Academy?

Miss Isabella wanted her to trust in God's notion of divine protection. Neala would have appreciated a few words from the headmistress on precisely how one best manifested such trust in a non-corporeal Being, when nobody here on earth was inclined to believe her.

If only she hadn't insisted that Abby borrow her cloak. No, if Abby hadn't worn that cloak, Neala would still be a blind duck in an open field. And despite their refusal to countenance such a possibility, both Miss Isabella and Liam conceded that it had been a person who shoved that boulder, not nature. But like the headmistress, the wiry coachman considered it nothing beyond a nasty prank, unlikely to be repeated.

Without warning, a bucketful of terror numbed her limbs as though she'd plunged them into a frozen pond. Neala jabbed her scalp with a hairpin. The brief pain didn't help.

Nobody believed her. To be blunt, nobody wanted to believe her, and how could she blame them? She herself didn't want to believe her assertions. Not for the first time, Grayson Faulkner's image pricked its way willy-nilly into her mind. Now there was a man with little use for speculations. Yet despite his uncivil behavior toward

Neala, for some inexplicable reason she found herself thinking about him. A lot. One moment she'd be immersed in fear and desperation; the next, her wayward brain dragged out an image of Mr. Faulkner.

Oh, he was a good-looking fellow, with his black hair and those blue eyes that… Well, mostly the expression in those blue eyes flayed her like a fish. But there had been a time or two, in Miss Isabella's parlor, and the next day, when he'd followed her in the woods, that she'd glimpsed something in his expression that made her skin feel too hot.

Quit behaving like a headless chicken, Neala. She would never see the man again and even if she did, more likely than not her skin would feel hot from anger or embarrassment. Flumagudgin. She didn't even understand why she kept thinking about Grayson Faulkner, when she needed to invest every scrap of energy in staying alive.

The sentiment seemed to echo in the crowded, stuffy coach.

Stiffly, with trembling fingers Neala dug around in her reticule and tugged out the only heirloom left to remind her that she had been part of a family, whose roots stretched back for centuries. After removing her gloves, she wrapped her fingers around the cool weight of Grandfather Shaw's crest badge.

He had so loved to talk about the badge. Originally fashioned from hammered silver, it had been worn on an ancient clansman's bonnet, held in place with a leather strap during battle. The present badge now sported a symbolic silver strap and buckle that circled the crest, along with some assorted colored-glass chips set in various places. Her grandfather had valued this badge more highly than gold. The central crest, he loved to remind her, had been given to Neala's great-great…well, a great many great-grandfathers ago, after he saved the clan chief's life. During the generations that followed, the eldest sons determined to distinguish themselves in similar fashion, to bring honor to their branch of the Shaw clan.

Yet as Adrian had reminded her throughout their childhood, it was Neala who had inherited Grandfather's name. And it was only Neala—granddaughter Neala—who was allowed to hold the crest badge. Growing up, the privilege had consoled her when Adrian kicked her shins under the dinner table or teased her about her curly mane of hair.

But they'd been family. Even now Neala liked to believe that, had Adrian been willing to take his place as the only remaining male child in the Neal Shaw branch of the clan, Grandfather would have bequeathed the badge to him.

But Adrian had scoffed at what he considered naught but sentimentality. He refused to be saddled with the antiquated notion of family honor, much less worship a stupid object that probably wouldn't fetch two dollars at an auction.

And he had run away. Neala's breath caught in her throat as a horrid possibility leaped into her mind. *What if Adrian had not run away after all?* What if the killer had discovered his whereabouts, and Adrian was not missing, but dead?

A fog of numbness shrouded her. Dead. Everyone in her family, everyone but her. All that remained of the Shaw family was Neala, a trunkful of letters, journals and papers—and the old crest badge that Neala had kept hidden from the auctioneers. And if she couldn't discover who was trying to murder her, and somehow stop them, that lineage would end forever, along with the fierce pride symbolized in the badge she clutched with desperate fingers.

White Sulphur Springs, West Virginia
August 1890

Sunbeams streamed through the trees, transforming the resort grounds into a multi-green patchwork of light and shadow. In striking contrast, all the buildings, from the four-hundred-foot-long Old White Hotel to the hundred cottages scattered over forty acres, glistened in their coats of blinding white paint. Greenbrier's White Sulphur Springs—"the Old White," longtime guests affectionately called it—lay nestled with the serenity of puffy white clouds in a deep blue sky between three gentle peaks of the ancient Appalachian Mountains.

Through the early-morning mist shrouding the trees just beyond the rows of cottages, Howard's Creek threaded a silvery path along the upland valley that stretched westward between the mountains. Here was a magical place, where whispers of Indian legends mingled with Old South manners. The ravages of the War Between the States had vanquished neither its gentility nor the sulphur springs from which gushed forty thousand gallons of water daily.

Over the past weeks, for at least a few hours each day, Neala allowed herself to lay aside her circumstances, instead thanking the good Lord for such a peaceful place. 'Twas difficult to dwell upon threats of death when every breath filled her lungs with pure mountain air, and the sounds of nature rang through her ears. Birds warbled, squirrels scampered among the boughs of oak, sugar maple and pine, while chipmunks darted among the laurel and rhododendron; on this morning, the air was dew dripped with a nip of autumn just around the corner. It was a fairy-tale scene, complete with a doe and two half-grown fawn slipping through the trees behind the line of guest cottages dubbed Paradise Row.

Neala always suppressed a smile whenever someone referred to "the cottages." Most of the brick structures had been constructed fifty or more years earlier by wealthy Southern blue bloods out to impress, and it took a stretch of the imagination for Neala to equate any of them with her notion of a cottage. Some of the rows resembled miniature versions of the main hotel, with miles of stairs and endless rows of columns to support the long porches. Presidents and society's elite spent entire seasons in those "cottages," graciously mingling with guests of unremarkable stations. Lesser-known families, bachelors and more plebeian guests were housed, like Neala, in spotless but plainly appointed rooms either inside the main hotel, or in the smaller rows of one-and two-room cottages.

The atmosphere at the White was unlike any other resort hotel in the world, Mrs. Frances Wilkes often remarked. "The quality of its guests might be exclusive, but the atmosphere is most democratic," she liked to remind Neala in her cultured Southern accent. "Even those prattling publications acknowledge the sociability here at the Old White. I trust you'll find no cause to disagree."

Since her arrival Neala had befriended two housemaids and one of the groundskeepers, along with a shy debutante from Pennsylvania and an elderly Confederate general. On matters of democratic sociability she found it easy to agree with her status-minded guardian.

Unfortunately, in other areas she and Mrs. Wilkes remained perpetually at loggerheads. Neala refused to agree either to the elderly woman's matchmaking efforts, or to her insistence that Neala allow her to provide costumes "appropriate to the guests at the Old White."

To be sure, there were a number of debutantes who might cast a pitying glance at her simple day and evening frocks and lack of adornment in a place renowned for ladies' fashions. Since professors' daughters weren't accustomed to grand fashion, Neala ignored the glances with the same sunny indifference with which she faced down the autocratic Mrs. Wilkes.

A sensation of timelessness permeated the air here, a peacefulness that banished haste and softened the sharp edge of anxiety. Her sleep was more restful, less riddled with nightmares of an unknown murderer. It was as though life both past and future was restrained inside a stoppered bottle, allowing a freedom from "vexatious rules of etiquette which hem in fashionable life at home," according to one of the many treatises on White Sulphur Springs scattered about the hotel's various reading rooms.

For Neala, that meant the freedom to wander about on her own, another issue upon which she and Mrs. Wilkes disagreed.

"You've changed, in a most disappointing fashion, from the accommodating child I remember," she liked to fuss, chin tilted imperiously. "The docile companion I anticipated seems to have grown into one of those disagreeable females who claim they wish to be emancipated. Stuff and nonsense. Intelligent women have always enjoyed the power they wield in their homes. This longing for emancipation, as though they were slaves, will lead to nothing but chaos, you mark my words. I daresay such notions on your part must be laid at your father's doorstep. Edward was always annoyingly progressive in his principles."

"Father was respected by everyone, because he treated people as Christ commanded," Neala responded, earning a rusty laugh and a pat on the cheek.

"There, now. That's the sweet girl I remember. You needn't defend your father to me, child. He may have been less than an adequate provider, but he was a good enough father and husband, despite his over-idealistic notions."

Neala forbore from trying to explain that her "emancipation" rose from necessity rather than inclination. She wandered alone in order to regain confidence. She refused to live the rest of her life cowering in her room because she was alone, without an escort, protector, or even a friend. If she could not achieve a semblance of serene independence here at White Sulphur Springs, likely there was no sanctuary this side of heaven she would find peace—until she discovered who was trying to kill her, and why.

Of course, like Miss Isabella, Mrs. Wilkes refused to believe that members of the Shaw family had been murdered, or that Neala herself was in fact hiding from the murderer or murderers. As far as the elderly widow was concerned, so many tragic deaths had weakened Neala's sensibilities; what she needed was a healthful dose of the waters, and a healthy focus on the living instead of the dead.

Sometimes Neala was almost tempted to believe her. Mrs. Wilkes's personality burned fiercely despite her almost eighty years. A quintessential matriarch of the Old South, her bloodlines included several senators, a governor and even European royalty. Her third husband had purportedly owned half the state of Alabama.

On this sunny morning in August, as usual she and Neala were on their way to taking the waters at the domed springhouse down the hill from the main hotel. Neala would have enjoyed the daily pastime more if the water didn't originate from a sulphur spring, which engendered a burned-match odor to the liquid. She could scarcely swallow the stuff without grimacing.

Today she was pensive, having spent until the wee hours of the night poring through the diary her grandmother Annie had kept the first year she and Grandfather Neal were married. Och, to have a love so strong as theirs...

"Must I be inflicted with a gloomy face this morning?" Mrs. Wilkes demanded, her walking cane thumping along the path.

"Sorry." Neala offered a wan smile. "I fear I stayed up too late, reading Grandmother's diary."

"Pish-tosh. You can be most vexing, my girl. Every Southerner since the War Between the States has a tragedy to share, grief to bear. You're only entitled to one life here on earth. Seems to me you could expend yours better than forever prattling about near-tragic accidents and untimely family deaths, and poring over a trunk of worthless papers. I've spent the better part of these past weeks introducing you, outfitting you properly, even instructing you on the finer points of a schottische so you'll be prepared for the Grand Ball tomorrow night."

She paused to nod regally to a couple strolling past in the opposite direction. "People come here to celebrate the joys of social intercourse, not wallow in their respective melodramas. I lost my first husband after only seven months, my second one in the War, and poor Vernon to Kentucky bourbon. I told you about Vernon, didn't I?"

"Yes, ma'am. He drank too much, and one night tripped over a boot scraper, fell and cracked his skull."

"Died on the spot. I didn't carry on about it then, and you don't see me carrying on about it now. Nor did I ever concoct implausible stories of sinister goings-on." She slanted Neala one of her censuring looks. "Haven't had anybody attempt to toss you off Lover's Leap, or accost you on a walk up Prospect Hill over these past months, have you?"

"No, ma'am." But that didn't mean it wasn't ever going to happen.

After they finished drinking their glasses of sulphur water, Mrs. Wilkes led Neala away from the crowd of other guests, down another of the many walking paths that crisscrossed the grounds.

"My letter from Isabella yesterday was most interesting," she announced. "For some reason beyond good sense, she has decided to enlist the help of a private investigator to look into the matter of the dislodged boulder. Good heavens, the incident occurred over two months ago."

Neala failed to suppress a gasp of indignation. Mrs. Wilkes slanted her a look before continuing. "I do not pretend to know what she hopes to accomplish. Private investigator indeed! I plan to tell her of my profound distaste in associating with such a person."

"She didn't tell me, or I would have dissuaded her," Neala said. "Besides, if anyone hired a detective, it should be me." And she had considered doing so, but only briefly since she had no means of paying such a person for services rendered.

"Balderdash. I absolutely forbid it." Mrs. Wilkes nodded to a noisy group dressed in riding apparel, spoke severely to several bright-eyed belles whose high-pitched giggles "offended the restful atmosphere," then turned back to Neala. "However, this…person has already agreed, and will be arriving here within the week to interrogate you. You needn't look like that. I plan to send the upstart packing myself. Now—no, you may not interrupt me, girl."

Ruefully, Neala complied. Later on, she would telegraph Miss Isabella, and—

"Neala! Are you paying attention?"

"Yes, ma'am." With considerable effort she forced her attention back on the widow.

"As I was saying, I noticed George Watlington—with that equestrian party heading for the stables—sizing you up. You could do worse. Only mark against him to my knowledge are those ears of his—big as the handles on a soup tureen. One could only hope the children would inherit yours." She inspected Neala's. "It's a blessing for a woman to have ears like you, small, flat against the head. Too bad about your hair—much too rebellious. We'll have to instruct Lallie to pin it up securely for the ball, show off your ears. Made to wear earrings. Speaking of that, I must insist you borrow my rubies tomorrow evening."

"That's very kind of you," Neala offered meekly. "I promise to look dazzling for you, Mrs. Wilkes."

"Bah! Matters not a whit to look dazzling for me, and you know it. Far better to dazzle the Watlington fellow. Now, I'll hear no more on the matter. It's time for breakfast. After that, you will accompany me to the post office. I'm sending Isabella a strongly worded reply about the inadvisability of indulging the weak minds of vulnerable young women. Private investigator indeed!"

Chapter Ten

The following night a thousand guests milled about the grand ballroom and spilled outside, crowding against the large window bays opened to view the proceedings. Streamers of multicolored veiling hung suspended about the cavernous room; the grandstand, alcoves and door arches had been lavishly decorated with greenery and garden roses. Even the two rows of pillars that ran the length of the room had been festooned in the colorful streamers. Debutantes floated across the floor in colorful sweeps of heliotrope silk, pink satin and white chiffon, full of life and a certain awareness that all eyes were trained upon them from the toes of their dancing slippers to the carefully arranged hair piled atop their heads. Jewelry winked and sparkled in a dazzling display around their creamy necks and dangled from their ears. The gentlemen's formal black tie and tails and snowy white shirtfronts offered a perfect counterpoint to the rainbow of color.

Reporters from newspapers and magazines all over the country prowled among the guests like hungry alley cats—another example of what Mrs. Wilkes referred to as the "vulgarization of our way of life." In Neala's first week at the White, an earnest gentleman with kind brown eyes had sidled up to her at the evening ball, inveigled her name before Neala realized his occupation, and was avidly peppering her with questions about Mrs. Wilkes when her mentor had steamed across the room and dispatched the fellow with a single look.

No member of the press had bothered Neala since.

Tonight, clad in a quiet plum-colored evening gown that muted even the Burmese rubies Mrs. Wilkes insisted she borrow, for the most part Neala watched the proceedings with a crush of other spectators. Mrs. Wilkes, along with a number of other habitués, held court from a row of chairs arranged for them at one end of the floor. The orchestra was in fine form, and several times gentlemen, including the large-eared Mr. Watlington, wove their way through the crowd to ask Neala to dance. She agreed mostly to please Mrs. Wilkes.

She also knew better than to confess to the matchmaking dowager how often wistful speculations about Grayson Faulkner continued to tease her heart. Now, if Mr. Faulkner suddenly appeared and asked her for the next dance…

Neala would turn him down flat.

The romantic atmosphere here must have affected her common sense.

She gave herself a mental pinch, then turned to the woman beside her and launched into an animated conversation.

By a little past midnight, the heat and noise battered at even the stoutest set of nerves, and the clash of perfumes and flowers and gentleman's hair pomade was making Neala's head swim. Over the hours more than one elderly guest had had to be escorted outside to inhale a reviving draft of chilly mountain air. Smashed into one of the window bays between a middle-aged couple from Ohio and a rowdy trio of young men making calves' eyes at the debutantes, Neala tried in vain to spot Mrs. Wilkes to see if the elderly woman needed to retire, though Neala's concern would doubtless be met with nothing less than a sharp rebuttal.

The dancers gathered in the center of the dance floor for another waltz, and with a stab of guilt Neala decided to savor her final moments of a sight she would never be part of again. Miss Isabella, and the rest of the students back in Virginia, would expect a detailed accounting.

Movement swelled outside the window as more onlookers seemed to converge behind her. Neala tried to wriggle forward on the window seat to escape the crush. Perhaps if she could stand…

Someone grabbed her arm; she glanced over her shoulder, but the lady from Ohio shifted just then, stumbling against Neala. Their gazes met in commiserating glances. But when Neala inclined her head to hear the proffered apology, she felt gloved fingers close around her arm again. She half turned, attempting with little success to discover who was trying to gain her attention—or haul her out of the way.

"So sorry," one of the young men to her left exclaimed as he was pushed sideways to collapse beside her onto the seat. "Odious bit of a crowd, isn't it?"

The fingers slipped away from her arm. Laughing, Neala started to warn the young man about the impatient onlookers outside the window who wanted them out of their way. At the same instant she opened her mouth, the orchestra struck the opening chords for Strauss's "Vienna Waltz." She waved him away instead and they both turned to observe the dancers. As she tried again to wriggle forward, she felt her arm clasped for the third time. Only now the tug was unrelenting, forcing her to lean her head back toward the window. Warm, bourbon-scented breath tickled her neck, just beneath her right ear.

"You couldn't hide forever," a hoarse voice whispered. "It's your turn now. You'll have to die. I'm sorry..."

Applause burst around her, the music soared, and the swell of a thousand conversations hummed through the ballroom as the dancers whirled around the floor.

Neala sat immobile, frozen in place, like a hapless butterfly pinned against a board.

For the first twenty-four hours after the ball, Neala barricaded herself in her room. After arranging for room service to deliver her meals, she sent word to Mrs. Wilkes that she was feeling poorly due to the excess activities of the ball, and planned to rest for a day or two.

Not surprisingly, the widow appeared at her door within an hour to personally demand explanations, and to change Neala's mind. Neala weathered the onslaught in polite silence. Then—equally politely—she promised to join Mrs. Wilkes at two the following afternoon, for a watermelon tea on the grounds. Hopefully, she reasoned, by that time she would be able to shore up her defenses adequately and behave with sufficient aplomb to mollify her irate sponsor.

At any rate, what would be gained by cowering in her room for the rest of the season? The murderer had discovered her whereabouts. He had approached her directly in the midst of a thousand oblivious guests. If he was determined to carry out his threat, a watermelon tea sufficed as well as her bedroom at the hotel as the site of her demise.

Miserably uncertain, Neala spent most of the day seated at her desk, reading through family documents yet another time, or wandering about the small room. Every so often she gazed forlornly out the window, where carefree guests strolled along the paths, lounged about on blankets spread over the long grasses, played croquet—all of them without a care in the world because *they* hadn't been told they had to die.

By the following morning, fear, restlessness and boredom propelled Neala out of her hiding place hours before the two o'clock watermelon tea. Heart rattling her rib cage, she marched along the hall, down two flights of stairs and outside to the grounds. Then she sat on one of the wooden benches wrapped around several of the larger trees, where she was visible to *everybody.* Surely the murderer would not carry out the deed in view of several hundred witnesses.

Almost an hour passed before her heartbeat settled to a calmer rhythm and she didn't jump whenever someone strolled by or spoke to her.

"Miss Shaw?"

Neala whipped her head around, then smiled a genuine smile. "Mr. Crocker, how nice to see you. I trust you've had no more run-ins with a wasps' nest?"

The groundskeeper removed his cap and smiled back shyly. "No'm, no wasps lately."

The question had become a silly yet enjoyable ritual they shared each time they happened to meet. Neala had first encountered Mr. Crocker several weeks earlier; she'd been strolling along one of the paths behind Alabama Row that led to the footbridge over Howard's

Creek when she spied Mr. Crocker frantically attempting to escape a swarm of wasps. Using her parasol, Neala leaped into the fray, swatting and shooing until both of them finally collapsed in relief on the steps of one of the cottages. Despite Mr. Crocker's protests, Neala had fetched some baking soda and water, made a paste and applied it to his myriad stings. He'd been panicked that his carelessness might cost him his job, since he'd only been employed by the hotel a week earlier. Neala assured him that nothing of the sort would happen, but she would speak to the head groundskeeper on Mr. Crocker's behalf. Ever since, whenever he caught sight of her, Mr. Crocker made a point of speaking to her, and Neala inquired about the wasps.

"Were you commandeered into helping clean up after last night?" she asked next.

"No'm. I've been over to the cottages, trimming the bushes. Um…did you attend? The Grand Ball, that is?"

The smile on Neala's face stiffened, but she answered readily enough. "Oh, yes. And it *was* grand."

"I imagine all the gentlemen asked for dances."

That startled a laugh out of her, and helped her relax back into naturalness. "Hundreds of them! Why, all those debutantes turned into wallflowers, I was so besieged by partners."

"You shouldn't belittle yourself," Mr. Crocker murmured. His sallow complexion turned red, and he wiped a grass-stained hand across the back of his neck. "Begging your pardon, Miss Shaw. I've no right to address you in such a manner."

"Pish-tosh," Neala retorted, borrowing one of Mrs. Wilkes's favorite expressions. "I'm not a wealthy debutante. Frankly, I never entertained hope of ever being one." Mr. Crocker's bony but not unattractive face revealed such bemusement a wash of friendliness swept over her. "In fact," she shared impulsively, "what I'd really like to be is an intrepid lady reporter for a New York newspaper, like Miss Nellie Bly."

The groundskeeper looked shocked. She realized belatedly that blurting out such personal information was perhaps not wise. Sighing, she waved a dismissive hand. "Don't mind me. I've a bad habit of speaking before I think. My mother is forever reminding me— Oh!"

The pain struck without warning. Stricken to silence, Neala could only stare at the groundskeeper while tears leaked from the corners of her eyes. Fumbling, she tugged out her hankie and dabbed at the moisture. "I—I beg your pardon, Mr. Crocker. It's just that sometimes I forget. My mother—she's dead, you see. Both she and my father were killed in a carriage accident. It's been over a year now, but sometimes..." Her voice trailed away helplessly.

Mr. Crocker looked extremely uncomfortable. After an awkward expression of sympathy, he announced that he should return to his work, crammed his cap back on his head and scuttled off across the lawn.

Neala berated herself for her blabbermouth. She should not treat a man she had met less than a month earlier as though they were lifelong friends. Worse than the sin of familiarity, however, in light of her circumstances she shouldn't presume upon the friendship of anyone. Her acquaintance with Mr. Crocker, along with the several guests she met with regularly, might already have placed them in danger.

What rattled her bones was the potential harm to Mrs. Wilkes.

Trains arrived and departed from the Old White daily. Come Friday, Neala planned to be on one of them.

At a little past one in the morning, the third night after the ball, she wandered over to the window because once again she was unable to sleep. Shoulders slumped, she gazed out at the moonlit night, scarcely aware of its silvered beauty. Never had Neala felt so alone, so conscious of the symbol of the heirloom momentarily cradled in her hands.

Abruptly she leaned forward, her attention drawn to a movement at the edge of some trees, a little ways beyond one of the gas-pole lamp fixtures that illuminated the path. That looked like… Yes. It was a person, a man, walking with the swift soundlessness of a wraith. Or a murderer? The crest dropped from her hand and fell to the carpet with a muffled thunk as Neala abruptly realized she had been standing in an open window, with a parlor lamp blazing away behind her, illuminating her silhouette. *Brainless peahen*, she railed at herself even as she braced her palms on the sill and leaned farther out, peering from her third-story perch over the moonlit grounds.

There was no sign of the shadowy figure. For all she knew, she'd conjured him up out of exhaustion, fear, and a fanciful imagination.

Muttering to herself, Neala turned out the lamp, retrieved the crest and laid it back inside the box with her mother's diary. Time she acknowledged the fear, accepted that her sleep would be riddled with nightmares, and climb into the wretched bed anyway.

Gray couldn't get over the changes. Of course, the last time he'd been dragged to White Sulphur Springs with his family, he'd been fourteen and miserable. Idly he twirled the walking cane Aunt Bella had thrust into his hands at the last moment. Made him look more the part of Harrison Faulkner's youngest son, she said, eyes twinkling because she knew his feelings quite well.

Breath spiraling upward in a chilled misty vapor, cane twirling, he stood on the edge of the Chesapeake and Ohio railway platform, listening to the fading creak-and-clatter of the train while he absorbed the changes.

For one thing, he was standing on a train platform. He recalled without fondness that years ago the trip from the family home in Richmond had been in their cumbersome coach, required six days of travel, and his sister—married and "in the family way"—spent most of the time whining, or emptying the contents of her stomach, once all over his new half boots.

"Evenin', sir. You be needing a buggy ride across to the Old White?"

Inexcusably inattentive, Gray spun halfway around in a crouch, one hand reaching for the gun, his other hand gripping the cane like a sword. *Blamed idiot.* He cudgeled instinct back into his persona as the "respectable son of Harrison Faulkner." "Sorry," he apologized to the colored man dressed in the hotel's uniform. "You startled me. I was…miles away."

"Ah. Well, here's a better place to be for you, I'm thinking. Nothing clears a man's soul like a season at the White."

That, Gray thought, was a matter of opinion. "You may be right. I think I'll walk across instead of ride. It's a beautiful night, and I feel the need for some fresh air, after that train trip."

"I could fetch yo' bags over if you like, then," the

porter offered, eyeing the pile of luggage stacked beside Gray. "Shame to spoil such a fine walk, totin' all those cases. Got a full moon tonight, big and round as a silver dollar."

Good killing moon, a cattle thief once told him. "Yes. Thank you. I'm staying in the third cottage along Baltimore Row." Gray effected the bored drawl of inherited wealth, while inside he cursed himself roundly for giving in to Aunt Bella's pleas. As for Neala Shaw… Well, he'd promised his aunt two weeks.

In a hundred yards, however, with a night sky lit by that full moon, and nostalgic aromas of wood smoke, meadow grasses, and the resiny tang of something unique to White Sulphur Springs flooding his senses, Gray felt a loosening inside himself.

Against all expectations to the contrary, he realized he was glad to be here. For over two hundred years weary souls had found their way to the springs in this secluded valley, and gone away refreshed. The worn slopes of the Appalachian Mountains more resembled blue-green forested hills compared to the stark soaring grandeur of the Rockies, but they offered something Gray had forgotten existed.

Peace.

He strolled at an ever-decreasing pace, past Virginia Row, expanded now he saw by more than half a dozen cottages. All of them gleamed as white as the moon, their silhouettes illuminated by electric lights, courtesy of the group of businessmen who had bought the place up a decade earlier and transformed it back into a world-class resort.

When he reached the central hotel he stopped, studying the plain but dignified grandeur of its porches and columns. The owners who had refurbished the resort in the late seventies had built a four-story wing on the western flank. Just what the place needed. More fancy rooms to entice more guests.

Neala Shaw was inside the main hotel. Number 323, Aunt Bella had told him. Her windows overlooked the back lawn, and Neala wrote her what a pleasure it was to see the sunset behind the mountains. What was it about the girl that roused his aunt's fierce maternal instincts to such an intense degree? Gray had puzzled over the question for days, ever since she'd written, begging him to help. Isabella Chilton had always been protective of her students, but in all the years he'd known her, she had never laid aside that steely common sense, nor her resolute faith in a God who was supposed to care when even a bird dropped dead.

His aunt's beliefs in a sovereign, all-loving, all-knowing God always made him feel as though he were locked inside a very small cage placed in the center of a very large city. Bad enough to be saddled with a set of inbred ethics he couldn't escape, but Gray refused to accept that every breath he drew was monitored by the Almighty. He'd endured plenty of that suffocating attention when he was growing up, thank you very much.

With a single head shake he focused instead on the unpleasant possibility that his aunt's concern for Neala might be justified.

"Mind you, I haven't informed her of my changed mind," Aunt Bella had wryly informed him. "Neala's possessed of a vivid imagination along with her overdeveloped sense of responsibility. I didn't want her charging back up here to nag the sheriff into an early grave."

All right, Miss Shaw, Gray challenged her silently. *Let's see how you prove your case to me.*

A reluctant grin tickled his mouth as he recalled her reaction on their previous meetings. Definitely not the sort to cower beneath the bedclothes, or cover her eyes and screech like a steam kettle.

Moonlight stitched a lacy pattern through the trees and across the vast lawn. Eyes narrowed, Gray thought for several long moments, then casually made his way around the main hotel, noting the darkest corners, the location of trees, shrubs, paths and lamplights.

A single window in the back glowed yellow against the ghostly white of the main hotel. Gray absently noted that it was a third-floor window; he was about to head for his cottage when a silhouette appeared. A slender but definitely feminine silhouette. When she leaned out, the golden lamplight behind her framed a head of riotous curls spilling over a pale face and tumbling down her shoulders. With the careless disregard of a coquette, she propped her elbows on the opened sill and stared out into the night.

Neala Shaw.

The woman possessed the self-protective skills of a lemming.

Gray's job as bodyguard commenced right now.

Chapter Eleven

A knock on the door echoed through the room with the resonance of a thunderclap.

Neala jumped, fumbled for the bedside lamp, then froze. If she turned on the lamp, whoever was out there would see the strip of light and expect her to open the door. If the room remained dark, they might go away.

On the other hand, if this was the murderer, he might conclude she was asleep, affording him the perfect opportunity to pick the lock and slay her in her bed.

Or it could be a frantic hotel clerk, alerting guests to a fire.

An urgent summons to Mrs. Wilkes—she was ill, injured. The guest across the hall needed immediate medical assistance…

Heart pounding in concussive thuds, Neala stood rooted to the floor. What to do, what to do—a weapon. She should be searching for a weapon, something with which she could defend herself.

The knock sounded again, this time louder, with an overtone of impatience. "Miss Shaw?" A man's voice carried through the panel. "It's Grayson Faulkner. I know you're in there." There was a pause, as though he were giving her time to absorb his words. "Open the door," he finished, and it was not a request.

Lord, I know I told You I'd accept anyone, but did You have to send him as Your chosen bodyguard?

She turned on the lamp, tightened the sash of her night robe with fingers that trembled, then marched across the room. "I certainly will not open the door," she managed to say civilly enough for having to raise her voice to be heard through the thick panel. "It's two o'clock in the morning. You scared the curls out of my hair, Mr. Faulkner. Go away and come back at a civilized hour."

There was no reply. Frowning, Neala took a cautious step forward, thinking to lay her ear against the door to see if she could hear the sound of retreating footsteps. Instead came the sound of a key rattling the lock. Even as she leaped to grab the knob, it turned in her hand. The door swung open, almost knocking her off her feet, and Miss Isabella's outrageous nephew stepped inside, shutting the door behind him. In his hand he held an odd-shaped key that bore no resemblance to Neala's room key, but before she could challenge him about it he'd tucked it away.

He scowled down at her, arms folded across his chest. "What were you thinking, standing in front of a lighted window? If the killer wanted to put a bullet through your heart instead of pushing a boulder over a cliff, you offered the perfect target."

So he'd been outside somewhere on the grounds, spying on her? *Again?* "I had already reached that decision myself." She waved toward the darkened room. "See? No more lights. There was no need to frighten me half to death by pounding on my door." She clutched the lapels of her bed robe more closely. "Besides, I'm already frightened enough."

"Good," he snapped. "Perhaps you'll be more inclined to obey me when I tell you what to do." His startling blue eyes wandered over Neala with an intensity that noodled her knees.

Annoyed, she stiffened the knees and ordered her spine to follow suit. "Why did you come, Mr. Faulkner? Surely you explained to your aunt that you, well, that you don't like me very much." Speaking the words aloud somehow gave them more power; instead of returning his glare, Neala stared just beyond Mr. Faulkner's shoulder. Between fright and humiliation, she was inches away from howling like a toddler.

"I'm here," came the sardonic reply, "because my aunt believes I can protect you. She also believes I might have more success tracking down the unknown person or persons who apparently will go to extraordinary lengths to dispose of you."

Despite herself, Neala's lips trembled. "I believe there's only one, a man. Two nights ago he, ah, spoke to me." She finally met his gaze. "I was sitting on a windowsill at the Grand Ball, s-surrounded by other guests. He grabbed my arm, pulled me backward, and whispered in my ear that he—" she scrabbled for breath, finished levelly enough "—was sorry, but it was m-my turn to die. By the time I was able to turn around to search for him…" Her voice trailed away.

Sparks seemed to leap from Mr. Faulkner's eyes, sizzling into air that all of a sudden crackled. He took a step forward, stopped, pinched the bridge of his nose and muttered something beneath his breath. Then, startling Neala so badly she flinched, he clasped both of her hands in his much larger ones and tugged her toward him. "All right," he murmured. "All right." Warm fingers gently stroked her taut knuckles. "I'm here now. I'll take care of you. Try to not be afraid."

Neala gaped at their clasped hands. "Mr. Faulkner, I don't understand you. I was expecting you to accuse me of making it up. Like you did the hunter… I don't understand."

He gave her hands a final squeeze, then released them with a short laugh. "Well, it's like this, Miss Shaw. I've come to realize you don't lie worth a— You don't lie well."

"Thank you so much. But—"

"Besides which every last soul at the school, not to mention Aunt Bella, praise you to the skies for your charming personality, your unassuming manner, and your 'laudable loyalty,' I believe was the way the school secretary—Miss Crabbe?—phrased it. And over the past couple of months I've—" He stopped, ran a hand over his beard-stubbled jaw, started to speak, grimaced. "I don't like being wrong, Miss Shaw," he finally admitted. "But I wish I'd searched the woods that day, instead of simply following you. You might not be in this predicament now if I'd done what I'm trained to do."

"If what I've come to believe is true, there's nothing you could have done." Neala fiddled with the crochet edging on the sleeves of her robe.

"Why do you say that? Go ahead, tell me whatever it is you need to tell me."

"What? I mean, how could you possibly—?"

"It's your eyes," he offered unhelpfully. "You've an easy face to read, Miss Shaw. So what is it you're debating whether or not to tell me?"

"Oh. Well. Um… I've been studying and thinking on things ever since I arrived here, back in June." She gestured to the large steamer trunk in the corner of the room. "Gone through all our family papers, diaries and letters countless times. I practically have them memorized. And…" She hesitated again.

"Tell me," Mr. Faulkner repeated, still with extraordinary patience.

Patience? From Miss Isabella's nephew? If he'd remained the churlish and disdainful man she remembered, Neala might have been able to stand her ground, insist that an interrogation wait until morning.

But she was exhausted, tired of the fear, tired of the sense of isolation. Weary of shouldering a burden crushing her beneath the weight of its sheer irrationality. "I think someone has been killing off everyone in my family," she blurted, then steeled herself for the response.

He merely inclined his head. "Why?"

Now there was a question. "I don't know." Her voice wavered. Heat flooding into her cheeks, Neala abruptly swiveled and escaped to the other side of the room, where the massive trunk offered at least an illusion of protection. "I don't know," she repeated. "I've thought and thought about it, but come up with nothing. I mean, my father was a professor at the University of Virginia. My uncle and grandfather owned a small freight company. It was successful, and highly respected. But we're just folks. Nobody famous or remarkable, much less wealthy. Yet after the man whispered to me the other night, I've had to accept that for some reason, he's possessed of a blind hatred for everyone in the Neal Shaw family."

"Neal Shaw? Your father?"

"My paternal grandfather. I was named after him. My

mother lost two babies before me, so when I was born—" She blinked rapidly. "Mr. Faulkner, could we please continue this discussion later?"

"Certainly. Can I trust you to keep away from the window, and to remain in this room until I come to fetch you?"

"I don't see why I should—"

"In that case," Mr. Faulkner interrupted as he strolled across to the pegs on the wall and proceeded to unbuckle his gun belt, "I'll be remaining here, with you."

"You most certainly will not!" Tears forgotten, Neala stalked across to the door and flung it open. "I appreciate very much your—your kindness. But contrary to what you believe about me, I'm not some mealymouthed young miss to be manipulated or…or managed. You leave this instant, Mr. Faulkner. I will not be bullied, do you understand?"

"Then you have a problem, Miss Shaw. I will not be dictated to, particularly when it comes to honoring a promise to my aunt." His lip curled upward in a mocking half smile. "I think we can both agree you've little chance of tossing me out of here. And no doubt you've heard all the stories about Harrison Faulkner's infamous youngest son. I daresay your old family friend might raise a ruckus when she hears we're sharing a room, but—" he shrugged "—it's your choice."

For as long as she could remember, Neala had played the role of peacemaker, pacifier, placater. She tried to get along with everyone, particularly her brother. But as she sifted through Mr. Faulkner's insulting ultimatum, an alien urge to rebel, to call his bluff, swelled inside, propelling her back across the room. Hands fisted on her waist, she stopped directly in front of the infuriating man. "After I write Miss Isabella a letter to inform her of your behavior, I'm going to bed. If you insist on ruining my reputation that will be *your* choice. Not mine. My conscience is clear, Mr. Faulkner, in my eyes, and the Lord's."

For a moment he did not respond, and the air in the room seemed to pulse in rhythm with Neala's heartbeat. Then a muscle twitched at the corner of his beard-scruffed jaw and astoundingly, he laughed. "Game and set to you, Miss Shaw," he finally drawled. "I should have expected it, given your disposition."

"My disposition?" What about his? Neala pressed her lips together to keep from blurting the question aloud. First he held her hands and reassured her. Then he laughed. *He'd laughed.* No longer could she pigeonhole him as an older version of Adrian to be placated, nor ignore him as an ill-tempered misogynist.

But since she could no longer anticipate his reactions, she couldn't bring herself to trust him entirely either.

"What *are* you going to do, then?" she asked at last.

"I'm going to leave you. No, not consign you to the jaws of a killer. You needn't look like that. I meant, I'm leaving you and your clear conscience to hopefully peaceful dreams." He paused, surveying the room. "However, since it's possible I'm not the only one who saw you silhouetted in the window..." in several long strides he crossed the room, fetched the cane-bottomed chair shoved beneath the small library table "...put a chair against the door. Like this." He demonstrated, then placed the chair on the floor beside the door. "Think you can manage?"

This time Neala could only nod.

"Good. Then I bid you good night." He swept her an

obviously mocking bow. "Is ten o'clock this morning, in the main parlor, agreeable with you?"

Her ears tingled from his laughter, her mind's eye reeled from the warmth in his eyes and the reassurance in his voice, but Neala scraped together enough sensibility to answer with a simple affirmative.

"Fine." He rebuckled his gun belt, touched two fingers to his homburg and put his hand out to the doorknob. Then he turned back. "You're certainly a different—and I'll admit intriguing—kettle of fish. In fact, Miss Shaw, I think I've changed my strategy toward protecting you." One eyelid lowered in an unmistakable wink. "Sleep well."

The door closed quietly behind him. As Neala stood, motionless, she heard him use his odd-shaped key to lock her door.

Still dazed, she carefully jammed the back of the chair beneath the knob. Then she wandered over to the bench at the foot of her bed and sat bonelessly on its cushioned seat.

"Miss Isabella," she pondered aloud, "what have you done?"

At the moment, it felt as though her former headmistress had supplied a fox to protect the henhouse, and she couldn't help but wonder whether Mr. Faulkner or an unknown killer posed the greater threat. One to her life, the other—her heart.

He hated this place. He especially hated having to spend hard-earned money in order to blend in, though much of his wardrobe had been acquired through judicious robbery. Even that necessary endeavor angered him. He considered thieving beneath him, the dishonorable handiwork of ignoble riffraff.

Why did Neala Shaw choose this place? His initial elation at having finally tracked her down was completely negated by having to associate with people who represented everything he despised. Pompous jackanapes, every last one of them, with their puffed-up sensibilities, their aura of smug complacency. Probably not a single one of them able to tie his own shoelaces, much less survive in forest or factory for weeks on end. If one of them tried to blend in to his world… The mental picture amused him. Easier for a hurdy-gurdy monkey to sip tea in the Old White's dining room.

He, on the other hand, had perfected the art of the chameleon. An anonymous chameleon, that was him. In other circumstances he had been able to function more like a wraith, invisible and unsuspected.

Here, regrettably, invisibility would not serve his purpose. Thus, he'd adapted accordingly. Hiding in plain view while he waited for the right opportunity to carry out his mission was almost more exhilarating than years of careful, meticulous planning so that he could never be recognized. Fancy that. A magician as well as a chameleon, practicing finesse and sleight of hand.

People could be such fools. Other people, not Neala Shaw. From her he had come to expect more, because she had managed to slip through every one of his snares. He could privately admit to relief and, until now, a certain measure of pride in her.

But now… He plucked a large tulip tree leaf from an overhead branch and systematically shredded it to confetti. Now Neala had proven to be no better than any other weak-brained woman.

And it was all because of that irritating man. For over a week now he'd watched her succumb to every lure Grayson Faulkner cast her way. Why couldn't she see that his supposed courtship was a sham, a ploy where Neala would become just another fool in a ritual designed from the beginning of time to end in humiliation for either or both participants?

He was not a fool, however. Nor was he an out-of-control madman, both of which traits would result in his capture. Regrettably, Faulkner—and he hoped to find out more than just his name by dinner that evening—could not be disposed of. The man was a philanderer, but he had nothing to do with the Mission. Personal honor demanded that innocents, however despicable, be spared. More to the point, both his and Neala's deaths would bring a locustrian plague of authorities, all of them determined to unearth the person who had tarnished the Old White's impeccable reputation.

Therefore he must somehow find a way to separate them, or give in to the highly risky solution of suffocating Neala in her room.

There they were. He fixed an urbane smile on his face, and as they passed he tipped his ridiculous straw boater. The moment they were out of sight he paused to strike a match on the sole of his shoe, turning to light his cigar so he could watch.

They walked closer together than they had a week ago, and Neala's expressive face had lost some of that pale, drawn look. She actually looked pretty this morning, with a spring to her step never present when she strolled the grounds with the old widow woman, or by herself.

He viciously ground the match beneath his heel. This was what happened when sentiment was allowed to sway one's will. All those times when he'd followed Neala on her solitary strolls, he'd watched the faces of people light up when she was with them, watched her friendliness to lowly hotel employees as well as illustrious guests. And he'd decided to grant her this one last pleasure. He'd waited for years. He would have waited for her to finish out her last season on earth, here at White Sulphur Springs.

No longer.

He'd thought Neala Shaw different, almost worthy of redeeming the name bequeathed to her by the man who had ruined it through his betrayals.

With a shake of his head he realized he was staring after them more than was wise. Cigar clamped between his teeth, he strode off across the deep grass, for the first time eschewing the path. There were plans to be made. He no longer felt regret for having to kill Neala Shaw. And he never should have warned her, never should have allowed his emotions to sway him.

That was one mistake he planned never to make again.

Chapter Twelve

For the first time in the two weeks since he'd arrived, Gray found himself simply enjoying the role of hotel guest, and suitor. The latter was a role he'd never expected to embrace, much less entertain passing fantasies of turning pretense into reality. Pretending to court Neala in the grand fashion of White Sulphur Springs suitors had simply offered the most plausible way to remain constantly in her company.

No wonder Aunt Bella had given him that cat-in-the-cream smile when he'd shared the plan he'd devised to protect Neala.

Gray shook his head. Contrary to all his expectations, Neala had turned out to be an entertaining companion, curious about everything, with an unself-conscious friendliness to which even a cynical Gray was not immune.

She was, unfortunately, a nightmare to protect, even as her suitor. Friendly, curious young women always spelled trouble. But Neala's impulsiveness added a volatile element to the mix that left Gray perpetually feeling as though he were trying to tie back a pair of butterfly wings without irreparably tearing them.

Thus far she'd climbed a tree with the giggling twelve-year-old daughter of a state senator; innocently insulted an elderly Yankee colonel by informing him that the North's victory did not absolve them of blame, since it was Yankees who had purchased and transported all the slaves from their African homes; and cajoled Gray to help gather a bouquet of wildflowers for a sick chambermaid.

This morning they were walking along Howard's Creek, one of Neala's favorite pastimes and thus far the most benign of her pursuits.

"Oh, look, Grayson!" she exclaimed, pulling him back into the present. "Over there, a pair of Canadian geese. Aren't they beautiful?"

"I don't think you've pointed out anything in the last week that you haven't considered beautiful."

She gave him a sunny smile. "That's because nature is part of God's creation. Of course there's something beautiful in everything."

"Algae?"

"It's a pretty shade of green."

"Dirt?"

"Things grow out of it."

Enjoying teasing her, Gray tucked her hand through his arm as they walked. She'd almost stopped jumping whenever he did so. He smiled to himself. "Mosquitoes?"

"Food for frogs."

"Ah. And no doubt you find frogs beautiful?"

"Oh, no you don't!" She laughed, pulled free and skipped ahead of him a few paces. "You just want to lure me into a comment about toads turning into princes from a kiss."

"Well, I'm no prince, but hopefully you no longer—Neala! Watch out. You're too close to the edge!"

Even as he spoke, the bank crumbled beneath her feet. Gray lunged forward as Neala, arms flailing, tilted toward the creek. He grabbed one delicate wrist, hauled her backward, then—because he couldn't resist—gathered her into a close embrace. The smell of violets, starched linen and warm woman filled his head.

"Oh, my!" Neala's hands fluttered against his chest. "Thank you. I…um… G-Grayson? You can let go of me now."

The feel of her lissome form awakened in Gray a waterfall of feeling that caught him off guard. He knew how it felt to desire a woman, but tenderness? A longing not merely to satisfy a physical urge, but for the simple joy of holding her close?

He all but shoved her away, yet even as he struggled to distance himself from her, he watched his hand lift, felt the warmth beneath the index finger he lightly brushed across her rose-hued cheek. "You need to watch your step," he murmured absently.

"Yes," Neala agreed.

For several seconds they stared at each other, while all around them insects darted about the long meadow grass, the creek water bubbled gently beside them, and the summer sun bathed them in peach-toned light. Somewhere in the woods a bird trilled.

"Mrs. Wilkes would peel me like a grape if I'd showed up for lunch dripping wet," Neala said eventually, the words breathless and hurried.

The reminder of their luncheon engagement with Frances Wilkes effectively wiped the smile from Gray's face. The bizarre emotion that had turned his blood the consistency of syrup dissolved in a welcome rush of irritation. The old woman was about as subtle as a stick of lighted dynamite, and more than once even Neala had remonstrated with her about her heavy-handed matchmaking. Unfortunately, Frances Wilkes had met Gray's parents some years earlier, when her third husband was still alive. To the matrimonial-minded dowager, the challenge of taming the infamous Grayson Faulkner, with his impeccable family pedigree, was irresistible.

"We better head back to the hotel." Without touching her again he swiveled and started walking back the way they'd come. "You might have been spared a dunk in the creek, but you'll want to freshen up." Half-angrily he scanned their surroundings, realizing that a man with a rifle and reasonable aim could have bagged his bird, and Gray to boot, all because of Gray's inattention. Some bodyguard he made—and it was Neala's fault.

Either do the job, or find someone else who will.

He paused, sucking in a deep breath while he waited for Neala to come abreast. When she smiled up at him as though nothing had happened, he didn't know whether to be relieved or miffed.

"Why won't you teach me how to shoot your gun?" Neala asked then, not for the first time. "Yesterday one of the maids loaned me a Sears Roebuck catalog. Did you know there are small derringers a lady can carry inside her purse? Think how much better protected I'd be."

"Do you realize that the more you pester me about it, the more determined I am to refuse?" Unlike his mother and sisters, or most other women, Neala didn't pout or invest significance into a trivial incident that after all had been— well, trivial. "Besides which *ladies*—" he emphasized the word "—do not carry a pistol in their purses."

"I wouldn't have to pester you if you'd teach me,"

Neala retorted, ignoring his dictum. “What happens if you’re hurt, and unable to protect me?”

“What happens if you end up shooting me instead of the killer, in your hurry to retrieve my gun, or the one concealed in your purse?”

Neala emitted an unladylike sniff. “I’ll have you know my grandfather taught me how to use a sword when I was all of ten years old.” She flashed him an insouciant grin, the last of her uncertainty banished. “Of course, it was one of those wispy English swords instead of a stout Scottish claymore. He told me I wouldn’t have been able to lift the one his great-granda carried.”

“You and your grandfather were close, weren’t you?”

The smile in her eyes faded. “Not for a long time. But when I was older…yes, we grew very close. You see, they named me after Grandfather because everyone believed my mother could never carry another child full term. Then Adrian was born, and Grandfather tried to force my parents to rename me, so Adrian would have the name of Neal.”

Gray privately thought the old man heartless, but he’d learned the futility of making any negative reference, however oblique, to anyone Neala cared about. The woman was loyal, he’d grudgingly admitted. Loyal, fearless, and more stubborn than any Scots Highlander. She bore scant resemblance to her heritage with her froth of nutmeg-brown curls and innocent brown eyes, but despite his determination to remain distant, Gray found himself increasingly drawn to her undaunted spirit.

“Did you brandish a stick at your grandfather, threaten to behead him with the sword if he stole your name and gave it to your brother?”

"I was only four." Her shoulders lifted in a light shrug. "I'm afraid I made a poor showing of courage. I hid inside a cupboard. I thought if nobody could find me, they couldn't take away my name. Of course Father and Mother categorically refused, and everything turned out all right. Grandfather eventually apologized, but it was years before I quit being afraid that I was going to die, because of my name."

Gray stopped short on the path and turned to stare down at her, outraged on a fundamental level he refused to examine. Instead he focused on the hint of a possibility. Was it possible she was targeted because she bore her grandfather's name? "What do you mean, you were afraid you were going to die?"

"Oh, I had a cousin—Grandfather's first grandchild—so of course Uncle Alexander and Aunt Matilda named him Neal. But he died when he was four—the same age I was when Adrian was born. I know now that I was being irrational, but..." She shrugged again. "Don't glare at me like that. I'm perfectly all right now. At any rate, I was afraid Grandfather was disappointed because I was a girl. I spent a lot of time with him, trying to prove myself. And like I told you, we became very close. I think that's why he gave me the crest badge. Our other two cousins died of typhus, back in the seventies, so that left only me and my brother."

She paused. "Adrian always insisted the clan crest ought to be his, as he would be the only male heir left after Grandfather and Father were gone."

"Understandable," Gray murmured, adding casually, "so your brother coveted the crest?"

"Well, yes. I suppose that's one way to put it." They

walked a few paces in silence before she added in a wistful tone, "Adrian's not a bad person. He just, well, he *was* the only male heir, but he possessed neither the name nor our family's most precious heirloom. Somehow in his mind he grew to be resentful, mostly because of the name." She sighed. "I wish he hadn't run away."

"Mmm." Gray casually took her elbow and they resumed walking. So Adrian kicked up a fuss about the crest badge after all the other male relatives died, did he? And then conveniently disappeared after the death of his own parents. An ugly worm of suspicion squirmed its way into Gray's mind, one he knew he'd need to investigate further. But not, he determined, until Neala had learned to trust him completely.

"I'd like to see this famous heirloom," he said. "Is it here with you, or locked away somewhere?"

"I keep it with me. At some point, after the War of 1812, I believe, it was turned into a brooch. But it's heavy, and I haven't worn it here, except in the evenings when I need my cloak. I promised Grandfather— Oh, hello, Mr. Crocker!"

Gray stiffened into alertness as he watched the approach of a tallish man dressed in the simple shirt, trousers and over-apron of a groundskeeper. Pleasant-looking enough chap, though the sun had pinkened his fair skin the hue of a poppy.

"My, you may have escaped the hornet's nest last month, but your face!" Neala was exclaiming. "Did you forget your cap, Mr. Crocker?"

"I'm afraid so, Miss Shaw." He glanced at Gray. Something Gray recognized as incipient jealousy flickered behind a pair of light brown eyes. "How are you doing this fine morning?"

"I'm doing well, thank you very much. I haven't seen you much these past weeks, so you won't have met my friend Mr. Faulkner." As though the now beet-red groundsman were another guest, Neala introduced him to Gray; of the three of them, only Neala seemed unfazed by the strained atmosphere. "When we return to the hotel, I'll fetch some vinegar from the dispensary," she continued, fussing over the other man in a manner that instantly raised Gray's hackles.

Before he could stop the movement, he had taken hold of her hand and looped it through his arm, covering the hand with his own. "Leave the poor fellow alone," he ordered with a crocodile's smile. "He's old enough not to need mothering."

"Oh, everyone enjoys a bit of feminine coddling," Mr. Crocker refuted, though he did back up a step and refused to look at Gray. "You're very kind, Miss Shaw. But you don't need to fret about me. I'll be fine."

After shooting Gray a look of dislike, the groundskeeper departed.

"You were rude," Neala said, tugging on her hand. "And it was plain you hurt his feelings."

"You were much too familiar with the hired help." Gray tightened his hold of her hand. "Especially under the circumstances. You've had other conversations with Crocker, I take it?"

"And intend to have many more. I never took you for a snob, Mr. Faulkner. Just because he's a groundskeeper doesn't place him beneath my notice. Frankly, I'm more comfortable around him than I am most of the guests here."

"My rationale has nothing to do with social or economic status, *Miss Shaw*. My concern is that you know nothing about this man. What if he's the one who's trying to kill you, and he's adopted the guise of a lowly gardener in order to be near at hand every day, waiting for the opportunity?"

"The same thought occurred to me…but then I have that same thought over every man I encounter here." She shook her head. "What am I supposed to do? For the first week I stayed glued to Mrs. Wilkes, until I realized my cowardice might cost a dear friend her life. I couldn't stop thinking about my friend Abby, back at the Academy, and how she almost died when that boulder crashed down. So I started wandering on my own, waiting to see what would happen."

"It's a miracle you're still alive."

"Perhaps." For a few steps they walked in silence. Then her face brightened and her shoulders squared. "I like to think that I have the Lord's protection, and now, yours as well." Without warning she leaned to scoop up an acorn, then tossed it at Gray.

He snagged it out of the air without looking away from Neala, watched with a puff of masculine satisfaction as her eyes widened with admiration. Little minx. Trying to test him, was she?

"So…based upon your reaction to Mr. Crocker, am I to conclude that you're going to be rude to every man between sixteen and sixty who condescends to speak to me?"

"Only the ones I haven't investigated, and those I'm satisfied have no desire to kill you." She winced, the air of mischief fading. Good. He was beginning to wonder if her cavalier attitude was the product of a character flaw, rather than a deliberate effort to maintain her sanity while living the nightmare of her present circumstances.

Somehow he needed to discover a way to make her more suspicious of every person—except him.

The irony would keep Aunt Bella chuckling for a week.

"What did you find out about George Watlington?" Neala asked. "Before you arrived, Mrs. Wilkes was determined to marry me off to him."

"Fine by me, if you'd rather die of boredom instead of a sadistically arranged 'accident.'"

After a stilted moment, he impatiently tugged at his too-tightly knotted tie. "Sorry. But you asked." He kicked a pebble on the path with the toe of his boot and sent it flying into the grass. "Thus far I haven't discovered anything that incriminates—or absolves—every man here. George Watlington's nice enough, but he likes to gamble. Peter Vandermoot, another of your would-be suitors, came here to pick a gullible young lady such as yourself who wouldn't notice how many mistresses he keeps tucked away in several New York brownstones."

"What? He doesn't! He was so kind to me. Until you arrived, at any rate."

"They're all kind, you little innocent, because that's typically the fastest way to get what they want. An infatuated woman has little brain to speak of. Even less common sense."

Abruptly she yanked her hand free, stepped back and gathered up her skirts. "Mr. Faulkner, I may be grateful for your protection, but I refuse to listen to any more of your disparaging remarks. Enjoy the rest of the walk by yourself. I'm going to return to the hotel and freshen up as you rudely suggested earlier, before we meet Mrs. Wilkes. Hopefully the murderer won't accomplish his deed between here and there."

Before Gray realized she actually meant to dart off without him, she'd set off across the lawn, skirts frothing about her heels. Alternately railing at himself and Neala, he followed more slowly, unwilling to garner more attention than they already had.

Knowing Mrs. Wilkes, it promised to be a long and painful luncheon.

Chapter Thirteen

Some years earlier, a race track had been built in a flat meadow across Howard's Creek, much to the dismay of the dignified Old South guests. But despite its lack of universal appeal, the races were well attended.

On this particular day several were scheduled for that afternoon. Neala, still smarting from Mr. Faulkner's regression to the persona she'd first met so many months earlier, informed him that she planned to attend the races. With or without him. The luncheon with Mrs. Wilkes had been an utter disaster, since her sponsor was completely smitten with the man who had succeeded in twisting Neala up like a skein of wet yarn. What a bother! Who cared that his pedigree rivaled a European aristocrat, or that his notoriety merely enhanced his desirability among elderly dames and eligible belles alike? Neala Shaw had neither the time nor the inclination to lose her heart over an ungodly man who plainly could not be trusted with it.

After the meal, Neala escaped to the sanctuary of her room until it was time to go to the races.

Of course, Mr. Faulkner had moved out of his Baltimore quarters and somehow contrived to be given the room next to hers. With only a wall between them, Neala's sanctuary no longer offered the same pretext of self-reliance. Never mind that she slept more securely at night, knowing Grayson Faulkner watched over her.

He was still a cynical man who switched moods as capriciously as a bee in a flower bed.

At a little before five, Neala hurriedly gathered her hair at the base of her neck, grabbed a shawl and sneaked down the hall as silently as she could. Grayson neither opened the door of his room as she passed, nor accosted her in the lobby. She was aware of the risk in attending the races without his protection, but at the moment she was more determined to prove a point. She had survived without Grayson Faulkner for two months, she had emerged unscathed from several attempts on her life, and ultimately she prayed she would continue to do so.

She was through being pummeled by his contrary personality—one moment the confident and charming companion, the next a hard, cryptic man whose attitude toward the gentler sex left Neala feeling frostbitten.

A party of young women who thus far had failed to snag at least one proposal from an eligible bachelor invited her to ride to the race track in a buggy they'd commandeered from the stables. Either too old, too young, or—as with Neala—without a name, extraordinary beauty or connections, the three other women made for lively and uncritical companions, far more so than most of the debutantes. With only a slight niggling of guilt, after asking one of the bellhops to inform Mr. Faulkner of her whereabouts, Neala climbed into the buggy.

By the time they arrived at the races, the crowd milled eight deep around the track. Chatting and flirting, her companions wormed their way through to a spot on the rail, Neala safely ensconced in the middle. For a few moments she enjoyed the spectacle, exchanging comments with the others while struggling to keep her balance in the enthusiastic crush of race goers. When someone trod upon her foot, she jerked back—and without warning memories of the Grand Ball swooped down, taunting her with how close she had been to death. How the murderer had talked to her. How he had even touched her.

She was alone.

No. She was safe, surrounded by other women and countless other harmless hotel guests. Nobody could hurt—

She was alone.

Alone.

Faces swam around her in a dizzying swirl. The air, thick with toilet water, pomade, dust and horses thickened until she could scarce take a breath. A buzzing sound intensified in her ears.

When a hand closed around her arm, Neala didn't think. She reacted, jerking backward into the rail while she rammed her elbow into a man's midriff.

"Oomph. That hurt! Miss Shaw, you promised never to be out of earshot. I ought to handcuff you to— Hey!" He managed to deflect her free hand before she smacked his jaw with it.

"Are you all right, Neala?"

"What's going on? Is that man accosting her?"

"No—that's her new beau!"

"Neala, you look dreadfully pale…"

Through the clamor of voices, Neala managed to grasp one blessed fact: the man holding her firmly, both hands now around her upper arms, was Grayson Faulkner. *Not* the murderer. She sagged, gasping in air, only realizing then how close she had come to swooning like a pea-brained idiot.

His voice murmured close to her ear, "All right now?"

She tried to speak, but nodding her head seemed simpler.

Around them the crowd's attention shifted as voices shouted out that the race was about to begin. Pressed from all sides, Neala felt Grayson's arm wrap firmly about her waist. His commanding voice ordered people to give her room to breathe.

From the other end of the ring the starting pistol rang out. Neala struggled to focus on the clutch of horses thundering down the track, but fear dragged at her lungs and weakened her limbs. Beside her, someone burst into excited screams for horse number two; on the other side several people yelled for Burberry, horse number six. Everyone surged forward, straining to see. The protective arm sheltering her fell away.

The horses rounded the first bend, less than fifty feet from where Neala stood. Excitement finally swept her along in its momentum, dousing most of the panic. She leaned forward, caught up in the drama.

Something hard plowed into her back.

Neala lost her balance and fell against the rail with such force the thin wood splintered.

With the sound of galloping hooves and screaming voices flooding her senses, she toppled onto her knees into the dirt track, directly in the path of the horses.

Gray didn't know how it happened, nor did he care. He only knew that clutching hands had yanked him away from Neala, and because of it she was about to be trampled to death. Diving headfirst onto the track, he rolled over her, wrapping her in his arms. A cacophony of screaming and shouting, thudding hooves and choking dust swirled around them. He felt several blows, but only peripherally. Somehow he managed to roll them back underneath the fence, into the grass, where dozens of hands appeared to help.

"Get back, give us room!" he ordered, then spoiled the effect by coughing until his eyes watered.

"Is she dead?"

"I never saw anything like it in my life…"

"What a magnificently brave gesture…"

"Blamed foolish if you ask me. Both of 'em should be dead…"

The roaring in his head stabilized, then vanished altogether. With more force than politeness Gray shoved aside the hands attempting to pat him down, to pull Neala away from his death grip. "Fetch Dr. Dabney," he snapped next. "Now!"

Carefully he lifted himself off her limp body. Advice, exclamations of horror and excitement whirled in the air, coating like dust. Gray scarcely noticed. Frantically he searched for blood, for splintered bones. She was unconscious, but her breathing was steady, and even as he finally allowed himself a shuddering sigh of relief she stirred, eyelids fluttering. A garbled moan whispered between dirt-caked lips. "Can I get some water, a cloth?" he asked, without looking away from Neala.

Seconds later he was handed a large napkin and a collapsible metal cup filled with water. "Thanks. Easy does it," Gray spoke to Neala as he carefully dabbed her mouth and face. "Don't move, Ne—Miss Shaw," he corrected himself. *In a public venue protect her reputation as well as her life...* "Just be still, now, and let me make sure nothing is broken."

"I say, is he getting fresh with her?"

"Shouldn't you wait for the physician?"

"Is there any blood?"

"Neala! Neala?"

A young woman pushed her way through the crowd and dropped to her knees beside them. Because he recognized her as one of Neala's friends, Gray didn't order her to leave.

"Oh, sir, is she all right?" she asked, stretching her hand to fleetingly brush trembling fingers against Neala's.

"I think so. Here—let me shift her around, examine her head. If there's no evidence of cranial injury, how about if we lay her head in your lap?"

"Oh, certainly!"

His own fingers none too steady, Gray probed Neala's scalp, dislodging pins until his hands filled with a mass of tangled, dust-coated curls. A dusky bruise smeared her forehead, but he thought that particular blow occurred when she hit either the railing, or the ground; he'd seen the damage a horse's hoof could inflict, and he thanked whatever gods were listening that Neala mercifully had been spared. Gently he probed her shoulders and collarbones, felt her stir, then stiffen.

"What…you *doing*?" she mumbled. Her eyelids finally lifted, and a pair of smudged brown eyes dazedly searched his face. "Grayson…did you know there's blood…on your lip? I have a hankie…" Her arm actually twitched as she made as though to search for it, and she didn't seem to notice her lapse into familiarity.

Gray needed to remove her from the crowd, as soon

as he collected the strength. For the moment, he captured her hand, held it. "Never mind my blood. We need to find out how badly you're injured."

"Neala, dear Neala." Her friend brushed a lock of hair from Neala's face. "Can you see me? It's Dora. Do you know me?"

Gray watched the emotions streak through those defenseless eyes. He could read each one as easily as if he were inside her head—confusion, fear, dawning awareness…and embarrassment. "Dora. I'm so sorry. Someone pushed me. Are the horses all right?" She blinked a time or two, focused back on Gray. "Are you all right, Mr. Faulkner? Did they push you, too?"

"Neala, he saved your life," Dora exclaimed, undisguised adulation plain in her voice. "He threw himself right into the path of the horses to rescue you!"

Behind them Gray heard more feminine demands to be let through, that Neala was their friend. The crowd around them was growing; doubtless a near-tragedy provided more entertainment than a humdrum horse race. Human beings were ever a bloodthirsty lot.

The murderer was likely one of the onlookers, standing a yard away from Neala, yet Gray wouldn't know it.

Rage pumped through his veins, flooding out the fear for Neala that had sheeted him with ice. If the bounder chose to lift a knife or even a gun to finish the job, at the moment Gray doubted he'd even be able to draw his own weapon. Even if he managed to, he couldn't very well fire into a crowd of teeming hotel guests, whose only crime was morbid curiosity.

He hadn't felt so helpless—so impotent—since he'd watched Marty die in his arms.

He didn't realize the crowd had drawn back and

grown quiet until he felt a light hand brush the fist he had pressed against his thigh. He blinked, realizing he'd been searching every face that surrounded them, and that doubtless his gaze reflected the rage. With difficulty he dropped his head, inhaled several more calming breaths, and focused back on Neala, wrapping his fingers around her wrist. Beneath them, her pulse thrummed a rapid tattoo.

"Mr. Faulkner," she whispered, her eyes dull with awareness, "he tried again, didn't he? The killer…he tried again."

"What are you talking about, Neala? Are you sure a hoof didn't strike her head, Mr. Faulkner?"

"Did she say the chap tried to kill her?"

Like a flash fire voices rose afresh, speculating, questioning, demanding answers. Neala's other friends shoved their way through, their questions peppering him like buckshot.

With a bitten-off oath Gray abruptly lifted Neala into his arms and surged to his feet, forcing the onlookers to scramble backward out of the way. "I'm taking her to the infirmary. The doctor can meet us there." He pinned Dora with a look. "Don't repeat a word of what you just heard. Do you understand? Not a word to your friends, or to anyone else."

"I—all right. But I don't understand. What—"

"There's nothing to understand. She's overwrought, frightened, only half-conscious. You'll cause incalculable harm to her reputation by repeating nonsensical words. Clear a path!" he shouted in a voice honed on subduing hard-bitten criminals.

Against him he could feel the warmth of Neala's slight weight, the tentative flexing of her hands on his shoulders, her breath in his ear. *She could have died, right in front of him. Just like Marty.*

"If you ever run off without me again, I'll let the killer have you."

She shuddered once, then seemed to shrink within herself, making Gray even more angry, this time with himself. Stupid, heartless cad.

"You've a right to be angry." The words drifted on a sigh between them. "But I'd appreciate it if you'd save the lecture for later. Otherwise I'm afraid I might enrage you more by weeping." He heard her swallow twice. "I'd really rather not. My nose always turns red and becomes stuffy. I detest stuffy noses."

He never would have expected to feel like smiling after a near-death experience, but the urge blindsided Gray like a punch to the solar plexus. In his entire life, he could not remember a time when the threat of feminine tears provoked the urge to laugh. Without exception, tears hardened his heart into what one mewling woman had called "a lump of lead, like the bullets you shoot from your gun."

Of course, never in his life had he met a woman like Neala Shaw.

"I'm not as angry with you as I am myself," he heard himself admit. "I should have guessed that, after this morning's walk, you'd finally do something to rebel against our sham courtship."

"Not completely." She pressed a hot cheek against his neck, and Gray had to strain to hear the rest. "Not like Adrian… He lied, about where he was going. I didn't lie." Gray felt a tear dampen his skin, slide down beneath his collar. "Told bellhop to tell you where I was going. So you'd know. You'd know…" Her voice broke.

"Yes," Gray said, "I knew. I found you, Neala. You're safe now."

She lifted her head. Tear-dark eyes blindly stared over his shoulder. The swelling bruise mocked his statement. "For how long?" she choked out. "How much longer will I be safe, G-Grayson?"

The answer to her question that popped into his mind unnerved him, so Gray didn't respond at all. Holding her close against his chest, he carried her the rest of the way to the hotel clinic in tomb-like silence.

Chapter Fourteen

Upon hearing about Neala's misadventure at the race track, Will Crocker debated over the advisability of risking a visit to her room. Rumors of her physical state flew thick and fast. She was mortally injured. She was only bruised. She'd broken bones.

Worst of all for Will was the uniform consensus that her suitor, Mr. Faulkner, had carried her away from the track. In his arms.

In the end he couldn't help himself. The following afternoon, after cleaning up as best he could, he hurried down to the head groundskeeper's quarters. Lloyd owned a cracked but full-length mirror, and he was generous about allowing other workers to borrow it whenever they had their half day off and wanted to spruce themselves up. Well, it wasn't Will's half day off, but he still wanted to look the best he could.

He studied his reflection glumly; compared to that arrogant Grayson Faulkner, Will more resembled a train-hopping hobo. Angrily he swiveled and left the room. Looks, he'd learned, could reflect how much money a man possessed, but looks could also camouflage. At the moment he was a lowly groundskeeper. But one day, that would change.

As he cut furtively behind trees and cottages to avoid questions from fellow workers, Will fixed a picture in his mind of Neala. People liked her—well, most people liked her. Some of those high-nosed debutantes—the "belles," they were called—treated her the way they treated Will, as though she were invisible. That was another connection between them, he reminded himself. With Neala, he never felt invisible. To Will's way of thinking, Neala was far more beautiful than any of the White Sulphur Springs belles. She smiled at him as if he were a real person. She'd turned the humiliating experience with the wasps into a shared secret between just the two of them. And she'd revealed a sliver of her mind that Will figured she hadn't shared with anyone else.

A newspaper reporter, of all things!

Though the very idea outraged his sense of what God intended a woman to be, Will didn't care. She was changing something inside of him, something that, if acted upon, would turn his entire life upside down.

If his mother knew what he was thinking—what he was doing—likely she'd throw one of her bad fits in an attempt to control him. Will smiled grimly. Oh, he understood her, right enough, understood from years of experience that the best tactic was to allow her to maintain the illusion that he was her meek, obedient son. She'd been dealt a loser hand, right enough, and he'd spent most of his life helping her atone for it. But this time things had changed.

This time he would have to be more firm about his own goals. As he approached the main hotel, Will decided that after his visit with Neala, he would write his mother. He wouldn't be there to calm the inevitable hysterics, but he also wouldn't have to defend himself from her fists, or flying crockery. Hopefully, by the time he was able to return home for a visit, she would listen to the details of what he planned to do.

As he slipped inside, he realized that he needed for his mother to understand something he scarcely comprehended himself. He also realized a groundskeeper's presence in these cool, largely deserted hallways constituted a significant risk, one he would not have been willing to take two months earlier. Fortunately he passed only two guests, who after mildly curious glances at him continued without comment on their way.

Sweat gathered in his armpits, the small of his back. With each step, a growing seed of doubt sprouted more leaves. Perhaps he shouldn't be exposing himself this way. Opening himself to more ridicule, or worse, condescension. What if Faulkner was there? Or the tyrannical widow?

Only the memory of Neala's friendly smile propelled his feet to the third floor, down the hall to her room. Sure enough, Faulkner was sitting on a chair just outside the door, his arms folded across his chest, the gun openly displayed at his side. A gun, at White Sulphur Springs! The management should do something other than fawn over the man, but Will knew they wouldn't because of the Faulkner name.

If a nobody like William Crocker strapped a gun to his waist, he'd be in jail before sunset. His mother was right about one thing. Life wasn't fair.

Will's jaw jutted; he walked right up to Faulkner. "I'm here to see Miss Shaw." He forced himself to sound courteous instead of demanding. "I heard about the mishap, at the track yesterday? Is she all right?"

"You're one of the groundsmen? Crocker, right? The one we spoke to briefly the other day."

"That's right. Will, Will Crocker."

Despite himself he shifted uneasily. There was something about the way those lake-blue eyes stared at him, as though they were peeling him like a grape and exposing his naked soul. Faulkner's right hand rested on the butt of the gun.

With the resolve cultivated over the years, Will maintained his air of polite calm. He also knew instinctively that, should he move in a way that Faulkner didn't care for, the barrel of that gun would likely be sticking in his face. Belatedly he remembered his cap, whipped it off, stood twisting it in his hands. "She's special, is Miss Shaw. Not like most of the others… She's been nice to me."

"I saw that."

The dry tone stung. "I'd like to speak to her," he repeated. "I won't stay long—I know it's unusual, but…" He stopped, words sticking in his throat. He'd as soon take a bullet than beg.

"Wait a moment. I'll see if she's awake," Faulkner announced unexpectedly. He opened the door, went inside and shut it in Will's face.

For a few shard-tipped seconds Will considered barging in. He had as much right as that uppity bruiser to pay Neala a visit. More, if truth be told.

Fortunately the door opened again almost immediately.

"Come in," Faulkner invited in that same irritating dry tone. "She's delighted you're here."

Will brushed by without even glancing up; Neala was ensconced in a lounger, with a light quilt covering her from the waist down. Several bouquets of flowers were scattered about, reminding him anew of her popularity, as well as his own cloddishness in not bringing her flowers himself, and him a groundsman.

Sunlight poured through a window behind the lounger, highlighting her pale face, a bruise on her forehead and a couple of scratches on her cheekbone. But she was alive. And her eyes were smiling at him. He ignored the widow seated in a rocking chair nearby even though her expression conveyed more plainly than words that lowly hired help deserved about as much welcome as a chamber pot that needed to be emptied.

"Thank you so much for stopping by, Mr. Crocker," Neala said, and Will focused his attention on the only person who was glad to see him.

"I don't mean to intrude," he began. The old woman made a noise deep in her throat, and Will felt a band of red climbing his cheeks.

"You could never intrude." Neala awkwardly gestured toward the room. "I know we're breaking all manner of propriety—"

"Absolutely," the widow interrupted testily. "Which is why I shall remain here, and visits with members of the opposite gender will be strictly limited to ten minutes."

Dressed in black, with a diamond stickpin flashing at her throat, she reminded Will of a buzzard circling in to feed on its carcass.

"Mrs. Wilkes, do stop intimidating every male who crosses the threshold." Neala smiled at Will. "Don't pay her any mind. She reacted the same way to several other gentlemen callers."

Will looked away.

"I beg your pardon," Neala said. "That remark didn't come out the way I intended."

"Another reason I plan to remain here," Mrs. Wilkes put in, laying aside a small embroidery hoop. "All this drama has muddled your mind as well as your mouth." She peered at Will over dainty spectacles. "Well, don't stand there gawking at her, Mr. Crocker. You've obviously come to inquire as to her health. Kindly do so before she commits another faux pas."

Will half turned to leave.

"Please, Mr. Crocker," Neala said. "Think what a favor you've accorded me, giving me someone else to talk to. Here—pull up a chair. Tell me if you've encountered any bees, or forgotten your cap again."

Gratefully Will started for the chair, but Faulkner abruptly materialized in the doorway, grabbed the chair and plonked it down a good three yards away from Neala. Then he went to the other side of the lounger to stand beside her, looking more than ever like a scowling bodyguard instead of a devoted escort.

An escort who apparently ignored, with the old widow's blessing, those ten-minute limitations on visiting.

Will would ponder the implications—later. "I've not forgotten my cap anymore," he said to Neala as he sat down. "But I did forget to bring you some of the black-eyed Susans I was pruning earlier."

When she gave him that shy, delighted smile, the one that made him feel more alive than he'd felt in years, Will wondered if his life could ever be the same, when the time came for him to leave White Sulphur Springs.

Chapter Fifteen

Four days after her nightmare day at the races, Neala gave in to Grayson's persistent bullying to accompany him for a walk about the grounds. The fact that she was still afraid chafed both spirit and mind, because she had never considered herself a spineless person afraid of her own shadow. As a devout believer, she was assured that God Himself watched over her, protected her, strengthened her.

Yet ever since the head-ringing had ceased, and she had worked the stiffness out of her knocked-about muscles, Neala was afraid to be alone. And she was more confused than ever. Why would God allow such dreadful calamities, when for all her life she had tried so hard to be a good person and a faithful follower?

Mrs. Wilkes produced a pragmatic maid, hired to remain in Neala's room overnights; Neala was too grateful to protest any more intrusions upon her privacy. An Ulster Scot brimming with self-confidence, Deirdre McGee towered over Neala, more resembling a stevedore than a lady's maid. She certainly snored like a stevedore, but Neala surprisingly found a modicum of comfort from the noise. Surely no self-respecting assassin would risk tangling with an Amazon whose snores fair shook the bed.

Truth be told, Deirdre was almost as tall as Grayson. Grayson himself pronounced Deirdre an acceptable night watchwoman, he called her with a grin.

"At least she saves me from camping outside your door every night. I'm told Mrs. Wilkes is relieved."

Neala tried to emulate his matter-of-fact attitude. But the realization that he had been prepared to sleep outside her door jangled her nerves almost as much as her fear of another murder attempt. She didn't understand Grayson at all. Every time she remembered regaining consciousness, felt his strength surrounding and protecting her, her stomach flip-flopped like a beached trout. Cravenly she admitted to herself that one of the reasons she didn't want to go for a walk was because she would be alone with Grayson.

"Here. There's a south wind blowing." Deirdre handed Neala her plain straw hat, to which she had nimbly fastened a spray of silk flowers. "This 'twill keep that sheep's head o' hair from curling about your face. And mind you don't come back with a crop of freckles."

"You're worse than Mrs. Wilkes," Neala complained with a small smile. "Sometimes I'm tempted to shear my head like a sheep."

"Himself wouldn't be liking that a' tall."

A light blush heated Neala's cheeks. With the passing of every hour her feelings toward Grayson seemed to shift and alter like windblown desert sand. When his manner was aloof, almost abrasive, Neala simply erected her shield of friendly tolerance toward an irritable puppy. But when he looked at her in a certain way, when the cold blue of his eyes deepened and seemed to pour over her like water from a lovely sun-warmed lake, her heart squeezed until it was difficult to breathe, and her palms turned all clammy. Because she simply did not feel the time was appropriate for entertaining such feelings, Neala found it easier to provoke Grayson than to risk having him catch her gazing at him with calf's eyes.

Which was why for the past twenty-four hours she had resisted going for a walk. If Grayson were forced to come to her rescue again, Neala wasn't sure she could control those jangled feelings clamoring inside for release.

"Himself doesn't have any say in what I choose to do with my hair," she told Deirdre firmly as she pinned the hat equally firmly in place.

"Ah-mm," Deirdre responded. "Keep telling yourself that, lassie."

A knock sounded. Reflexively Neala froze, then sidled over behind her bed, her gaze fixed on the door. Shaking her head, Deirdre lumbered over, yelled through the panel to ask the knocker's identity, and opened it with a resigned flick of a gaze toward Neala so that Grayson could enter.

"Miss Shaw still shies at every noise, Mr. Faulkner."

Gray dropped his homburg on the writing table and strolled across to Neala. "She's cause enough," he said. When he reached her, in a surprise move he lifted her hands, carried them to his mouth, and dropped a light kiss on the back of each one. "But that's going to change." He tugged her gently around the bed, then led her across the room. "Starting right now." He returned his hat to his head while never releasing his firm grip on Neala's forearm. "The first outing is always the hardest," he murmured. "Trust me, Neala. I won't let him close enough to even think about harming you."

"Aye, you do that," Deirdre added. "Bring her back with a bloom to her cheeks. I'll be seeing you tonight, miss. Ten o'clock, without fail." Shutting the door, she handed Grayson the key, then walked past them down the hall, her heavy skirts practically wide enough to brush both sides of the walls.

"Her father was a dockworker from Derry," Neala said, watching her dignified passage. Words spilled forth as she battled a stubborn case of the flutters. "And she told me her mother was the only daughter of a Scottish minister who was killed in the siege. They emigrated to Pennsylvania. Deirdre has six brothers. Six! Apparently she grew up on stories of battles rather than baking. By the time she was fourteen she could arm wrestle—and win—half the boys who worked in the steel mill where her father worked."

"Where on earth did Mrs. Wilkes dig her up?"

"She knows everything about everyone. I believe Deirdre was a nanny for some acquaintance of Mr. Carnegie, and Mrs. Wilkes met her here last year when that family came down for the season. They're letting me borrow her right now."

Grayson chuckled, the low deep-in-his-chest laugh that tripped Neala's heart up and set it to pattering. "Between you and Mrs. Wilkes, every guest here is wrapped around your little fingers."

"Everyone except the man who wants to kill me."

Beneath her fingers she felt the muscles in his arm flex. "Let's talk, all right? While we walk?"

Anything was easier to bear than having the heart flutters over a man who didn't like females, especially cowardly ones. "All right. Will you be able to talk and keep watch?"

"I reckon I'll manage," he drawled. Then, more seriously, he said, "We've both read through everything in that trunk over the past several days, and I think it's time to take the next step."

"Next step?"

For a moment or two he didn't respond. Neala opened her mouth to inquire again, then closed it when Grayson resumed talking.

"I've had people looking for your brother," he said.

"Adrian?" The world tilted; the breeze stilled. "Did they find him? Is he… Is he—?"

His hand covered her fingers, and Neala realized she'd been practically clawing his arm.

"Last fall, his name was on the passenger list of a schooner whose destination was Charleston. My contacts haven't picked up any further information. But he was alive a year ago, Neala."

Her breath expelled in a long sigh. "Thank you. You don't have to keep looking for him, Grayson. But I appreciate your efforts."

"I don't know why you care. I've heard and seen no evidence of familial responsibility on your behalf. In fact, more than once I've considered the possibility that—" He stopped. "Never mind. Let's talk about your grandfather, hmm? I've come up with a plan."

Stung by his uncomfortably accurate summation of her brother, Neala grappled with hurt for a moment before she decided to simply be grateful that at least Adrian could still be alive. She pinned a smile on her face. "What's your plan?"

"Since the best we can determine all the deaths are limited to your paternal grandfather's side of the family, I'm thinking we need to investigate Neal Shaw more closely. So—" he glanced down at her, then hugged her arm to his side "—I'm leaving for North Carolina day after tomorrow," Grayson announced quietly. "And you're coming with me."

"I see." Neala chewed over his words for a few moments. "That sounds like a good plan to me. Deirdre shouldn't..." She plowed doggedly ahead. "What I mean is, it's unfair to expect Deirdre to be my faithful watchdog during the day as well as all night. I'm sorry I'm not brave enough."

"Don't be ridiculous. I'm relieved." He glanced down. "You may not have noticed, but basically I didn't give you a choice in the matter of coming or no."

"Oh." The tightness crushing her middle loosened a bit. "That's true. You didn't ask, you ordered." Yet instead of feeling resentment over his high-handedness, a long-absent sense of freedom trickled through her. Freedom—and security, because she would be with Grayson.

She sifted through possibilities, her enthusiasm growing. "Do you know, I should have thought of going to North Carolina myself, last spring. We knew Grandfather settled in Wilmington, but never the address where he lived. I doubt there's anyone still alive who knew him. I mean, it has been fifty years."

"That's why it's known as detective work. Here's your chance to do some investigating like your favorite heroine, Nellie Bly."

"You're absolutely right. And I shall do so even when you laugh at me, like you're about to do." They exchanged smiles, but Neala's faded swiftly. "How do we slip away from here without alerting the murderer?" she asked, her voice quavering a bit on the last word.

Gray stopped suddenly, and before Neala could draw

a breath he'd pulled her off the path beneath the boughs of a monstrous hemlock.

"Shh." He wrapped her in an embarrassingly close embrace, dropping his head until his lips brushed her ear. "I think someone might be following us. I need for you to relax, put your arms around me as though we're about to share a kiss. Can you do that for me, Neala?"

Share a kiss? "Um…of course. Are we?"

He'd turned his head slightly, his gaze scanning the rows of cottages off to their right, then the trees lining Howard's Creek, where they were headed. "Hmm? Are we what?"

"Nothing." Neala plunked her forearms against the soft lawn shirt and casual jacket he had worn that day. His necktie, she noted, matched to perfection his deep blue eyes. "Is this acceptable?"

"Only if you're about to shove me away." He returned his attention to her, searched her face a long uncomfortable moment. Something flickered within the blue gaze, something silvery and ominous that backed up the breath in Neala's lungs. "Here," he murmured, "like this." He drew her arms up and placed them on his shoulders. "No, don't stiffen up. Relax, Neala. I promise, this won't hurt."

"I think you're taking undue advantage of me, Mr. Faulkner," Neala muttered against his shirtfront. "There's nobody following us at all."

Grayson went still. Then, very softly, he said, "If I'd wanted to take undue advantage of you, Miss Shaw, I could have done so on many other occasions than this one. Furthermore—" his hand burrowed between them to cup her chin "—if there's advantage being taken here, more likely it's all on your side."

"M-my side?"

"Mm-mm." His other arm shifted to embrace her waist, and the hand holding her chin slowly slid up to a couple of wayward curls dangling in front of her ear. "I think it might be this hair you love to hate." His fingers lifted the curls, which wrapped around them in hairy chains. "I can't seem to stop wanting to do this. I've never felt hair so soft, yet so strong it defies every attempt at control."

His voice deepened, and Neala's knees decided to buckle. "Mr. Faulkner… Grayson. I don't think this is—"

"Shh." His head dipped and he cut off her protest with a light but electrifying kiss. "You think too much, love. This is the Old White. We're surrounded by eligible bachelors and available belles who contrive to steal a kiss or two at every opportunity." He kissed her again, another teasing brush that singed every nerve along Neala's spineless spine.

"Fine," she managed to say, and hauled herself out of his arms. The effort felt as though she were trying to wrest herself free of a vat of molasses. "We can kiss, then. But you may *not* call me terms of endearment. They're lies, and I won't have it." Breathless, she struggled to control the annoying trembling, and was forced to bite her lip as well as lock her knees.

"Most women," Grayson mused to the branches above their heads, "enjoy my, ah, terms of endearment."

"I'm surprised you even know any," Neala sputtered, "seeing as how you don't regard women very highly. Unless you're taking advantage, that is."

"Little cynic. You surprise me, Neala." He grinned wickedly, and Neala to her utter stupefaction found herself grinning back. "I was frankly halfway steeling myself for either a slap or a swoon."

"Stuff and nonsense," she retorted. "Your sisters read too many gothic novels. I grew up watching my friends turn flirting into an art, instead of reading about it. Pretending to evade a kiss is a time-honored device to allow a pursuing male to feel the matter is in his hands, when of course it's the—" She stopped, a blush hotter than the summer sun scalding her cheeks. She could not believe what had dribbled out of her wayward mouth, and almost yielded to the temptation to flee like the simpering damsels in gothic novels.

"I'm—"

"If you apologize, I'll kiss you again. And this time it won't be a mere touching of our lips."

Wide-eyed, Neala searched Grayson's face, tried to determine if the light in the back of his eyes was laughter or irritation. "I don't know what to do with you," she whispered, half to herself. "Nothing seems to be the way I thought. The way it's supposed to be. I don't understand you—I don't understand anything." Her voice wobbled. "Everyone in my family but my brother is dead, and I don't know why. Now the murderer wants to kill me. It's not right. It's not fair. And—and I can't even pray like I used to, can't hear God talking to me anymore."

The painful revelations burst forth, smearing the tranquil air with their corrosive sense of betrayal. "All my life I've trusted God. Ever since I was a child. I sat on Grandfather's knee, and I could recite all the Beatitudes to him when Adrian couldn't even manage the Twenty-Third Psalm. I only missed church once, because I had the measles. I've tried, for my entire life, to be good. To honor God because—" she gulped back a sob "—because I t-trusted Him."

"Neala…"

She flung up her hand, pressed her palm against his lips. "No! Don't say anything. This is all your fault, anyway. Yours, and Mrs. Wilkes, for harping on the illusion that you're courting me, until I don't know what's real and what's not. Well, for your information, Mr. Blacksheep-of-the-family Faulkner, I don't want to marry you. Right now, I wouldn't marry anybody even if I did want to because it wouldn't be fair. Do you understand me?"

"If you don't lower your voice, you'll be able to ask half a dozen or so interested guests if they understand. I confess I don't, but—"

"Flumagudgin. You don't understand. I don't understand."

Oh, the glorious freedom of tossing all restraints aside, prying open the locked box of her feelings and heaving them over the side and into the whirlwind. "Understanding is irrelevant. All that matters is that you promised to protect me, and to help me find out who is trying to kill me. Seducing me is *not* necessary. You can kiss me if you must—but only while we remain here at the Old White." She lifted her chin. "After we leave, you will not take advantage due to propinquity."

"I've never responded well to ultimatums," Grayson answered in such a mild tone Neala's passionate tirade abruptly collapsed. "I don't want to marry you, either, so we can snip that particular thorn and be done with it."

He took a step closer, but his hands were clasped behind his back so Neala was unalarmed.

"As for the rest, seems to me you're placing a bit more blame on God for all your troubles than is probably fair. From the little I recollect, God's not the one responsible for all your woes. Mankind's the culprit, love—sorry. *Neala*." He arched an eyebrow. "I may still call you

Neala, right? You've not objected to that familiarity, nor have you shown any reservations about calling me by my Christian name."

Was there a trap buried somewhere within the smooth-tongued sentences? Neala didn't know. She did know, however, that she was drained, and bewildered, by her outrageous behavior. "I much prefer my Christian name over terms of affection," she said tiredly, "and since I've been calling you Grayson for weeks, it would be hypocritical to object now."

"Fine. Now, as I was saying, God isn't killing off the members of your family. The responsibility for that falls squarely on the deranged but nonetheless human individual inflicting the mayhem. He's the one to whom you ought to direct all this wrath and hurt." He lifted a hand and Neala automatically tensed, but he only brushed a windblown lock of hair off his forehead. "As for divine protection, I have to say in my experience—which I'm sure you'll concede is far broader than your own—that there is no such thing. God's in His heaven, I suppose, but I've witnessed precious few examples of proof that He intervenes in human affairs."

Diverted, Neala studied him for a moment. "Do you really believe that?" she finally asked. "How can you? Of course God intervenes—" She stopped.

For almost eighteen months she had been pleading with the Lord to help her understand, to give her peace. Patience. Perseverance. And thus far she was limping along blindly, sliding into despair instead of peace. Resignation instead of patience. And in another second she might throw her hands up and ask Grayson to stake her like a sacrificial goat, just so she could get her murder over with.

What kind of Christian did that make her?

"I'd be seven kinds of fool to believe anything other than what I said," Grayson retorted, his voice short. "You're far better off depending on your own resources, using the mind God gave you, and strengthening whatever skills are necessary to survive. When you left Sumner you came here, didn't you? Not because God told you to, but because you thought this would be a safe place."

"Sumner?"

"Sorry." He shrugged. "The Isabella Chilton Academy for Single Females. When I was a boy, the place was a family estate, known throughout the South as Sumner. I still think of it that way. At any rate, you left because you made the decision to do so. Now that you've been discovered, another course of action is called for on our parts. Ours, not God's. When we leave here for—"

He clamped his lips together. "Never mind," he muttered next, and before Neala had time to blink twice he'd casually whipped out an arm and tugged her back against his chest. In movements too swift to block he deftly removed hat pins until he lifted off her hat and dropped it to the grass. "I think I need another kiss," he whispered against her mouth, and followed words with action.

Only this was no brief, almost teasing kiss. This time he lingered, drawing Neala into a blinding cocoon where shooting stars burst into Catherine wheels behind her tightly closed eyes and the ground beneath her feet seemed to dissolve.

When he finally released her, he pressed her cheek against his chest and rested his against the top of her head. His arms held her close. Beneath her ear she could hear the thunderous beating of his heart, feel his rapid breathing stir her hair. "Neala Shaw," he eventually murmured, then heaved a long sigh. "Since I don't see the Almighty sending along any other reinforcements, I will protect you to the best of my ability. But I can't help but wonder…" he finally set her back, his hands clasping her upper arms, thumbs moving in restless circles that did little to calm Neala's own runaway pulse "…who's going to protect me from you?"

"What do you mean?" It was a fatuous question at best, but there was no help for it. Her mind was naught but the remnants of sparks from those Catherine wheels. "Are you… Do you mean the murderer might harm you, to get to me? If so, I release you. I don't want anyone else hurt because of me. Please, Grayson. I couldn't bear it."

"All right. Don't worry about it, Neala, it's all right. I can take care of myself." He squeezed her arms, smiled at her, a strangely bemused smile. "Believe me, I've been in far more dangerous circumstances."

"Oh. Well, then…" She couldn't seem to stop gazing up into his face, couldn't stop a tickly smile of her own. "I'll try not to worry about your safety, but I will warn you that I find your notion of God dreadfully hilter-skilter. Furthermore, just because I'm muddleheaded right now doesn't mean I'm wrong. On our trip to North—"

"Shh." Instantly his palm covered her mouth. His smile disappeared. After tugging her back into his arms, he lowered his head so that his lips brushed her ear. "Neala… you deserve to know," came a husky murmur that tripped her breath anew, "the first time I kissed you was deliberate. You see, somebody really is following us, and I needed ah…a plausible maneuver, to confirm what my instincts were telling me."

"Very clever," Neala murmured, then cleared her throat. "Who was it?"

"Couldn't tell." He shrugged. "I do know today's not the first time, however."

"Oh." A shiver that had nothing to do with being kissed under the trees danced along her veins. "But you kissed me again. Why did you—I mean, it wasn't…"

He lifted his head, muttered something beneath his breath Neala decided she was better off not knowing, then cupped her face in his hands. "Someone should have taught you prudence years ago. Looks like I'm stuck with the job." His teeth flashed in a quick smile.

"It's not a joking matter."

"How do you know I was joking?" He pressed his thumbs against her lips. "Shh. We'll discuss it later. Right now, I need you to listen. Until we're on the train—and then only if I tell you—don't mention our plans out loud. Not where we're going, not when we're going. Nothing. Don't tell anyone, particularly Mrs. Wilkes."

"Deirdre?" Neala queried hazily. Grayson had rendered her incapable of concentration. His eyes were bluer than a blue jay's feather, and his hands…oh, but they were warm, warmer than—

"I've already told Deirdre. We need to maintain a point of contact here, and I can't think of anyone safer. That woman could outsilence a tombstone if the situation merited it." Finally he released her, stepping back and casually adjusting his cuffs. "But absolutely nobody else can know. Not your friends, not the maid, or the bellhops. Nobody but Deirdre."

"I understand," Neala said, and swallowed hard. He sounded as though he genuinely admired Deirdre McGee. "I understand, Grayson. I won't tell anyone other than Deirdre, or talk about it."

All at once she felt exposed, stripped to her drawers, vulnerable and frightened and ashamed. He had kissed her only as a diversion; now he lectured her as though she were six years old. Obviously she was an inferior bolt of cloth compared to her nightly bodyguard. Yet not only had she allowed his kisses—she had reciprocated, which certainly couldn't speak well for her character.

Even more unsettling than her questionable decorum, however, was her wavering faith. No longer was she blithely confident of God's protection. Instead, somehow over the past few weeks she had willingly entrusted her life to Grayson Faulkner, and she was terribly afraid that she had just handed him her heart as well.

Chapter Sixteen

Wilmington, North Carolina
September 1890

The sultry, cloying month of August grudgingly gave way to September. In North Carolina, however, the fry-an-egg-on-stone temperatures refused to acknowledge summer's passing. Gray lounged on the warped front porch of Uriah Coolidge's boardinghouse, where he and Neala had spent a fruitless ten days searching for people who remembered Neal Shaw, of Strathspey, Scotland, and the address where he had lived here in Wilmington, North Carolina.

Dressed casually in uncollared shirt and light flannel trousers, Gray nursed a tepid lemonade while he waited for Neala to return from her visit with the octogenarian grandmother of a woman who for some reason refused to allow a man in her rambling old house. Neala had promised to try and discover the answer to at least that mystery.

Gray leaned his head back against the wicker rocking chair and contemplated the peeling paint on the porch ceiling. Uriah's wife had run the boardinghouse with the punctiliousness of a martinet, according to the older residents. Meals were plain but plentiful, floors swept, whitewash applied spring and fall. After she passed, Uriah hired a decent cook, but he let things go some, though when he took a notion he was a dab carpenter, and a pure genius with flowers. Gray liked the man, but more than once found himself marveling that Uriah still grieved the passing of his wife, even after four years. Most marriages, as far as Gray could tell, consisted either of long-suffering tolerance, passionless friendship, or—he slumped down in the rocker with a reminiscent smile—in the case of his youngest sister, a mind-numbing succession of battles as fierce as any fought in the War.

Then there was Aunt Bella and Uncle Everett. Sighing, he straightened in the chair and set it to rocking. Their marriage defied both convention and all Gray's preconceptions; the wealthy eldest son and heir of one of the South's most prestigious families had married, of all things, a governess. They used to laugh at the timeworn cliché of it, Gray remembered. Yet over the two decades of their union they forged a legacy that withstood every societal spear, every bit of anecdotal wisdom that had prophesied a doomed relationship.

Everett and Isabella Chilton contradicted every scrap of reality Gray had accepted as truth since he was old enough to wonder why his mother and father never shared a bed.

Aunt Bella insisted the reason for their abiding relationship was Jesus. "He's the glue, the reason a man and a woman cling together and transform two ordinary, ornery individuals into a couple. A united entity that paradoxically strengthens their individuality while cementing their couple-ness as well."

The notion that one could only have a successful marriage if one were a devout believer annoyed Gray.

During his travels over the past decade, he'd met a lot of married folks who did not consider themselves Christian. It was inconceivable that none of them would be allowed to enjoy a life of connubial bliss simply because they did not consider Christ as the head of the household.

He might tackle Neala with the subject. Certainly she possessed more knowledge of Scripture than a rebellious backslider like Gray. He appreciated the fact that she didn't force her faith on anyone, including him. On the other hand, she never tried to hide its importance in her life. Come to think of it, he decided he found her steadfast faith in God almost as annoying as his aunt's. And yet, somewhere deep inside, a part of himself he'd considered long dead seemed to be quickening, prickles of pain in a frostbitten limb. Aunt Bella and Neala had suffered devastating losses, yet both of them faced life with far more optimism than Gray. Sure as he was sitting on Uriah Coolidge's front porch, Gray knew they would credit that optimism to their faith in God.

Abruptly uncomfortable with the train of thought, Gray stirred in his seat, gulped another swallow of lemonade, tried to steer his mind onto another subject. How was he supposed to ask her anything, when she'd absented herself for—he yanked out his pocket watch and glared at the time—two hours? She'd been gone two hours, and it was high time for her to return.

All right, she'd warned him that she enjoyed visiting, expressly ordered him not to "sit on the porch waiting for me all by yourself. Talk to somebody. You've been a detective. Do some detecting."

The smile slowly returned over the memory of her ferociously serious face as she delivered the lecture, just before she left, while a soft wind blew tousled brown curls all about her cheeks and forehead until she'd smashed them beneath her hat. Gray heard her mutter some preposterous expression. Then she'd laughed, waved a hand and set sail down the walk, unaware that he'd watched her until she turned the corner three blocks away.

With a long, cleansing breath, Gray allowed himself the luxury of thinking about nothing but Neala. With each passing day he was growing more accustomed to the strange, still uncomfortable emotions she aroused, even when she wasn't in the room.

She was frightened, yet refused to dissolve into uselessness, or endless bouts of weeping. When she did cry, it was brief, honest, and without apology. Gray found it most unsettling that Neala's occasional emotional lapses did not automatically raise his hackles.

She was homeless, for all intents and purposes orphaned and indigent. Yet she befriended everyone she met, without guile or greed. For some reason, she seemed to simply like people. In the eyes of the world she was helpless, at Gray's mercy, shunned by polite society because she was traveling unchaperoned with a man.

Except by their second night at the boardinghouse, every resident including Uriah was enchanted, and had promised to do what they could to aid her search for her grandfather.

His mother would have ostracized her; despite her overt matchmaking Frances Wilkes would snatch her bald-headed, as Gray's old mammy used to say, and send her off to a convent or something. Then she'd come after Gray with her knitting needles. Aunt Bella… He slugged down the rest of the lemonade and slammed the glass on top of the wicker side table. Aunt Bella would understand, he told himself staunchly. She would understand, because she knew his heart, and Neala's.

The thought of Neala's heart unraveled something inside, something he feared he would never figure out how to wind back together. Because whenever she looked at him with those guileless brown eyes he could see…he could see…

Abruptly he stood, and stomped down off the porch into the blistering sun.

Infuriating female. Where had she taken herself off to? Just because he had determined they were safe here, that their midnight exodus from the Old White had been successful, didn't mean Gray was willing to allow her more freedom than he felt was wise. Yes, he'd agreed she could pay a visit on her own. But he also remembered how he'd watched her marching down the road, and how he'd barely throttled the urge to chase her down. That she was willing to undertake the task without him testified more to her courage than to Gray's confidence in her safety.

He flipped open his watch again. Should have been back an hour ago. How long could it take to ask an old woman if she remembered one Neal Shaw, and what she remembered?

For several moments he paced the hard-packed earth in front of the boardinghouse. Then, with a frustrated oath he set off down the street. If his heart was beating faster, it was due to the heat, not because he was; the feelings roiling around his gut were annoyance, not fear for her safety.

But he was responsible for her, blast it.

He never should have agreed to let her go by herself, never should have let the big-eyed waif with her stubborn chin and determined expression talk him out of his responsibility. If something happened to her, if he'd slipped up somehow and the murderer had found out where she was, he didn't know how he'd survive it.

For the first time in years, Gray found himself wanting to believe everything that Neala claimed about God. Like his aunt, she believed the Almighty kept a divine finger on the pulse of every creature, including nondescript birds nobody else cared about or even noticed. To Gray's way of thinking, that either made God a sadistic busybody or, as Neala insisted, an all-loving caretaker, Who was as concerned about Gray as He was Neala.

But if God cared, if God were omnipotent and omniscient, His lack of interference in Neala's plight made no sense. And Neala's faith was faltering because of it.

Gray realized with another unnerving jolt that he didn't want Neala's faith in God to be misplaced.

When he heard her voice, calling his name, and saw her waving her arm, he quickly thrust the uncomfortable thoughts aside. But he couldn't ignore the urge to thank God for her safe return as he lengthened his stride to meet her.

She was smiling; he could see the smile yet he could also see her eyes, and their expression quickened his pulse. "What is it?" He reached her and clasped her hand. "Neala? What is it?"

"I found out," she said breathlessly. "I found out where he lived, Grayson! But I learned more than the address."

Her voice rose, and without thinking twice Gray took her other hand and tugged her close. "Tell me."

"Grayson, Grandfather eloped! He and Grandmother met at their boardinghouse, fell in love and they eloped!"

White Sulphur Springs, West Virginia

She was gone. For two days, Will trudged through the hours, halfheartedly performing mindless tasks. In between he wandered the grounds, hoping for even a glimpse of Neala.

By the third morning he was forced to accept the truth that she was gone.

Why had she left without telling him goodbye? Rationally he accepted that his feelings toward her were one-sided, futile. But he could not quell the longing any more than he could squash the bitterness twining upward through his insides, like the infernal poison ivy with which the groundskeepers waged a ceaseless war.

On a dreary morning early in September, Will packed up his meager possessions and set off for home. Momma had been writing him twice a week, asking when he would return, demanding information he did not want to share. He dreaded their reunion, and despised himself for it. Something inside him had changed over the past several months at the Old White, something fundamental. Life-altering. His lifelong goals remained the same, but from now on there would be significant modifications in how he achieved them.

Rutter, Virginia

It was late, almost ten at night, when Will reached the lane leading to their house. Crickets chirruped without pause in the stultifying darkness, and somewhere a whip-poor-will called its mate in a mindless repetition that grated his nerves. As a child, he'd been constantly tormented by a couple of snot-nosed brats who lived next door to his grandmother. They used to threaten to whip him, taunting him that God sent a bird demanding that they "whip poor Will."

Grimly Will thrust the memory aside. The future would be different, he vowed with every step down the lane. Different, and brighter.

"William? Is that you?"

His mother appeared in the doorway of the house, the single lantern she held outlining her spare form beneath a shapeless sack dress.

"It's me, Momma!"

When he reached her he dropped his battered suitcase and wrapped her in a cautious hug. "It's good to be home," he said, and released her before she could stiffen.

"It's so good to have you back. I've waited so long, William. I was frightened that you were never coming home. I was afraid that you'd changed your mind, that you were going to betray me like everyone else."

Will casually grabbed his suitcase and stepped inside. "You know better than that. I love you, Momma—I could never betray you. We're in this together, remember?" Slowly his gaze swept the room. "Momma," he finally said, "you knew I was going to be home this evening. Why didn't you clean? I remember how you used to always want me to come home to a—"

"I told you I was afraid you weren't coming!" She crossed her arms across her flat bosom, glared at Will with reproachful eyes. "What use was there to clean? What use is there to do anything, if you're just going to give up? That's what you've come home to tell me, isn't it? That you're giving up our dream?"

Wearily he set about picking up the untidy little room. "I'm never giving up on our dream," he promised her as he collected old mail and scattered newspapers, stacking them in a neat pile. "In fact, I've made a decision, one that will finally bring the dream within our grasp. I want to share with you what I've decided. But not—" he held her gaze until the defiance faded from her expression "—until you promise that you'll start taking better care of yourself when I'm not here."

"I try, William. It's just taking so long. I'm not a young woman any longer, and look at you. Half your life is gone and still we live in a miserable hovel. We've let your grandmother down. And all I hear are promises, promises that never come to pass." Her bottom lip quivered.

Sighing, Will walked over to her. The lantern light was unflattering, giving her the sullen appearance of a hard-bitten cracker. Her lace collar was faded and grungy, ripped in two places. When he realized he was comparing his mother with Neala Shaw, Will had to close his eyes.

"Momma, we're closer now than we've been in over twenty years. I promise to tell you all about it in the morning, after I've had a decent night's sleep."

"Never mind that *I'll* never be able to sleep, wondering what's going on inside your head. I know you, William. There's something changed about you, something I'm not sure I like."

Her voice was rising as she worked herself into one of her tantrums. This time, fortified with what he'd decided over the last weeks, Will refused to be swayed, regardless of the outcome. "Momma, I'm going to bed," he repeated firmly. "I'm exhausted, and I need time to think. You can either go to bed as well, or you can stay out here."

"Don't you treat me like a child! I'm your mother, and I deserve respect. You don't understand—"

"I understand perfectly," he interrupted. The power sweeping through him was heady, like the occasional glass of champagne at the Old White he used to sneak on weekends. He should have stood up to his mother years ago, instead of trying to appease or apologize or simply allow her to manipulate him. *I've had enough, Momma.* "Now you must understand me. All my life I've done whatever you asked, applied myself to the goal of reclaiming what is rightfully mine—a goal *you* determined for me. The goal remains. Only the means of attaining it will change."

He paused, waited. His mother did not respond.

"That's all I plan to say on the matter until morning." Ignoring the hectic color splotching her face, Will leaned down and pressed a kiss against her quivering cheek. "Good night, Momma."

"For you, perhaps. I doubt I'll ever have another good night, thanks to my selfish son." She clamped Will's arm in a frenzied grip. "Don't you walk away from me! If you do, I promise you'll be sorry."

As gently as he could Will pried her fingers away, then held her hand so she couldn't lash out. "Threats won't work anymore, Momma. I've changed. You might as well start accepting this, because I'm not going to change back. And it's all because of her." He grimaced, steeling himself.

"All because…" she hissed, head tilted, muscles in her throat quivering like a rattlesnake's tail. "Who are you talking about, William? Tell me, tell me this instant."

Stoically Will surveyed the woman who was his mother, the woman he had idolized, struggled to please, and after forty years finally managed to free himself from. Whatever her reaction, he may as well endure it now than wait until morning.

"Neala Shaw," he stated, and watched all the color leach from her face, leaving her as pale and haggard-looking as a corpse. "I met her, talked with her. She's not at all like those White Sulphur Springs belles. She's not like any woman I've ever known. And that means, Momma, that I'm changing our plans."

He half expected her to lunge for him, to scream invectives, to strike out—all reactions he'd grown used to over the years. This time, however, she surprised him. Worse, unnerved him.

"I'll see you both in perdition first," she said, lips barely moving.

Then she walked around him as though he were invisible, went inside her bedroom and shut the door.

A chill skittered through Will's body. As though he were invisible. For a long time he stood, teetering on the edge of a black, bottomless pit because a snide little voice inside his head warned him that his mother had just renounced him. And he was fading, fading into the darkness, indistinguishable and overlooked, as he had been his entire life.

Neala, he thought, repeating her name in a litany. Somehow he would have to find her again, before it was too late for them all.

Chapter Seventeen

Wilmington, North Carolina

". . . and it was the town scandal for years," Neala finished, bewilderment spilling over as she shared the story.

Because the afternoon remained unpleasantly warm, Grayson had insisted on renting a hack to drive to the street where, almost sixty years earlier, Neal Shaw had met and fallen in love with Annie Bremmer. Neala scarcely noticed their surroundings; immersed in the past, she let the words flow while her mind grappled for understanding. Insight.

"But I don't understand why it was a scandal," she confided. Again. "There's nothing wrong in what they did. I asked Mrs. Percy if she could try to recall anything else that would explain." She sighed, absently twirling a lock of hair around her finger. "She wasn't very helpful. All she remembered, she kept telling me over and over, was that it was a scandal."

She peered sideways, into Grayson's face. "You have that look again."

"What look would that be?"

"The one like you just swallowed a bite of cake I baked for you, but it tastes like…like coal dust, and you don't want to tell me."

"Mmm. Very colorful," was the unhelpful response. "Neala, I can think of one or two salient causes for a scandal. They lived in the same boardinghouse, which would make it very easy to yield to temptation, and then—"

"Grandfather would *never* have behaved in such an ungentlemanly manner. It wasn't sordid. They fell in love. It's the most romantic story I've ever heard."

"I thought you didn't read gothic novels," Grayson inserted.

His teasing jab worked. Neala swatted his arm. "This is not a novel. This is my family's history. We have to find out what happened. If it really was a scandal, or just gossipmongering that over the years took on a life of its own. That happens, you know."

"Neala, after all this time, second-or third-generation hear-say is the most we can hope for. We'll do the best we can, but you need to prepare yourself for disappointment."

"I'm prepared. But I can also hope for a—a Godly serendipity." Determinedly she lightened her voice, thrusting aside Grayson's pragmatism, and her own qualms. "At least I'm riding in a buggy down the street where they met, and fell in love." More enthusiastically, she finished, "We can park the buggy, take a stroll, just like they must have done."

Despite the bleak, even sordid possibilities swimming beneath the surface, for the first time since Mother and Father were killed, and Adrian deserted her, anticipation buoyed Neala's heart. At last, she was doing more than running away, hiding like a coward while helplessly waiting to be murdered.

"I think this is the street," Grayson said, deftly turning the horse onto a broad tree-lined avenue flanked with elms. He slanted a look toward Neala. "You all right?"

"Perfectly. Well… I, ah, I don't know." She shifted on the seat. Inside her gloves, the palms of her hands had dampened; her fingers chilled. "I thought I was—in fact I couldn't wait for this moment. Now, I feel a bit anxious. Like you reminded me, this could very well turn out to be nothing but another dead end."

"Then we'll just move along to the next clue," Grayson calmly replied. "That's the way it works."

"Of course. You would know, wouldn't you?" She gave him a quick smile. "But I still wish it would work faster."

"Mmm. I remember feeling that way once, until the band of outlaws I was chasing with a U.S. marshal decided to ambush us. Things happened so fast I suffered nightmares for a year."

"You did?"

He nodded. "I did. The marshal was shot in the back. I took one in the shoulder, and for about a half hour I was convinced my time was up."

Neala turned on the seat so she could watch him. He sat there, relaxed and competent, loosely holding the reins and talking, though his eyes were never still, constantly searching out their surroundings, a habit, he'd told her, that had saved his hide more than once. Neala still struggled to reconcile the image of that man with the unruffled one sitting beside her now, a man who seemed both a kind friend, yet an enigmatic stranger. Then there was the urbane gentleman at White Sulphur Springs, who fit among the more exalted guests as to the manor born.

She supposed he *was* born to wealth, seeing as how the Faulkners could stand shoulder to shoulder with the

Vanderbilts, Carnegies and Hunts. Not for the first time, Neala wondered why Grayson had separated himself from his family. Miss Isabella refused to divulge any personal information other than the fact that he had endured a difficult childhood. Mrs. Wilkes, on the other hand, peppered Neala with his connections, his striking looks, his wealth, and that she was only too happy to overlook his notoriety if a marriage between Neala and Grayson could be arranged.

That thought triggered a now familiar sensation of stumbling over a log and falling, not to the ground, but into a bottomless abyss.

"You're staring at me. Why?"

Neala quickly averted her gaze but she knew Grayson had spied the hectic blush because he reached across and lightly stroked his finger down one hot cheek. Since they'd left the Old White he hadn't kissed her, or even embraced her. But he certainly seemed to, well, touch her frequently. Never in any manner that would arouse her ire, or that could be labeled disrespectful.

Just enough to keep her middle a-twitter, as Grandmother used to say.

"Such a blush. Now you've aroused my curiosity."

"I was wondering what happened to make your childhood so awful you renounced your family," Neala blurted out, unsurprised when his face hardened into that of the man she'd first met, the one whose heart seemed encased in an iron vault.

"Who's been your informant," he asked without inflection, "my aunt or Mrs. Wilkes?"

"Neither of them," Neala replied. "Miss Isabella mentioned in passing once that you'd had a difficult childhood, and have spent most of your adult life out west, that's all. Mrs. Wilkes glossed over all your peccadilloes because she was determined that I land you for my husband."

"Ah. Well, we've both determined that that particular fate is not likely to occur between us. Like I've told you before, I plan to shun the institution of marriage until I've drawn my last breath."

"I'm quite aware of your feelings on the subject," Neala returned with stilted dignity. "As you should be aware of mine, which preclude not only marriage at this time, but marriage to you at any time."

"Now that we have that settled—" he turned to face her and for a tingling second Neala forgot to breathe "—I'd still like to know what you were thinking to bring a blush to your cheeks that near burned my finger." He returned his attention to the road, then added coolly, "If it was speculation about my childhood, since the curiosity is about to eat you alive, I'll satisfy it—to a degree."

"Fine. Whatever you're comfortable sharing, Mr. Faulkner."

For a moment the only sound between them was the steady clip-clop of the horse's hooves and the faint crunching of the buggy wheels in the packed-dirt street. Then, they both turned to glare at each other, the glares melting into rueful smiles.

"Sorry," they both said together, which prompted laughter, and the atmosphere lightened into the comfortable camaraderie of the past several weeks.

"I'm touchy on the subject of my childhood," Grayson admitted. "But since you're entrusting your life to my care these days, I suppose it's only fair to trust you with my own. In a manner of speaking."

"I didn't mean to pry." Neala hesitated, then laid her

hand on his forearm. “You needn’t tell me anything, Grayson. I trust you, regardless of whatever happened that turned you so sour in your views toward women. I…um…appreciate you moderating your attitude while you’re protecting me.”

“It has been an effort.”

She balled her fingers and punched the muscular forearm. “And here I was actually thinking about how you unsettle my insides, and that sometimes it’s difficult to bre— Oh!” Swiftly she turned away, staring sightlessly at the passing houses. “I can’t believe I said that,” she mumbled in a small voice.

“Neither can I.”

Suddenly he pulled the buggy to the side of the road, stopping underneath the sloping branches of a hundred-year-old elm. “You, Neala Shaw, are by far the most complicated, convoluted woman I’ve ever known. Certainly the most…indiscreet. I don’t know what I’m going to do with you.”

As long as he didn’t kiss her again she was prepared for just about anything. Neala clamped her bottom lip between her teeth to make sure she didn’t speak the thought aloud. “Hopefully you’re going to keep me alive,” she offered eventually. “And perhaps help me discover who hates my family enough to kill everyone in it.”

For some reason, verbalizing the last sentence out loud, on a quiet, well-mannered street in a lovely Southern town on a somnolent late-summer afternoon, ignited the fuse on all the roiling emotion Neala had managed through sheer will to tamp down some place deep out of sight. Without warning icicles frosted her spine. The humid air thickened until she couldn’t seem to breathe; a sensation of unreality whirled her into a dizzying vortex where visions of all the members of her dead family pressed closer and closer. "Grayson…" she barely whispered. "Grayson, everyone's dead. They're all dead but me. He wants to kill me. Someone wants to kill me and I've done nothing wrong…"

"Easy, love. You're all right."

Somehow his hand was on the back of her neck, pressing her head down, down. She wanted to fight the pressure but the dizziness was making her nauseous and weak. Vaguely she heard his voice, speaking words she didn't understand except for the tone. She'd never heard him speak so gently. She tried to tell him, but what emerged sounded more like a gasping croak and she gave up. *I give up, Lord. I'd rather go ahead and die than suffer this unbearable waiting.*

"No, you don't want to die. Besides, I'm not going to let you."

"Is your wife unwell, sir?"

"Just overcome by the heat a bit."

"Would you like to bring her inside? We live right here."

"Do come in," a feminine voice urged.

Her soft Southern drawl sounded like Mother. Fresh pain squeezed Neala in a vice but the whirling vortex had slowed. She tried to sit up, mortified to her bones, but Grayson's hand firmly held her.

"Let's wait a bit, love," he said. "I don't want to risk your passing out on me."

"Oh, do bring her inside, out of this dreadful heat. Dolly, could you fetch us some smelling salts, please?"

"Yes, ma'am."

"I'm all right," Neala whispered. "Please, Grayson… I'm all right."

"Of course you are." He finally allowed her to sit up, but his hand cupped her chin and she was subjected to an intense scrutiny that made her close her eyes. "If you're sure it wouldn't be too much of an imposition," she heard him say, "I think perhaps we'll accept your kind offer."

"She looks so pale. Do you need my husband to help you carry her?"

"Thank you, no. I can manage."

She had never been so humiliated in her life, but Neala simply couldn't find the energy to protest. It was as though everything that had happened in the past eighteen months had ambushed her, like those outlaws who had ambushed Grayson. "So sorry," she mumbled without opening her eyes. "Don't understand…"

"You've been carrying a load that would have crumbled a lot of men, certainly every woman I've ever known." Before she quite knew how he'd managed it Grayson was on the street, on her side of the buggy, and lifting her into his arms. "Frankly, I've been waiting for something like this to happen."

He'd been waiting for her to swoon—well, almost swoon, like some silly widgeon. Did that mean he now viewed her with the same sneering contempt with which he viewed all women? The prospect distressed Neala more profoundly than she liked, especially when she felt her eyes sting.

"I'll see to your horse," the man's voice said. "Evie, can you hold the door for them?"

"Yes, dearest," the woman whose voice sounded so like her mother's responded.

"Hold on," Grayson murmured in her ear as he began following the woman called Evie.

"You broke your promise." Desperately Neala swallowed,

squeezed her eyelids tightly together. "You called me 'love.' I told you not to use terms of endearment."

"So you did. Sorry, love."

If she'd possessed the strength she would have punched him again. Since she didn't, Neala gave in and relaxed against him like a sack of potatoes. Just for a little while…

Chapter Eighteen

Moments later, Neala was ensconced on what was regrettably known as a fainting couch. The woman, a plump but pretty lady who looked to be in her late fifties, hovered over her with smelling salts, which Neala refused with sufficient firmness for Gray to wave them away. He was crouched beside her on the floor, his face inches from hers. The concern Neala read there reassured her, and within moments she was able to sit upright and apologize for making a spectacle of herself. The couple introduced themselves as Alton and Evie Young. Mr. Young discreetly retired to the other side of the parlor to spare Neala further embarrassment.

"We were out for a drive, exploring where my grandfather lived when he came over from Scotland," Neala explained. At Gray's gentle insistence she took another swallow of the blackberry tea Mrs. Young's maid, Dolly, had provided. "There used to be a boardinghouse on this street. He met my grandmother there."

"How delightful." Mrs. Young beamed. "Well, I can tell you that at one time there were several boardinghouses along here, one of them just two doors down. That one burned down, I'm afraid."

"Burned down?" Neala echoed blankly. "Oh." Swallowing hard, she stared down into the dark swirling tea, but her mind had gone as blank as a fresh sheet of foolscap.

"What about the other boardinghouses? The one we're looking for would have been used in that capacity back in the 1830s," Grayson continued. "We haven't been able to find much else out about it, other than the name of the street, and that—" he hesitated, glancing at Neala, and whatever he saw in her eyes must have provided enough impetus to forge ahead "—that a large magnolia tree grew near the front porch."

And Grandfather used to snip petals off the flowers and sneak them into Grandmother's room. Until the day she died, Grandmother loved the scent of magnolia above all other flowers. Trying with little success not to tremble, Neala handed the cooling tea to the Youngs' maid, who after a quick troubled look at her, took the cup and saucer and whisked from the room.

"Goodness to gracious," Mrs. Young suddenly exclaimed. "Your grandparents must have lived two doors down, then, in the house that burned. I remember that magnolia. Our family's lived on this street since before the conflict with the British in 1812. My mother told us about that boardinghouse, way back when I was a girl. As I recall it wasn't too long after the fire that the Sandersons bought the lot and built their home there."

They'd found the place after all, only to find that it had burned. Only two houses down. She was sitting less than a hundred yards from where her grandparents had lived. Dizziness set the room to spiraling until Neala realized she was holding her breath; Grayson's hand covered hers, soothing with reassuring strokes, and after a moment the dizziness receded. Without fanfare Grayson shifted to sit on the couch beside her.

"Do you remember anything else your mother told you?" he asked Mrs. Young.

"Not much, I'm afraid. You all never would have discovered anything by driving up and down the street. Only reason I'm sure of the place is your mentioning the magnolia tree. It was the largest magnolia on this street in its day. But the fire damaged it, and the Sandersons eventually had to have it cut down, oh, going on 'bout thirty years now. Mr. Young and I used to love sitting on the porch when that tree was in bloom, smelling the sweet scent." Her eyes misted. "I reckon we're near about the only folks who still remember. Lots of families had to leave back in the seventies, don't you know. Times were real bad then. Quite sad, really."

"Someone torched the place, I believe you told me?" Mr. Young queried, as though to keep his wife from rambling. "The fire was not an accident."

"Yes, dear. Didn't I say so? The lady who ran the boardinghouse died, along with several residents. Oh—surely your grandparents weren't—no." She fanned herself with a hankie she tugged from her sleeve. "How silly of me. You wouldn't be here in our parlor now if your grandparents had perished, would you, honey?"

"No, ma'am," Neala replied faintly. Instead her grandparents had lived to produce children and grandchildren so they could be hunted down, one by one, exterminated like vermin. She didn't realize she was digging her nails into Grayson's hand until he pried her fingers open, then laced his through them, all the time keeping an attentive gaze upon Mrs. Young.

"My mother was only a child," the lady chattered away, "but she said the neighbors talked about it for years."

"I imagine they would," Grayson returned amiably while his thumb burrowed beneath their intertwined fingers to stroke Neala's palm in mesmerizing circles. His calm strength and vitality seeped into her bones like an unguent. "Did they ever discover the perpetrators?"

"There were a lot of rumors, but nobody was ever charged," Mrs. Young said. "Here, dear, you're looking flushed now. Should I have Dolly fetch a cool cloth? It's no wonder, learning that your dear grandparents almost perished in a fire."

"No, thank you. I'm fine. Truly." Or she was as fine as was possible considering she was sitting beside a man who was not her husband, soaking up his tender attentions while listening to stories of fires and deaths and waiting on tenterhooks to learn something about her grandparents.

"What were the rumors?" Grayson prodded after glancing down at Neala. A corner of his mouth twitched.

"Well, I don't rightly recollect all of them." Mrs. Young folded her handkerchief and made an elaborate production of stuffing it back in her sleeve. "Something about someone left a candle burning. Or that one of the gentlemen was purported to be a heavy pipe smoker, and fell asleep in his bed."

"The rumor she doesn't want to tell you fed the gossip mill for years," Alton Young put in dryly. "The one where a woman dressed all in white, or a ghost, if you want to venture into the supernatural, heaved a lighted torch through one of the windows, then disappeared, never to be seen again."

"A woman?" Neala frowned, struggled to collect the scattered pieces of information in her still-scattered brain. While she sorted through her thoughts she finally slid her hand free of Grayson's, under the pretext of smoothing down the pleats in her rumpled shirtwaist. "Why would a woman do such a thing?"

"Women commit countless crimes for a number of reasons," Grayson said.

Neala doubted if the Youngs heard the nuance of cynicism coloring the words.

"Did you tell me your grandfather's surname?" Mrs. Young asked. "I don't recall."

"Shaw." Neala spoke through stiff lips. "Neal Shaw."

"Wait. Everything is coming back to me," Mrs. Young announced excitedly. "Oh, my soul and body!"

"What? What is it?" Neala pressed a fist to her midriff. "Did you know—did your mother know—my grandfather?"

"Not as well as she knew the woman with whom he eloped. Her name, as I recall, was Miss Brind… Breem… Bremmer! That's it! Miss Bremmer."

Neala smothered a cry. Mrs. Young stood, her face plainly revealing distress. Mr. Young walked across and put his arm around his wife's shoulders. "It was a long time ago. Just tell them what your mother told you. They deserve to know."

Nervously Mrs. Young twisted her hands. "Miss Bremmer—she was your grandmother?"

Mouth dry, Neala nodded.

"Yes, well, she was a teacher—Mother was one of her pupils. She thought the elopement very romantic, of course, though she told me she cried for days because she loved Miss Bremmer."

"Her name was Annie," Neala whispered. "Annie Bremmer."

"Ah." She shook her head. "Well, now, what I haven't told you, since I've just now remembered, is the reason for the elopement." Apricot color tinged her plump cheeks.

A giant snake wrapped Neala in its coils and squeezed. Grayson could not be right. She didn't want to believe that her grandparents—

"It's not what you're thinking," Mrs. Young hastily interrupted. "Leastways, Mother never mentioned…um… *those* sort of rumors. However, I'm terribly sorry to be the one to inform you, Mrs. Faulkner— What is it, honey? Here, drink some more tea. Oh, dear. Dolly took it away. I'll ring for more."

"No need." Mr. Young stepped forward. "Here, Mrs. Faulkner. A glass of mineral water." He handed her a crystal goblet.

Anything to divert the phrase Mrs. Faulkner *from clanging in her ears like a fire-alarm bell.* Neala grabbed the glass and took a quick swallow, which of course set her to coughing again. Eyes streaming, she glared up at Grayson, who had the effrontery to smile at her. And shrug.

"I beg your pardon," she told Mrs. Young. "You were saying?"

"Well, I do hope this doesn't upset you further, but I have to tell you that your grandfather and grandmother ran away on the very day your grandfather was to have married another woman."

Oh, no. No. This was even worse than the usual reason couples were forced to marry in haste. "Another woman?"

she eventually murmured. "Grandfather…jilted some other woman? On their *wedding* day?"

"I'm afraid so. And seeing as how it was Judge Rutledge's only daughter, you can imagine how the scandal was difficult to live down. The Judge ended up paying a sharecropper to marry Letitia, I believe was the daughter's name, and sent them off to somewhere in another state to live."

After leaving the Youngs, for several blocks Neala and Grayson drove in silence. Above them the sun burned through the late-afternoon haze, while the steady clip-clop of the horse's hooves beat in rhythm with Neala's overflowing heart. She wanted to fling out her arms and embrace the moment with an excitement as glowing as the sunset. Words abruptly bubbled up in a froth of emotion.

"I've been so disheartened, and my faith was even wavering," she exclaimed to Grayson. "And yes, I'm disappointed by Grandfather's behavior. And I feel dreadful for poor Miss Rutledge. Why do you suppose her parents forced her to marry someone else?" She shook her head. "Never mind, I think I understand. My parents were most concerned about my future, especially after I turned down my second proposal."

"You've refused two offers of marriage?"

"Yes. Oh, never mind all that. It's not important. I just hope Miss Rutledge developed an affection for her husband." And she mentally winged a thank-you heavenward to her own parents, for not forcing her into an arranged marriage. "I know my grandparents loved each other very much, or they never would have eloped in the first place. When Grandmother died, Grandfather refused to leave her grave for two days. So you see, he never meant to hurt Miss Rutledge, he just loved my grandmother too much to not take her for his wife."

She stopped, thoughts crowding her mind faster than her tongue could translate them into words. "I just realized…we have a name, Grayson! When I least expected it, God gives us a clue. Miss Rutledge."

"Might be we just happened to be in the right place at the right time."

"Stuff and nonsense. The timing was right because the Lord arranged it. He knew when we'd be passing that part of the street, so He arranged for the Youngs to be there."

"I suppose He also arranged for you to pass out in the buggy?"

Provoked with him, Neala blew out an exasperated breath. "In the first place, I did *not* faint. In the second, it wouldn't matter to me if I had. Otherwise the Youngs would have passed by, like two ships in the night, and we never would have learned what we did."

Beside her Grayson muttered something beneath his breath. "If God really wanted to help," he observed impatiently, "He would have provided the state and city where the jilted bride and her poor dupe of a husband were exiled to. Along with the name of the dupe."

"Oh, stop being so cynical. You, Grayson Faulkner, can scoff all you like. But what happened today was not chance or happenstance or coincidence. And someday you're going to find yourself in a place where you'll admit that God cares about us, that He watches over us, that He loves us. And you'll be thanking Him for it."

"And someday, Neala Shaw, you're going to realize that humans are not puppets dancing to God's tune. If He wanted puppets, He wouldn't have created humans with free will. Most of the time," he added with a bite to his voice, "humans choose their own tune, not God's. You believe He cares for you. But I've learned that kind of faith doesn't mean He's going to protect you from all harm. More than likely, He'll stand by and let the murderer have his way with you the same as He did the rest of your family."

For the rest of the journey, they sat side by side in a silence that now seemed as wide and deep as the ocean.

Chapter Nineteen

White Sulphur Springs, West Virginia

For a week he scrounged for information, waited and smoldered. She'd escaped. Again. The failure was insupportable, something that ate into him like a canker, ruined his sleep, and sent him prowling the grounds of the hotel resort until the moon waned in the sky.

After days of subtle investigation, he was still unable to ascertain the whereabouts of either Neala Shaw or that interfering Grayson Faulkner. He wasn't a man. He was a predator, swooping in for the kill, claiming a woman he had no right to. Regrettably, neither the old widow nor the giant of a woman hired to sleep in Neala's room offered any useful information. He'd charmed the widow one evening at dinner and, on another afternoon, under the guise of hiring her as a nanny had plied the Irish skirt with questions.

The sense of hurt, even betrayal, fomented and bubbled. Over the last eighteen months he had come to regard Neala as his own. He alone was responsible for her life—and for her death. Like a secretive shadow he had stalked her, watched her, learned her personality with all its fascinating idiosyncrasies. When she allowed Faulkner to dupe her, she had betrayed the man who knew her the most intimately. *Him.* Watching her seduction at the hands of that profligate filled him with indescribable hurt.

As September slipped into October, hurt escalated to rage. Neala was going to pay for her defection. She had chosen to allow Faulkner to spirit her away. Therefore something would have to be done to bring her back, something he would not relish, nor be able to enjoy. Neala would pay for that as well.

He'd made it a practice to avoid doing away with bystanders. It defaced the nobility of his mission. Now he was forced to break his rules, to kill an innocent bystander, because nothing less would be able to lure Neala away from her seducer, and return her to White Sulphur Springs.

Once he settled on his decision, he focused his attention upon the victim: Mrs. Frances Wilkes.

For three days he observed her every move, all her daily habits and rituals, and concluded that the task was too risky to accomplish in broad daylight. He could arrange it, of course, and the challenge appealed to his pride. But he simply didn't want to take the time testing his craft and cunning on someone who amounted to nothing more than a pawn.

A simple suffocation in her bed would have to suffice. He was sorry for the indignity of it, but his purpose must take precedent.

Two nights later, with a sliver of a moon shrouded in clouds, he changed from the neat English woolen jacket and striped trousers he'd worn for dinner and the concert on the lawn into what he referred to euphemistically as his night clothes: every item from soft-soled shoes to the wig was black. He waited until all sights and sounds of other guests faded, and the only sounds to be heard were the interminable chirping of insects and a light southerly breeze that aided his cause by pushing more clouds over the moon.

Once more he had made himself invisible.

At a little past two in the morning, he crept through deserted lobbies, down long corridors until he arrived at the widow's suite of rooms. He'd thought about entering through the window, but that would have been too simple, outraging his sense of professionalism.

When he reached her door, he paused, readying himself for the task, forcing rage to life. It curled upward through his body until it propelled him through the door and across the parlor to a sumptuously arranged bedroom incongruous with the almost Spartan bedrooms of other guests. These quarters reeked of wealth and prestige. He didn't even hesitate as he selected one of the embroidered pillows gracing a chair near the bed.

For a long moment he stood over her, watching the rise and fall of her chest beneath the bedcovers, listening to the soft snores that occasionally passed her lips. Then, fueling the rage to swamp out any insidious remnants of regret or conscience, he leaned over and pressed the pillow over the widow's face.

Wilmington, North Carolina

The telegram arrived before breakfast. Gray read it through twice, crumpled the piece of yellow paper and savagely hurled it across his bedroom. With helpless fury seething around him, he stalked from his room, slammed the door and strode outside, the openmouthed stares of several early-morning residents following in his wake.

What would this do to Neala? For months she had kept her spirits high, refusing to succumb to despair, except for that one brief episode in the buggy, before the Youngs came along.

Even the couple's happenstance arrival she regarded as divinely inspired.

So what kind of God helped one person, about the same time as another one was being slaughtered like a sacrificial goat? As clearly as if the murderer instead of Deirdre had sent the telegram, Gray knew the motive for Frances Wilkes's murder, and he had no doubt of its effectiveness.

His vow to protect Neala was about to be tested in a lake of burning fire.

Eventually the rage burned itself into manageable flames, and Gray retraced his steps to the boardinghouse.

Neala waited on the front porch. She was sitting, alert and unsmiling, in the same wicker rocking chair where Gray had waited for her a week earlier.

"Mr. Coolidge told me a telegram arrived for you," she said as he walked up the steps. "Is something wrong in your family? Do you need to leave? I'll be all right, and can—"

"How about if you hear what the telegram says before you plan what we're going to do?" He sat down beside her on the edge of a glider and propped his elbows on his knees. How best to break the news? Tease her into relaxing? Just tell her and get it over with?

"Grayson, I can tell something has happened, as can

the residents who witnessed your departure from the house. What is it? Just tell me and you'll feel better for it."

She looked so sweetly earnest that for a moment Gray found all he could do was to look at her, absorb her goodness and her pluck. There was something different about Neala Shaw, something he couldn't quite put a finger on. Whatever it was, she stuck in his brain like flypaper, even when she wasn't around. Perhaps it was her innocence, but he didn't think so. Innocence for the most part in a female was either calculated or boringly predictable, two descriptions that could not be attributed to the woman sitting beside him.

Her courage? She was carrying a frightful burden, yet still she could scrape together the resilience to meet each day with a smile.

What would this news do to her?

"Grayson…"

Sighing, he worried his hair with his hands, then lifted his head and faced her. "Neala—" he reached and folded her fingers within his "—the telegram was from Deirdre."

"Deirdre? Why would she send— No. No. Don't tell me, I don't want to hear this, Grayson." She tugged at her hands though her gaze was fixed upon his and it implored him to say anything but the knowledge already filling her eyes.

So he told her as fast as he could, to get the deed done. "Mrs. Wilkes is dead. She died in her sleep, but we both know this likely wasn't due to natural causes."

All the color leached from her complexion, and the hands Gray held might as well have belonged to a corpse.

"My fault," she whispered through lips that scarcely

moved. "This is my fault. He's telling me this will keep happening if I disappear so he can't find me."

"Yes."

For an interminable moment she seemed to stare through him. Then she sat up straight, gently but firmly separating herself from Gray. "I'm going back to the Old White," she said. "And I'm going alone. I don't want you anywhere near me. I want you to go back to the Academy and make sure Miss Isabella and all the students are safe."

"I don't think so." It took a monumental effort to keep his voice calm and matter-of-fact, even more of an effort to rope-tie the fear. "From this moment on, Neala, you will not leave my sight. As for my aunt and the school, I'll make arrangements for their protection. I have a lot of connections, and a lot of friends who'd be only too happy to spend a few weeks squiring a group of young ladies around."

"Thank you for that. It's difficult enough, remembering what happened to my friend Abigail." She stopped, swallowed several times while she stared up at the peeling-paint ceiling. "I can't think about Mrs. Wilkes right now. I just can't, or I won't be able to function." Her lips trembled and she wound her fingers together. "And I can't allow you to continue protecting me. I…can't."

The embers of rage reignited. Gray stared down at his knees for a protracted moment. "If you think for one second I'll stand by while you whistle yourself back to White Sulphur Springs on your own—which we both know is precisely what the murderer wants you to do—then let me disabuse you of that notion."

"I know you're far too honorable to send me into the mouth of the lion. That's why I'm not giving you the option." She licked her lips. "I renounce your protection."

With a stifled growl he leaned forward, clamping his hands on the arms of the rocker and effectively trapping Neala. "You're stuck with me, Neala Shaw. I gave my word to protect you, and that's precisely what I'm going to do. Even if I have to marry you to accomplish it."

The words punched out, a one-two blow that left him reeling, because they couldn't be stuffed back down his throat. Furious with himself, with Neala, with the untenable circumstances, Gray abruptly straightened, swiveled on his heel and stomped to the end of the porch. A cardinal chittered from the branches of a dogwood. The bold red color reminded him too much of blood; with a stifled sound he snatched up a dirt-covered spade lying on the railing and hurled it at the bird, who flitted off to parts unknown with a contemptuous chirp.

Just like the infernal madman who traversed the country with impunity, seeking out Neala Shaw. Until and unless Gray could catch him, neither he nor Neala would ever know another moment's peace.

He heard a floorboard creak and turned around, bracing himself.

"I know you didn't mean it," Neala said. She stood a scant yard away, freckles accentuated in her too-pale face, her brown eyes wretched. The effervescent mass of curls was strangled at the base of her neck within the clasp of an enameled clip. "Don't worry, Grayson. You haven't frightened or offended me. I appreciate the gesture, but it's impossible." Above the simple white shirtwaist, the pulse in her throat fluttered like butterfly wings.

Irrationally piqued by her stilted refusal, Gray leaned back against the porch railing and folded his arms across his chest. "Because neither of us wants to marry the other? Under the circumstances, I don't think our wants matter. Unless you're willing to allow me to remain with you every hour of the day without the legality of marriage, I don't see much of a choice for either of us."

For an interminable span of time Neala stood without responding, staring at him as though she could somehow force him to dematerialize, or worse, imprint her will upon his. *Not a chance, sweetheart.* He'd learned before he was out of short pants how to circumvent women and their torturous schemes.

"Marriage is sacred," she finally whispered. "Ordained by God. I can't marry a man who trusts neither God nor the nature of a loving relationship between husband and wife."

"I'll concede the point," Gray said. "On the other hand, marriage is also a legally binding contract between two parties that more often than not is arranged for reasons other than God and undying love." He stepped closer, his voice hardening. "It's time for you to face some unpalatable truths about the world, Neala. People seldom cooperate with your idealized notions of how they should act. Life doesn't work like that. Most people are greedy, selfish and immoral. They act out of self-interest, not altruism or nobility."

"In that case," Neala whipped out, "you should have no trouble doing what I asked. Leave me. Go pursue your own godless life. Regardless of what you think of me, I don't want another death on *my* conscience."

"Neither do I!" Grayson shouted back. He snatched Neala into a fierce embrace. "I don't want your death on *my* conscience." Much like his earlier impetuous declaration, words spewed forth from someplace so deeply buried he hadn't known it existed. "Regardless of what you think of me, I'm not a misogynistic heathen who doesn't care a fig for anyone but myself. I spent a miserable childhood with a mother who refused to let me grow up, who smothered me with overprotectiveness until I ran away so I could learn what it meant to be a man."

"I didn't mean—"

"And I vowed," he swept on, "that I would show my mother—my entire family—that I could not only take care of myself, I could take care of others." He glared at her, indifferent to the moisture stinging his eyelids. "I wanted to *help people*! I wanted to protect the innocent, pursue justice! I wanted to prove I could stand on my own!"

With an oath, he shoved Neala away from him. "So don't stand there in your pristine righteousness and call me a godless heathen, when all I'm trying to do is to save your life!"

Breathing hard, he clamped his mouth shut until his jaw throbbed. He couldn't believe what he'd just done—manhandled her, shouted at her, doubtless terrified her out of her wits. He was no better than the conscienceless fiend trying to kill her.

Then Neala spoke. "I'm sorry, Grayson," she said, her words contrite. "You're right. What I said to you was cruel, and untrue. Will you forgive me?"

Forgive *her*?

Gray blinked. "You're not making sense. I'm the one who should beg for forgiveness. I had no right to shout at you." His throat felt as though a vicious genie had dumped a shaker full of hot sand down his gullet. "To grab you."

"Oh, that's nothing." She waved away his execrable display of temper as though he'd done nothing but spit in public. "You should hear my brother. He used to screech like a steaming kettle when he didn't get his way. Father, now, he was mild tempered, but Grandfather would bellow when he was angered. Grandmother once told him he sounded like a wounded moose, which of course only made him holler louder."

Tentatively she reached out a hand, and almost in a daze Gray clasped it in his. "You didn't hurt me, or scare me. I don't have a problem with spilled tempers," she promised him earnestly. "I just don't know what to do about…us." The words quavered as she tried a smile that barely tipped the corners of her trembling lips. "Grayson, I don't know what to do."

Very slowly, Gray drew her closer, until he could rest his forehead against the soft crown of her hair. "Neither do I, Neala," he finally confessed against the curls. "Neither do I."

Behind them someone cleared his throat. Gray's head whipped up as he automatically pulled Neala behind him.

"Oh. Mr. Young." Gray nodded to the older man, and ignored the heat he could feel spreading across his cheeks. As far as Alton Young knew, Gray and Neala were a happily married couple enjoying a spot of canoodling on the front porch.

"I'm on my way to work," Mr. Young said as he mounted the porch steps. He tipped his bowler to Neala. "The streetcar passes a block down, so I told Mrs. Young I'd stop by on the way to bring you this." He held out a piece of folded paper. "Last night we got to talking, and she recollected that the daughter of one of her mother's friends keeps an ear to the ground, concerning all the goings-on in Wilmington society. Nothing would do but we had to pay a visit then and there. Thought your missus might be glad to know the name of the sharecropper fellow old Judge Rutledge married his daughter off to."

Gray took the paper, opened it up. "Hiram Buxton, married Letitia Rutledge, September 1832. Moved to Twin Oaks, North Carolina."

Neala turned around to beam at Mr. Young. "This is wonderful! Thank you so much, Mr. Young. Please tell Mrs. Young how grateful I am—we both are."

She was practically vibrating with excitement and before he even thought twice Gray wrapped a restraining arm around her shoulders. "As you can tell, this means a lot. But—" The noose tightened around his neck. He gave a mental shrug, and jumped. "My wife's obviously forgetting that the circumstances which necessitated Miss Rutledge's marriage to this man were doubtless painful rather than celebratory."

"Well, Mrs. Young wondered about that, but since this happened so long ago, and far as we know all these folks have gone on to their rewards, there didn't seem to be any harm in letting you know."

"Of course not," Gray said, but kept his thoughts to himself.

Courtesy of the wifely reference, Neala now stood like a cornstalk on a frigid winter day. Gray squeezed her shoulders once, then stepped forward to shake the older man's hand.

After Mr. Young tipped his hat and set back off down to the corner to catch the trolley, Gray glanced down at Neala. "Go ahead, rip a strip off my hide for referring to you as my wife," he said. "But be warned, I'm not in the best frame of mind for any more fireworks. Besides which, I think we have more important matters to discuss." He waved the paper in her face. "I'm thinking we need to pay a visit to Twin Oaks."

For a moment Neala regarded him in silence, head tilted to one side while her fingers absently played with a dangling curl. "I won't tear any strips," she said at last on a long sigh. "But one day I'll have to write the Youngs to explain. If I live long enough."

"What kind of talk is that, from my upbeat little Christian woman—oof!" He rubbed the ribs Neala had just elbowed. "All right. If you promise not to make any gloom-and-doom remarks, I promise to keep my, ah, endearments, under control."

Neala shrugged. "Grayson," she said next, the words dragging, "why would an eminently respected, prestigious judge marry his only daughter off to a sharecropper? She was the one who was jilted, after all."

"I've had a thought or two on that since Mrs. Young first shared the story yesterday. You might not like the tenor of them."

"They probably echo mine," she returned bleakly. "I just don't want to believe Grandfather was that irresponsible."

Gray could think of a few less flattering descriptions, but he figured Neala had enough to contend with. "The woman he married might not have been with child," he finished levelly, "but I'd bet my boots that the woman he left waiting at the altar was."

"I think so, too." She half lifted one hand, shook her head. "Grayson…that would mean I have another relative. An aunt, or an uncle—Letitia's child. If we can find them, I'd have family."

"Neala." He kept his voice gentle. "I'll find them for you. But you need to accept that they might not want anything to do with you. After all, you represent everything they lost, because your grandfather chose to marry Annie Bremmer instead of Letitia Rutledge."

Up went her chin and back went the shoulders. "They might be the only family I have left. I'll just have to find a way to convince him or her that we *are* family. And together we may stumble over a clue that unearths the Shaw executioner."

Gray decided no answer was the smartest response. As he led Neala across the porch to the front door, it also occurred to him that right now might be an auspicious time for him to see if her notion of God was worth pursuing. His gut warned him that they would need any and all divine assistance that might be flung their way, over the next few days.

But at least the news about Letitia Rutledge had successfully diverted Neala from the death of Frances Wilkes, and returning to White Sulphur Springs on her own.

Chapter Twenty

October, 1890

On the long train trip back to White Sulphur Springs, Neala argued with her conscience, debated with her mind, and ignored her heart, in a vain attempt to convince herself that her actions were necessary. Even honorable. She could not face herself in the mirror every morning if she did not pay her respects to Mrs. Wilkes. What difference did personal safety or family history matter when compared with the monstrous act perpetrated against a woman whose association with Neala had cost her life?

Nor could she ever hope to re-stitch her tattered self-respect if something happened to the man with whom she'd stupidly fallen in love, because she wasn't brave enough to try and survive on her own. In the dark, stuffy coach car, she prayed. Prayed for courage. Prayed God would at last heed her prayers and protect her, because she possessed not a shred of an illusion that Grayson Faulkner would be doing so any longer.

Grayson.

Blindly Neala stared at her reflection in the train window. Beyond the greasy pane of glass an indifferent world slid past in darkness, while the rhythmic clickety-clack of the train wheels rushed toward a destination that would lead either to absolution—or her own death.

By now Grayson would know she was gone. Would he bother to read her letter, or would he rip it to shreds and consign Neala Shaw to the fate she deserved? Mrs. Oppenheimer, the aging spinster who had roomed next to her, had proven to be an artful accomplice. She'd told Grayson that Neala needed some time alone, that she planned to take supper in her room and would see Grayson in the morning. After the meal was over, Mrs. Oppenheimer would give him Neala's letter.

God forgive her for the lie. Because after choking down a few bites of her meal, Neala had set the tray aside, then slipped down the servant stairs, out the back door and into the hack Mrs. Oppenheimer had arranged to take Neala to the depot. Grayson was contentedly eating supper with the rest of the boarders, not knowing that yet another woman had betrayed him.

Throat tight, Neala leaned her head back against the antimacassar and closed her eyes. *Lord, what else was I to do?* She never could have convinced him to save his own life at the expense of her own. What decent man would? For all his notorious shenanigans and caustic attitudes, Neala had come to know him better, to see the goodness in him he could no longer see in himself. On the surface Grayson might be portrayed as the reckless, wayward youngest son, but Neala had watched him sit and chat with Mr. Coolidge for hours, though the landlord tended to repeat every other sentence until her eyes crossed. Over the course of these past few weeks, Grayson had also spent many idle hours playing dominoes with Mrs. Oppenheimer, and entertained an excessively shy schoolteacher with stories of the western frontier.

As for Neala herself… She swallowed hard several times, and tried to erase from her mind the memory of his tenderness. His kisses.

Though it may cost her her life, and the love of her life, Neala was willing to accept the consequences in order to save Grayson. Sadly, he would never see it that way. She stirred in her seat, clasping and unclasping her hands.

Lord, he'll blame himself. Not only would he never forgive her for leaving—if the killer succeeded this time—Grayson would never forgive himself for failing to protect her. Oh, but this was too much!

Neala knew he had begun to feel something for her other than tolerance and exasperation. Not love, certainly. But at least perhaps a sort of affection. She also knew her actions would likely forever harden his heart not only toward her, but toward all women, yet another burden to crush her. No longer would he play parlor games with lonely widows, nor draw out shy schoolteachers.

Never hold her again, never tease her or call her *love.*

But he would be alive.

Why did she have to fall in love with him?

Nothing but burdens. Her life for the past two years had reaped nothing but more boulders, tripping her up, crushing her, smashing her world into so many fragments she would never be able to put them all back together. And so far as she knew, this solitary journey might be one of her last nights on earth.

It wasn't right that she had to endure this alone, afraid, full of regret and—and—

In a jerky motion she sat up, startling the sleeping governess from South Carolina who shared the seat. Neala apologized, the woman grumbled something, turned and dozed back off seconds later. Neala felt as alone as she had the day Adrian disappeared from her life.

And she was angry at God.

There. The awful thought was laid bare in her mind, and she half steeled herself for a lightning bolt to strike her dead and save the murderer the trouble.

Bleakly she sat, desolate and lonely, wondering with every mile if she would ever know why she had never measured up enough for anyone. God claimed to love everybody, but He hadn't spared a thought for a nondescript woman whose name wasn't even her own.

She had wasted her entire life, struggling to either compensate for the void, or to fill it through her own actions. Neither was sufficient. Oh, her parents had loved her, yes, but mostly because compared to Adrian she'd never caused any trouble. Grandfather had finally come to love her, but he'd wanted her to be a boy.

She didn't want to think about Grandfather.

So…what about her brother? Adrian… Her hands fisted in her lap. Face it. He never really loved her at all. She'd been nothing but a convenience, someone to fetch and carry and bail him out of trouble.

As for the Isabella Chilton Academy, if she'd been there longer, perhaps the ties would have become strong enough to allow the affection Miss Isabella and the students had shown her to blossom into a deeper love, bonds that finally would have blessed her with a sense of her own worth.

Such speculations were futile, chasing the wind.

What would it matter if she did return? After four months she was naught but a memory in the tides of their lives, like a finger pulled from the ocean. Just as the waters flowed over and completely erased where her finger had been, so would memory of Neala What-*Was*-Her-Name fade from Miss Isabella's mind, Abby's, Liam's, Mr. Pepperell and Miss Crabbe—until even her existence would be forgotten.

She was doomed to dribble out her remaining days in isolation and despair. Drifting like a severed branch down the stream of life, without the comfort of knowing that at least one person cared whether she lived or perished.

If this was life, she no longer possessed the stamina to fight. Her faith was shattered, her courage wavering, and hope? Well, at the moment her only hope was to find out where Mrs. Wilkes was to be buried, and to be able to ask her forgiveness over her grave.

She supposed she could hope that the murderer would be swift.

Right now, death would be a relief.

The train pulled into the station at two o'clock on Thursday afternoon. All around her autumn colors poured like spilled paint over the earth in breathtaking hues of red and orange and gold. The air was crisp, unlike North Carolina, with an invigorating clarity that partially lifted Neala's spirits. Clutching her cracked leather valise, the only luggage she had brought along, she waited until she knew her legs would do their job, then lifted her chin and faced her future.

An hour later she was sitting in the manager's private office, sipping hot tea while he informed her of the circumstances surrounding Mrs. Wilkes's death.

"It was her maid's off day, or we would have discovered her sooner, perhaps before—" He coughed, then hurriedly continued. "At any rate, without her maid, and without you here, she wasn't missed until lunchtime, when she was to have met several other ladies in the dining room. They'd planned an outing to the Chalybeate Spring."

Without her here. The cup and saucer rattled as Neala carefully set them on a piecrust table next to the chair. "Does the physician think she suffered?" she asked.

"Likely not," Mr. Eakle tried to reassure her. "He thinks she suffered a massive heart attack in her sleep, and never woke. In some ways, you can consider it a blessing, since she would not have suffered."

"She was having more difficulty breathing," Neala recalled slowly, longing to believe Dr. Dabney's diagnosis. That in fact Mrs. Wilkes *had* expired from natural causes.

"Of course," Mr. Eakle continued, his gaze avoiding Neala's, "I feel I should warn you that the Vances' nanny put up a bit of a fuss. Apparently she had some connection with you?"

Neala managed a nod.

"Ah." Though plainly mystified, the manager did not pursue the matter. "Well, I frankly didn't pay her much attention. But since you were Mrs. Wilkes's protégée, and apparently Miss McGee was a companion of sorts?"

"That's as good a way to define it as any," Neala murmured.

"Ah. Yes, Miss McGee assured me, most strongly, that she planned to tell nobody but you and Mr. Faulkner, myself and Dr. Dabney. I've debated over these past few days, on the advisability of bringing the matter to your attention." He hesitated, then planted his forearms on his desk and leaned forward. "Miss Shaw, since you've explained Mr. Faulkner's absence I am more reluctant than ever to mention this. I fear this claim might cause you unnecessary distress."

"I'll be fine," Neala replied faintly. 'Twas a good thing she was seated, for the bones in her limbs were dissolving. The ceiling seemed to have descended so that its weight bore down upon her shoulders. "Tell me what Miss McGee said?" she eventually prompted, though she knew the nature of the answer. Had known it all along. Knowing, however, was not the same as confronting its reality face-to-face.

Mr. Eakle shook his head, shrugged. "She apparently thinks Mrs. Wilkes did not expire from natural causes. But since her only reason for making that claim is some sort of decorative pillow that was out of place, lying on the floor, I believe, nobody paid her hypothesis much credence."

"You're saying…" she drew in a trickle of air and let the words fall where they may "…that Miss McGee believes Mrs. Wilkes was…smothered in her sleep? Using a—a pillow?"

"There. I knew I shouldn't have told you, Miss Shaw. I can see the revelation, bizarre though it may be, has upset you. Please, sip some more of your tea. Shall I call Dr. Dabney?"

"No. I'm fine. Can I… I mean, where…ah… Mrs. Wilkes… Where is her—her body?"

"Oh, I say. That is…" He cleared his throat, his fingers nervously smoothing over his lapels. "At the depot," he said at last, flushing. "We telegraphed her nearest relative, a great-nephew, in Alabama. Apparently it was Mrs. Wilkes's desire to be buried in Charlottesville, with her first husband. Unfortunately, there won't be a train until the day after tomorrow."

He finally looked across at Neala. "It seemed more… discreet, to have the remains lie in state elsewhere than her rooms here in the hotel. I have a trusted chambermaid packing up her possessions." He cleared his throat again. "Candidly, I was hoping, since you've returned, if you might lend your assistance, being the closest to family Mrs. Wilkes has in the area?"

"Of course. I'll do anything I can to help." Neala stood, shored up her crumbling composure. "It's the least I can do." Seeing as how she'd left Mrs. Wilkes all on her own. Undefended. "I should never have left."

"Miss Shaw, there was nothing you could have done." Mr. Eakle walked around the desk to briefly clasp her hand. "Over these many years Mrs. Wilkes has cultivated many good friends here at the Old White, and certainly a fond loyalty among all of us on staff. Please do not distress yourself over your absence, and believe we are taking the best care of her as can be arranged."

"I have no doubt of that. The great-nephew—will he come here, or Charlottesville?"

"It is my understanding that he will travel directly to Charlottesville." The manager walked back around his desk, searched a stack of correspondence until he picked out a folded piece of paper. "Here is his letter." He held it out. "Read it, if you wish."

Neala took the letter, pretended to scan the lines and handed it back to Mr. Eakle. "She is—was—a very dear friend of my family."

"Mrs. Wilkes had shared that with me. She also told me about the deaths of your parents. You've not had an easy time of it, have you?" He hesitated. "Under the circumstances, I believe we could arrange for you to stay in your old room, free of charge." His hands fluttered through some papers. "I'll also provide a key to Mrs. Wilkes's suite. Thank you again for your assistance."

"I'm honored to help," Neala repeated mechanically. *The key to Mrs. Wilkes's suite.* Hurriedly she changed the subject, asking if Deirdre was still with the Vances.

Plainly relieved, Mr. Eakle's face cleared. "Why, yes. Though I believe they plan to leave within the week. Ah, you may recall that the season closes October 15?"

"I remember." Neala offered her hand, thanked Mr. Eakle, and wandered back out into the main lobby. Plenty of guests still strolled about, but the crowds and the liveliness had definitely slowed. After selecting a vacant chair in the middle of the reading room, she sank down to collect her thoughts. She longed to seek Deirdre out, if only for the comfort of her presence. But she didn't, because that would put Deirdre at risk. She also knew she should go straight to Mrs. Wilkes's rooms, but at the moment the prospect was too daunting.

What to do, what to do? She could go for a walk, wander over the footbridge and along Howard's Creek, allow the soft sound of the water to soothe her soul. *He leadeth me beside still waters, He restoreth my soul.* Ha! Defiantly, Neala closed her mind to further tidbits of Scripture. She was in no mood for empty words and false hopes.

Restive, Neala smoothed her skirts, then rose and marched from the lobby out onto the piazza, down to the path that led back to the depot. She would cajole the station agent into allowing her to pay her respects to Mrs. Wilkes, then she would walk by the creek and enjoy the fall colors.

Come and get me, she challenged the despicable man

who had promised to take her life. *If you're still here, come and get me.*

Neala possessed few illusions about her capacity to defend herself, though she planned to try. Not for the first time since she'd boarded the train, she lifted her hand, cupping the clan crest brooch she had pinned to her traveling cloak. The colored-glass chips gleamed within the hammered pewter, reminding her that regardless of her isolation, she was a Shaw, and Shaws did not flinch from the valley of the shadow of death.

Nor did Shaws blench at responsibility.

When she reached the depot, the station agent was immersed in passengers, but the kindly colored attendant approached to ask if he could be of assistance. Upon hearing her request, he led her across to the baggage room, unlocked the door, and ushered her into a small storage room in the back.

"They put her here so's not to disturb the guests," he said with a wry smile. "Reckon some folks don't see that she ain't here noways. Just a shell inside that box." Wise chocolate eyes studied Neala. "Don't you fret none, miss. I've knowed Miz Wilkes since afore you was born. She's up there with the Lord, sure as you and me be standing here. And she's directing His affairs, I expect, same as she did down here. Don't be sad."

He left her then, and Neala slowly approached the plain wooden coffin resting upon huge blocks of ice. Tentatively she laid her hand on the lid, and tears slowly splashed down her cheeks. "I'm sorry," she whispered in a choked voice. "So sorry. I miss you, and I hope you didn't suffer." *Perhaps I'll see you soon, along with Mother and Father.*

Neala no longer expected to feel the Lord's presence,

surrounding and sustaining her. She no longer enjoyed the protection of the man she had grown to love, or the Goliath of a woman who kept the nightmares away or the indomitable sponsor determined to marry her off.

"Half your desire is fulfilled," Neala told Mrs. Wilkes then, and swiped away tears falling more freely now, soaking her face, but she didn't care. There was nobody to see her, nobody to chide, ridicule…or comfort. Like Grayson had in the buggy, holding her close, supporting her. Caring for her as nobody in her entire life had ever cared for her. "I fell in love with him," she finished, her voice breaking. "I fell in love, and so I left him."

The words hung in the close, dank air.

When the spate of grief passed, Neala lifted her hands, and slowly unpinned the clan crest. "I don't deserve to wear this right now." Dullness filmed her heart. Feeling nothing beyond the numbness that had invaded her limbs, she gently laid the clan crest on top of the coffin. Her actions did not seem illogical or irrational, but inevitable.

Stolidly she pressed a kiss to her palm, then placed her hand over the crest for the last time. "Goodbye," she whispered, to both of them.

Then she set her face and her feet toward Howard's Creek.

It was a little past four in the afternoon.

Chapter Twenty-One

Slanting sunbeams gilded the clear water of Howard's Creek. A pair of mallards floated near some cattails. As Neala pensively enjoyed the ducks, a delicate white crane swooped down into the shallows. How lovely, she reflected, to be a bird, confident of your territory, contented with your lot in life.

Of course, if she were a bird, doubtless some hunter would bag her before breakfast.

Sighing, she continued strolling by the creek, her walking boots almost disappearing in the sun-warmed grasses. Every noise, however innocuous, wedged the breath in her throat and sent chills racing down her spine—the breeze rustling through the tree branches, the two guests strolling by, the startled groundhog who flattened the grass in his rush to flee from her. She could not, could *not* endure the suspense another day.

If unaccosted and alive by dusk, she would request a boxed supper, which she would consume on the bluff above the creek, within the darkest grove of trees she could find. During the day the collection of winding paths was a favorite destination for courting couples, but after dark the place was deserted, so the murderer faced little risk of exposure. Neala would consume her last supper, then wander the paths, which all bore names—Lover's Walk, Courtship Maze, Hesitancy, Rejection. Now there was the perfect path for Neala. She would consume her last meal there—no. In an even more fitting gesture, she would stake herself out at the end of the path dubbed Lover's Leap. The murderer could accomplish the deed by tossing her off the high bluff that overlooked Howard's Creek.

Would anyone appreciate the irony?

When a man stepped out from behind a clump of sumac and jutting boulders she jumped like a scalded frog. Then she recognized him, and her thundering pulse steadied. "Goodness, but you startled me!" She scraped up a smile. "It's Mr. Lipscomb, isn't it?"

"For the moment, anyway." He stood in front of her, a half smile showing beneath the trim mustache and full beard.

Though they'd encountered him infrequently, both Neala and Mrs. Wilkes had been favorably inclined toward the dapper gentleman, who always exchanged pleasantries but never intruded. Neala felt a soft spot for him because he sported a head of curly black hair as unmanageable-looking as her own.

"I...um... I'm taking a walk, before supper. It's a lovely afternoon, isn't it?" She willed the prickles coursing over her skin to subside and her mind to pretend everything was normal. She was merely a guest, out for a stroll along the creek.

"Yes." He sighed, his hand reaching inside the Norfolk jacket he wore. "And I hope it turns out to be a lovely evening."

He withdrew a folded-up handkerchief and a small stoppered bottle, his gaze never leaving Neala's as he opened the bottle and tipped the contents into the handkerchief. "This will be much easier for us both if you don't struggle. I don't want to hurt you, Neala."

Neala blinked. All pretense of normalcy evaporated as the truth settled into her. *Mr. Lipscomb?* It was as much relief as surprise. "So, it's you," she murmured. "I had no idea."

"I know. At first, I never intended for you to know." He took a step toward her. "We'll talk later. Too much risk here, out in the open."

Of course. He should have waited an hour. She studied the soaking handkerchief, from which emanated an unpleasantly sweet odor. "Is that some poison, then? You're going to suffocate me with it, like you did Mrs. Wilkes?"

His eyes flickered. "No," he told her in a soft voice that instilled a bizarre sort of comfort, "this is only to render you unconscious. I really am sorry about Mrs. Wilkes. But you've only yourself to blame. You shouldn't have run away, especially not with that man." A chilling shadow chased across his countenance. "At any rate, I didn't have time to hunt you down again."

"Why?"

He shook his head. "I'll explain later. I'm glad you're not trying to run, Neala. I'd like to think it's because you believe me when I tell you that I've decided not to kill you after all."

The quiet statement plunged her more deeply within the mists of a surreal world, where anything could be said, everything exposed without terror because she was only reading a story. Nothing would actually happen.

Lurid melodrama was not wreaked upon ordinary people like Neala Shaw.

"Good girl," Mr. Lipscomb said. He lifted the handkerchief. "Let me do this, and when you wake up, we'll talk."

Panic belatedly jolted her into action. Neala swept her arm up, knocking his hand away. "No!"

She leaped backward, then turned to run.

He caught her in less than half a dozen strides, clamping one strong arm about her middle while the other pressed the handkerchief over her mouth and nose. "Don't," he whispered in her ear. "Just breathe, and let go. I'm not going to kill you unless you leave me no choice…"

The words followed the darkness coiling around her like a monstrous snake, squeezing her into oblivion.

Once, when he'd been a raw eastern tenderfoot dumb enough to try and hide his inexperience, Gray stupidly accepted a dare to ride a wild mustang the other wranglers had whipped into a frenzy. The horse not only tossed him on his backside, but stomped the stuffing out of him before the wranglers dragged him free.

The pain from the bruises and cracked ribs was nothing compared to the pain he was fighting from Neala's betrayal.

The time he'd been shot, terrified he was about to die? A mere hiccup of discomfort, compared to the excruciating awareness that not only did she not trust him, despite the fact that he had shown her more respect, more gentleness—more of himself—than any other woman except his aunt…she could very likely already be dead.

No. She was not dead. He wouldn't think it, he refused to believe it, banished the possibility from his mind.

Anger, that's the ticket. He was angry with Neala for pulling such a thoughtless and dangerous stunt. In fact, when he found her, Gray chewed over the satisfaction of inflicting her with the worst of his undiluted temper.

As for the stoic German crone who aided and abetted her escape, lying to Gray with the expertise of a professional huckster, well, he was satisfied she'd think more than twice the next time she came between a man and his woman.

The phrase ricocheted around the stagecoach in which Gray was riding. It was four o'clock in the morning, the western sky as black as his thoughts, and he was sore from eighteen hours of travel in some of the most uncomfortable conveyances ever devised by man. He was grateful for the few hours of sleep he'd managed atop a pile of mailbags in the baggage car of a northbound freight train he'd hopped outside of Sanford.

The stage wheels bounced into a rut, throwing him sideways. Groaning, Gray jammed himself against the corner, crossed his arms and tried, mostly in vain, to stop thinking about Neala.

When Neala woke, for a befuddled moment she didn't know where she was. Blinking, she realized her mouth was very dry and that she felt vaguely queasy. She realized she was lying down, in a bed. But something wasn't right. Was she sick?

Stirring, she tried to sit up, but the effort intensified a sensation of vertigo and she lay back, closing her eyes as foggy and unpleasant memories pummeled her. So she wasn't dead yet, then…

"Neala? Wake up. Please wake up so we can talk. I've been waiting all night."

The voice was familiar, but she couldn't place it immediately so she reluctantly obeyed the plea to open her eyes. A man's face swam into view. "Mr. Crocker?" she whispered, mystified. "I— Did you find me? He didn't kill me. It's… Mr.….Lipscomb…" Her head throbbed, her mouth wouldn't work properly, and the only thought that didn't float away was that she was still alive.

She tried to smile for Mr. Crocker. "Saved me," she whispered. "You…saved my life."

The groundskeeper's eyes clouded, and he ducked his head. "I did," he eventually admitted in a low voice. "But you'll have to help me, to keep you alive."

"Help?"

The bed sagged when Mr. Crocker sat down beside her. A flutter of disquiet whispered through Neala, but she couldn't shift away, much less vocalize a protest.

"Neala." He lifted a hand to smooth hair from her forehead, and Neala flinched. Mr. Crocker's face fell. "Try not to be scared," he said. "I'll take care of you."

"Where is Mr. Lipscomb?"

A half smile flickered as Mr. Crocker rose, walked away, returning momentarily with a canvas sack. "Meet Mr. Lipscomb," he said, his voice deepening, altering intonation so that he sounded exactly like the debonair gentleman from Kentucky.

Neala watched slack-jawed as he tugged a tousled black wig from the sack and casually fitted it over his balding pate. Next he produced a fake beard and mustache, transforming within the blink of an eye to Mr. Lipscomb, dressed in the garb of a lowly groundskeeper.

The deceit triggered the beginnings of outrage, deep inside. "Why?" She fought for lucidity; her body refused to cooperate. At the moment she could only lie there like a useless heap of rags, courtesy of the man standing above her.

A man she thought she knew. An unassuming, congenial gentleman who had turned out to be neither unassuming nor a gentleman.

Grayson hadn't trusted him from the first time they'd met.

Grayson, another man she thought she had known. And she'd been wrong about him, as well. "Sorry," she whispered, as desolation chilled her halfhearted attempt to regain consciousness and fight.

If she'd trusted Grayson more, she wouldn't be having to fight all alone.

"Neala! You must wake up!"

Startled, Neala blinked, tried to focus on Mr. Crocker. "You…lied to me."

"I told you, it was necessary." His hand closed over her upper arm, and he administered a light shake. "Don't go back to sleep. I need to explain, I want you to understand me, Neala."

She understood all right. She understood he was a scheming, deceitful… Her thoughts floated away. Eyelids drooping, she listened in a half doze while he talked.

"…and mostly because I needed to be able to follow your movements without risking exposure. Worked beautifully, didn't it?" As though embarrassed, he briefly turned his head and cleared his throat. "Over this past year, every time you managed to escape made me furious—yet relieved. Because the more I watched you, the more I realized you represent everything I've ever wanted. You're not like all the other women I've known. You noticed me, even when I was just Will Crocker, a lowly groundsman, instead of a wealthy gentleman. That's why I decided to warn you, the night of the ball. It seemed fitting somehow. Fair."

He rubbed his hands together. "Then I thought of something even better."

Chapter Twenty-Two

The stage pulled into White Sulphur Springs a little past seven o'clock Friday morning. Within another hour Gray ascertained that as of the previous afternoon Neala Shaw was still alive, and that he could find Deirdre McGee with the Vance family. After securing a room, where he cleaned himself into respectability if not affability, Gray made his way outside to the grounds behind the main hotel, where he found Deirdre reading a book while a group of children played croquet. When she caught sight of him, she laid her book aside and stood.

"Mr. Faulkner. I've been hoping you would come." She studied him, tapping one long finger against the corner of her mouth. After a moment the aura of censure dissipated. "I…see. So you were not after abandoning her to the wolves, as it were. She's a mind of her own, that girl."

"Lack of a mind, I'd say. At the moment I'm sorely tempted to abandon her to those wolves." They both sat down on the bench. "Actually, the little fool abandoned *me*. Left in the middle of the night." He reined in the runaway emotion. Deirdre's face revealed far too much sympathy. "Have you talked with her?"

"She refuses to have aught to do with me either. Sent a note yesterday, when she arrived, informing me that she'll not risk anyone else she cares about so I was not even to acknowledge her, should we cross paths. I would imagine the reason for her abandonment of you to be the same."

"If she cared a plugged nickel about me, she wouldn't have crept off in the middle of the night." Never mind what Deirdre assumed, or what Neala said in the letter she'd written to him. Actions, to Gray's way of thinking, most certainly did speak louder than a handful of tear-splotched words asking his forgiveness, urging him to forget about her.

"The lass would not be thinking clearly, what with the death of Mrs. Wilkes," Deirdre pointed out, her brogue thickening. She flicked Gray an apologetic smile. "Begging your pardon, Mr. Faulkner, but I was fond of the lady, don't you know. She was a grand dame, and didn't deserve to die, not like that."

"Nobody does. Even Neala, who's all but staked herself out for the fiend. Have you seen her at all, even from a distance?"

Deirdre shook her head. "But then, I've been at my duties to the children there, keeping them out of trouble and helping the Vances pack." She paused, added quietly, "I'll be leaving with them day after tomorrow. If Neala won't have me with her, there's naught I can do."

"It's all right." He failed to keep the bitterness out of his tone. "God knows there might be little I can do myself."

"Did you know how she fretted about your views of God?"

Gray made a derisive sound. "Her views aren't much better, to my way of thinking. Right now she's probably deluded herself into believing that all she needs is God's protection. That when she confronts this madman she'll convince him of the error of his ways, talk him into turning himself in, then take meals to him in prison."

"Wouldn't surprise me," Deirdre replied. "She's a stout heart, Mr. Faulkner, and a way about her that draws people."

"She's a foolish heart, and her naïveté about people is about to get her killed."

"Then I expect you better be off about your duty, hadn't you?"

And with that Deirdre picked up her book, called to the children, and left Gray standing in fulminating silence.

When Neala next awoke, the room was dark save for the flickering flame in an oil lantern on top of a bureau standing against the far wall. She had no idea of time, whether it was day or night, or how long her captivity had lasted. She supposed she ought to be afraid, but she felt nothing, not even gratitude that she was still alive, much less a compunction to pray for divine intervention.

God was not a loving heavenly Father, just a distant, austere Presence, dispensing judgment and justice at His whim, doling out tidbits of comfort when He so desired, never mind the needs of His suffering children. Yes, He was the Author of life. But He never lifted a finger to protect the innocent from senseless slaughter.

A shiver tapped with frost-tipped fingernails down the back of her spine. She should plot an escape, not lie here wallowing in a stupor of drugged self-pity. But Mr. Lipscomb—no, not Mr. Lipscomb. Will Crocker, the groundsman who she'd thought was her friend—Will Crocker, the villainous wretch, would hunt her down again.

For a while Neala idly watched the lantern flame, while she tried to drum up some outrage. Vaguely ashamed of the apathy, she finally rolled onto her side and managed to sit up. Cascades of curls drifted across her face, spilled over her shoulders and down her back. Neala didn't care. The room seemed to expand and shrink around her; blinking her eyes several times did not dispel the fuzziness. Chloroform made for an excellent jailer.

At the moment, if she attempted a grandiose dash for the door, she'd collapse on the plank floorboards like an underbaked soufflé.

So where was Will?

Disinclined for anything beyond a cup of hot tea, Neala cleared her throat again. "Will? Hello? Are you here?"

Her abductor materialized in the doorway. Blearily Neala watched him cross to her, dressed in the dapper attire of Mr. Lipscomb.

"It's about time," he said, his head tilted to one side while he examined her with a thoroughness that roused her from some of the stupor.

His neatly pressed suit and spotted silk necktie made her feel more disheveled, even sordid. She gathered the mass of hair and, ignoring Will's presence, tried to plait the strands into a braid; neither her hair nor her fingers cooperated. Fine. She would ignore her hair as well. Neala lifted her chin. "I'm very thirsty. Is there anything to drink?"

"Of course. I had some refreshments delivered." A corner of his mustached mouth twitched. "Mr. Lipscomb is a particular, private individual, who faithfully orders the same tray every Friday morning. The bellhop who delivers it is quite friendly, because I tip him very well. Nobody suspects a thing, Neala. I told you, I'm very good at what I do."

At last a ripple of anger sloshed over the apathy. "It's not something to brag about." If her legs hadn't still felt noodly and the room weaving about, Neala would have been tempted to cannon into Will with the express intent of knocking him flat on the floor. "I liked you better as a groundsman."

"I know. That's why you're not dead."

Leaving her slack-jawed and silent, he returned moments later with tepid lemonade and a plate of soggy sandwiches. No utensils she might have used for a weapon were included with the meal. Nor would he allow her to eat at the table in the other room. Like an invalid—or the condemned prisoner—she was forced to eat sitting up in the bed. But Will did produce the mother-of-pearl hair clip she'd been wearing when he abducted her, handing it to her without comment.

Humiliated, Neala scraped the mess of curls together at the base of her neck, fastened the clip, then turned to the tray. Her stomach churned but she choked down the food. It was difficult, holding on to anger when one was weak from hunger and trepidation.

If only she had listened to Grayson.

If only. Was there any other phrase in the land that could equal that one, for proclaiming the agony of abandonment by everything and everyone you loved? Including God?

When she finished eating, Will removed the tray and set it on the floor, then pulled a straight-back chair next to the bed and sat down. "You're awake, and I've fed you. Now we're going to talk." He leaned forward. "I used to wonder why they named you after him," he observed almost dreamily. "All through the years, I wondered. I'm glad my mother was wrong. You're nothing like him."

Impatience abruptly tightened his face and the dreaminess vanished. The light brown eyes turned opaque, like muddy water. "Before I share the rest of my plans, tell me where you've hidden the crest badge. It's mine, you know. I've been searching for it all my life." Without looking away from Neala he scooped up the glass of her half-finished lemonade and downed it in a single gulp. Against the dark contrast of false beard and mustache his lips appeared almost red, shiny from the liquid.

Anger stirred inside Neala like a bucket of hissing snakes. She shimmied backward on the bed until her spine pressed against the iron rungs on the headboard. "Will Crocker, you may have successfully abducted me. But you most certainly do not have me." If only she possessed the strength to dump the bucket of snakes over his head. "Nor do you have *my* family's crest badge."

Wait. The badge. His comment about her being named after Grandfather. Why would he care about the badge, or her name, unless… No. Oh, no. Dry-mouthed, Neala sensed what was coming, and resisted with every drop of sluggish blood in her body. In a futile and childish reaction she squeezed her eyes shut.

Instead of reacting with more anger she heard Will laugh. “You can’t run or hide anymore, Neala. It’s like God’s will. You can’t escape it. Or me. *I’m* God’s will.” Another laugh grated her ears, this one full of bitterness.

Reluctantly Neala opened her eyes, drew up her knees, and clasped them with clammy hands while she waited for the man in front of her to finish destroying her life.

“Grandmother and Momma used to tell me that, you know. Tell me over and over that I was God’s will. And I never understood, it was the same as the neighbor boys who thrashed me. I hated them, hated my name. Hated *you*. I never understood—until I slipped into your room one day, when you were out with your seducer.” He spewed the word as though spitting out a vile potion. “I held the crest badge in my hands and realized they were right all along. The crest badge was meant to belong to me, just as you are meant to belong to me. To *me*.”

Time ticked into immobility, like a clock winding down, as Will ceased the verbal onslaught. A welter of emotions swirled around the air between them, sucking the breath from Neala’s lungs. As the silence stretched, crushing knowledge settled irrevocably inside her heart.

“Your grandmother was Letitia Rutledge,” she said dully. “The woman my grandfather jilted.”

“He ruined her. *Humiliated and ruined her.* Her, and my mother.”

Before Neala could blink his hands were around her throat, thumbs pressing against her windpipe. “She was forced to marry a country bumpkin because she was carrying Neal Shaw's child. A sharecropper. A nobody who treated her like she was a slave."

A dark flush stained his cheeks. "I'm Neal Shaw's firstborn male progeny. You have no right—for half a century nobody's had the right to the name, to the family heirloom—but me. Not that pompous Alexander Shaw, or his two whelps. Not your stuffy, insignificant father or your coward of a brother. My name should be William *Shaw*, and my mother should be living in that mansion on Grace Avenue in Richmond. *I* should be wearing the clan crest. Not you."

With each word, his fingers squeezed her throat more tightly. "I'm finally taking the name that should have been mine forty years ago. Now—" he lowered his face until they were inches apart "—tell me what you've done with the crest badge."

"I was told that Miss Shaw was staying in this room. She checked in yesterday afternoon," Gray queried the maid who was loading up mop and buckets and soiled linens outside Neala's room. "What do you mean, you haven't seen her?"

She finally glanced up from behind the large push cart holding all her supplies. "Well, she ain't been 'round. I put away her things, like, but I don't know nothin' else."

Gray dismissed the sullen maid, then shut the door and spent several moments thoroughly searching the room. In her impulsive flight from North Carolina, Neala had scarcely packed enough to fill the single case now tucked away in the chiffonier. He found nothing of value in his search, not even a slip of paper in her handwriting, or a handkerchief carelessly left on the counterpane. Setting his jaw, Gray headed for Mrs. Wilkes's suite of rooms on the first floor.

The parlor was meticulously clean—and jarringly silent. When he reached the widow's bedroom he paused, staring at the bed while his chest tightened and impotent rage swam through his veins.

There was something despicable about murdering an elderly woman in her sleep, something lacking in the villain's moral fiber that rendered him more monster than human being. Such a person did not deserve to live.

If he'd harmed Neala, if she was—

With a muttered oath he swiveled on his boot and stalked out, slamming the door behind him. The Old White covered forty acres, with cottages and service buildings scattered everywhere. Gray planned to search every inch of the grounds, every one of the buildings.

By noon he learned that after Neala arrived the previous day she had walked back across to the depot. For the few moments it took Gray to walk there himself he nursed the illusion that she'd been smart enough to board the first train passing through. That faint hope was snuffed out the moment he talked to Hank, the old porter, who kindly led him to the storage room where Mrs. Wilkes's coffin lay on huge blocks of ice. Grimly Gray set about searching every dusty corner until he determined that at least Neala had not been murdered and stuffed behind the stacks of steamer trunks and crates.

Finally he approached the coffin—and discovered her prized crest badge lying on top.

She'd been here. At some point in the last twenty-four hours, Neala had been inside this room. And for some reason, she had left her most valued possession behind.

A clue, in hopes Gray would discover it? Or, knowing Neala as he did, more likely she'd left the crest in a gesture of renunciation, and perhaps atonement, since she blamed herself for Mrs. Wilkes's death.

A puff of empathy dusted over Gray. *My fault.* He remembered the words she'd spoken, that she believed with all of her anguished heart to be true. *This is all my fault.*

"In a pig's eye," Gray declared now, empathy rapidly displaced by frustration—and fear.

He scooped up the crest, studied it in the dim light, surprised by its weight and, upon closer examination, its monetary value. Obviously Neala knew next to nothing about gemstones; she'd declared the crest to be mostly of sentimental value. She seldom wore it, explaining to Gray that it was far too heavy for spring and summer costumes, and her light woolen shawl. On the few occasions she'd needed her heavy cloak, Gray had idly noted the badge pinned to her shoulder, but his attention had been focused on Neala, not an unremarkable cloak or a cumbersome Scottish memento of only sentimental value.

Perhaps he should have remembered the first rule of investigation: notice everything.

Well, he was noticing now. Two deep red rubies, probably Burmese, winked at him from the metal strap and buckle that circled a hand holding a dagger. Three smaller emeralds of equally fine quality were embedded in the dagger's shaft, while a narrow rope of cornflower-blue sapphire chips formed the base of the hand.

Neala's sentimental crest badge, with its motley collection of what she'd assumed was colored glass, would fetch a hefty fortune, particularly if the gemstones were pried free and sold off.

For several moments Gray stood silently, almost absently caressing the badge's contours. Eventually he noticed the lettering engraved along the top half of the metal strap and buckle, no doubt added back in the thirties or forties, when Queen Victoria's fondness for Scotland invaded England with far more success than her northern neighbor ever enjoyed politically. The light was too dim to read the words. Gray walked behind the coffin, shoving aside some trunks in order to reach the storage room's solitary window. He turned so the light fell directly upon the crest.

"Fide et fortitudine." He read the Latin phrase aloud. Fidelity and fortitude—no. If he recalled his Latin, the correct translation would be *by* fidelity and fortitude.

Chest tight, Gray returned to the coffin. After a somber moment's reflection, he removed his hat. According to Hank, Mrs. Wilkes would depart the Old White for the last time on a four o'clock freight train, bound for Charlottesville, Virginia. One hand resting on the coffin, the other holding Neala's clan crest, Gray spared a brief moment to bid Mrs. Wilkes farewell. "I'll find the man who did this," he promised her aloud. "And I'll find Neala. Rest in peace, Mrs. Wilkes."

Somebody ought to be able to rest in peace.

He left the storage room and motioned to Hank. "I need for you to hold on to this until I return," he told the porter, and handed him the badge. "It belongs to Miss Shaw. I'd hate for it to be misplaced, or lost."

They shared a look of wordless communication.

"Don't you worry, suh," Hank said as he withdrew a large paisley handkerchief and deftly wrapped the crest badge inside its folds. Then he tucked everything inside the inner pocket of his uniform. "I'll keep it safe, whiles you fetch Miss Shaw. I reckon it be your job, keeping her safe."

His job. As Gray made his way back to the hotel, he faced squarely that keeping Neala safe was no longer merely a job. *By fidelity and fortitude.* "Hold on, love," he whispered. "Hold on to your faith, and your fortitude, for both of us."

Chapter Twenty-Three

Breathing hard, Will stared down at the woman he held captive, whose creamy complexion was now mottled with red and bruised-purple splotches because he was choking her. His fingers were wrapped around that soft, slender throat not in a caress—but to kill.

With a strangled groan he yanked his hands away and stepped backward, two steps, then three, his gaze transfixed upon her face. The darkness had consumed him, causing him to almost kill Neala despite his resolve to achieve his lifelong goals, not through her death—but through marriage.

She gasped, then coughed, tears leaking from the corners of her eyes as her body spasmed back to life.

"It's too easy," Will murmured, trancelike, his gaze falling to his hands. "Too easy to take someone's life." Finally he blinked, focusing on Neala once more. "I don't like who I am, don't like what my mother and grandmother turned me into."

He swiveled, walking unsteadily to the other side of the room. For several long moments he stood without moving, until the bloodlust finally subsided. The darkness receded, and he regained the sense of self, the man he longed to be.

Silently he fetched more lemonade, then held her so she could swallow, closing his eyes to savor the feel of her soft hair, the shape of her head. When she pushed his hand away, he set the glass aside and sat back down, watching her. Waiting.

After a long moment, she sighed. One trembling hand lifted to cover her eyes, then dropped back onto the bed. "What Grandfather did to your grandmother was…a grievous sin," she whispered, her voice papery thin. "I—I can't blame you for being angry. For feeling betrayed."

Her understanding gutted Will. He had expected fear, even hysteria. Perhaps anger, given the spark of temper he'd briefly witnessed. But not this—this softness, this compassion, toward the person who had threatened her. He didn't know how to react, what to say. How to explain the longing he had tried to strangle out of his entire life, like he had almost strangled Neala.

"I have something to ask you," he eventually confessed. "I don't care what Grandmother and Momma told me about your grandfather, because I—"

"Our grandfather," Neala interrupted softly. "Mr. Crocker—Will. We share the same grandfather. We're… family."

The word pricked him on the raw, all the more because her declaration ruined the moment of his own. "We're no more 'family' than a flock of wild geese flying south for the winter. But when we marry, *then* we'll be family."

"Marry?" she spluttered. "Marry…you?" Now temper licked through the words, banishing all trace of the compassion. "I can't believe you'd have the—the audacity to suggest such a thing. It's monstrous, sickening. This

prattle about marriage is a form of torture, isn't it? Like pretending you've changed your mind about killing me."

Relief at the outburst spread inside Will. Long inured to his mother's emotional outbursts, he found anger and contempt more palatable than displays of softness or compassion. "I knew it would take time to convince you." Calmer now, he quietly padded across the room and opened the top drawer of the bureau. "Time, unfortunately, is not something we have a lot of." After retrieving what he wanted, he returned to Neala. "Defy me if you must. But you won't be the only one to suffer the consequences."

"What is that supposed to mean?" She pressed her fingers against her temples as though holding a headache at bay, then laid her hand over her bruised throat. "I can't believe I actually felt sorry for you. You've treated our family—*your* family, not just my family—like a flock of wild geese! Shooting us down, one by one, because your grandmother and your mother poisoned your heart. Our grandfather was wrong, but your grandmother was, too. She had no right to inflict her lack of forgiveness on you, and your mother. They ruined your life, and now you've ruined an entire family—what could have been *your* family."

"You don't know what you're talking about. I've only done what had to be done. And will continue to do so." Slowly he tugged at his tie, loosening its constricting folds. She used words, trapped him with them the way he set up snares for rabbits. Momma had warned him, but he hadn't wanted to listen.

"Why didn't you write Grandfather?" Neala persisted, swiping her dampened eyes in a gesture reminiscent enough of his mother to prick his own temper. "Why didn't your *grandmother* write him? He would have accepted her child as his own. Yes, it might have been awkward, but if he had known, he would—"

"He did know."

The assertion fell between them like sulfuric coals, filling the air with their stench. Neala blinked once, twice, shook her head in denial. With a hiss of rage Will whipped off the tie, balling it in his fist. "My grandmother showed me the letter she wrote, demanding that he take responsibility for her and his baby—my mother. And do you know what your grandfather wrote back? *Do you?*"

Dropping the tie, he reached forward and grabbed her shoulders, shook her. Hard. "Answer me!"

It was as though his anger fueled Neala's. "I don't know!" she yelled back. "You let go of me, Will Crocker! Remove your hands this instant!"

Will released her abruptly and took two backward steps, but Neala was too incensed to notice. Oh, but she was weary of the role of peacemaker.

Of being nice.

"I will not be treated as your kicking post another minute! Not one more minute! Do you hear me? Whatever Grandfather said or didn't say, whatever he did or didn't do, *is not my fault*. What's more, I don't care what he wrote your grandmother! You don't like the name you have, but at least it's yours. You didn't have someone trying to take it away from you because you were only a girl. You didn't have a brother who resented you his entire life when he should have— Oh, why am I bothering?"

She glowered at him, funneling a lifetime of resentment into the bubbling core of her first temper tantrum.

"You don't care. Nobody cares. It's a good thing Adrian at least disappeared somewhere even you couldn't find, isn't it? Otherwise he would have been one more goose in your gunnysack."

"Your brother's a cur," Will muttered sullenly. "He wasn't worth my time tracking him down."

"Ha! He's just better at covering his trail than I was. Maybe at least he found some happiness somewhere." Furiously she swiped her dripping nose and unwanted tears with her sleeve. She was a prisoner, wasn't she? Doomed prisoners didn't bother with gentility. "I had dreams, like my brother. Like you." The words tumbled free, gathering fresh momentum. "I entertained longings for the future. I had hopes. But not anymore. You…destroyed every one of them. You should have been my cousin," she finished, pain thickening the statement. "It's a shame you're not a very good marksman. I wouldn't be here now, waiting for you to finish your—your life's mission, making all of Neal Shaw's legitimate children pay because he made the mistake of falling in love with someone else."

For a humming moment, Will stood there, staring down. "I never realized it, but you have a shrew inside of you, just like my mother. I don't like it, Neala."

So nothing good blew in on the storms of an unleashed temper, not even satisfaction. Nor did Neala much care for the debris littering her heart in the backwash, especially when that terrifying opaqueness once again darkened her captor's eyes, giving them a reptilian chill that boded nothing promising for her future.

"I do have to leave for a little while now," Will announced suddenly. "I can't trust you, of course." He reached behind his back, then produced a pair of metal handcuffs. “These will keep you from trying to escape. I’ll try to fix it so you can sleep.”

Stupid of her to have expected otherwise. Dully she assessed her options—door, window, physical attack—and discarded them all. Will remained stronger, quicker, and certainly more ruthless. She needed to make the effort however, and shoved herself forward on the bed.

Then Will was beside her. The room tipped into a slow swirl as he looped the chain on the handcuffs through one of the bed rungs, then handcuffed her wrists together. “If you want to stay alive, keep quiet.”

Next he removed a snow-white linen handkerchief. “This will help,” he said as he gagged her mouth with it. His hand closed over her forearm, just above the cuffs, in a fleeting caress that chilled her to the bone. “To avoid further discomfort, keep still.”

The door shut behind him. Neala was alone with a bitterness that splashed her soul like acid heedlessly spilled on unprotected skin.

By two o’clock, Gray reached the conclusion that nobody had encountered Neala on any of the paths leading from the depot back to the main hotel. Or if she had, regrettably nobody he talked to had witnessed such a meeting.

By four o’clock, he discovered that the groundskeeper Neala had befriended had given notice and quit the previous week.

“Did he give a reason?” Gray inquired of the head groundsman.

“Nay.” The gaunt Irishman shrugged, then spat a wad of tobacco. “But would no’ surprise me if ’twere the woman. He was sweet on one of the lasses—not a belle, mind you. The lad knew his place, right enough, when it came to mingling with belles and blue bloods. But seems she left, and he grieved, something fierce, I recollect. Never knew her name. Will always kept to himself, like."

"Any ideas where he may have gone?"

"No, sir. Like I said, Will kept to himself. Nice enough, never a moment's trouble. Did his job in fine fashion, don't you know."

The suspicion crawling through Gray's mind settled coldly in his gut. "His name was Will?"

"Aye."

"Will—what was his last name?" he asked, wanting to be sure.

"That would be Crocker."

"Did he supply you with any references when he was hired?"

"Wouldn't be knowing that. You'd have to check with Mr. Eakle, the hotel manager."

"Do you know what Will did on his off days?"

The other man winked. "Now why would I be knowing what the man was up to on his own time?" He pushed the brim of his flat cap up on his forehead, his ruddy countenance sobering as he studied Gray. "Sorry to be so little help, lad. But the truth is, I never saw him when he weren't workin'."

Gray thanked him, tipped the man a quarter and left him to his business. A headache thudded at the base of his skull; the back of his spine itched like blazes. Why hadn't he taken Crocker more seriously? That day, the day Crocker paid a visit to Neala after she'd almost been killed at the racetrack—the signs were unmistakable—and Gray had ignored them. At the time he'd been more annoyed with the groundskeeper's effrontery than suspicious, despite the fact that Crocker's infatuation with Neala blazed forth plain as a wall-eyed pike. Gray might have wanted to toss him out the window, but he could hardly blame the poor fellow when he'd been struggling with the same uncomfortable emotions himself.

Now he cursed himself for not paying closer attention. Infatuation rendered men's brains the consistency of mud.

But unrequited infatuation could also turn to hatred. No doubt Crocker had accepted as truth Gray and Neala's sham courtship, since Gray had gone to great lengths to convince every guest and every employee of the Old White that verisimilitude equated with truth.

But for Neala the sham courtship had swiftly become fact. She was neither experienced enough, jaded enough, nor manipulative enough, to be able to hide her feelings from him. Briefly he closed his eyes, struggling against an avalanche of self-condemnation. *He* was experienced enough, jaded enough, and manipulative enough, to ensure the affections of a young woman whose arsenal of female arrows remained sheathed.

Neala hadn't smothered him with pleas or expectations, had placed no demands upon him. In fact, the contrary woman had renounced his protection altogether, and run away. While he might tell himself that her actions spoke louder than what he'd seen in those expressive brown eyes, he knew he was deceiving nobody but himself.

As for his own feelings…

Hoist on your own petard, aren't you, pal? Yessiree, despite himself Gray had succumbed to his own fabrication.

Though he despised himself, he at least could be man enough to admit that his heart was irrevocably lost to the only woman on earth who hadn't demanded it. Which made the "esteemed" Grayson Faulkner with all his wealth and family connections, all his hard-won skills and fierce independence, the equal of an inconsequential groundskeeper. If God was really up there, all-seeing and all-knowing, no doubt He considered that Gray deserved every one of the boulders avalanching his way.

What if Will Crocker couldn't accept the seeming loss of Neala's heart to another man? Instead of getting himself roaring drunk, or looking for another pretty face to pursue, what if he'd determined to seek revenge on the woman who had rebuffed him?

His brains were turning rotten. Tales of rejected lovers had fueled the gossip grist mill here at the Old White for decades. And to Gray's knowledge, not a single discarded male ever took a nosedive off Lover's Leap. Outside of a few illegal duels, none of them had resorted to murder, either, particularly the murder of an innocent friend of the erstwhile sweetheart.

Like countless other guests from European princes to genteel Southern paupers, Will Crocker had merely slunk off to lick his wounds. This was Greenbrier's White Sulphur Springs, not some two-bit hotel over a saloon, or vaudeville on Coney Island with its exaggerated villains, heroines and heroes.

Yet over the years Gray's idealism, sanded down through brutal reality, had been forced to accept that most acts of murder were crimes of passion as opposed to the cold premeditation with which the Shaw family had been stalked and subsequently slaughtered.

God knew he'd witnessed one of those inexplicable crimes of passion himself.

Which meant *Crocker* might be responsible for Mrs.

Wilkes's death, and Neala's disappearance from the hotel. Will Crocker, lowly groundsman. Not the elusive, cold-blooded bounder who'd been dispatching members of the Shaw family.

Gray was probably tracking not one, but two killers.

Too much. Such a likelihood was too much for a man to handle.

For the past twenty-four hours he'd fought his way through a foreboding cloud of uncertainty. Now the cloud chilled, whirled around him in a sucking vortex until it swallowed him up completely. He could scarcely breathe. Mind spinning, he collapsed onto one of the many benches scattered about the grounds. Dropping his head, he propped his forearms on his knees and stared unseeingly at the grass between his boots. Two ants trudged their way between the blades. With a quick move, Gray could grind those ants into oblivion with his heel.

A sensation of profound inadequacy seized hold, suffocating in its intensity. Right now he felt as powerless as those ants looking up at his descending boot heel. He didn't know which way to turn, how to proceed. Neala might already be dead—and all of Gray's experience and touted capabilities had proved worthless. Like Marty. Just like Marty. Even if he telegraphed for reinforcements, odds were they'd arrive too late. So like a mindless chump, he sat on a bench and did nothing.

As though in a dream, Aunt Isabella's voice drifted across his mind, sorrowfully reproaching him for his hard heart, his unwillingness to allow God to be a part of his life. To guide his path, offer counsel and direction. "Why would I want to?" he groused aloud. What had God ever done for him, to foster the kind of faith his aunt—even Neala—professed?

Where had God been throughout his stifled childhood, or his painful journey to adulthood? When Marty's life was snuffed out, like Mrs. Wilkes's, for no reason? *No reason.* Black despair savaged his insides.

A faint but insistent voice deep inside his mind pointed out that his life without God certainly hadn't provided the faculties he needed to survive this present darkness.

With a guttural groan he surged to his feet. He absolutely did *not* want to hear that voice. But in vain Gray struggled to erase from his mind the vision of Aunt Bella with her knowing eyes, or the sound of Neala's confident assertion that God would protect her.

All right. *All right. If You keep her alive, I promise to give You a try.*

The vow squeezed through his denial. Once the thought entered his mind, however, Gray realized he couldn't ignore the tantalizing possibility that faith in God might actually help him. He felt numb, weightless, yet his knees threatened to buckle beneath the unbearable strain of not knowing. But what could it hurt, to see if Neala's and Aunt Bella's views of God possessed any merit?

Almost unconsciously he resumed walking, his footsteps taking him along toward Howard's Creek. She loved walking by the creek. Used to babble much like the water, about how peaceful it was, about the ducks and geese and mockingbirds and swallows and every other species of fowl she felt compelled to point out to Gray; about the smell of wild grasses and damp earth and some floral fragrance neither of them could identify. Every time they ventured forth for a stroll, Neala insisted upon a walk along the creek.

Awareness punched through Gray with the sharp crack

of a rifle shot. *She would have come here to walk, after she saw the coffin.* To heal, to soothe the pain. Gray knew it as though Neala were standing here explaining her feelings.

Charged with fresh strength, he retraced his steps until he reached the bridge that led back to the hotel. Then, stropping his senses to razor-edge concentration, he methodically commenced a search of every square inch of turf. He didn't know what he was looking for, but he did know that if Neala had left any trace, no matter how infinitesimal, he would find it.

Chapter Twenty-Four

Late-afternoon sunlight cast a luminescent glow over the earth, turning the still water of Howard's Creek to a shimmery silver-gold. Oblivious to the beauty of his surroundings, Gray scoured every inch of the ground along the creek bank.

Thirty minutes later, he spied a lady's glove lying in the long meadow grass, next to a large outcropping of boulders and towering sumac. Disbelief all but knocked him backward into the creek. It was Neala's glove. Dizzy with the relief—and some unidentifiable emotion he couldn't describe—Gray held the scrap of soft leather against his face, inhaling the faintest tang of the vanilla lotion she liked. When his fingers traced over the indentation where a button was missing, he almost broke down. Three days earlier Neala had grumbled about having to find a haberdasher to purchase another button, and how she detested needlework.

"I'm too impatient," she'd admitted. "This is the third button I've lost. I never sew them on tightly enough."

It could have been any glove, but it wasn't. It was Neala's. What he wouldn't give for a good tracking dog… Instead, Gray tucked the glove inside his breast pocket, over his heart. Then he examined every inch of the ground surrounding the spot where he'd found it.

Behind the boulders, pressed deep into the dirt, he found two footprints. Shoes, not boots, roughly size elevens. Weight on the right foot concentrated on the heel, which was more worn on the left side. Little disturbance in the earth around the prints. So, he'd been lying in wait, had he? Probably followed her, then cut around through the trees until he discovered this isolated spot.

He wouldn't have had much time beforehand to prepare, which told Gray the man was not only determined, but daring. But who was it? Will Crocker, or someone as yet unknown and unidentified?

Sheathing his mind from the fear, Gray poured sixteen years of experience into the task of backtracking the trail of those two footprints. They led across the meadow, past the bathhouse and onto the path leading to the spring. Gray ignored the curious stares of several strolling guests, ignored the deepening gold cast to the light, ignored the pressure building inside his chest. He would search nose to the ground if necessary, to filter through the hundreds of smeared prints marking the packed-dirt walkways, until he found a print that matched the ones by Howard's Creek.

All right, he knew he was crazy to even try. Knew the odds against him were laughable, they were so immense.

But he'd found Neala's glove.

An hour later, eyes straining in the purpling shadows of dusk, back muscles on fire, he tripped over a tree root a little ways past the Georgia Row cottages, and went down on his knees. Winded, fighting exhaustion, for a moment he didn't move; the urge to give in, to just roll over and let life crush him, gnawed his vitals like a cornered rat. He lifted a hand to swipe at his eyes, blinked several times to regain his focus.

Twelve inches from his knee, a size-eleven footprint, with the weight listing to the right side and the left heel more worn down, waited for his inspection. A light wind stirred the tree branches above him, and a dying sunbeam highlighted the print.

For a pulsating second that stretched heavenward, Gray stared unblinkingly. A single boot print might offer little in the way of conclusive direction, or even the identity of the wearer. But for Gray, the sight of it came close enough to answered prayer to lift him off his knees and to his feet.

Whoever made this print had to be either a guest, or an employee.

Gray set off at a run for the main hotel. The register would supply names. And hopefully Mr. Eakle, or one of the other hotel employees, would supply the knowledge.

Unless she'd been murdered and hastily disposed of—a possibility Gray refused to accept—the murderer would not risk exposure by using the cottages as part of his abduction scheme. Most likely he'd been on foot. There had been no sign either of hooves or buggy wheels near the path by Howard's Creek. Regardless of whether Neala had accompanied him quietly, or as—he flinched from the thought—an unconscious bundle, her abductor couldn't travel very far, most likely within a one-to three-mile radius. Whether this footprint had been made before or after he snatched Neala, its presence indicated that in all likelihood the man—and Neala—were still within reach.

Somewhere within that one-to three-mile radius, he would find Neala.

And she wouldn't be dead. *She was not* dead.

God? If You're really up there, and You care, please don't let Neala be dead.

Fuming, Will locked the door to the second chamber with a vicious rattle, so that Neala would hear. Her tirade had made him late; as Mr. Lipscomb, he always took a stroll about the grounds in the late afternoons, but he could see through the window that the sky was streaked with deepening shades of rust-colored orange. The pole lamps scattered over the grounds had been lit, and the square nickel alarm clock on the mantel was relentlessly ticking toward six. He hurried across to his valise, which he'd left open on top of the library table in the corner of the room, and snatched up a fresh white collar and cuffs from the neat stacks of Mr. Lipscomb's clothes.

Then he realized he'd left his necktie in the room with Neala.

Kill her off now, and be done with it. She's never going to agree to your plan, and if she does it's a lie. She'll flee at the first opportunity. A guttural sound escaped and he paced the room, crushing the collar and cuffs while he struggled to silence the inner taunts, tried to formulate a plan when every moment brought his mother one step closer to discovering his lair.

To calm himself, he fetched the gold pocket watch and vest chain he'd treated himself to and fastened it in place. The cigars. He mustn't forget the cigars that Lipscomb smoked during his evening stroll. Only two remained in the cigar box. Well, he wouldn't be needing the affectation after tomorrow anyway, he reminded himself. Too bad. He'd developed a fondness for the taste of tobacco, and decided that he might cultivate the habit when he became William Shaw, gentleman and proud owner of a centuries-old heirloom unlike any other.

An image of Neala, lying bound and gagged on the rumpled bed, slowed his movements as he tucked the cigars inside the flap pockets of his jacket. The words she'd hurled at him rang in his ears. With a muffled curse, he smoothed the collar, then yanked it in place around his neck. It was wrinkled, but once he put on the coat nobody would notice, especially this late in the day.

The clock dinged six.

He fumbled with the button on the stupid collar. Stupid laundress had applied too much starch again. And the stupid button was too small for a man's fingers.

A firm knock sounded on the outside door. Rattled, Will dropped the collar, his gaze riveted to the door. Another knock, this one more forceful, made him jump.

"Just a moment," he called.

He retrieved the collar, but he'd never get it and the cuffs fastened in time so he tossed everything back into the valise, then feverishly checked his appearance in the oval mirror over the parlor fireplace.

He looked acceptable, despite that unfortunate scuffle with Neala. The fastidious, somewhat prissy gentleman of means from Kentucky. No resemblance whatsoever to Will Crocker, even without cuffs and collar, or necktie. Wig, mustache and beard remained in place, and above his vest the blue pinstripe shirt sported only a few wrinkles. The gold watch and chain polished the look nicely. He looked the very picture of a gentleman enjoying a peaceful afternoon in his private rooms.

After a last calming breath, he started back across the

room—and remembered the valise. Lipscomb was supposed to remain until the last day. His valise would certainly not be on display, nor packed to the brim. "One moment," he called again, frantically closing the case and dropping it in the farthest corner, well beyond the light from the bulb hanging from the ceiling.

Drawing a deep breath, he fixed a smile on his face, and opened the door. Grayson Faulkner stood on the porch. The dying sun rimmed his silhouette in livid hues of orange, yet cast the rest of his body into the shadows of approaching night.

Will blinked, then collected himself. He was the honorable Geoffrey Lipscomb, and he had nothing to hide. "Hello… Faulkner, isn't it? We met a time or two."

"Yes." His gaze swept Will in a comprehensive survey, then moved to the room behind. "I understand you're remaining here until the last day?"

Will nodded. "I enjoy the fall colors. How about yourself? Planning to finish out the season as well?" He paused, investing what he felt was an appropriate amount of inquiry in his tone. Confidence poured over him in a welcome flood tide. "Is there something I can do for you?" It was a temptation not to laugh aloud in his face.

"I'm speaking to all the remaining guests," Faulkner said. "Trying to find information about Miss Shaw. Neala Shaw."

"Ah, yes. The young woman who accompanied you on several occasions, when we met on the grounds earlier this summer. Seemed a charming lady."

The other man obviously had no idea that the woman he sought was a dozen paces away. The novelty of it swelled inside Will. For a sliver of a second he was tempted to share his accomplishment, longed to feel the satisfaction of someone complimenting him on his mind, on a job well done.

"That's right." Faulkner's expression had turned to stone. "Miss Shaw. Have you seen her lately?"

Will professed confusion. "Why, no. Why do you ask? A lovers' quarrel?"

Their gazes met, and for some reason a chill danced between Will's shoulder blades. His palms began to sweat but he maintained eye contact, keeping his expression politely curious.

"Not a quarrel," Faulkner said. "There's a strong possibility something may have happened to her." He paused. "And if it has, I plan to see that the person or persons responsible pay. Dearly."

"Do you mean to tell me…some sort of foul play? Surely not, Mr. Faulkner. Things like that don't happen here at the Old White. Why, that's tantamount to sacrilege. Surely the young lady has departed, and chose not to inform you. Perhaps her feelings did not mirror yours."

Too much, he warned himself. Too much. And yet, the temptation crested, sweeping Will into the backwash. Casually he tugged out the watch, flipped its lid open. "I say, I'm about to order up a late tea. Would you care to join me?"

For a deliciously frightening second he thought Faulkner would take him up on the offer. Then the other man shook his head.

"Thanks, I'll pass. I'm checking every cottage on the grounds. Every one," he repeated, eyes bluer than the late-afternoon October sky boring into Will. "I won't rest until I've found Miss Shaw."

"Well, I wish you success, and pray the young lady is well. It's a trifle late, but after tea I plan to take my usual afternoon perambulation about the grounds, before going to supper. I'll keep an eye open for Miss Shaw."

"Thanks." After a last lingering look, Faulkner swiveled on his heel and left.

Will shut the door, and clamped a hand over his mouth to stifle the wild laughter.

Forty minutes later, Gray completed his circuit of all remaining occupied cottages; he returned to the main hotel, where Superintendent Eakle assured him that every room in the main hotel had also been searched. No sign of Neala Shaw had been reported, outside of her belongings in her old room.

Restless, Gray returned to his own room, where he spent several moments writing out his thoughts, grappling with something—a feeling, a hunch. Perhaps it was foreboding, or fear. But something nagged his mind, vexatious as a chigger bite.

One by one he listed the remaining guests. Several, he decided, justified further scrutiny. The mantel clock chimed half past the hour; his stomach growled, reminding him he hadn't eaten much in the past thirty-six hours.

Something else to lay at Neala's feet, when he found her.

His skin felt as though it were on fire. In a surge of motion Gray stood, flung aside tablet and chewed-up pencil, strapped holster and gun in place, stuffed arms in his jacket and fled the room. He may as well go feed his belly. He wasn't about to while away two hours feeding the fear.

Halfway across the lobby Deirdre McGee hailed him. "Glad to catch up with you, Mr. Faulkner," she said. "I just met a woman. I'm thinking you need to meet her as well. She claims to be Will Crocker's ma."

"His *mother*?"

"Aye. My reaction as well. But that's what she says. I happened to be at the front desk, fetching the last of the mail for the Vances. Jimmy hands me the mail, then introduces us after telling Mrs. Crocker I might have some information as to her son's whereabouts."

"And why would Jimmy think that, Deirdre?"

She pulled a face. "I've not said a word, Mr. Faulkner, so don't be flaying me with those eyes of yours. But 'twas no secret that guests thought I was lady's maid to Miss Shaw, nor that poor Will carried a torch for her. Most of the staff heard of it, the day she was almost trampled at the racetrack."

"I know." He inclined his head in a tacit apology before shifting his attention to the thin, washed-out-looking woman standing with arms defensively crossed, in the corner of the lobby. Her gown was neatly pressed, but the style was a good fifteen years out of fashion, as was the hat on her head. She certainly looked more like a mother than a jealous woman who had chased her lover down. But why was she here at the Old White?

He didn't know if Will Crocker's mother's appearance was coincidence, or divine providence. But he couldn't help but remember Neala's words, the day they'd met the Youngs, and learned about Letitia Rutledge.

"Someday," she'd told him with the facile confidence that used to provoke him beyond measure, "you're going to find yourself in a place where you'll not only admit that God watches over us, you'll be thanking Him for it."

Gray set his jaw. "You told me Crocker left two weeks ago. What did Mrs. Crocker have to say to you?"

"She's that concerned about her son, she says. Claims he went home spouting plans about a woman he planned to marry, then disappeared. She's looking for him."

"What?" A passing bellboy stopped dead in his tracks, eyes rounded as he gawked at Gray. Gray lashed himself back under control. "Crocker told his mother he was going to *marry* Neala?"

"Aye, and if you hope to learn anything else, you'd best plaster a friendlier look on your face, laddie."

Jaw twitching, Gray tried to relax his taut neck and shoulders. "I didn't plan to roast her alive." Heat prickled the back of his neck.

"I'll introduce you," Deirdre murmured, and administered a light pat that almost dislocated his shoulder. "She's a mother, distressed over her son, same as you're distressed over Neala. You'll do fine, Mr. Faulkner. Myself, I'll not be able to stay but a moment. The Vances are expecting me." She tugged a slip of folded paper out of her pocket, hesitated before thrusting it out for Gray. "We leave in the morning. This is the address where I'll be. Would you mind, if you find Neala—"

"I will find her."

The corner of Deirdre's mouth flickered. "Aye," she murmured. "You will. Would you let me know?"

Gray took the slip of paper. Then, dragging his gaze away from the slight form of Mrs. Crocker, he looked across into the kind face of a woman who, much like Aunt Bella, saw far more than most other people. "I'll let you know," he promised. Then he brushed a kiss against her cheek that colored up lovely as a summer tea rose. "Thanks, Deirdre. You're a rare one, for a woman."

"Aye, that's what they all say." Charmingly flustered, she gestured across the lobby. "She's waiting."

"Then let's not keep her waiting any longer."

All right, God, Gray thought as Mrs. Crocker rose, staring at them with hope and fear blazing from her eyes, *let's see what You have to offer.*

Chapter Twenty-Five

"This is the gentleman I was telling you about, Mr. Grayson Faulkner." Deirdre introduced him with an encouraging smile to Mrs. Crocker. "If anyone can help you find your son, he can. Now I must be off, but rest easy. It will be all right," she promised. "Mr. Faulkner will make it so. 'Tis in his nature, don't you know, to take care of people."

Before Gray could growl a retort, she'd whispered goodbye, strolling with her immense dignity down the long hallway.

"Mr. Faulkner." Beneath an old-fashioned black bonnet, feverish bright eyes latched onto Gray. "You know my son, William?"

"I've met him, yes." Would have been less awkward if Deirdre had remained another few moments. He scraped up a smile that hopefully mirrored Deirdre's. "He was one of the groundskeepers here. Did you know that?"

"Of course. I wouldn't be here otherwise, now would I? My boy wrote me every week, until—until—" Two spots of color smeared her bony, wrinkled face.

"Until what, Mrs. Crocker?"

"Until this young woman—Miss Shaw's her name—turned his head," she declared. "William's shy, not one to chase the ladies. I brought him up to respect women. When he told me about her, I was very concerned."

Gray ran a hand around the back of his tense neck. "Why don't we sit down, Mrs. Crocker?" He gestured to a cluster of chairs off to the side, beyond the glare of the incandescent electric lights installed several years earlier. "Tell me when you last saw your son."

For a tension-spiked moment he was afraid Mrs. Crocker might bolt on him. Thin body poised for flight, fingers strangling the handles of her worn carpetbag, she stared at the waxed floorboards for a long time before speaking again. "You the law?"

He lifted an eyebrow at the tone. "I have been," he admitted. "But at the moment, no, I'm not the law. Why? Has your son committed a crime?"

Mrs. Crocker's head reared back. "My son is a decent, God-fearing man, not a criminal. He has lived a good and obedient life—until now. Until her. That woman. Neala Shaw. She's the one who's filled his head with nonsense, she's the one who caused him to turn into a stranger to his own mother."

A dull pickax hacking away at the base of his skull would have been more tolerable than listening to this tripe. "Why do you say that?"

"I know what I know. He ain't no skirt-chaser." With her mousey hair scraped in a severe bun and her narrow, wrinkled face, she could have been anywhere from sixty years and up, yet she talked as though her son were fourteen instead of a man pushing at least two-score years.

An uncomfortable tightness constricted Gray's throat. Grimly he quelled a spark of empathy toward Will. "You claim Miss Shaw caused some kind of rift to occur between you and your son? I find that hard to believe. Have you met her, Mrs. Crocker?"

A quick negative jerk of the head was the answer. Then she said, "You know her, Mr… What did you say the name was?"

"Faulkner. And yes, I do know Miss Shaw."

Something akin to despair seemed to flatten out the sharp angles of her face, leaving her looking old and sunken. "You don't believe me. She's worked her evil on you as well. I can see it plain on your face."

Control thin as a thumbtack, Gray planted his hands on his knees. "Mrs. Crocker, I don't know much about your son, and I don't know what he told you, but I do know Miss Shaw. She is not the woman you have described. She in fact enjoys a sterling reputation here at the Old White, among staff as well as guests."

Stubborn memories mutinied against his resolve not to think about Neala. Everyone who met her responded to her sunny, generous personality—himself included. Even the sour housemaid's face lit up when Neala wished her a bonny day in an exaggerated Scottish burr.

Raw pain savaged his insides.

"Are you calling my son a liar?"

Pain and poignant memories evaporated. "I'm not calling him anything of the sort, Mrs. Crocker. I'm merely enlightening you. People who have met Miss Shaw do not share your opinion of her. Without exception they find her a charming young woman."

Mrs. Crocker suddenly emitted a strangled sob, and covered her face with her hands. "I'm sorry, so sorry," she sniffled, tears thickening the words. "It's just… I've been so worried. It's been over a month since he was home. I ain't been able to find my way here… I'm afraid something's happened to him. Something bad."

Gray fought the automatic urge to snarl, then bolt for the hills, far away from yet another distraught mother who thought all she had to do was turn on the tears and every male within hearing distance would buckle at the knees. But if he yielded to impulse, he would lose possibly his only lead to Will's whereabouts. To Neala's. So he waited in stony silence while Mrs. Crocker spilled out a largely unintelligible litany of fears, woes, worries and desperation about her missing son.

A trickle of memory meandered into his mind, then flowed faster until images and phrases drowned out the sound of Mrs. Crocker. Neala had wept in his presence, without apology or shame. And Gray remembered suddenly how he'd felt when she sobbed her heart out against his shoulder, how the comfort he'd ungrudgingly offered had produced a grateful smile. Even now the memories kindled a need to provide that comfort again.

Somehow Neala's forthright bouts of tears had cleansed them both, fostered intimacy instead of hindering it.

There was protectiveness as well, he realized. Protectiveness, and for the first time in years, contentment. She demanded nothing, which paradoxically released him to offer more of himself than he'd been willing to share with any other woman. Perhaps…just perhaps that was all most women wanted when tears flowed. Comfort. Arms that offered a protective bulwark, if only for a few moments, from whatever produced the tears. Not control, not guilt. Determination settled inside Gray, and he found himself relaxing back in the chair while he waited for Mrs. Crocker's lamentations to run their course. For Neala, he could be patient. He could even be…prayerful.

Eventually Will's mother sat back, sighed, and stiffly dug inside her disreputable-looking carpetbag, dragging out a crumpled, none-too-clean-looking man's handkerchief. She dabbed her eyes, her temples, and even wiped her nose, then twined her hands together in her lap. A spur of reluctant pity flickered within Gray. But despite the pity, he couldn't afford to drop his guard toward a woman whose son may or may not have murdered Mrs. Wilkes. Fifteen years left calluses as well as caution.

On the other hand, he hadn't bolted for the hills, much less snarled.

Because of Neala. Neala…who would probably inform him that his transformation was God's doing, not her own. Since he'd prayed more in the past twenty-four hours than he had since he was a small boy, Gray wasn't in a position to argue over her naive faith in God, especially considering the timely arrival of the woman sitting across from him.

"I beg your pardon," Mrs. Crocker finally said. "William gets very impatient with me when I weep."

"I'm afraid I, too, am guilty of such an insensitivity," Gray admitted gruffly.

"Well, Mr. Faulkner." Abruptly she rose to her feet, forcing Gray to hurriedly follow suit. "Sitting here won't find my son. That rather large young woman assured me that you would assist me." Noisily she cleared her throat, dabbed her mouth with the handkerchief. "But I'm sure you're much too busy for the likes of me. I can find my own way to his quarters."

"He's not there," Gray told her quietly. "I checked myself, earlier today."

"But he might be there now," Mrs. Crocker insisted. "You don't know my William like I do. He can be…secretive." Her eyes moistened anew. "That's one of the reasons I'm so worried."

"Why is that?" Despite his rising sense of urgency, Gray casually took her arm in a gesture of support. Its weightless fragility surprised him. "Tell me about it, while we both go and check his quarters again, hmm."

"Mr. Faulkner?" Jimmy called from behind the desk as they started across the front hallway.

Gray glanced down at Mrs. Crocker. "One moment." He gave her elbow a light squeeze, then hurried back over to the desk clerk.

"Here's the list you asked for, of the names of all guests who are first-timers this year. I'm going off duty, but I thought you might want this before tomorrow."

"I do. Thanks, Jimmy." He tipped the grateful young man a half dollar, turned to leave, then retraced his steps. "Jimmy, do you happen to know which of these guests arrived after Miss Shaw, this past June?"

"Let me see." He studied the list Gray handed back to him for a moment. "To the best of my recollection, that would be these folks here. The Stamfords, Burlingtons… Mrs. VanPeter, Mr. Lipscomb…and Mr. Lyle." He looked at Gray. "The Stamfords and Mr. Lipscomb are the only guests who haven't left yet. Does that help?"

"You've no idea, Jimmy."

Pulse pounding, Gray strode across to Mrs. Crocker. Keep calm, stay polite but firm. "Mrs. Crocker, something urgent has come up that demands my immediate attention. I need you to remain here, for just a little while, all right?"

"No. I refuse to be left behind like a stray puppy." She

gripped her carpetbag and glared up at Gray. "It's William, isn't it? You're lying to me, you're—"

The supernatural calm enfolding Gray cracked. "I'm not lying to you! Mrs. Crocker, this has nothing to do with your son. Understand? Nothing."

He wasn't surprised when her shoulders hunched, because he was practically shouting at her. She hugged the carpetbag to her as though to buffer herself from his words.

All right, he *was* shouting. He felt like a man tied between two freight trains steaming off in opposite directions. It was imperative that he investigate this lead immediately; yet Mrs. Crocker offered his best prospect for finding Will. He couldn't afford to alienate her. Pinching the bridge of his nose, Gray sucked in a single calming breath and managed with an effort to moderate his tone.

"I want to find your son every bit as much as you do," he began. "But there's something I must see to immediately. Something vital that has nothing to do with your son. Would you wait here for me?" The urgency stomped his chest now with hobnailed boots, but Gray scraped up a coaxing smile. "Please? You've not eaten since you arrived, have you? How about if I arrange for you to be escorted to the dining room? They serve supper until eight. You choose whatever you like to eat, enjoy a good meal. I'll be back before you're finished—" he gestured to a bellboy, who snapped to attention at once "—and… um…and I'll have dessert with you. Then together we'll find your son."

"I don't…" Her throat muscles worked convulsively, her gaze darting between the ebony-faced bellboy and Gray. Then, with eerie suddenness, the wildness left her face. "Very well, Mr. Faulkner," she said. "Thank you. Your kindness… I appreciate it."

"I'll see you, soon I hope," he promised her as he slipped several bills to the bellboy.

"Yes, I expect you will," was the dull reply.

But Gray was already halfway to the door. The list had finally connected together the torn scraps of a picture that had nagged his brain for several hours. He marked the gathering darkness as he plunged down the steps to the grounds.

Lipscomb. Mr. Geoffrey Lipscomb, a man who claimed to be from Kentucky yet whose accent more resembled the distinct refined drawl of Tidewater Virginia or North Carolina, overlaid with the lightest dusting of a mountain twang. He could have recently moved to Kentucky, of course. But regardless of his home of origin, Lipscomb was not who, or what, he appeared to be.

He'd been perspiring heavily for a brisk fall afternoon. A man relaxing in the privacy of his room, with nothing on his mind save enjoying the fall foliage, should not have been sweating like a horse after a race.

Another image clicked into place: the wrists of his cuffless shirt. They'd been soiled. Not covered with dirt, not anything that would have immediately alerted Gray. But a man of means able to afford two rooms in cottages on Alabama Row, one who had made a point to present himself as a wealthy, dandified gentleman, would not wear soiled shirts no matter how casual the occasion.

And his hair. That outrageous head of curly black hair. Neala had remarked upon his hair every time they'd met Mr. Lipscomb, about how she empathized with anyone cursed with thick, curly hair. She'd wondered aloud how often he had to pay a visit to the barber, since whenever they met him, Mr. Lipscomb's hair almost brushed his collar.

When Gray talked to him this afternoon, the hair… What was it about his hair that chafed Gray now? As he sprinted across the grounds toward the cottages on Alabama Row, the blurred image suddenly sharpened in focus—Gray, standing on the porch; Lipscomb, lounging in the doorway. Sunset-tipped light had streamed around Gray directly onto the other man, illuminating his features with pitiless clarity.

The hair on the right side of Lipscomb's head had completely covered his ear. The hair on the left side, however, scarcely brushed the top of the earlobe.

Either the Old White's barber was going blind—or Master Lipscomb wore a toupee. More likely a wig, which would disguise not only the shape of his head and his real hair color, but would also completely change his appearance.

For the third time in twenty-four hours, Gray found himself praying.

Chapter Twenty-Six

Neala watched Will while he paced the floor beside the bed.

Ever since someone knocked on the door earlier, he'd been behaving strangely, either laughing—a guttural yet out-of-control sound that peppered Neala's skin with goose bumps—or pacing in that silent manner of a trapped wild animal.

All of a sudden he swiveled, crossed over to the bed. "We're leaving."

He reached toward her, hurriedly removed the gag, then fumbled the key into the handcuffs and released her wrists. The obscene clang of metal against metal jangled over the roaring in Neala's ears. "I'll give you a moment or two to make sure you can walk. Promise to be sensible, so I'll be able to keep you alive."

He tossed the threat at her in the same tone as one might order a breakfast tray.

Light-headed, her fingers numb and her limbs uncoordinated, Neala massaged her wrists and arms until the worst of the discomfort eased. The activity not only restored circulation, but gave her something other than abject self-pity on which to focus.

Slowly she maneuvered to the edge of the bed, shakily forcing herself to stand. When she was confident of her balance, she lifted her gaze to Will. "Let me go. My life is not your responsibility." It was difficult, forcing her tongue to form words when her jaw felt ossified, and her lips were dry as dust. "All you have to do to keep me alive is to let me go free."

"You will always be my responsibility."

Neala managed to choke back the hot denial. Distractedly she turned to straighten the bedcovers, fluff the pillow—anything to channel her antagonism into something noninflammatory.

"If we don't leave," Will continued, the words hoarse and low, "I might end up killing someone again."

Neala's hands stilled. She turned, for the first time openly searching his face. Droplets of perspiration dotted his forehead and temples. His Adam's apple bobbed convulsively as he swallowed hard, several times. His eyes… His eyes stared back at her, and they were black with fear.

"Will…" she whispered. "Who are you afraid is going to come through that door?"

Primitive rage flashed so swiftly she wouldn't have caught it had she not been watching every flicker of an eyelash. Then, as though redonning a mask, his expression reverted to the urbane Mr. Lipscomb, who seldom manifested emotion of any kind. "You're mistaken, Neala. I'm not at all afraid. I will, however, allow you to decide if you want the death of your former suitor on your conscience. Go ahead, try to escape. He cares nothing about you, remember? Show me that you care more for your own skin than his. Try to escape, Neala."

Her head reared back. "Grayson," she breathed. "That's the person who knocked at the door, isn't it?"

Will ignored her question, no doubt an answer itself.

Oh, but her heart fairly convulsed with fearful joy. Grayson had come for her after all. She hadn't expected him to, had given up any hope that she would ever see him, or anyone else on earth, again. She expected to die, and hours earlier had resigned herself to the inevitable. Yet Grayson had refused to give up on her. *She hadn't even told him she loved him.* Surely he realized his actions needlessly imperiled his own life. She had in fact done her best to ensure that he would not follow her.

But she wished she'd at least told him in the letter that she loved him.

A notion sparkled in a distant corner of her mind.

"You never looked at me like that," Will's abruptly petulant voice intruded, demanding her attention, snuffling the twinkling revelation. "Not once. Even when I explained…" His hands closed into fists. "I told you, I don't like what I've become. I want to put the past behind us. But I can't, not when I'm afraid you'll do something reckless." His gaze shifted toward the other room, then back to Neala. "Something stupid. Grayson Faulkner deserves killing for what he turned you into."

Keep him talking. Keep him distracted. Keep his mind…anywhere but on the possibility of killing Grayson. She shuffled one foot forward, stopped. "If we're leaving, I need my shoes."

As she had hoped, the non sequitur disconcerted Will. But instead of turning his back to her, he sidled to the other side of the bed, bent down, then tossed her traveling button-top boots into the middle of the bed. "You have two minutes."

Knees stiff, she retrieved the boots, and stumbled to the chair by the bed. "I'll tell you where to find the crest badge, if you promise not to harm Grayson," she tried next, keeping her gaze on the task of fastening buttons with fingers that still felt like uncooked sausage links.

Time stretched, quivered in air gone thick as Grandmother's sugarcane syrup.

"You think you can bribe me," Will finally said. All of a sudden the tips of his shoes bumped into hers. "You think you can bribe me?" he repeated, then snatched her to her feet. One hand shackled her wrist in a vicious grip. "You'll use your most precious possession—that's what you call it, isn't it?—you'll bargain with the legacy that should have been mine, to save the life of the man who ruined you?"

"Grayson didn't ruin me, Will. You did. As for the badge, what it symbolized to me doesn't exist anymore."

Red suffused Will's pallid countenance. But he didn't rail at her this time, merely hauled her across the room, indifferent to her uncoordinated scrambling. "Now I know why you won't marry me. I think I'll have to kill him after all."

Fear and fury geysered up in a heedless spray of words. "You'll never have the chance! I won't let you!"

She swung her free arm up and punched his jaw with her fist. The force of the blow knocked his head sideways and sent pain streaking up her arm. Will staggered, and the crushing hold on her wrist slackened. Neala tore herself free and ran for the door, fought with slippery fingers to turn the knob. Behind her, Will shouted a warning, cursing her as he leaped across the room. She felt clawlike fingers brush her shoulders and then the door opened and she flung herself forward, her gaze glued to the next door, and two seconds of freedom. With those two seconds, she could scream a warning.

She might have succeeded in her escape had her knee not buckled in the dash across the parlor. Staggering, she wavered, and by the time she regained her balance Will was there, blocking the outside door with his body. Breathing hard, he plastered his back against the panel. Watery light from the parlor lamp revealed a trickle of blood oozing from the corner of his mouth.

"Faulkner will be disposed of." He wiped the blood away with his hand, then reached inside his jacket. "But despite everything you've done, Neala, I still want to keep you alive." He withdrew his hand and flicked open the blade of a pocketknife. "Unless you hit me again."

Neala eyed the length of the blade, which could easily slice through a large potato, not to mention her throat. Resolve wavered. The prospect of imminent death lost its appeal when she was no longer handcuffed to a bed and drugged senseless, especially when Grayson was risking his own life to save hers.

"I won't hit you again, Will," she promised, joining him at the door. The odor of sweat and macassar oil rolled over her, making her head swim, but she forced herself to stand docilely, and waited for an opportunity.

Watching her, Will opened the door a few inches. The faint tang of pine trees and wood smoke wafted through the crack. Fresh air she hadn't breathed in over twenty-four hours dispelled some of the nausea and quickened her senses, filling Neala with yearning so intense she leaned forward.

Like a lightning bolt Will's hand flashed out, clamping her forearm in a punishing grip that seared all the way up her shoulder.

Neala struggled to twist free. "You're hurting my arm."

The fingers tightened. "Payment for my jaw, dear."

He shoved the door all the way open and dragged her out onto the porch. Twilight blurred the cottages to ghost-white structures, while the mountains loomed dark and forbidding all around them. Yet freedom spread like an unguent into Neala's skin, reviving senses and spirit. She wanted to lift her arms and embrace the night, but stifled the impulse, having learned that any movement on her part would precipitate swift, and painful, retaliation from Will. So she focused on a small bright star winkling just above the mountains, savoring the resurrection of her lost faith. *Lead Grayson like Your star led the wise men, Lord...*

"Come on. We have to hurry," Will growled as he hauled her down the porch steps with a recklessness that made Neala tumble against his side. He wrapped her in a bone-crushing hug. "Be careful!"

"Then slow down! I can barely see," Neala retorted. "Do you want to risk my turning an ankle? What if I break it? I couldn't walk. You'd have to carry me, leave me—or kill me."

"Shh!" She felt the prick of steel against her throat. "Stop taunting me when I've told you I don't want to kill you." He moved the blade so it rested against the side of her neck. "But I can hurt you, Neala. And I'll do it where he can see, make him feel as helpless as he did when he watched his friend die."

So, he knew about Grayson's friend. The implications checked her recklessness even more than the knife at her throat. What else was going on inside a mind twisted from birth, whose sense of right and wrong Neala could scarcely comprehend?

Quiet enfolded them, a malevolent, waiting silence. Only a week earlier these grounds and cottages had teemed with life—guests strolling the lawn, riding horses and bicycles, enjoying board games or cards in the shade of the columned porches; children chasing hoops while their parents enjoyed a picnic lunch and the band tuned its instruments in the bandstand.

Now the Old White more resembled a cemetery.

Suddenly her gaze caught on a distant figure, moving fast across the lawn. Briefly one of the pole lamps lighting the pathways highlighted a silhouette—a man, who promptly disappeared into the shadows. A gasp escaped before Neala could swallow it back.

Beside her Will stiffened and muttered something unintelligible under his breath. He seized her elbow and dragged her after him as he set off in the opposite direction. "Keep up," he ordered, adding in a goaded undertone, "It's too soon. I'm not ready for this."

Another long row of gleaming white cottages materialized beneath the trees. Behind them, the twilight faded into night and darkness fell with the suddenness of a guillotine blade. Will didn't hesitate; with Neala squirming against his side, he muscled her up the long staircase onto the porch of another one of the cottages. Neala opened her mouth and managed a single scream—Grayson's name—before Will's fist slammed into her chin.

"Now you know how it feels," he hissed.

He kicked open the door and dragged her across the threshold, slamming the door behind him. After shoving her into a chair, he turned to grab the washstand, dragging it across to bar the door. The white ceramic bowl and pitcher tumbled to the floor and smashed into pieces.

Neala groggily righted herself in the straight-back chair, blinked away tears as she tentatively pressed her fingers against her throbbing chin. The room was dark, every shadow coiled to pounce.

Will struck a match, lit one of the gas lamps over the fireplace. "You shouldn't have tried to yell." Feeble light trickled across the room as he returned and stood over Neala. He wiped his hand across the back of his mouth, all the time staring reproachfully at her.

"And if I yell again? Will you hit me—or just use the knife?" She wriggled her jaw. Like her knuckles, it throbbed in protest but nothing seemed to be broken. She hoped she would never be called upon to hit anybody else, including Will. "I don't plan to cooperate anymore, Will."

"You never have shown much common sense, have you?" he muttered, staring down at her. Yellow light deepened the brooding cast of his mouth beneath the false mustache; beads of sweat pearled across his forehead. "You shouldn't *warn* me that you don't plan to cooperate. You're like a child, Neala, with no awareness of danger. You think you can taunt me into making a mistake. Only you're the one making a mistake."

Shaking his head, he thrust his hands inside his jacket pocket, then stood there, swaying slightly. "Never mind. He knows we're here," he muttered. "I have to think." He moved across to the barricaded door, shoved the table again as though to test its effectiveness. "I have to think about what I'm going to do," he repeated. "With both of you."

Unnerved, Neala sat motionless, straining to listen for Grayson while reality punched her as though she were bread dough. She *was* an idealistic ninny, a foolish, reckless dunderhead. She had actually deluded herself into believing in her powers of persuasion, that her desire for people to act reasonably would be honored, that her innocence would shield her from mortal harm. Even when she lay trussed to the bed with a gag in her mouth, in the darkest reaches of her mind she had still believed that, despite God's desertion, she could somehow wriggle her way out on her own.

Because He had not answered her prayers the way she wanted, she had given up on God—and committed the grievous sin of presumption, by assuming His power and authority, claiming it for herself to wield as she saw fit. Oh, she hadn't sinned on purpose, like Will, nor at the time even realized her presumption. But ignorance of her folly did not displace the sin of it. 'Twas a miracle she wasn't already dead.

God, dear God. Forgive me. I didn't mean to... Don't allow Grayson to die because of me.

A single tear of utter humbleness trickled down her cheek. *Lord? Please, will You help us out of this mess?* Not that she deserved it, but because...because even when she'd turned her back on God, He loved her enough to stay with her. All along, even though she hadn't "felt" Him, even though she had cast her faith into the darkness and set out on her own path—her own *wrong* path, God had remained close by. The Almighty ruler of the universe loved her enough to hurt with her, to wait patiently for her to open her heart back up, and believe in the power of His love.

She should have been a better witness to Grayson, when she'd possessed the opportunity.

Even as she mentally prostrated herself before the Almighty, for the first time in her entire twenty-three years she grasped the extent of her gullibility and her…yes, her pride, along with her almost irrational predisposition to assume everything would work out all right because she'd always tried to be an obedient Christian.

But she'd learned her lesson at last. And the message burned to ash a lifetime of misconceptions.

Sometimes God allowed things to go terribly wrong, even with devout Christians, not because He didn't care, or because He was bent upon punishment—but because He had given mankind the gift of freedom of choice. And most of the time, people seemed to choose wrongly. Even those who claimed Christ as Savior and Lord.

Welcome to the human race, Neala Shaw.

Footsteps clattered up the porch outside.

Chapter Twenty-Seven

"Lipscomb!" Grayson's voice roared through the door panels as though they were made of thin cotton. "There's nowhere you can run. Nowhere you can hide. Give it up, man." There followed a brief pause. Then Grayson added, "Don't you think there's been enough killing? Let Neala go. You don't want to kill her—I don't want to kill you. Open the door."

Neala slowly slid forward to the edge of the chair, then wobbled to her feet. Heartbeat thrumming in her ears, she took one step, then another. One more second, and she would make a dash for the door, try to shove the table out of—

"Don't move," Will warned. His eyes were black with violent emotion. He glared first at Neala, then the window behind her, finally at the door. "Don't," he repeated, only this time the word emerged more as a plea than a threat.

"I'll give you ten more seconds, Lipscomb. Or should I call you by your real name—William Crocker?"

"My real name will be William Shaw!" he burst out in a maniacal scream, yanking the curly black wig from his head and flinging it into a corner. Next he attacked the mustache, clawing and ripping it from his upper lip. He seemed to have forgotten Neala altogether when he stomped over to the door and commenced pounding on the wood with his fists. “William Shaw,” he bellowed. “William Shaw. *William Shaw!* I’ve planned for this my whole life, and you will not stop me now!”

The tirade ceased as suddenly as it had erupted. Chest heaving, he slewed back around and faced Neala, paralyzing her with the unadulterated fury blazing from the black pits of those eyes.

He was going to kill her after all. Frozen in place, Neala twined her fingers together and fought the spike of terror that locked her throat. *Grayson... God, take care of Grayson.* When Will shifted she jolted as though he’d stabbed her through the heart, but he… Why, he wasn’t even looking her way any longer. Instead his gaze seemed fixed upon the room’s only window.

What if he tried to escape through that window?

The prospect jarred the panic loose, cudgeled it into resolve. She was neither drugged, nor bound, and she categorically refused to stand here like an ice block while Will squirmed through that window. As long as there was breath in her body, she would do what she could to—

Stand still, and wait upon the Lord. *The Lord will fight for you; you need only to be still.*

The verse winked into her mind, like a firefly dancing in the night. Awareness suffused her veins, saturated her with a yearning to believe. To—*know*. She felt as though she’d been transported into a bright, soundless vacuum where nothing existed but Neala, and the longing. She held her breath—and did not move. *Are You... Are You here?* Tingling warmth spread from the crown of her head downward.

Knowledge rife with expectation joined the firefly dance. The time had arrived for her to choose: she could try to stop Will through her own efforts—or she could obey the instruction she had just been given, trust the One Who had illuminated her mind.

Stand still...for it is by faith you stand firm. Once again the words of Scripture flashed through her mind, unbidden but as real as the flickering light keeping the darkness at bay in this small room. Neala forced her feet to stay glued to the floor. *All right, Lord. I'm, ah, waiting for You to do something.*

Her suspended sense of time shattered when Will screamed out, "I know you're still out there! Where are you? Don't you play games with me! I'll kill her, I mean it." He yanked out the knife and started across the room toward Neala.

Terror-roughed chills skated down her spine. Did God intend her to be the sacrificial lamb?

Will lifted the knife, and from somewhere more knowledge poured over her, through her, galvanized her limbs, pushed her forward. Instead of running, she met Will in the middle of the room. "Put that knife away, Will Crocker!" The words gushed forth in a torrent. "You told me you were tired of killing, you even asked me to marry you! Now look at what you're doing! Marriage requires mutual love, and you don't begin to know what that means. Love doesn't take. It gives. It doesn't threaten—it protects."

"You don't understand anything." Will thrust the knife in front of Neala's face, its point inches away from her nose. "Back off, Faulkner!" he yelled. "If I don't hear you leave, I'll slit her throat. By the time you break in her blood will be spilling all over the floor."

"No," Neala told him calmly, utterly at peace. "No, Will. You don't want to do that."

"Don't tell me what—"

There was no warning. With the explosive force of a summer deluge, the door splintered open, flinging the washstand to the floor. Will lifted the knife over his head. Neala automatically raised her arms to protect her throat. But instead of stabbing her, Will jerked around and hurled the knife toward the man charging through the doorway like a runaway bull moose. The point missed Grayson's ear by a whisker and thudded harmlessly into the ruined door post.

"Grayson!" Neala screamed.

She launched herself at Will, grabbing his arm and hanging on with all her strength until Will's elbow jammed into her midriff. Gasping, Neala fell to her knees, then rolled aside in a tumble of skirts and petticoats.

Grayson, weapon drawn, savage intent darkening his face, started across the room. Even as Will grabbed a poker from the fireplace, Gray's leg kicked out, his foot connecting with Will's wrist. The poker spun into the air, landing with a clatter on the floor and out of immediate reach.

Will feinted sideways, swiveled toward the door, but before he managed two steps Gray had holstered the gun and latched onto Will's shoulders. He toppled the other man like a tiger attacking its prey, slamming him to the floor and following him down.

Neala staggered to her feet, then darted across to tug the knife out of the wood. "I've got his knife, Grayson!" she called breathlessly.

Grayson didn't acknowledge her, and after a horrified glance Neala realized that he was as out of control as Will, and most likely would kill the other man with his bare hands if someone didn't bring him to his senses. After a reproachful glance heavenward, Neala approached the thrashing bodies, hands outstretched. Oh…the knife. Hastily she folded it up and thrust it inside her skirt pocket.

For a moment she hovered, terrified because she might distract Grayson and allow Will to get the upper hand; even more terrified that if she stayed out of the way, Grayson would be the one committing murder. Galvanized by the ugly possibility, she sucked in a sustaining breath, steeled herself—and Grayson pinned Will facedown, wrapping his forearm around the other man's neck.

Pulse thumping in her ears, Neala stepped closer and stretched out a hand to brush the bunched muscles of Grayson's shoulder. Her gaze collided with Will's.

His face was mottled a dusky-red, and his eyes were bloodshot and wild, yet his expression reached inside Neala and twisted her heart like a dishrag.

"Grayson." She stepped closer, rested her hand more firmly on his shoulder. "Grayson, stop. You're killing him. Stop. I'm all right. I'm—"

The words died in her throat when Grayson whipped his head sideways. "He hurt you. For over a year he's tried to kill you. Now he's going to pay." He uttered the words with pitiless matter-of-factness.

"If you kill him, you'll be the one paying." She shifted her hand to skim her fingertips across his cheekbone. "And so will I. Grayson…don't. I—I love you. Please don't kill him."

She hadn't intended the words, had in truth not realized how much she did love him, until she watched him choking the life out of another human being and knew, deep inside her soul, that if he succeeded the man she loved would die as well.

The strange fluttering drifted over her again, into her, settled her pulse to a slow, deep throbbing and her heart to racing. Love…casts out fear…love forgives…keeps no record of wrongs. God's love endures forever… His love for His children never fails… Love…gives people strength and hope and grace and—

Determination.

"Grayson! Let him go and listen to me! You big lunk, *I love you*! So you better look at me and say something about that."

A shudder rippled through his body. Then, almost as though he were plowing his way through a mud hole, Grayson released the chokehold on Will and sat back. For a moment he didn't move, then slowly rolled off the other man. Will coughed, wheezed in air, and made a feeble attempt to rise before he collapsed to sprawl unmoving on the floor.

Grayson's head lifted until the blue eyes focused on Neala.

"I love you, too," he murmured in a rusty-sounding voice. Tears glittered, and he lifted the hand that had been choking Will to swipe at the moisture, never looking away from Neala. "You have a bruise on your chin, and your cheek." A muscle twitched at the corner of his mouth. "There's a cut on your neck, and your wrists are—"

"Fine," Neala hurriedly interjected, the lightness dancing around her until she thought she might float away with it. "Grayson, I'm all right. You came for me."

A crooked sliver of a smile briefly appeared. "I

shouldn't have had to." He shuddered. "Neala… Neala…" His eyes closed briefly, and when they reopened they were full of more tears. "Of course I came. Did he…hurt you? I mean—hurt you worse than I can see?"

Will stirred. Gray calmly planted a knee in the small of his back, his gaze never leaving Neala.

"I'm not hurt anywhere that matters. I'm fine. Fine." In the blink of an eye she erased twenty-four hours of pain and humiliation, eighteen months of uncertainty and fear. The past had lost all power to haunt her, and therefore no longer mattered. She reached and touched his cheek, where a tear left a dusty trail of moisture. "I never thought I'd see you cry."

Incredibly, a blush stained his cheekbones. He searched her face, and with a tenderness that reduced Neala to a puddle, gently ran one finger over the bruises, then tangled in a lock of curling hair that had spilled over her forehead. "I've cried," he admitted in a husky whisper. "Especially when I thought I'd never see you again."

"I'm sorry for everything I did."

One eyebrow arched quizzically. "I'll remind you of that—later."

With the lithe grace that still amazed Neala, he levered himself up, then hauled Will to his feet and shoved him down in the chair. "Unless you feel up to a second bout, stay there."

Shoulders bowed, Will ducked his head and didn't respond. Defeat clung to him like layers of caked mud. His lethargy pinched Neala's conscience—though only a little.

"Come here, love," Grayson then ordered her in a very different tone.

Still floating in that otherworldly cloud, Neala took

two steps. Suddenly shy, she dropped her gaze to her shoes. Heat crept into her cheeks.

"We have a mountain of unfinished business," Grayson murmured, his warm hand tipping her chin. "But just to set the record straight—" He slid a steely glance down at Will, then brushed Neala's lips in a light but mesmerizing kiss. "This woman belongs to me," he announced with the authority of a desert sheikh, which bothered Neala not a bit. "You're alive only because of her. Don't tempt me to alter that condition by doing something stupid. Like moving."

"Grayson…perhaps you should tie him up?"

Grayson smiled down at her, drew her close to his side, and before her dazzled eyes the gun appeared in his hands. "I think you might be right," he murmured. "Trouble is… I don't have any rope handy."

Giddily they grinned at each other. "I know where we can find some," Neala said. "If you like, I can fetch—"

"Move away from my son!" A pale, gaunt woman stepped across the broken doorway. She lifted a small but deadly pistol—and pointed it straight at Neala. "You scheming, lying jezebel, how dare you poison my son against me!"

For Gray, time seemed to evaporate, sucking him into the past with a punch that left him disoriented. *A woman, with a weapon aimed at someone he loved.*

"I know your reputation, Mr. Faulkner. So if I see your fingers so much as twitch, I'll pull the trigger." Mrs. Crocker flicked a malevolent glare his way. "I'll shoot her, and you, too. Both of you are liars. Full of deceit."

"Momma!" Will struggled to his feet. "Momma, don't. It's over. Don't do this."

"It's not over." She jerked her chin toward Neala. The gun didn't waver. "Where is it? Where's the clan crest, whelp of a faithless philanderer? I've waited for this moment for over fifty years. Where is it?" The question cracked like a whip. "I know you have it. William told me he'd discovered it in your room. That he'd held it in his hands."

The clan crest? Obviously she was aware of its value, and was willing to commit murder over it. Gray was disillusioned, but unsurprised. Beside him Neala shifted her weight as though she might try to distance herself. Gray wasn't about to allow even a few inches between them. He curved his hand about her waist, drew her closer to his side, and felt the subtle relaxation of her body.

"You want Grandfather's crest badge?" she asked Will's mother. "I'll give it to you, but you'll have to let us go so I can retrieve it. I…left it somewhere. Let us go, and I p-promise to give it to you. By right it belongs to your son."

"No!" Will cried out. "I don't want it anymore. I'm tired." His voice cracked. "I'm tired, Momma."

"Neala, I don't think you should—"

"I don't believe you." Mrs. Crocker stepped closer, her expression murderous. "Yer jes' trying to trick me, same as you tricked my son." Her shaking finger moved to the trigger of what looked to be an old Colt .22 pocket revolver.

The skin at the back of Gray's neck crawled, but he didn't dare go for his own weapon. He might enjoy a reputation as the fastest draw on both sides of the Mississippi, but speed mattered not a bit when confronted by an irrational woman with a loaded revolver, whose heart was poisoned with decades of festering hate. "Mrs. Crocker, put the gun down. Then we can talk, and you—"

"Don't talk to my mother like that," Will interrupted.

Some of his bluster had returned, but Gray noted the caution stiffening his body. His gaze shifted between Neala, his mother and the Colt .22 ferociously gripped in her shaking hand. "Momma," he continued hoarsely, "Neala's not the problem. It's the man. Grayson Faulkner's the one who deserves to be shot like a cornered rat. Keep the gun trained on him, while Neala and I fetch the crest badge."

"No! You won't go anywhere with her." Her pallid face crumpled, much as Gray had witnessed in the hotel. "William…how could you think of marrying this creature?"

"Because…" Will inched around Gray, just out of reach. "Because I—because I thought if we married, I'd have the name as well as the crest, Momma. But she refused, and I don't care about anything now. Don't you see? Nothing matters."

"I see you've forgotten everything my momma and I taught you all your life, that's what I see."

Her mouth worked; a tremor quaked through her bony frame and for an instant the gun wavered. But even as Gray's muscles bunched to reach for his own weapon, the deadly little revolver was leveled at Neala again.

"You never should have been born," she spat. "If my mother had taken care of things, my father and that treacherous female who stole him would have burned in a lake of fire. Now God's justice will be served at last. Me and my son, we'll finally get what's ours."

"Your mother started the fire at my grandparents' boardinghouse!" Neala exclaimed. "Everyone thought it was just a story, but it wasn't, was it? Your mother was Letitia Rutledge."

Her lips flattened into a thin white line. "You ain't fit to say her name."

"Madam," Gray inserted in a deceptively smooth tone, "if you shoot Neala, I promise you won't live long enough to enjoy holding that crest badge in your murderous hands."

"Grayson…wait." Neala grabbed his left hand and squeezed. "Mrs. Crocker, Will's right. I promise you, I'm not going to marry your son." She glanced up at Grayson, her gaze vaguely apologetic. "I'm sort of hoping to marry Mr. Faulkner, if he'll have me."

"No! Not *him*!" Will flung himself between Gray and Neala, grappling for Gray's Smith & Wesson at the same moment his fist swung toward Gray's cheekbone.

Reflexively, Gray jerked sideways so the blow only grazed his chin. Desperate to protect Neala, he pivoted, thrusting her behind him with one arm while with the other he wrestled Will for control of his weapon. Vaguely he was aware of Mrs. Crocker screeching like a steam kettle, of Neala scrambling out of the way, of Will yelling and cursing.

The air exploded with an earsplitting roar.

Chapter Twenty-Eight

God... Oh, God. Please. Don't let her... No...

Wild with fear, Gray planted his palm against Will's face and shoved, wrenched himself free and staggered across toward Neala. She hadn't fallen, she was still standing. She was alive. Standing on her own two feet, not spiraling into a boneless heap on the floor with blood gushing forth. But beneath the tumble of dust-coated curls her face was stripped of color, blank as a corpse.

"Neala?" Somehow Gray managed to say her name. He couldn't feel his feet or his knees.

Behind him, Mrs. Crocker burst into loud gulping sobs.

Slowly Neala turned toward him, lifted a shaking hand to her face. "I—why, I'm okay," she whispered, and blinked. The awful blankness vanished. More frantically she ran both hands over her face, head, and neck. Then she looked across at Mrs. Crocker. "You missed," she said.

Gray wrapped her in a hug that caused her to squeak in protest. "Sorry," he choked out. "Let me see, let me make sure." As he murmured the words he was running his hands down her arms, her back, her side. "Easy, love. It's all right. You're all right."

He couldn't think over the relief, couldn't translate into action the potential for danger that still existed.

Somewhere within his resurrected conscience he managed a garbled prayer of thanks.

Her arms crept up and around him in a tentative embrace. "I felt the bullet go by," she noted in a pedantic little voice. "Neither Will nor Mrs. Crocker is as good a shot as you are. Did I tell you that Will was the hunter who shot at me last spring?"

The gun. Will. Gray's stomach leaped into his throat as her words jabbed him back to reality. "Get behind me, darling."

"What about—"

He kissed her hard, and shoved her behind him once more. "Stay behind me," he repeated as he slipped the Smith & Wesson from the holster. A swift survey of the room marginally relaxed his muscles; Will's attention had been diverted to his mother—not Gray and Neala. He seemed to be trying to persuade her to hand over the Colt .22.

Mrs. Crocker refused to relinquish the gun, twisting and turning, batting at Will's hands. She screamed a sewer full of abuse at her son, terms of endearment usually reserved for babies, invectives and pleas to rid the earth of all Shaws. From where Gray stood, Will's mother had completely shed herself of sanity.

A slender hand tapped his shoulder. "Perhaps I should try to help," Neala ventured.

The hairs at the back of his neck seemed to ignite into flames. Without turning his head, he clamped his free hand over Neala's. "Stay out of the way," he commanded with far too much harshness. He couldn't help it. Terror burned his gut like live coals. If Mrs. Crocker managed to free herself, if she regained control of the pistol…

"I'll keep them distracted. You slip out the door. Please, Neala. Please, love. I can't bear the thought of seeing someone else I love die, not like this."

Because he couldn't help himself, for one precious moment Gray turned to Neala, leaving his back exposed. But he had to look at her, had to know that she understood. Had to fill himself with her love, because these might be their last moments together. Chest tight, he scraped together a semblance of a smile. Reverently he skimmed one finger along her temple, down her damp cheek, to the point of her chin. "This will be the last time I ever want you out of my sight. I promise," he said, inwardly tensed for the agonizing impact of a bullet.

Neala searched his face, her eyes huge, liquid with unspoken words. "All right, Grayson." Her hand crept up to rest over his heart. "I will always love you," he thought she whispered.

The screaming abruptly stopped.

Ears still ringing, Gray shifted his attention to the two Crockers even as his hand urgently pushed Neala toward the door. Will was talking to his mother in a low, strained voice, most of the words inaudible; he looked as though he were embracing her in a hug. Mrs. Crocker hung limply in his arms, but at least she was silent.

The sinister little Colt .22 pocket revolver was nowhere in sight.

Prickles feathered the back of Gray's neck again, this time more insistently. He adjusted his grip on his Smith &

Wesson, at the same time moving in front of Neala as she edged toward the door.

Will didn't even turn his head their way, but the mumbled words now drifted clearly across the otherwise silent room. "...and I know this is hard for you. But right now I don't know what else to do. I tell you I'm tired of the killing. I'm just...worn out."

"I...nothing to live for," Mrs. Crocker returned plaintively, her words muffled since her face was pressed against Will's chest. "You've betrayed...left me nothing. I've lost you. Lost...only thing...ever mattered to me."

Gray bent until his lips brushed Neala's ear. "Duck outside and run for the main hotel. I'll keep them distracted. The staff should already have telephoned the sheriff's office."

"All right, Grayson." Neala's hand shifted until her fingers twisted in the collar of his shirt. "But I don't like it. You better be careful yourself."

"Faulkner!" Will called out. "It would be best if you left." A portentous silence thickened before he added leadenly, "Take Neala with you. I'm—I'm not going anywhere."

And he was a three-tailed raccoon. "Not a chance, Will. You and your mother are—"

Mrs. Crocker erupted with an inhuman shriek, wrenched free of Will, then slapped his face, hard. Staggering, he sidestepped and before anyone could react, she snatched the revolver out of her son's hands and darted around him to the front door, blocking the way.

"I won't let you give up like this! You're nothing but a coward! A weak-minded coward and you'll roast for what you've done to me! All of you will!"

She lifted the gun, pointed it straight at Neala.

"Momma! No! *No!*"

Gray's finger tightened on the trigger—and Will leaped in front of him and Neala. Once more the crack of a gunshot ripped through the room.

Only… Only Gray felt nothing. No molten pain, no spurt of warm blood soaking his shirt. He stared down at his gun. He hadn't taken the shot, he knew he hadn't. What—?

Almost in slow motion, Will sank to his knees, his gaze upon his mother. Both hands clutched his chest. "No more killing," he whispered.

Eyes wild, Mrs. Crocker stared down at her son. *"William?"* Mouth quivering, she took a step forward. "William?"

Will shuddered. A moan leaked from his half-open mouth and he lifted one of his hands in front of his face. Bright red blood dripped from fingers curled like claws.

Gray heard Neala gasp. Taking no chances, however, he kept his weapon trained on Mrs. Crocker and didn't move toward the fallen man. "How bad is it?" he asked Will.

"Not sure…" He started to sway.

"No… My son. My son…" Mrs. Crocker dropped down, threw her arms around Will. "I'm sorry, baby. I'm so sorry. Please don't leave me, William. It will be all right. I promise. You'll marry her, it will be all right. You'll be William Shaw… William?"

Eyes glazing, Will slid free of his mother's arms to lie motionless on the floor. Gray quickly knelt and with more force than gentleness snatched the gun from Mrs. Crocker's unresisting hand. Rising, he holstered his own gun, shucked the remaining bullets from the pocket revolver, then flung it through the open door, out into the darkness. For the first time in hours he managed a deep breath.

When he turned back around, Neala was crouched by Will, her hands pressing a snowy-white handkerchief against his chest. Within seconds the handkerchief was soaked with blood.

Like Lot's wife, frozen into a pillar of salt at the sight of something too unbearable to imagine, Mrs. Crocker stared at the tableau of her son and the woman she had come to destroy.

Grayson crossed the room, knelt by Neala. His arm went around her shoulders and she rested her head against him. Tears stood in her eyes.

"He saved both our lives," she murmured.

Eyes cloudy, Will wheezed a single rattling breath. "Tired…of the killing," he repeated. His head rolled so that his gaze fell upon his mother. "S-sorry."

His mother didn't respond.

Neala touched his cheek. Will slowly focused back on her face. "Thank you, Will. Thank you, for saving both our lives."

Something came and went in the dull brown eyes. When Neala leaned down, her face almost brushing Will's, it took the last of Gray's remaining control not to haul her back and away into the safety of his embrace. But something beyond his ability to comprehend wrapped around his arms, gently but authoritatively pressing him to stillness.

Even when Neala brushed a fleeting kiss to Will's brow.

"Your name should have been Shaw," she told him then. "Grandfather was wrong. Please forgive him, Will."

A shudder rippled through her body, and Gray watched in utter bafflement as her face seemed to soften, while at the same time light infused her in ethereal radiance. He could not tear his eyes away. "You see, I'm forgiving you for everything you did, that brought death and grief to my family." The tears flowed freely down her cheeks. "I forgive you, Will."

But Will shook his head in a single renunciatory gesture. His lips moved soundlessly. The dark hopelessness in his eyes deepened until his lids drifted down. A final breath sighed past his lips.

Gray forced himself to look across at Mrs. Crocker, who hadn't moved, hadn't blinked. She exhibited no sign whatsoever that her son had just died, by her hand, much less that she remained a threat to Neala, or himself. "Mrs. Crocker?"

No response. Still cautious, Gray slipped his hand beneath Neala's elbow. "Come along, love," he said, and helped her to her feet. "It's over now. It's all over."

"Yes." She swallowed noisily. "Grayson…he saved our lives. But he—but he…"

"I know."

The strange sensation tugged at him again, an uncomfortable weight of, well, of *knowing* that demanded acknowledgment, only Gray couldn't seem to find the words. "I don't want to end up like Will," was what came forth, almost on its own volition. He held Neala a little ways from him and cupped her face in his hands. "I want to feel forgiveness," he whispered. "And… I want to give it. To you. To my—" he blinked hard "—to my own mother, as well as…them."

The smile Neala gave him took his breath away. "Oh,

I think we'll both be surprised," she murmured, "how easily we'll slip into the miracle of grace."

He couldn't help it. Despite a dead body at their feet and a catatonic woman who may or may not have been aware of her surroundings, Gray dipped his head and pressed a kiss to his beloved's lips. Life seemed to leap between them. Life—and a love that had triumphed over evil, over death.

Aunt Bella doubtless would have plenty of spiritual applications. For the first time in his life, Gray realized he looked forward to hearing every one of them.

Hands entwined, he and Neala turned to Mrs. Crocker. Neala squeezed Gray's hand, then freed herself to gently tug Mrs. Crocker to her feet, guiding her away from the body of her son. Grayson grabbed a bedspread and draped it over the corpse.

A moment later, he ushered the two women around the wreckage of the door and onto the gallery of the cottage. Shining from the deep black night sky, the rising moon cast a brilliant white light above the gentle silhouettes of the mountains. A single moonbeam streamed through the trees onto the grounds, almost, Gray thought in a fanciful turn of mind, as though it were lighting the way.

Aunt Bella, he promised his distant aunt, I think your prayers for me have finally been answered.

When Mrs. Crocker reached the bottom of the long set of stairs, she roused, looked around dazedly, then burst into heaving, uncontrollable sobs.

And Grayson Faulkner, misogynist and hater of female tears and histrionics, swung up into his arms the woman he had almost killed—the woman he could have killed without compunction—and carried her across the lawn toward the main hotel. Beside him, her step jaunty and her head up, Neala commenced a running discourse on God, peace and God's Presence in their lives even when they couldn't feel it, see it, or believe it.

And Gray could only nod in agreement.

Chapter Twenty-Nine

Isabella Chilton Academy
October 1890

Departing rain clouds scudded across the eastern sky, blown toward the ocean by a frosty northwestern wind. Bundled in cloaks and hats, a small party of mourners gathered in the midst of a small copse of ancient trees, their leaves tipped in gold and scarlet. Tucked beneath a massive chestnut, a new granite headstone marked the single grave where William Crocker had been laid to rest.

"Still say he deserved naught but a pauper's grave," Liam Brody grumbled. "As for this fancy-dancy headstone..."

"He saved my life, and Grayson's," Neala responded with a coaxing smile for the crusty stable master. "I couldn't bury him in the family cemetery, but it didn't seem, well, fair, condemning him to a pauper's grave."

"Well, I can't promise no' to spit on the grave, when there's nobody else about."

Beside her, Grayson chuckled. Across from them, Miss Isabella cleared her throat, and Liam subsided, but

Neala watched the two men exchange nods of masculine accord.

"I think this spot is most appropriate," she said. "After all, these woods are where Grayson and I met for the first time."

She sneaked a footstep closer to her fiancé, basking in his warmth and the newfound peace that had erased the lines scoring his forehead over the past few months. Inside her gloves, she pressed the fingers of her left hand together to better savor the unfamiliar weight of her betrothal ring. "If Will hadn't been shooting at me," she continued, "who knows if Grayson and I would ever have shared more than a passing acquaintance?"

"Are you going to hold that over me the rest of our lives?" Grayson leaned to brush his lips to her temples in a feathery caress, then glanced across at his aunt. "Why don't you go ahead and say some words over the grave? The wind's picking up."

Expression thoughtful, Miss Isabella repositioned a strand of silver-gray hair the wind had tugged loose. Then she lifted her Bible and thrust it out, over the grave, to Grayson. "I think it would be far more appropriate for you to be the one to say some words."

After a stunned moment, Grayson reached and took the Bible, muttering something unintelligible. He clutched it awkwardly, and an endearing blush crept up his neck. Then he took a deep breath, and the corner of his mouth kicked up. "I can see this business of talking to God isn't going to come easy," he confessed. "Frankly, I'd rather just recite the Lord's Prayer and be done with it. But—" he looked down at Neala so tenderly her eyes stung "—I've ignored, denied, or given lip service long enough. So—" red stained his cheeks "—let's, ah, pray."

He bowed his head and closed his eyes. Neala couldn't help but dart a quick look at the other bystanders, her heart squishing to a puddle as every one of them obediently bowed their heads.

"God…ah, I don't understand much about You yet," Grayson began, "but I've come to believe that understanding isn't necessary for…for knowing that You're God—and I'm not. And that faith in You makes me a better man, but not a saint. A stronger man, not a weaker one. And…" Neala heard him swallow hard "…and a man who wants to honor his promises, not just today when it's easy, but for all the days I have left on the earth. So if Your Son can forgive all the bad things I've ever done, I need to forgive Will Crocker, for the bad things he did. Because, in the end, he did a good thing, God. He did a good thing."

Neala instinctively lifted her hand to cup the clan crest, pinned securely on her cloak. While her faith in God and family had faltered, Grayson's had taken root and sprouted. As she listened to his halting yet heartfelt prayer, she realized all over again that her husband-to-be had protected not only her life—but her heritage. It was because of Grayson that she'd been able to forgive her grandfather, seeing him with a clearer—and more understanding—eye.

On the other hand, she could scarcely comprehend that what she had assumed all of her life were colored chips of glass were in fact priceless gemstones.

Grayson's voice deepened, snapping Neala's attention back on his words.

"In a bizarre kind of way, in the end, I think I understand how Will felt," he said, then paused.

When Neala heard him swallow, she couldn't resist

an upward peek. Her eyes filled, because Grayson's eyes were still closed tightly—but a single tear had tracked a damp path down his hard-boned cheek. When he opened his mouth, she hastily dropped her head.

"I don't know all the right words yet," Grayson finished huskily. "Just…help me to be the man, and the husband, I need to be. And…well…thanks."

For several long moments, silence hovered over the small group.

Then, "Amen," Liam boomed out, the Irish brogue ringing a benediction.

"Amen," Miss Isabella echoed, and the other mourners followed suit, clustering around her to speak to Neala and Grayson. Neala was surprised to see Jocelyn Tremayne hovering behind the other students. Her solemn face spoke of a haunting sorrow deeper than words; Neala wondered with a guilty pinch if this simple graveside service had reawakened the young widow's grief over her dead husband. Or if Neala and Grayson's obvious happiness filled her with loneliness instead of shared joy. She would have gone to her, but Abigail approached, hands outstretched.

"I'm so happy for you," she said, the genuine warmth of the words belied by her own sadness that, like Jocelyn's, lurked deep behind her smile.

Neala wrapped her in a fierce hug. "We'll be nearby, remember. The site Grayson found for our house is just on the other side of these woods. Scarcely an hour's walk on a pretty day."

Miss Isabella laid a hand on her nephew's shoulder. "Since they'll be living here at the Academy while the house is being built, this is as good a time as any to say welcome home. And that I'm as proud of you as if you were my own son."

"I used to wish I was," Grayson replied gruffly. "After Pamela Crocker, though, I think maybe I can look a little more kindly on my own."

"That Mrs. Crocker's a horrid woman," Nan Sweeney put in, ever the dramatist. "Are you sure there's no risk of her escaping from that asylum in Georgia? What if she did, and tracks you and Neala down, and—"

"Nan," Miss Isabella interrupted, but Gray shook his head.

"It's all right, Aunt Bella. Besides, even though you'd never admit it, I'm sure you've thought the same. I know, I know. You don't worry, you pray." He winked, and Miss Isabella's face pinked up like a rosy-cheeked infant. "I promise you, Mrs. Crocker is no longer a threat to anyone but herself. I talked to the sheriff in White Sulphur Springs, before we boarded the train. He confided that she'd pretty much gone round the bend. Wouldn't speak to anybody—anyone alive, that is. But she did talk to her mother, and Will, like they were there in the room with her. Sheriff said he'd never seen anything like it." A muscle in his jaw twitched. "Two generations who allowed hate to deteriorate into madness. It's unnerving, realizing the effect parents have on their children's lives."

"Mmm. I'll remind you of that sentiment," Miss Isabella remarked pointedly, "when you and Neala have your firstborn. And remind you how even prodigal sons such as yourself can be restored, with a lot of prayer and a bit of God's grace."

"And a bit of soul-searching on my part," Grayson muttered. "You've made your point, Aunt Bella. No more lectures, please."

"Have you set a wedding date?" Abigail asked shyly.

"We're waiting to see if we can find Adrian first," Neala said. "And… I want to finish my studies here at the Academy."

"I'll have two-dozen chaperones to contend with," Grayson joked. "Our courtship was a lot more satisfying at the Old White, when I had you mostly to myself."

"Well, don't be thinking the pair of you can slip off without me knowing about it." Liam slapped a hand on Grayson's shoulder. "Not that I'll be doing anything, mind you. I'll just be knowing."

More laughter rippled through the group. Then, as though by some prearranged signal, one by one, faces turned away and people drifted off, heading for the warmth of the Academy, until only Miss Isabella remained with Neala and Grayson.

"Don't dally too long," she said. "There's a bite to this wind, and rain in the air."

Neala started to speak, but the headmistress lifted a hand. "You both need to say a private farewell." She studied them a long moment before her gaze rose to the brilliant forest canopy. "While you're about it, perhaps you can bid farewell to a number of preconceptions and misconceptions as well. There's more to marriage, my dears, than avowals of undying love."

For a few moments after Miss Isabella departed, Neala and Grayson stood together in peaceful silence.

"You probably ought to know that I don't think I'd be here, like this, if Will had done to her what he did to Mrs. Wilkes," Grayson eventually admitted.

"I wouldn't blame you." Neala approached the headstone and lightly laid her hand on cold granite. "Grayson, do you wish you'd killed Mrs. Crocker?"

He came to her, stripped off his gloves and dropped them to the ground, then cupped her face in his bare hands. "No. But I would have, if she'd shot you." The warmth of his fingers reached deep inside Neala, calm and caressing. "I didn't want to kill Mrs. Crocker. I'm glad I didn't have to. My finger was on the trigger, pulling it back to fire. But—something stopped me, the same way you stopped me from choking Will. I know now that 'something' was God. And it occurred to me that one of the reasons I couldn't bring myself to pull the trigger was because of the day my best friend died, and I killed a woman."

He set her a little ways from him to search her face. "If what happened in Philadelphia had never occurred, I don't think I would have held back with Mrs. Crocker."

Cautiously Neala nodded.

"For over a year now that whole tragedy has been eating away at me, in a way killing the last of my humanity. I couldn't see any sense to it, couldn't get out from under the awful *unfairness* of it." A frustrated sound escaped his throat. "I didn't know what to do. So I blamed God."

"Did you know that I gave up on God after Will murdered Mrs. Wilkes?"

"What?"

Smiling a little, Neala nodded. "She was sort of my camel's straw. All my life, I'd tried to be a good person, even after everyone in my family died, or left me. I blamed myself for Mrs. Wilkes's death. By the time Will abducted me, I didn't care about anything. I didn't even care about dying, because I never expected to see you again. I felt abandoned, by everyone, including the Lord."

She was watching Grayson closely enough to catch the muscle twitch in his jaw. "I also felt I deserved it," she added contritely, "because I'd deceived you."

"It's over," Grayson put in roughly. "I don't want to talk about it, not now. Not ever."

"Okay. But does it help, knowing that I felt God had abandoned me?"

"No. You should have known better, about both of us."

"Are you going to rub my nose in it the rest of our lives?" Neala mimicked the words he'd spoken to her earlier.

"Only the first ten or fifteen years." His hands slid inside her cloak, up her arms until his thumbs could caress her throat. "Don't ever leave me," he whispered. Then his mouth covered hers.

A gust of wind shoved them, splattering their faces with the first drops of rain. Grayson wrapped her in another bear hug and turned so that his body protected her from the weather. "I figured something else out, about God," he confessed against her temple.

Neala murmured an unintelligible sound of encouragement, and with a long, peaceful sigh Grayson continued. "I figured out that Marty and Mrs. Wilkes didn't die because God turned a blind eye. They died because two bitter, twisted people killed them. I can accept—now—that God allows senseless deaths not because He doesn't care, but because He gave mankind the freedom to choose."

"I tried to explain as much to Will." Neala burrowed deeper into Grayson's protective bulk after a raindrop splashed onto her nose. "He wouldn't listen."

"Mmm. I'm not sure he knew how."

A lump formed in her throat. "I know."

As though he could read her mind, Grayson jostled

her a bit. "A senseless tragedy last year in Philadelphia turned out to be the catalyst I needed to do the right thing last week at White Sulphur Springs." He pressed another kiss to her temple, then one to the corners of both eyes. "Something good came from something awful." His voice thickened. "It still doesn't make much sense, because I don't believe God deliberately engineered circumstances so that Mrs. Wilkes and the woman who killed Marty would die. But I feel different inside now. At peace with myself, with everything that's happened, the bad and the good."

Laughing a little, he clasped her shoulders, then took a couple of backward steps, until he was leaning against the trunk of a massive chestnut. "If you don't kiss me again I'm liable to start babbling like a circuit-riding preacher."

"I love listening to your babbling almost as much as I love kissing you," Neala told him, her own throat aching. To satisfy them both she stretched on her toes to plant a kiss at the corner of his mouth, where the lips were curved in a smile. "You might be interested to know there's a verse, in the New Testament. The Book of Romans. It captures what you're saying perfectly. We'll have to read it together. Someplace…dry."

More raindrops splattered them, and the wind set the trees around them to swaying. They exchanged another kiss, then turned to face William's grave one last time.

"Goodbye, William," Neala said, then because the urge welled up and spilled over, she dropped to her knees and bowed her head while rain began to fall in a steady patter. "Lord, help us to remember always, that even when life is tossing its worst our way, that You're still beside us. And no matter how afraid we are, or angry, or hurting, or grieving over things we can't understand, that if we choose to trust You with our lives, You will always plant flowers in our hearts, instead of thorns."

Beside her, she felt Grayson kneel as well, felt his arm wrap around her shoulder in a firm, comforting grip.

"Help us to choose to look for the flowers, Lord. Amen."

Grayson helped her to her feet. For a moment they stood, staring down at the grave.

"How about," he finally said, "if we plant some flowers on his grave, next spring?"

"I think that would be a good thing to do," Neala said. "How about…forget-me-nots?"

Hand in hand, they turned their faces and their steps toward the Academy. All around them rain and cold wind blew, dulling the brilliant fall foliage and darkening the sky. Likely they would be soaked before they reached shelter, but neither Neala nor Grayson cared.

"We're in for a lecture," Grayson commented.

"Not," Neala returned with a conspiratorial grin, "if we hide out in the stable with Liam until the storm passes. He installed one of Mr. Bell's telephones there, this past summer. It connects to the main house, so he can call Miss Isabella and let her know we're safe and sound."

"Just what I need. A cantankerous Irishman for a chaperone."

"Did I mention that he and Mr. Pepperell spend every Friday evening playing chess—in Mr. Pepperell's cottage?"

"Ah. And today's Friday, isn't it? So you think that, after he telephones the main house to assure everyone of our safety, he'll trot right on out in the storm to play chess, leaving us alone in the stables?"

Neala swiped a hank of damp, wind-tossed curls out

of her face. “Absolutely. Liam loves his chess game. Besides—” she blinked raindrops away as she grinned up at her beloved “—the entire school has been praying that you and I would realize we’re a perfect match. Abby told me, when we returned last week.”

Grayson paused to tug her cloak tighter and pull the hood over her head. “Then by all means, let’s head for the barn. I’m still fairly new at practicing my Christian faith, but even I know God has a fondness for stables.”

Their laughter rang through the rain and the wind, which whisked it upward toward heaven.

* * * * *

SPECIAL EXCERPT FROM

Love Inspired® HISTORICAL

Evicted from her home, Joanna Nelson and her two children seek refuge on the harsh Montana plains—which leads her to rancher Aidan McKaslin's property. When outside forces threaten their blossoming friendship, Aidan decides to take action. Can he convince Joanna to bind herself to him permanently or will it drive her away forever?

Read on for a sneak preview of High Country Bride *by Jillian Hart!*

"Where are you going to go?"

His tone was flat, his jaw tensed, as if he was still fighting his temper. His blue eyes glanced past her to where the children were going about their chore.

"I don't know." Her throat went dry. Her tongue felt thick as she answered. She trembled, not from fear of him—she truly didn't believe he would strike her—but from the unknown.

Of being forced to take the frightening step off the only safe spot she'd found since she'd lost Pa's house.

When you were homeless, everything seemed so fragile, so easily off balance. It was a big, unkind world for a woman alone with her children. She had no one to protect her. No one to care. The truth was, Joanna had never had those things in her husband. How could she

LIHEXP89584

expect them from any stranger? Especially this man she hardly knew, who seemed harsh, cold and hard-hearted?

And, worse, what if he brought in the law?

"Let me guess. If you leave here, you don't know where you're going and you have no money to get there with?"

She nodded. "Yes, sir."

"Then get you and your kids into the wagon. I'll hitch up your horses for you." His eyes were cold and yet not unfeeling as he fastened his gaze on hers. "I have a shanty out back of my house that no one's living in. You can stay there for the night."

"What?" She stumbled back, and the solid wood of the tailgate bit into the small of her back. "But—"

"There will be no argument," he snapped, interrupting her. "None at all. I buried a wife and son years ago, what was most precious to me, and to see you and them neglected like this—with no one to care…" His jaw clenched again, and his eyes were no longer cold.

Joanna didn't think she'd ever seen anything sadder than Aiden McKaslin standing there in the slanting rays of the setting sun.

Without another word, he turned on his heel and walked away, melting into the thick shadows of the summer evening.

Don't miss
High Country Bride *by Jillian Hart,*
available October 2018.

www.LoveInspired.com

LIHEXP89584

SPECIAL EXCERPT FROM

Love Inspired®

When Amos Burkholder steps in to help the Miller family, he soon discovers that middle daughter Deborah disappears for hours at a time. Where does she go?

Read on for a sneak preview of Courting Her Secret Heart *by Mary Davis, available September 2018 from Love Inspired!*

Amos Burkholder looked out over the Millers' fields to be plowed in the spring. He couldn't help but think of them as partly his. Of course, they weren't his fields, and he might not even be here to do the plowing and the planting. But if he was, he would take pride in that work.

Bartholomew Miller appreciated everything he did around the farm, so Amos worked harder than he ever had at home.

Bartholomew had never had a son to help him with all the work around the farm. How had he run this place without sons?

But on the flip side, Amos's *mutter* had been alone doing the house chores, cooking, cleaning and laundry for six men. How did she do it without help?

On the far side of one of the fields, a woman emerged from a bare stand of sycamore trees nestled next to a pond. She walked across the field.

The woman came closer and closer.

Deborah.

Where did she go all the time? She had disappeared every day this week and would be gone for hours. He was about to find out.

With her head down, she didn't see him approaching. He stepped directly into her path a few yards in front of her. When it looked as though she might literally run into him, he cleared his throat.

She halted a foot away. She was so startled to see him there, she appeared to lose her balance. Her arms swung out to keep herself upright.

He reached out and took hold of her upper arms to stop her from tumbling to the ground. "Whoa there."

She gasped. "I'm sorry. I didn't see you."

"Where have you been all day?"

"What? Nowhere." She tried to pull free of his grip, but he held fast.

He shook his head. "You've been somewhere. You've left every day this week and been gone for most of the day."

"I—I went for a walk."

"Where? Ohio?"

"We have a pond just over there. I like to sit and watch the ducks. It's a nice place to think and be alone. You should go sometime."

"I did. Today. You weren't there."

Her self-satisfied expression fell. "I was for a while, then I walked farther."

He sensed there was more to her absence than a walk. "Where?"

"Why do you care?"

"With your *vater* laid up, I'm responsible for everyone on this farm."

"I'm fine. I can take care of myself. May I go now?"

He didn't want to let her go but did. "I don't want you to leave the farm without telling me where you're going."

"Are you serious?"

He gave her his serious look.

She huffed and strode away.

Where did she go every day? He had wanted to follow her, but he realized it was none of his business. But curiosity pushed hard on him. He still might follow her if she didn't obey. Just to see. Just to watch her from a distance. Just to know her secret.

Something inside him feared for her. Feared she would walk out across this field and never return. Feared her secret would consume them both. She was a mystery.

A mystery he was drawn to solve.

Don't miss
Courting Her Secret Heart *by Mary Davis,*
available September 2018 wherever
Love Inspired® books and ebooks are sold.

www.LoveInspired.com

LIEXP0818